A COVENANT OF LOVE

A COVENANT OF LOVE

GILBERT MORRIS

Tyndale House Publishers, Inc.
Wheaton, Illinois

© 1992 by Gilbert Morris

Cover illustration copyright © 2000 by Rick Johnson

All rights reserved.

Living Books is a registered trademark of Tyndale House Publishers, Inc.

Published in association with the literary agency of Alive Communications, Inc. 7680 Goddard Street, Suite 200, Colorado Springs, CO 80920.

Scripture quotations are taken from the *Holy Bible*, King James Version.

ISBN 0-8432-4272-9

Printed in the United States of America

05	04	03	02	01	00
6	5	4	3	2	1

We Have Saved the Best—!

Weep not because our love's first spring is past—
And hold no wake for trembling young delight,
For we have saved the best, my Love, 'til last!

O yes, I know the sands of time run fast—
For us these are but golden days and nights.
Weep not because our summer's love is past.

The wine we quaffed with our love's first repast
Has aged—and does more now than blur our sight,
For we have saved the best, my Love, 'til last!

We've sipped together from Time's silver flask;
We've heard, Sweetheart, love's golden chimes by night!
Weep not because our autumn love is past,
Swirled like aging leaves by winter's blast
Into some dreary grave far from the light,
For we have saved the best. My love, 'twill last
For us just long enough for earth's delight,
And then we'll drink forever from cask!

Weep not because our love's first spring is past—
For we have saved, my Love, the best 'til last!

CONTENTS

Part Four: Thunder over Sumter—1860

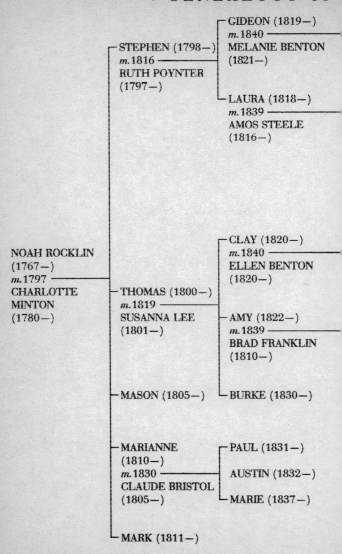

NOAH ROCKLIN
(1767—)
*m.*1797 ———
CHARLOTTE
MINTON
(1780—)

STEPHEN (1798—)
*m.*1816 ———
RUTH POYNTER
(1797—)

GIDEON (1819—)
*m.*1840 ———
MELANIE BENTON
(1821—)

LAURA (1818—)
*m.*1839 ———
AMOS STEELE
(1816—)

THOMAS (1800—)
*m.*1819 ———
SUSANNA LEE
(1801—)

CLAY (1820—)
*m.*1840 ———
ELLEN BENTON
(1820—)

AMY (1822—)
*m.*1839 ———
BRAD FRANKLIN
(1810—)

MASON (1805—)

BURKE (1830—)

MARIANNE
(1810—)
*m.*1830 ———
CLAUDE BRISTOL
(1805—)

PAUL (1831—)

AUSTIN (1832—)

MARIE (1837—)

MARK (1811—)

THE ROCKLINS ✦

- TYLER (1841—)
- ROBERT (1842—)
- FRANK (1843—)

- PATRICK (1840—)
- COLIN (1841—)
- DEBORAH (1842—)
- CLINTON (1843—)

- DENTON (1842—)
- DAVID (1842—)
- LOWELL (1843—)
- RENA (1846—)

- GRANT (1840—)
- RACHEL (1842—)
- LES (1844—)

PART ONE
THE RIVALRY—1840

CHAPTER ONE
A BALL AT GRACEFIELD

"CLAY Rocklin! You let me go this minute, you hear?"

Melanie Benton's voice was sharp, but her blue eyes were filled with laughter and her lips curved upward as she tried to pull away from the tall young man who held her easily. She showed no sign of alarm, but as he drew her closer, she glanced over her shoulder quickly, saying, "If my father sees us, he'll shoot you!"

Rocklin's grip on her waist tightened. "He can't see us," he said with a reckless grin. "This old scuppernong vine arbor is useful for something besides good wine, Mellie. From the house you can't see what's going on inside it. And I'd risk getting shot any time for a kiss from the prettiest girl in the county!"

Melanie turned her head aside just in time to catch his kiss on one satiny cheek. "It's a wonder some jealous husband hasn't shot you before this, Clay," she said sternly. But she was pleased by his words, as she was by his appearance.

Clay Rocklin was the most handsome of all the Rocklin men. He was six feet two inches tall, lean and muscular, and as Melanie tilted her head back to look up at him she thought, not for the first time, *He's too good-looking for his own good!* Clay was one of the "Black Rocklins," deriving his raven dark hair, black eyes, and olive skin from his father. The strain of Welsh blood that flowed through his veins showed in the strong, clean features: straight nose, wide cheekbones, deep-set eyes under black brows, and the cleft in the determined chin. He might have been charged with being too pretty save for the mouth that was too wide and the chin with the deep cleft that jutted out too aggressively.

The tendrils of the scuppernong vine overhead blocked out the warm April sun, throwing lacy patterns of shade on Melanie's face. Clay's voice grew husky as he murmured, "Mellie, you're so beautiful!" Then he kissed her, and as she stood there in his arms, Melanie tried to resist. She had always been able to handle Clay at such times, but now there was a power in his arms. Suddenly she found herself kissing him back with an ardor that she had never shown to any man. Then she realized that her hands were behind his head, and with a shock she pulled her lips away and pushed at his chest.

"I—mustn't!" she whispered. When he released her, she added, "You shouldn't do that, Clay!"

"I only did half of it, Mellie."

Though his answer angered her, she knew he was right. "Well, I shouldn't be letting you kiss me," she said. Her hands were trembling, and she turned suddenly, clasping them. "It's wrong."

He put his hands on her shoulders, turned her around, then put his hand under her chin. "What's so wrong with a kiss? Especially when you know how I feel about you."

"Clay, you've courted half the girls in Richmond," Melanie insisted. "And you've told most of them the same thing you're telling me."

A slight flush tinged Clay's cheeks, but he shook his head stubbornly. "A man's got to look around, doesn't he? Well, I've seen a few girls, but now I'm sure, Mellie. I love you, and I'll never love another woman."

Melanie was startled by the intensity in Clay's voice. She had never encouraged his attention; indeed, she had discouraged him frequently. They had grown up together, their families living only ten miles apart, bound by common interests. James and Alice Benton, Melanie's parents, ruled over the second-largest plantation in the county. But their holdings were only slightly less than Gracefield, the Rocklin estate.

Theirs was a feudal society, and it was no less rigid than the world of the Middle Ages. At the bottom of the pyramid lay the black slaves, owners of nothing, not even their own bodies. Over them, the poor whites, struggling for survival. Next were the shopkeepers and small businessmen, then the professional men—the lawyers and doctors who touched on all worlds.

At the top, at the apex of Virginia society of 1840, were the elite group of plantation owners whose estates ran into thousands of acres—and whose whims were law to the slaves and free whites who kept the cotton and rice flowing out of the rich earth. The South was ruled by this upper class, by men like Wade Hampton of South Carolina and the Lees and Hugers of Virginia.

The Rocklins and the Bentons, like most wealthy planters, liked to think of themselves as heirs to the traditions of knights and cavaliers, and they played the part stylishly. It was their code to practice chivalry toward women, kindness to inferiors, and honor among equals. They cultivated a taste for blooded horses, fine foxhounds, handmade firearms, and the Southern belles of affluent families. Many studied the arts of war, though seldom with the intention of actually using what they learned. A Mississippi planter, Jefferson Davis, stated with pride that only in the South did gentlemen who did not intend to follow the profession of arms go to a military academy.

In such a world, the marriages of sons and daughters were almost as carefully planned as those of the royal families of Europe. In the latter instance, only a young man of royal blood was considered eligible for a princess. Both the Bentons and the Rocklins would have stated promptly that the only candidates they would welcome into their family must come from the minutely small group that made up the "royalty" of Richmond.

The rigid caste system of her people was not in

Melanie's thoughts as she stood facing Clay—at least, not *consciously*. But in another sense, there was never a time when knowledge of such things was not with her. She could not have put her finger on a specific time when her parents had said to her, "You must marry a man who is from your world, Mellie; who is wealthy, cultured, and Southern." And yet, as she looked up at Clay, her blood still not cooled after his embrace, she was aware (as she had been for years) that he was one of the few men who would be welcomed without reservation by her parents.

Seeing her hesitate, Clay smiled roguishly and grasped her shoulders. "You do love me, Mellie! I know you do!" He would have kissed her again, but just at that moment the sound of a voice filtered through the arbor, startling both of them. They stepped apart quickly, and Melanie smoothed her hair nervously.

"Clay? You in here?"

Noah Rocklin's cane tapped on the stone walk that led from the house to the arbor, and his pace was so halting and slow that by the time he rounded the corner and saw his grandson and Melanie, the pair seemed calm and un-involved. "Here we are, Grandfather," Clay said quickly, stepping forward to meet the old man. "We were making plans for the ball tomorrow. Here, sit down and help us."

"No time for that, boy." Noah Rocklin studied them, his black eyes sharp as ever despite his seventy-three years. Time may have bent his tall figure and trans-formed his coal-black hair to silver, but he had lost none of the astuteness that had enabled him to create an empire out of nothing. Fifty years earlier he had stepped off a boat at the dock in Richmond, a penniless lad from the coal mines of Wales. With no backing, no influence, and little education, he had shouldered his way into the cloistered world of the rich planters of Vir-ginia. He had gotten his start by means of a bay mare who could beat any horse in the country for a quarter of a mile. Moving around from meet to meet, he had won purses, then invested in a worn-out farm that he bought for almost nothing. He had purchased one slave, Jacob, and in their first year together the two of them had wrenched a bumper crop of cotton from the woebegone farm. Noah still had Jacob, along with 160 other slaves—and that first farm of 120 acres was now lost in an ocean of over 50,000 acres, all rich, black land that sprawled over much of the county.

Only one thing held as much importance in Noah Rocklin's heart as his self-made empire, and that was his wife, Charlotte. She had brought him great joy and had blessed him with four sons—Stephen, Thomas, Mason, and Mark—and with his only daughter, Marianne. The fierce devotion Noah felt for Gracefield was nominal compared to his feelings toward his family.

Of course, Noah Rocklin's rise to power had not been unopposed—and the stories of his fits of anger were legendary. He had fought in the War of 1812, rising to the rank of major. When that was over, he had fought three duels, winning each with contemptuous ease. Perhaps it was because he recognized too much of his own fiery temper and wild youth in his grandson Clay that he scowled now, saying, "I heard about that trouble you had with Louis Waymeyer, boy. Bad business!"

"It was a matter of honor, sir!"

"Honor!" Noah scoffed, punching his cane against the stones angrily. "It was a brawl over a silly woman between two empty-headed young men!"

His remark caused both young people to redden, but Noah went on. "You're going to get your head shot off if you keep messing around with that kind of woman, Clay."

"Grandfather, you shouldn't speak that way in front of Mellie!"

"Why not? Why, boy, she's heard the story a dozen times—and I'd guess you got some of the minute details, didn't you, missy?" A stricken look came to Melanie's face, and he laughed loudly. "Why, I heard at least six versions of it myself, and the women don't let a thing like that die!"

Clay clamped his lips shut, saying nothing, but he noticed that Melanie seemed more amused than upset. It had been a piddling affair. He had cut Louis out with Dora Seller, and Louis had called him an unpleasant name. "I had to give him satisfaction, Grandfather," he insisted.

"If some of my family has to die, I'd rather see them die over something more important than Dora Seller's petticoats." Then he laughed again. "Look at her," he said suddenly, waving toward Melanie. "You thought what the boy did was romantic, didn't you? Well, you better watch out for this one. He's too much like I was at his age!"

"I think that's a great compliment to Clay, Major Rocklin," Melanie said with a smile and patted his arm. "If I get a husband half as handsome and romantic as you, I'll be happy."

"Romantic!" Noah recoiled as if she had put a snake on his arm. "I deny it, girl!"

"You can't," Melanie giggled. "Your wife showed me some of your old letters to her!"

Noah stared at her, then muttered, "I'll beat that woman! See if I don't—and it's long overdue!" He saw that his threat didn't impress the pair and changed the subject abruptly. "Stephen and his family will be on the 1:15, Clay. You get the large buggy and bring them here."

"Yes sir." Clay nodded. "How many will there be?"

"Why, Stephen and Ruth and the baby, of course. And Laura and that abolitionist she married."

"I'm surprised you'd let him come, Grandfather," Clay said, smiling. "You said before the wedding you'd horsewhip him if he ever stepped foot on Gracefield."

"Never mind what I said!" Noah snapped. "They'll have my great-grandson with them. He's bound to be an improvement over you young whelps I call grandsons!"

Melanie knew that the old man was fiercely proud of his grandsons, and asked, "Will Gideon be here?"

"Stephen said he would. I think he pulled some strings to get leave for him." Gideon, Stephen's son, was about to graduate from West Point, and this military career gave him a special favor with Noah Rocklin—indeed, with most of the family.

"I'll go along, Clay," Melanie said suddenly. When he gave her a sharp look, she added quickly, "To help Laura hold the baby. I'm sure she'll be worn out after that long ride from Washington."

Clay said stiffly, "Be pretty crowded in the carriage, Mellie."

"Oh, I don't mind," she answered with a sly smile. Clay walked off with a frown on his face, and she turned to see that Noah was studying her with his black eyes. "Why—I guess he doesn't want me to go, Major. But I am anxious to see Laura's baby." His shrewd eyes studied her for a moment.

"'Course it's the baby you're anxious to see. Who else would it be? Certainly not that good-looking soldier grandson of mine," he said dryly.

Melanie flushed uncomfortably and glanced away. "I think I'll go anyway. Clay won't mind," she said stubbornly, then walked quickly out of the arbor. As soon as she left, the old man pulled a very old silver flask out of his hip pocket. When he had taken two large swallows, he took a deep breath, then said, "Ahhhhhh!" He sat there, the sunlight creeping through the branches causing him to narrow his eyes. He grinned suddenly, saying out loud, "'Making plans for the ball tomorrow.' Ho! I know what you and that girl were doing, Clay Rocklin!" The thought amused him, and he lifted the flask again.

Suddenly a voice very close made him jump so abruptly that he spilled some of the liquor down the front of his shirt.

"Yas! I kotched you, din't I?" A tall, gangling Negro dressed in black pants and a white shirt had emerged from the far end of the arbor and approached to stand beside Noah. The Negro's hair was white as cotton, and

9

despite the lines which were etched in his face, his eyes were sharp. "You gimme that liquor, now!" he insisted, holding out a pink palm. "You know Miz Charlotte and the doctuh say you kain't have no mo'!"

Noah glared at the slave, saying defiantly, "Who cares what that quack says? Get away from here, Jake!"

"I won't do it! If you don't gimme dat liquor right now, I gonna tell Miz Charlotte!"

Noah stared at the slave, then suddenly lifted the flask and drained the last few swallows. Tossing the flask to Jacob, he laughed, "There! Now tell her whatever you like."

The tall slave shook his head in disapproval. He had been with Noah Rocklin since he was sixteen years old. The two of them had suffered together to bring Gracefield to where it was. Now that death was close, the two of them felt a special kinship that went beyond master and slave. Both knew that whichever of them went to the grave first would leave a massive gap in the heart of the other.

Carefully, Jake lifted the flask and licked the last few drops of amber liquor. Then he cocked his head and asked, "Marse Clay gonna marry up with Miss Mellie?" When Noah gave him a discouraged look and merely shook his head, a curious light came into his faded eyes. "I reckon she ain't made no pick yet. You reckon she's gonna pick Marse Stephen's boy, Gideon?"

Noah stared at the black face, so familiar to his sight, and knew that no detail of his family life was safe from this one. "Don't you have enough to do without keeping up with every case of puppy love on this place?"

"No sah, it ain't none of puppy love." Jake shook his head, thinking hard. Anything that touched Noah and Charlotte Rocklin touched him, and he saw trouble ahead. "It gonna be bad if she choose Marse Gideon, ain't it, Major?"

Noah got to his feet painfully. Leaning on his cane, he moved across the stone walk, but turned as he reached the edge of the arbor. His old eyes were filled with apprehension as he said, "Jake, it's going to be bad no matter *which* of those boys she chooses!" Then he moved out of sight, leaving the tall slave staring after him, his lips drawn up in a pucker and his brow wrinkled.

"Seem lak a woman ain't nevah happy lessen she causin' men trouble!"

The architect of the mansion at Gracefield had given much thought to the exterior grounds and the approach from the main road. A long, sweeping drive, lined with massive oaks and broad enough for three carriages, made a U-shape from the road to the mansion. The curve of the drive made a convenient place for carriages to wait until the balls were over.

Those arriving at the Gracefield mansion were often struck by the majestic beauty of the white frame building with white Corinthian columns across the front and down both sides. A balcony, set off by an ornate iron grill painted gleaming white, ran all the way around the house. Tall, wide windows could be seen on both floors of the house, the blue shutters breaking the gleaming white of the siding. The steeply pitched roof ran up to a center point, broken by three gables on each side, which gave light and air to the attic rooms. High-rising chimneys capped with curving covers of brick added further beauty to the building.

The house seemed to have been constructed for the purpose of formal balls; fully half of the space on the first floor was designated for that purpose. A pair of enormous oak doors opened into a spacious foyer. Upon entering, one's attention was immediately drawn to the broad stairway that divided the lower section of the house and curved to the right and left at the landing. At the left one could see the library and a large dining room; to the right, the ballroom. Behind these was a wide hallway that ran the length of the house. On the east was the very large, stately master bedroom. Most of the rest of the house was taken up by the kitchen and canning room, which were separated by a covered porch.

The second floor was composed of bedrooms, and in the largest and most ornate of these, Thomas Rocklin was helping his wife, Susanna, with the buttons on the back of her dress. "There . . . ," he said finally, then stepped back and took a careful look at her. "You'll be the belle of the ball," he pronounced. "You're as beautiful as ever."

Susanna gave him a smile. She was a handsome woman of thirty-nine, only one year younger than her husband. Her auburn hair gleamed in the lamplight, and the green silk dress she wore set off her blue-green eyes. Patting Thomas's arm lightly, she said, "Thank you, dear. And you'll be the finest-looking man." She gave him a quick glance of inspection, pulled his tie into line, and thought that he might just *be* the most handsome man at the ball. He had the blackest possible hair, with dark eyes and complexion to match. His bad habits had not yet put signs of dissipation on his face. For one instant, Susanna felt a wave of sadness and the thought came to her, as it had many times before, *I wish your ways were as handsome as your looks!*

But she allowed none of that to show on her face. Instead she said, "It's good to have Stephen and his family for a visit. I wish we could see more of them."

"Not much chance of that." Thomas shrugged. "I'm surprised my hardworking brother let himself be pulled away from that factory of his. Must be the first vacation he's had in two or three years." He glanced at the low walnut table close to the massive bed, then moved toward it and poured himself a drink from the cut-crystal bottle. "Stephen's changed a lot. He's become a Yankee peddler."

Susanna opened her mouth to say, "You shouldn't begin drinking so early," but cut the words off—he would only be angered by her interference. Instead she said, "I think Stephen came to show off his son. He and Ruth are very proud of Gideon's career."

"I suppose so. Do you think you can put up with

Ruth's ways while they're here?" Thomas gave her a gloomy look, for he had not yet completely forgiven his brother Stephen for marrying a woman from the North. He agreed with his father that Stephen's decision to move to Washington and go into business was due to Ruth, his wife. The fact that he had done well there did nothing to placate either Thomas or his father. Both felt that Stephen had somehow betrayed his legacy as a Southerner.

"Oh, Ruth's all right, Thomas," Susanna said. "And they're right to be proud of Gideon. He's in the top 10 percent of his class at West Point, and he's been asked to stay on after graduation to help train the new cadets. That's quite an accomplishment." Then she added with a smile that didn't quite come off, "Gideon's quite good-looking, and in his uniform he'll have every girl in Richmond after him—even if he is a Yankee."

"Gideon's no Yankee!" Thomas drank the rest of the liquor in his glass, then came to take her arm. "He's a Southerner. You can't take that out of a man. Come on, let's go to the ball."

As they came to the staircase, a bedroom door opened. "Ruth, how nice you look!" Susanna said with a bright smile as her sister-in-law emerged, followed by Stephen. "That must be one of those new Washington fashions."

"Oh, I bought it to wear to the president's reception," Ruth said. She was a blonde woman of forty-three, with quick brown eyes and a pronounced Northern accent. "President Van Buren thought it was nice, or so he said." She spoke of the president lightly, but both Thomas and Susanna knew they would hear of President Van Buren's opinion of Ruth's dress innumerable times. Stephen's wife was a ruthless socialite who structured her whole life by the political and social hierarchy that reigned in Washington. Her father had been in the House, and two of her brothers held offices in the federal service.

As Ruth continued talking about Washington, Susanna listened, but stole a glance at the two men at their sides.

13

The difference between the brothers had fascinated her from the time she had first met them. Over the years she had watched these differences grow. Now she noted again how, physically, they looked very little like brothers. The term "Black Rocklins" fit Thomas very well—as it did Mark—for both of them were dark in coloring. But the other two brothers, Stephen and Mason, were fair like their mother. Thomas seemed much taller than Stephen, though actually he was only two inches over the other's height. The illusion came from the two men's builds— Thomas was lean and almost thin, whereas Stephen Rocklin was thickset and muscular. Because of this, Stephen's five feet ten inches seemed even shorter when he stood next to his taller brother. He had fair coloring like his mother, Charlotte, and possessed the only pair of gray eyes in the family. There was a solidness about him, not just physically in the thick shoulders and strong hands, but in the spirit, that impressed all he met.

As they reached the bottom of the stairs, Stephen turned and smiled at Susanna. "I want your first dance, Susanna. If I don't get that one, these young fellows will never give me another chance."

Ruth gave her husband a look of irritation. She never liked it when he paid attention to her sister-in-law. She was a quick-witted woman and had long ago realized that Susanna Rocklin and her husband were mutual admirers. Yet she said nothing, choosing to go at once to where the attorney general of Virginia was speaking with Noah Rocklin.

Stephen's dancing, Susanna thought as the two of them moved over the polished heart-pine floor, *is much like the man himself—competent and steady.* He had none of Thomas's flair, on the dance floor or otherwise, but he was a man women and men alike would trust.

"We've all missed you," Susanna said as they swung around in a stately waltz. "I've never ceased to be sorry that you moved to Washington. Though it's only a few miles from Gracefield, it's like another country."

"I miss this place. Don't think I'll ever get over my longing for the South," Stephen said slowly. "But Ruth would never be happy here."

"No, I don't think she would." Susanna avoided the subject of Ruth, for it was somewhat of a delicate matter. As was the matter of their daughter Laura's husband, Amos Steele. Amos and Laura had been married less than two years, and none of the Southern branch of the Rocklins could understand why such a sweet girl had married an abolitionist. Tactfully, Susanna said, "Laura's baby is precious. Isn't it nice that we both have new grandsons the same age?"

Stephen grinned suddenly, looking much younger. "It's pretty sad I think, Susanna. All of us grandparents standing around bragging on each other's grandchildren, and thinking all the time how much more handsome *ours* really is!"

"Oh, Stephen! I don't do any such thing!" Susanna protested. Then, being an honest woman, she laughed ruefully. "You're right, of course. I guess we all feel that way. But your new grandson is every bit as handsome as mine!"

Stephen said with an unexpected burst of gallantry, "Well, Susanna, any grandson of yours would have to be handsome."

Susanna was taken aback by his remark. In all the years she had known him he had never paid her such a compliment. "Why, Stephen, you're getting positively gallant!" Then she smiled at him, adding, "We're growing older, aren't we? At a fancy ball and talking about grandchildren! Let's talk about *children*," she urged. "I don't feel so old doing that. And let me say first how impressed I am with Gideon. You must be very proud, the record he's made at West Point."

"Ruth and I are proud of Gideon," Stephen agreed, nodding. "He's going to be a fine soldier." He lifted his head and glanced over to where Clay and his son were talking, one on each side of Melanie Benton. "Clay is the

15

finest-looking young man here." Then he looked into her eyes and said seriously, "I heard about the duel. Too bad."

It was as close to being critical of Clay's behavior as Stephen would ever come. And he softened the remark at once by smiling. "I hope he doesn't challenge Gideon to a duel over Melanie. Arms are his profession."

The remark, lightly made and not intended to be serious, brought a line between Susanna's eyebrows. "I used to think that the two of them were just joking about their rivalry over her, but it's serious, Stephen. One of them is going to get a heartache sooner or later."

Even as she was speaking, Clay and Gideon were enduring some sly teasing over their rivalry. Taylor Dewitt, part of the group of young people that had clustered around Melanie and her two suitors, was saying, "Well now, Cadet Rocklin, looks like you got the inside track on all the rest of us." He winked at Tug Ramsey, the rotund nephew of the governor, adding, "I never can get over how a uniform makes a woman blind to real quality!"

"Oh, you hush, Taylor!" Melanie said sharply. "You've had too much to drink already."

"Why, Melanie, there's no such thing as too much to drink!" Dewitt smiled. "Like there are never enough beautiful women. That's right, isn't it, Clay?"

His remark was a sly jab, and not without danger, for though Clay Rocklin believed exactly the same thing, he was touchy about having remarks made on it. Everyone glanced at him with a certain degree of apprehension, the memory of Clay's duel with Louis Waymeyer vivid in their mind. The fact that Dewitt was a daredevil himself made the situation even more explosive.

Fortunately, Clay chose to ignore Dewitt's jibe. "You old degenerate!" He grinned at Dewitt. "I resent your remark. It's an insult to Southern womanhood." His smile took the sting from his words, and he added, "Cousin Gideon doesn't need any uniform to attract women. He's always been a favorite with the fair sex." Then he turned to

Gideon, who was taking all of this in with a faint smile. "Remember Lucy Ann Garner, Gid?" he asked. "I declare, that girl was so in love with you it was a shame!"

Melanie giggled then, for Gideon's solid features flushed and he looked very uncomfortable. "I remember that, Clay," she said, nodding, then explained, "Lucy was the daughter of the Baptist preacher who was here a few years ago. She was so taken with Gid that her father had to have a talk with him."

"I heard he brought his shotgun along for the talk," Clay said, his black eyes dancing.

"Oh, nonsense!" Gideon stammered. "You two always bring that poor girl up! She was like a sister to me."

A howl of laughter went up from the young men, and Dewitt cried out over them, "Ladies, look to your honor! When a dandy begins that old story about 'just being a brother,' it's time to flee!"

"That's right!" Tug Ramsey said, his blue eyes gleaming with fun in his round face. "As Doctor Johnson said, 'When a man starts talking a great deal about his honor, I start counting the spoons!'" Just then the music started, and Ramsey said, "Melanie, you can't trust either one of these two Rocklin boys, so I'll just claim this next dance."

He moved toward her, but suddenly Gideon was in front of him. "Ramsey, your uncle, the governor, has told my father some of the problems you've handed him. I don't think it would be safe for Melanie to be seen dancing with such a Don Juan."

He swept Melanie away while the group was laughing at the surprise on Tug's face, and only when the pair were swirling around the room did Dewitt say in surprise, "Well, I'll be dipped! I guess ol' Gid *has* learned something at West Point!"

"Learned what?" Clay asked at once, his dark eyes following the pair.

"Why, I guess he learned about maneuvering, Clay," Dewitt answered. "'Cuz I surely don't see any of *us* dancing with Melanie!" Catching the look of irritation on

Clay's face, he winked again at Tug Ramsey. "Maybe there is something in a uniform. Guess I'd better go sign up and get me one. Looks like that's what it takes to get the ladies around here!"

A small young woman who had walked up to the group in time to hear the last of the conversation said, "Taylor, that remark is an insult to ladies everywhere!"

Taylor Dewitt turned to her, a smile breaking across his lips. "I don't see how you can say that, Ellen. Everybody knows how I revere the ladies." That brought a laugh from everyone, for Dewitt was a womanizer of infinite proportions. "But it does seem that a uniform draws pretty girls to a man."

Ellen Benton shook her head firmly. "It's not what a man wears that's important. It's what he is underneath." Her remark caught Clay's attention, and he studied her as she carried on a lively conversation with Dewitt. Ellen was Melanie's cousin, the daughter of Melanie's father's only brother. She had come to Briarcliff Plantation after her parents were killed in a steamboat accident in Portland. There was some sort of scandal attached to her family, but what it was no one quite knew. The Bentons never spoke of it. All anyone knew was that Melanie's father had cut all communication with his brother.

Wonder what her father did to get cut off from the family? Clay pondered, studying the girl. *She's good-looking, but pretty free with men.* Ellen was not beautiful in the sense that Melanie was, but she did have large brown eyes, a wealth of dark brown hair, and a fine complexion. And there was a certain quality in her looks and bearing that caused men to turn and stare at her. Yet none of the young men of the county pursued her seriously.

She's got what it takes to draw men, but none of us is quite sure what to do about it, Clay thought as he watched Dewitt and Ramsey and the others. *She's something else— if she were just any girl it would be easier to pursue her. But she's the niece of James Benton, and it'd be a bad mistake to antagonize him.*

18

Suddenly Ellen turned to him. "Clay, ask me to dance."

"I was waiting for you to settle these callow youth," Clay answered at once, and soon they were whirling around the room. Several times she brushed against him, and the faint perfume she wore was sweet. She was not a tall girl, and when she tilted her head up to smile at him, he could not ignore the fullness of her lips.

As they danced, he was totally aware of her femininity, yet he was on his guard. Her free ways puzzled him, and he was aware that she was not a candidate for a serious courtship. Of course, he was drawn to her physically—but she was, in one sense, a nobody. Despite her uncle's wealth, there was a cloud over her past and an uncertainty about her future. And she was not a Southern girl.

As the dance went on, Ellen glanced at Gid and Melanie, then looked up at Clay. "I suppose Taylor was right," she said. "About girls liking uniforms. I didn't like what he said, but you can't deny the truth of it, can you?"

"Maybe I ought to join the army."

"Don't do that, Clay!" Ellen said quickly, her hand tightening on his. "It may be all right for Gideon, but it wouldn't be for you."

He looked down at her, admiring the perfect skin and the smoothness of her shoulder. "Why not, Ellen? Don't you think I could be a good soldier?"

"You would be good at anything, Clay Rocklin," Ellen said instantly. "But you are different from Gideon. He doesn't mind the monotony and the formality of a soldier's life. You have a free spirit. A life like that would be misery for you."

He was startled at her perception, but shook his head. "Father wishes I *were* a little more disciplined." He grinned briefly. "And Mother thinks my 'free spirit' is sinful. I'm a pretty big disappointment to them. Matter of fact, both of them wish I were more like Gid."

"As much as I admire your parents," Ellen said, "I don't think they're right in this case. The worst thing a parent can do is to try to make a child into something he's not. Wives make that mistake, too, don't they? A man has to be what he is, Clay. And what your parents don't see is that this is just a time for you to explore the world. Young people have to touch the world, and that means the bad as well as the good."

Clay was fascinated by her thinking—it was exactly the same thing he had said to himself many times. "What about you, Ellen?" he demanded. "What kind of life do you want?"

She smiled then, saying, "I'm like you, Clay. I want all that life has. It's soon over, isn't it? When I am old I want to say, 'I've had an exciting journey. I didn't refuse life because I was afraid of what people would say.'" Then she laughed out loud, in a charming manner. "I've shocked you, haven't I, Clay? Women aren't supposed to even *think* such things, much less *say* them to a man!"

Clay suddenly pulled her closer, excited by her manner and by the pressure of her full figure. "You're quite a woman, Ellen," he whispered, and as they danced on, he forgot about Gid and Melanie, which was exactly what Ellen wished.

Melanie had not been at all displeased with the way Gideon had stepped in to take her out on the dance floor. As he held her she was very conscious of the strength of his arms. "My, you've changed, Gid," she said with a smile. "You couldn't have done that two years ago. Are you sure you've been studying guns and marching and all that, and not courting those Yankee girls?"

Gid grinned suddenly. "My life's been one constant series of balls and picnics with beautiful women since I went to the Point," he said with a nod. "We have special classes in ballroom dancing and the fine points of courtship. Should have gone there years ago!" He pulled her closer, dropped his voice, and said, "Right now, page 84 in the manual on courtship would advise, 'As soon as you have wooed the young lady away from the lesser men, take her out to the garden for a breath of fresh air.'"

"Oh, I couldn't do that!" Melanie protested, but scant minutes later she found herself in the same arbor where she'd stood with Clay a few hours earlier. The night was so clear that the silver globe of the moon seemed huge against the velvety night sky. The music came to them, thin and faint, from the ballroom. The happy sound of laughter drifting on the wind was pleasant.

They stood there, looking out over the rolling hills, and finally Melanie asked, "Well, what does your old manual say to do now?"

"This—," Gid said firmly, and took her in his arms. It caught her off guard, for he had always been rather shy. She had known, in the way that beautiful young ladies know such things, that he liked her, but she had never been able to draw him out. As he kissed her, her idea that he had been without fire left her. There was nothing insipid in his manner now!

She pulled away, leaned back in his arms, and whispered, "Why, Gid! You've never done such a thing before!"

Gid stood there, taking in the beauty of her face, and then said slowly, "I was always afraid you'd laugh at me, Mellie. You were always the prettiest girl around. Every fellow wanted to be your beau. You could have had any of them. Still could," he added, then a light of determination came to his eyes. "But you're going to have to run me off this time! I haven't read any manuals on how to court a girl, Mellie. There was never anyone I wanted. But I love you. Always have, I think, since the first time Father brought me to Gracefield. I was nine, and the first time I saw you, I think I just fell in love."

"Oh, Gid, that's not possible!"

"I think it is," he said, and there was a rocklike certainty in his manner that made her nervous. She was accustomed to light flirtations, but Gideon Rocklin, she saw, would pursue a woman with the same dogged determination he had used to get to the top of his class at

West Point. "I guess that's about the only plan I have for courting you, Mellie," he said quietly. "Just to say I love you. And to promise that if you marry me, I'll do everything under God's heaven to make you happy." He shrugged slightly, adding, "I don't cut a very romantic figure. I know that."

Melanie understood at once that he was thinking of Clay, who cut a *very* romantic figure. The seriousness on Gid's face sobered her as she stood still in his arms. Finally she sighed, "Well, Gid, a romantic figure isn't everything." Then, knowing that it was time to break the scene off, she came up with a smile. "But I'll expect a little more in the way of courtship than a discussion of military tactics!"

Her remark brought a smile to his lips. Nodding, he said, "Maybe I'd better buy a manual on courtship, after all."

As she drew him down the stone walk, she glanced up at him. "No, you're doing fine, Cadet Rocklin. Do carry on!" They stepped inside and at once were engulfed by a world of music and color.

CHAPTER TWO

A CLOUD THE SIZE OF
A MAN'S HAND

GRACEFIELD Plantation was a little world dwarfed by the rolling hills of Virginia, yet it was complete in its workings. No tangible wall surrounded it, yet in some powerful spiritual manner, its limits were marked in the minds of the denizens who spent their lives within its boundaries. Even as a ship rolled onward over a trackless ocean with nothing to mark its progress, so Gracefield moved through time. The family and the slaves knew of the larger world outside Gracefield's borders, but for them its existence was vague and hazy—as was the distant shore to the sailor whose life was confined to the bobbing ship on the ocean.

Springtime and summer, fall and winter passed over the little world. Children were born, the aged died. Often, songs of joy, such as the happy shouting of slaves in their Sunday meetings or the jig dances of the parties, filled the air. At other times, the songs were slow and sad—when loved ones were lowered into the ground and covered over with the black earth, or when tragedy struck and the sound of weeping scored the long nights.

In all of this, though, there was order, for Gracefield was a microcosm of the larger world of men. Noah Rocklin was the archetype ruler: master, potentate, king, prince, emperor, congress, parliament, court. He ruled Gracefield with the power of a despot, and the Big House was no less the seat of authority than the Vatican or Buckingham Palace. Though he was growing old and the reins of power were slipping into other, more youthful hands, there was the certain knowledge that when Noah

23

Rocklin loosened his hands for the last time, there would be no loss of the order he had kept. Others would be there to guide, to direct, to govern.

Nowhere was the order of Gracefield more evident than in the world of the slaves, whose sweat sustained the kingdom of the Rocklins. For within their ranks was a rigid hierarchy. Those who toiled in the long rows of white cotton were the base. Without them, there would be no Gracefield, for cotton and rice could only be grown by many hands. The field slaves had no need of skill; all such work required was a strong back and endurance. In some minds, the less they knew, the better suited they were for the endless monotony of the task. What were dreams to a slave who went to the fields before dawn and picked cotton from a hunched position until it was too dark to see, with only a brief thirty-minute break to gobble down a dry piece of cornbread and swallow a drink of tepid water?

The second class of slaves was those who had mastered some sort of skill. Such a slave was Box, a tall, strong Negro who was the best blacksmith at Gracefield. He was such a valuable part of the place that no one would have suggested he ever demean himself by going to the fields. As for his wife, Carrie, she enjoyed a status envied by the wives of mere field hands.

The aristocracy, however, of the world of the slave, was the house slave—those who served as maids for the ladies of the Big House, cleaned the mansion, or cooked and served the meals for the white masters. These workers, it must be confessed, often were swollen with pride, feeling that the Negroes who worked the fields were far beneath them.

Still, even within the exalted positions of house slaves, adamant lines were drawn. And Dorrie, a tall, heavy woman of thirty-seven, ruled with iron authority. Charlotte Rocklin had chosen Dorrie at the age of six, seeing in the child a quickness of mind that was lacking in others. As the years had passed, Dorrie had learned every skill of keeping a large house in order. She had served as cleaning maid, kitchen helper, ladies' maid, and cook. Technically, she was still the cook—but most of the actual cooking was done by a thin woman named Dulcie.

Charlotte Rocklin was, of course, the titular mistress of Gracefield, but it was Dorrie who saw to the seemingly endless details of the Big House. And it was a rare thing for the two women to disagree over matters, for if anything, Dorrie was far more strict in running the mansion than Charlotte herself. Dorrie was a shrewd woman who, over the years, had built up a system that worked well for her. She had married a tall, handsome field hand named Zander, and through careful and discreet manipulation had gotten him installed as butler. Their sixteen-year-old daughter, Cleo, worked in the kitchen; their other daughter, Lutie, was a housemaid. Their twelve-year-old son, Moses, was the stable boy.

The morning after the ball, Dorrie had driven the house slaves hard, so that by noon the house was cleaned and sparkling. Then, after a quick break, she routed them out again, her large eyes sharp and her voice sharper. Coming upon Cleo and Lutie sitting outside on a bench sipping lemonade left over from the ball, she lit into them.

"Git youself in dis house! Whut you mean sippin' dat lemonade? You know dat ain't fo' you!"

"Aw, Mama," Cleo complained. "It was lef' over from the party!"

Dorrie snatched the pitcher from Cleo and cuffed her across the head. "De party ain't ovah yet, and you knows it. Now, you git them potatoes peeled or I'll do some peelin' my own self! And you, Lutie, go make up de yeller room."

"Who it for?"

Dorrie gave the fourteen-year-old an impatient shove. "Whut diff'rence it make? You jest clean it up good." Then she relented, saying, "Marse Mark come dis morning, and Miss Charlotte tole me dat her baby boy comin' in any time."

She had entered the kitchen as she spoke this, and Zander lifted his head to stare at her. "I didn't know dat." He was sitting on a high stool by the counter, carefully peeling potatoes, wearing a white apron over his black pants and white shirt. "Marse Noah threatened to run him off wif a shotgun do he come back."

Mark, the "baby" Dorrie had mentioned, was the youngest son of Noah and Charlotte Rocklin. He was twenty-nine years old, but to Dorrie he was still the baby. She had been almost a mother to him, and he had broken her heart as he had the hearts of his parents by his wild ways. A rebel from the time he could walk, he had brought such heartache to the Rocklins that Noah had finally thrown him out of the house. He had written from time to time, and even visited, but his visits were always tense affairs for everyone in the family.

"Lemme see," Zander said, "Why, it's been three years since Marse Mark been heah, ain't it now?" He studied a half-peeled potato, carefully cut a peeling from it, then grinned. "Whoo, now! Whut dat boy been and done dis time!"

"You shut!" Dorrie said sharply, for she would never allow anyone to criticize the young man in her presence. "And you bettah get dat good silver polished—and we gonna have de good plates, too, for supper."

Zander stared at her curiously. "If Miss Marianne come, it'll be de fust time de whole family's et together in a mighty long time." A doubtful look crossed his face, and he put down the bowl of potatoes, then said, "I hope dey ain't no big fuss lak de last time they all got together. Lawd! I thought dey was gonna start shootin'!"

Dorrie glanced around to where Dulcie and Cleo were working at the far end of the kitchen. "I tole you to shut!" she whispered. "They ain't gonna be no fighting."

Zander took off his apron, folded it carefully, then put it on the counter. He brushed the front of his shirt and pants, then straightened up to his full height. "Well, old woman," he said slowly, "If dem Black Rocklins gits through a meal without a fuss—it'll be 'bout the first time dat ever come about!"

Noah Rocklin's "study" was filled with a great many possessions—but few of them were books. One walnut bookshelf occupied a space along the west wall, and it was packed with books and magazines. Most were manuals dealing with some aspect of farming; the others dealt with history or law. The rest of the room was packed with mementos of Noah's lifetime. Over fifty guns, including rifles, shotguns, and pistols of all sorts, took prominence. The weapons gleamed in the afternoon sun that was streaming through the dormer window. It was Jacob's job to keep the guns well polished, and he took pride in this task. Paintings were hung randomly; most of them of family, but some of statesmen, generally from Virginia.

But Noah was not looking at his guns or souvenirs as he sat in his worn leather chair behind a huge flattop pine desk. He was considering his children. They were all there, all five of them, and it gave him a strange feeling to see them together. Glancing at Charlotte, who sat beside him in a straight chair, he saw that she shared that same feeling. Noah and Charlotte Rocklin were closer than most married couples. Always had been—but in the later years, their devotion had grown even deeper. She was, at sixty, more beautiful than she had been when he married her. Silver showed in her blonde hair, and the dark blue eyes were not as bright as when they had married—but no matter! In Noah's eyes, his Charlotte was still the fairest of all women.

Sensing Noah's emotion at seeing all the family together, Charlotte reached out and put her hand on his forearm. Though they never spoke of it, she realized that he was a sick man. Steadfastly she refused to envision life without him and lived each day as if it were forever. Now she gave him a quick smile, then turned toward the children, her quick mind going over each of them—what they were, and what she and Noah longed for them to be.

Stephen, the steady one. The firstborn, and the one she worried about the least. He was larger than she remembered, a solid man, strong and determined. His wife, Ruth, was an attractive woman, but she never had accepted the family. It had been a wrench when Stephen had left to make his life in Washington. Noah had grieved, but silently, speaking only to his wife of it.

Thomas, who could never find his way. Charlotte studied the handsome face of her second-born, admiring his perfect features. If only he could settle down! He had always been jealous of Stephen. Charlotte thought that he longed for the steadiness in his brother, which was sadly lacking in himself. But it was not too late. He was only forty years old. Again the hope flared in Charlotte that somehow this handsome, gifted man would awaken to the potential that God had given him. Glancing quickly at Thomas's wife, Susanna, Charlotte gave a fervent prayer of thanksgiving, for from the moment Thomas had married her, both Noah and Charlotte knew that if Thomas Rocklin were ever to become a complete man, it would be this woman who would show him the way.

Mason, the lonely one. Lost because when his wife died, most of him died with her. Nothing had given Charlotte more satisfaction than Mason's marriage to Jane Dent. It was a pairing made in heaven. Then she died, along with the child she tried to bring into the world, and the life went out of Mason's dark blue eyes. *It's been seven years,* Charlotte thought, *and, from all reports, he's never even looked at another woman.* He had fled Gracefield, and all the memories of Jane that it held, by going to join Stephen in Washington. But even his success in the business world had not given him any joy.

Marianne, the only daughter. She was blessed with Thomas's dark good looks and Stephen's determination.

Tall and willowy, she could have had her pick of the young bloods of Richmond. But she had married Claude Bristol. He was sitting beside his wife now, the French ancestry plain in his thin face. Too fond of cards and fast horses, he was dissatisfied with life at Gracefield, but tied to it by his inability to find anything more comfortable. "He's a weak man," Noah had once said to Charlotte. But he was Marianne's choice, and never did she by word or expression reveal any regret over her choice.

Mark, the wild one. At twenty-nine he looked exactly as his father had looked at that age: six feet one inch tall, with black hair and dark eyes. He was quick-witted, intelligent, charming—and lost! Of all their children, Charlotte and Noah knew this one the least. His early years had been a torment for them, and even now Charlotte felt a dull ache, looking at him and grieving over what might have been. She knew that he was a gambler on a Mississippi riverboat, and that was less dishonorable than some professions he had followed. She had not seen him for three years, and although the marks of dissipation were not on his face, his eyes were empty, and there was a hollowness in his manner.

Jacob came in bearing a tray. He poured coffee from the massive silver pot, and Mark said, "Jacob, I hope this coffee is better than the stuff you used to make."

The wrinkled face of the old slave was immobile as he looked at the young man, but a light of humor came to his brown eyes. "I ain't had no complaints—not since you left, Marse Mark."

"Don't try to get one on Jake, Mark," Claude Bristol laughed. He had fine teeth and smiled as he looked at the slave. "He's the one who caught you and me gambling with the Huger boys out behind the slave quarters, remember?"

Mark blinked; then as the memory came back, he nodded. "I guess I do remember, Claude. I don't know what Father did to you, but he made an 'impression' on me that day!"

Noah's lips curved in a slight grin as laughter went around the room. "Not enough of one, I reckon," he said when it died down. "Maybe I should have used a bigger stick."

Charlotte was dismayed at the look that washed over Mark's face, knowing how he had resented all of Noah's attempts to curb his wild ways. But Stephen said quickly, "Not as big as the one you used on me, I hope, when I sneaked off to see the circus at Richmond." He smiled gently, adding, "I thought it was worth a licking to see my first elephant. Well, I guess the only thing I can say about the thrashing you gave me was that I was willing to quit a long time before you were!"

Mark relaxed as the others laughed at Stephen. He knew that it was the only thrashing Stephen had ever gotten, and he knew his older brother had spoken up to take the attention from him. He felt out of place, as always, in the family. But recently he had felt some vague dread . . . and though it was never quite clear in his mind, it had caused him to respond to his parents' urging to come home for the gathering. *They all have roots,* he thought, looking around at his prosperous family. *All except me.*

He looked at his father and saw that age had eaten away at him. The fine, erect figure was bent and stooped, and even the fierce determination that had been part of Noah Rocklin's being could not hide the pain that grabbed him from time to time. Mark was a good gambler, which meant he could hide his emotions well, but the first glimpse of his father's ravaged face and withered frame had broken that control. His father had seen his reaction, but neither of them could bring himself to mention the illness that was cutting the life out of Noah Rocklin.

"I wanted to see you all alone, before the supper tonight," Noah said suddenly, his voice cutting like a knife across the small talk of the children. He let his eyes run around the room, pausing on each of them, as if weighing them in a balance, then added, "It's been a long time since we've been in the same room."

"Too long," Marianne said quickly. She patted Mason's arm, saying, "It's not as far from Washington as all that, Mason!" She had always been close to this brother—and to his wife, Jane, before her death. "You just wait, dear brother, and see what plans I have for you!"

"I suspect it will be the same plan you use every time I come, Marianne," Mason said, humor in his blue eyes.

"Why, I never—!"

"Your plan," Mason interrupted her, "is to parade every lady looking for a husband in front of me." Marianne sputtered indignantly, but he reached over and put his hand over her mouth. "Do you have a new crop this time? Or is it the same old bunch?"

Stephen laughed at Marianne as she broke away from Mason's grasp, and he said, "She's got one new one, Mason. A very rich widow from Savannah is here, shopping around Richmond for a husband. A Mrs. Sterling. Trot her out, Marianne," he urged, "and have her bring her stock reports."

"Stephen, you are awful—and you, too, Mason!" Marianne said sharply. "Mrs. Sterling is *not* shopping for a husband!"

As the joking went on, Noah looked up suddenly, catching Jacob's eye. The old man was watching him carefully, and he let himself wink. They had been together a long time, and Jake knew how much Noah needed this sort of thing. He let the talk between his children run on, taking little part, but studying them all. From time to time he would respond when one of them asked a question, and he felt Charlotte's warmth as the hour rolled on.

Finally he said, "I guess you all know that I never was a man to mince words—and it's too late to begin now." A silence fell across the room, and he let it stand for what seemed like a long time.

"It's good to see you all here, but I'm thinking this may

be the last time all of us are together." He felt Charlotte's hand suddenly grow tense as it lay on his arm, and he put his other hand over hers. His words had driven all the joy from the room, and now he smiled, a strange smile that touched his dark eyes.

"I hope I've brought you all up to face the truth. I've failed in so many ways. . . ." He paused then, dropping his head as he tried to find the right words. "Well, I've always been a stubborn man, but I'd like you to know that the one regret I have about coming to the end is that I could never say to you the things I wanted to say. So—let me say now, that despite all our bickering and fighting, I've always loved you."

The huge clock in one corner ticked loudly in the silence. "Well, why it's hard for a man to say that to his children, I can't say. Maybe it isn't for some men. I hope all of you will learn to say it often to your own children. Don't put it off. It's something they need to hear."

Marianne said gently, tears in her eyes, "You've said it, Father."

Noah nodded, but seemed sad. "It's easier to say to girls, I think. Harder to say it to boys—and hardest of all to say it to boys who have become men."

Stephen said, "I think we all knew you loved us, Father."

"Did you?" Noah asked, looking up quickly at his oldest son as if for reassurance. "Still, it needs to be said." He shook his head firmly, then went on, "Well, I'm not dead yet, but this world is a pretty deadly place, and any of us can go at any time. So I wanted to talk to you, just you, without your children. Not a sermon, but not far from one either. . . . "

He began to speak, and it was not like anything any of them had ever heard from Noah Rocklin—not even Charlotte. He was not a man given to long speeches, nor to talking about himself. But he did speak of himself, and it was of the dream he had cherished all his life. He told them how he'd begun even as a boy in Wales to dream of a place where he could grow and prosper and have his roots go down deep into the soil. The dream was to make a place that would last, a place where his children and grandchildren could be close, a place of family where they could be free to build a world for the future.

As he spoke, each of his listeners sat silent, amazed. This was the part of Noah Rocklin that none of them had ever known—except for Charlotte. Never before had he put into words the dream that had brought him across the sea, but now that he was dying, the words seemed to come like a spring breaking free from a dam.

Finally he stopped talking, looked around the room, and said, "Don't ever grieve over me. I've had a long life and a good one. I've had the best woman I've ever seen—" here he squeezed Charlotte's hand—"a good place to work, good friends. God has been good to me!"

Then he shook his head, adding, "But a man can do only so much to make his world. I've done the best I know how to make one for you—for all of you. But some things are too big for any man. This country is changing, and I'm afraid of what those changes will do to all of you."

"Why, this is a new country, Father," Thomas said. "It's growing. Changes are to be expected."

Noah shook his head, saying at once, "I knew a man who was with Washington at Valley Forge, Thomas. That was a terrible time. He told me about the bloody footprints in the snow made by men with no shoes. But they were fighting an enemy from across the sea. Oh, Washington's men were Englishmen, I know, but this was America, the New World, and my friend said that it was that dream that kept them going."

"That's right, Father," Stephen agreed. "Men can stand almost anything if they've got the right cause."

Noah studied his hands, saying nothing, then looked up. "That's the change I've been seeing these last few years, Stephen," he said in a voice that was suddenly fragile and weak.

"You mean the problem over slavery?" Mason asked.

"It's not just slavery, Son," Noah said. "That's the red flag that the abolitionists wave to get the crowd to shouting. But there's something lurking up ahead. It's not very big right now . . . ," he said slowly, then paused and seemed lost in thought. "It's like the story in the old Bible, when the prophet was praying for rain. I disremember where it is—"

"First Kings, the eighteenth chapter," Charlotte said promptly. Getting out of her chair, she went to a small table and picked up a worn black Bible. She thumbed through it until she found the place, then read, "And he said to his servant, 'Go up now, look toward the sea.' And he went up, and looked, and said, 'There is nothing.' And he said, 'Go again seven times.' And it came to pass at the seventh time, that he said, 'Behold, there ariseth a little cloud out of the sea, like a man's hand'—"

"That's it!" Noah exclaimed. "Something is coming to America. It's small now, but getting bigger every day. I saw it coming ten years ago. You remember, don't you, the debate in the Senate between Hayne and Webster?"

He referred to a head-on collision in 1830 over the matter of the tariff. But the issue went beyond that and became an arena when states' rights were thrown against national power. Robert Y. Hayne, a young and eloquent senator from South Carolina who was coached by John Calhoun, spoke in favor of the rights of individual states to govern themselves. Daniel Webster rose the next day, and his reply—which took two afternoons!—was a remarkable speech that Northerners had quoted and revered for years.

"I remember what Webster said," Stephen said suddenly. "He said, 'Liberty and union, now and forever, one and inseparable!'"

Thomas suddenly lifted his head, disagreement in his tone. "If a state has the right to join the Union, she has the right to leave it," he said harshly. The two men had fought this battle many times. "You wouldn't think the

Union was so great if you'd stayed here in the South, Stephen," he added. "The North is using our sweat to get rich. We grow the cotton; they pay us a pittance. Then they make it into clothing, and when we buy it back, it's for a king's ransom!"

It was not a new argument, and, as usual, what was said for the next few minutes was not pleasant. Stephen and Mason, having gone North, felt that the charges of the South were not entirely unjust, but that the issues should be solved in Congress. Thomas and Claude Bristol disagreed. Mark said nothing, but watched with sadness in his eyes.

"That's enough!" Noah said finally. He looked around the room, a bleak expression in his eyes. "You see how it is? If my own family is ready to come to blows over states' rights, how much chance is there that Congress can do better?"

"But you surely don't think it will come to a breakup of the Union, sir?" Claude Bristol asked.

"I think it might," Noah answered. "That's why I asked you all to come today. We may never meet again, as I said, and if we don't, I would like for you all to remember one thing." He paused, seeking the right words, then finally said, "If this small cloud that I see does get larger, and if there is ever a time when this country is torn apart—I want you all to remember that no matter how terrible the thing gets, you are all of one blood. And I don't mean just you five Rocklins and your children. I mean all of us who are Americans are of one blood. That's what Valley Forge was all about."

Noah turned away slightly so that his profile was caught in a shaft of clear white sunshine. The light was so bright that millions of motes danced wildly around the head of the old man, creating a profile that was almost spectral in appearance. This, those gathered around the table all felt strongly, was their source in the earth. Their very muscles and sinews came from the pair that sat quietly in the sunlight.

Finally Noah whispered, "May the God of all peace grant you his wisdom. For I know in my bones that you will need it in the days that are coming!"

Then he did something that none of them ever forgot—not ever! The head of the Rocklin family had been a nominal Christian during the latter days of his life, not given to much formal expression of his faith. But now he got to his feet and picked up his cane. With faltering steps, he moved around the desk and came to stand before Stephen. Slowly he put out his free hand until it rested on the head of his firstborn. He stood there, and Stephen bowed his head. They were like a statue, the two of them, so still did they become. Noah's lips were moving but they could not hear what he said. Stephen only knew that his eyes were suddenly filled with hot tears, and then he heard his father say, "God bless you, my boy!"

Noah moved unhurriedly around the group, and when he had repeated the simple action with each of his children, he moved to the door. Jacob opened it silently, waited for Noah to pass through it, then closed it quietly.

They all heard the sound of the cane tapping down the hall, and as it faded, each of them felt a stab of fear—there had been something in the nature of a farewell in the scene. No one wanted to speak. Finally, Charlotte got up and left the room, pausing only to say quietly, "God bless you all. Your father and I love each one of you very much." Then she walked out, and the rest of them followed without saying a word. The only sound in the room then was the ticking of the old clock and the cry of a whippoorwill somewhere off in the distance.

CHAPTER THREE

THE NEW PREACHER

"DORRIE, here's the seating arrangement for the dinner."

Dorrie, on her way from the dining room to the kitchen, paused long enough to take the list from Charlotte. She studied the paper, then nodded. "Yes ma'am, I'll tend to it." A frown came to her face, and she shook her head, adding, "It ain't gonna make Marse Clay happy."

"Why not?"

"'Cause you got him sitting across the table from Miss Melanie—and you got Marse Gideon sittin' right next to her, dats why."

"Oh, don't be foolish, Dorrie," Charlotte snapped. "He's close enough to talk to her, and that's all that's necessary."

"He won't like it none, Miss Charlotte," Dorrie argued. "And I don't think you got the rest of it right, neither."

Charlotte had turned to leave, but wheeled and stared at Dorrie. The two of them had ruled Gracefield so long that there were few disagreements, but Charlotte had learned to listen to the black woman, for she was shrewd. "Well, what's wrong with the seating?" she demanded.

Dorrie held out the paper and began pointing out various guests and their positions. She could read as well as Charlotte and had taught Zander and their children. Her brow wrinkled with discontent as she pointed at the paper.

"Well, in the fust place, you and Mistuh Noah is at one end of the table—and Mistuh Benton is away down at the other end. Now dat don't make no sense, Miss Charlotte! Mistuh Benton, he lak to talk to Mistuh Noah, and he kain't do dat way off down on tother end!" She

37

	Stephen Rocklin	Ruth Rocklin	Laura Steele	Amos Steele
Noah Rocklin	○	○	○	○
	○			
Charlotte Rocklin	○			
	○	○	○	○
	Thomas Rocklin	Susanna Rocklin	Amy Franklin	Brad Franklin

nodded emphatically, adding, "You and Mistuh Noah ought to be right across from the Bentons."

"Oh, Dorrie, we always put the honored guests at the other end of the table from where Noah and I sit! Besides, I've put Marianne and Claude down there to talk to them."

"Well, it doan make no sense," Dorrie said acidly. "And looky whut you done with the rest of it. You done got Marse Stephen and all his folks from up North on one side of de table, and on de other side you got all our own people."

Charlotte stared at the paper, then lifted her eyes to Dorrie, saying with considerable irritation, "They'll want to sit together!"

"Doan care whut dey wants! I says we needs to mix 'em all up! I spect dat oldest boy feel cut off enough, without lining him and his family up 'cross from de folks here like dey was all some kinda' show!"

Staring down at the diagram, Charlotte saw what Dorrie meant. She and Noah were at the north end of the huge rectangular table, and to Noah's left she had placed the visitors: Stephen and Ruth; then their daughter, Laura, and her husband, Amos Steele; and past them she had put Mason and Gideon. *All from the North*, Charlotte thought, *and all set off like they were nothing but guests.*

Across from them, at Charlotte's right, sat the people tied to Gracefield: Thomas and Susanna; Amy and her

Mason Rocklin	Jeremiah Irons	Gideon Rocklin	Melanie Benton	
○	○	○	○	
			○	James Benton
			○	Alice Benton
○	○	○	○	

Marianne Bristol	Claude Bristol	Mark Rocklin	Clay Rocklin

husband, Brad; Marianne and her husband, Claude; then Mark and Clay. Across from Clay sat Melanie, right next to Gideon. Except for the new minister, Jeremiah Irons, who was seated between Mason and Gideon, one side of the table obviously represented the Northern branch of the Rocklins, the other the Southern.

"Never mind, Dorrie," Charlotte said wearily. "Just put the cards down. After we eat, we can go to the drawing room and they can talk to anyone they please."

"Whut about dat niece, Miss Ellen? You ain't got her down, but she'll be here, won't she?"

Charlotte hesitated, then said, "She won't be here. Mrs. Benton said that Ellen was going to a dance in Richmond with Taylor Dewitt."

"Dat girl has got a wicked pair of eyes, ain't she now? Gonna have all de men folks fighting duels ovah her!"

"Oh, she's just a child, Dorrie!" Charlotte said impatiently.

"Chile my foot!" Dorrie sniffed. "She ain't got nothing but men on her mind!"

"Dorrie, don't meddle!"

Dorrie sniffed, but said no more. Hustling back into the kitchen, she spent the next two hours harrying the cooks, the maids, and Zander. Jacob, who was to serve as a second butler, was above Dorrie's control. He sat in a straight-back chair, smoking a corncob pipe and waiting patiently. When Dorrie had everything under control, she paused and fixed two cups of tea, then set one down before Jacob. He nodded, and he sipped the amber liquid as she related her grievance with the mistress over the seating. Finally she shook her head, her lips pursed together in displeasure, saying, "Miss Charlotte's gettin' old, Jacob. Time wuz when she could of fixed things better!"

Jacob closed his eyes, leaned back in the chair, and allowed a puff of blue smoke to escape his lips. He was tired, very tired, and the visitors from Washington had depressed him. The Rocklins were the only family he'd ever known, and he had grieved over the division that had come when Stephen and Mason had gone to live in the North.

"She's mighty tired, I reckon," he said finally. "So am I. But I don't see no way to make things bettah by swappin' folks around at the dinner table."

Dorrie sighed, sipped her tea, then nodded. "I know, Jacob. Breaks your heart, don't it? Might be bettuh if dey hadn't come. I doan lak whut's goin' on. Clay and Gideon chasin' the same woman." She lifted her eyes to Jacob and asked softly, "Do Clay really want dat girl? He done chase aftuh so many, I kain't tell 'bout him."

Jacob thought of the two boys, then said, "Dorrie, you know Clay, how he is. Always been jealous of Gideon. Always tryin' to best him at everything. I been thinkin' he may be after Melanie Benton jest 'cause Gideon likes her. I hopes she turns both of them down." The two of them sat there, talking quietly, until the sound of voices rose from the dining room, and at once they began serving the meal.

The dining room was a large rectangular area, flanked on the outside wall by large windows. There was room at the huge table for exactly twenty people, and every seat was filled. As the soup was served, a pleasant low-pitched buzz filled the room, and Charlotte felt a weight leave her spirit. She had been worried about the dinner, wanting it to go well, not only for Noah's sake, but also for the rest of them.

They progressed through several courses, with Jacob and Zander moving quietly and efficiently through it all, both of them tall and dignified in their uniforms. The maids, well trained by Charlotte and Dorrie, saw to it that no glass was empty for more than a few moments, and the food was delicious.

James Benton, a large man with a shock of white hair over a round face, beamed and said in stentorian tones, "Why, Charlotte, this is excellent! Excellent!"

"Thank you, James," Charlotte said, smiling. "Not as fancy as your Richmond dinners, I fear."

Benton held up his hand in protest. "Not true! Your table at Gracefield is legendary, my dear. Noah, may I propose a toast? To the master and mistress of Gracefield—the epitome of Southern culture!"

Noah tasted his wine, then said, "I offer a toast. To our family and friends from Washington. Though miles come between us, may no distance nor difference sever us."

Murmurs of "Hear! Hear!" ran around the room, and after the toast, James Benton gave a quick glance at the man sitting between Mason and Gideon Rocklin. He had been introduced to the new pastor of the Baptist church before the meal, but a streak of curiosity ran through the planter. "Rev. Irons," he said, "would it be proper of me to propose a toast to you? Or as a man of the cloth, perhaps you might object to the use of ardent spirits?"

Rev. Jeremiah Irons was of medium height and wiry build. He was not handsome, though his direct brown eyes and neat features were agreeable. From time to time during the meal, he had spoken with those seated close to him, particularly to Marianne and Claude Bristol, but also to Mark Rocklin. Now he looked at Mr. Benton and said with a faint smile, "Well, sir, the first pay I ever got for my services as a clergyman was a gallon of home-made whiskey." A laugh went around the table, and when Mark asked, "Did you sample it, Reverend?" Irons shook his head and said, "I must remain silent on that subject, Mr. Rocklin."

"You come from Arkansas, Brother Irons?" Marianne asked.

"Yes, Mrs. Bristol. From so far back in the woods I'd never been to a town before I was twelve years old."

Marianne looked at the hands of Jeremiah Irons and saw that they were hard, brown, and calloused. It made her like him the more, and she said with an encouraging smile, "We are glad to have you, Reverend. Some of us have been praying for a revival at our church for some time."

Irons studied them for a moment, then said, "I'm glad to be here—but I must warn you of two things. One of them you'll discover as soon as I start preaching Sunday morning. I'm not an eloquent man. The other thing, I think you know, and that is that I didn't bring a revival in my bag when I came to Virginia. Only God can give a revival."

Amos Steele, Laura's husband, spoke up at once. "Brother Finney would not agree with you there, Reverend." Steele was a Congregational minister himself, a devout admirer of Charles Finney, the prominent evangelist. A tall man with a dark complexion and piercing hazel eyes, Steele was a striking figure as he leaned forward to peer down the table at Irons. "Mr. Finney insists that bringing a revival of religion is no different from bringing a harvest of corn. He states that there are 'laws' of the spirit, and that if we do what God has commanded, the results must follow."

Irons answered, "I've read Mr. Finney's *Revival Lectures*. A great work, and he's a powerful man of God." He paused, then added, "He may be right, Rev. Steele. But even Mr. Finney says that no revival can come unless God's people repent and turn to God with all their heart."

Steele nodded his approval, but made the mistake of saying, "I think if you can bring your church members to see the wrong in owning another human being, you might have a revival."

At once the room was charged with anger. Laura put

her hand on her husband's arm, saying, "Amos, this is not the time to speak of that."

Steele gave her a direct look, then ran his gaze around the room. "It is always time to speak of righteousness," he said, then he seemed to brace himself, for the anger in the faces of those across the table from him was obvious. He felt a sudden regret that he had spoken, and indeed, he had promised Laura not to bring the subject up while at Gracefield. He was not a tactful man, but neither was he unkind. He had learned to admire and respect his father-in-law, Stephen Rocklin, as he did few other men. And he knew Mason Rocklin to be a man of high principle. But they had left the South—and presumably their Southern faith in slavery. Or so he had believed, but now he saw disapproval on Stephen's face, and it caused him to say, "I apologize. It was wrong of me to speak of my beliefs at this time."

Noah Rocklin said suddenly, "A man must hold to what he believes to be true, Amos." His simple words took the pressure out of the situation—for the moment. The dinner ran on, and nothing more was said about slavery.

Noah ate almost nothing, but watched the little drama going on at the far end of the table. He could not hear the conversation between Melanie, Clay, and Gideon, but he saw the tension in the two men. And he saw also that the parents of both were conscious of it. Certainly the Bentons didn't miss a word.

Alice Benton had said to Melanie before dinner, "I wish you wouldn't get those two young men stirred up. Wait until we get back home. You've got enough beaux there, heaven knows!"

Her words made no impression on Melanie. She was a fine young woman at heart, but who could resist the pleasure of having two men such as the Rocklin cousins vying for her hand? She sat next to Gideon—which caused Clay's eyes to burn with displeasure—and, as the meal progressed, showed her skill at handling suitors. Both men angled for the privilege of taking her to a party at a planter's house the next day; she neither encouraged nor discouraged either of them.

It had been Mark Rocklin who had started the conversation that led to the contest. "I saw something in Memphis last year that would have interested you, Gideon. Fellow named Colt who makes firearms gave a demonstration of his work."

"I met him, Mark," Gideon said. "He tried to get the army to approve his new rifle, but they turned him down."

Mark shrugged, saying, "Don't know about the army, but the rifle he demonstrated beat anything I'd ever seen. He called it the Ring Lever Rifle. Had a cylinder that took six bullets. Colt didn't do the shooting himself, but the marksman who did put six bullets in the bull's-eye in ten seconds. Fired so fast you couldn't even pick out the individual shots."

"Wish the army had bought them," Gideon said. "I'll probably be sent to the plains to fight Indians as soon as I graduate. Be nice to have men armed with those rifles."

"Better practice up on your shooting before you get there, Gideon," Clay spoke up. He grinned, adding, "At the last contest, I beat you pretty bad."

Stung, Gideon replied, "Yes, but I've had a little practice since then."

Clay shook his head. "I don't think practice helps much with shooting. Either a fellow has the eye and the hand, or he hasn't."

"Can't agree," Gideon said at once. "I've seen some pretty bad shots come to the Point, and they learned to hit the center."

Mark's dark eyes gleamed and he said idly, "Why don't you two fellows shoot to see who takes the young lady to the party?"

Clay cried out, "Just the thing! What about it, Gid?"

"You'll have to ask Miss Benton," Gideon said at once. He thought she would put a stop to it and was surprised when she said, "Why, that would be fun!"

"I don't think it would be proper," Charlotte spoke up, seeing the danger of such a contest.

But Clay would not be denied. "Most of our crowd is coming here for breakfast tomorrow. We'll have the contest after that."

Mark suddenly said, "I shouldn't have proposed such a thing, Clay. Let's have the contest, but make the stakes a cash purse."

"I could shoot better for the privilege of escorting a Southern belle to a party than for a few paltry dollars, Mark," Clay said with a grin. After dinner he said to his father, "I don't have a uniform to dazzle the ladies, but I could always outshoot Gid."

"Do him good to lose," Thomas said, smiling. "I never had any use for West Point, anyway."

The following morning brought a group of young men on horseback and young ladies in carriages. There were nine new guests in all, and the house was filled with laughter and high-spirited talk during the breakfast. They devoured mountains of pancakes, sausages, battered eggs, and biscuits, and as they ate Susanna tried to get Thomas to persuade Clay to abandon the idea of the shooting match. "It will cause hard feelings, I'm afraid."

"Nonsense!" Thomas said. He himself was excited by the match and had made a sizable bet with James Benton. He loved to gamble, and more than that, he wanted to see Clay beat Gideon. It was more than the simple desire of a father to see a son win. There was something much deeper than that. He knew it had something to do with the fact that he himself had never been able to best his older brother. He patted Susanna on the shoulder, saying, "It's just a bit of foolishness. The young people have to have their sport."

The shooting match had been mentioned at the breakfast, and at ten o'clock there was a parade from the Big House out to the south pasture. Jeremiah Irons had stayed the night, talking into the early hours of the morning with

Amos Steele, whom he liked but disagreed with heartily. Steele and Brad Franklin had been impressed as judges for the match. It was a beautiful morning, and not only the young people who had come for the holiday, but everyone moved out to where a line of huge oaks formed a boundary for a grazing pasture.

"Don't either of you two hit one of my horses," Claude Bristol warned. He was enjoying the whole thing, for like Thomas he was a man who liked the excitement of gambling. His wife, Marianne, did not like it and said so.

"I wish Mark had never thought of this foolish thing. He ought to know how competitive Clay and Gideon are."

"It'll be all right," Claude assured her. But Marianne saw that her mother was worried, and she wished that the whole incident were over.

Several of the young men had clamored to get into the match, and Clay had said magnanimously, "Come on. None of you can hit the ground with a rifle anyway."

Jacob had brought a dozen rifles from Noah's study, and there was considerable time consumed as the young men argued over them. Zander was sent to nail a board to a tree, then to fasten to it a piece of paper with a cross in the center of it.

Jeremiah Irons found himself standing beside Charlotte Rocklin as the men drew for turns. He saw that her eyes were worried, and he said, "It's just a match, Mrs. Rocklin. Young people must have their fun."

Charlotte turned and looked into his eyes. "And how old are you, Reverend Irons?"

He saw she had him and said sheepishly, "Well, I'm twenty."

"The same age as Clay, and Gideon is twenty-one."

Irons felt uncomfortable, but defended his position. "I guess I'm older than my years you might say. Missed out on most of the things young people do." He looked down at his calloused hands and laughed ruefully. "Guess I was too busy working to learn how to play." Then he said quickly, "Not complaining, sister.

But, truly, your grandsons are fine boys. They'll be all right."

Charlotte didn't answer, but she liked the preacher very much. They both turned to watch as six of the young men took shots at the target. After each shot, Zander put a circle around the hole in the target with an initial showing whose shot it was. Tug Ramsey, the rotund nephew of the governor, never even hit the target, but Taylor Dewitt and two others besides Gid and Clay did.

Mr. Benton called out, "Move back twenty feet for the second shot." In the next round two more dropped out, leaving only Dewitt and the Rocklins.

"Back another twenty feet!" Benton called out. They moved back, and it was Dewitt who dropped out that time. "Between you two," he said with a grin, stepping back.

They moved back again, and for the next ten minutes Clay and Gid took turns, each of them having three shots at the target. They stayed neck and neck, and Irons saw that the pressure was beginning to tell on Clay. *He thought he'd get an easy victory*, Irons realized. *I don't think he likes the pressure.*

It was true. Clay had expected an easy victory. He saw at once that Gid had improved a great deal, and the thought of losing to his cousin made him tense. At the beginning of the match, there had been a great deal of laughter and joking. When it narrowed down to Clay and Gid, most of that died away. A quiet fell on the field, broken only by the cries of the judges announcing the scores.

Gideon was heartily wishing that the thing had never begun. *Blast that fool Mark for thinking of such a thing!* he thought. He saw the pain in his grandmother's face and wanted to deliberately miss, but he found that it was not that easy. He had never loved a woman, and as silly as the contest was, it came to him strongly that the whole thing had become some kind of a symbol. He had glimpsed Melanie's face and saw that she was intent on the thing. So, calling himself a fool, he shot as well as he could.

The sun was hot, and the contest drew down finally to the last target. The scores were equal, and Mr. Benton said, "The man that comes the closest to the bull's-eye this time wins the match!"

The two men shot carefully, taking their time, and after each shot, Zander marked the result. After Clay sent his last shot home, Steele and Franklin took the target off and examined it. Then Steele cried out, "It looks like a tie!"

Clay nodded, his face grim, but Irons had been watching the faces of Noah and Charlotte. They were standing together, slightly to his left, and there was something fragile about them. Irons knew that Noah Rocklin was not well, and he admired him tremendously. He had already discovered that Charlotte Rocklin was one of the finest Christian women he'd ever met. He had been told this, and his visit had proven it to his own mind.

He was not a man to dominate, this young preacher, but the tension in the air and the potential for disaster made him step forward, saying, "Just a minute." They all turned to stare at him, and he took off his coat, saying, "I'm a little late to enter the contest, but I've got a good reason."

"What is it, Reverend?" Benton asked.

"Well, Mr. Benton, I was afraid I'd be embarrassed. I thought Virginia men could shoot. But I've got a twelve-year-old brother back home named Toby, and he could beat anybody I've seen here." He ignored the hard looks he got from the young men and added, "And *I* can beat Toby. So with your permission, Miss Melanie, I'd like to join myself to your other suitors."

Melanie Benton had a quick sense of humor. She liked the young preacher, and the idea of going to a party with him suddenly amused her. "I wish you luck, Reverend Irons," she said demurely.

"Put the target back up," Benton called to the judges, then turned to say with a frown, "I'm not sure it's proper for a man of the cloth to participate in such an affair as this, sir!"

"Oh, Jesus ate with sinners, Mr. Benton, so I suppose I can shoot with a few."

A tall young man named Bushrod Aimes nudged Taylor Dewitt. "He's a blowhard, ain't he, Dewitt?"

"Don't know until I see him shoot." A wicked light came into his eyes. "He better be as good as his brag. Otherwise he might get a ducking in the creek some time or other."

Jake had loaded one of the Hawken rifles, and as Irons took it, he said softly to the preacher, "This is Marse Noah's personal rifle gun, suh. Pulls just a hair to the left."

Irons flashed the slave a quick grin, then swept the rifle up and fired the instant it reached shoulder level. There was no hesitation, and when Steele looked at the target, he yelled, "Dead center!"

There was no need for a second shot, for he had bested the efforts of Clay and Gideon. Gideon came up at once, his hand out and a smile of relief on his broad face. "Fine shot!"

Clay nodded, but he was not smiling as he said, "Good shot, Reverend."

Bushrod Aimes was staring at the preacher. "I guess he don't get no bath in the creek, does he, Dewitt?"

"Nope. Matter of fact, if I ever got in a bad scrap, that preacher would be a pretty good fellow to have around!"

Irons handed the rifle back to Jacob, saying, "Fine shooting gun. It does pull a mite to the left, at that."

Turning, he approached Clay, who was staring at the ground. "Clay, I'll tell you what," he said casually. "Why don't all three of us take that party in? You, me, and Gideon."

Clay looked up quickly at the minister. Disgust and anger marred his eyes, but when he saw the friendly expression on Irons's face, he swallowed hard and forced a grin. "That's decent of you, Preacher," he said. "We'll do it."

Noah and Charlotte were watching as Clay suddenly seemed to lose his anger, and when the three men—Irons, Clay, and Gideon—went to Melanie, she laughed heartily and the tension seemed to dissipate. Irons left the others and moved to where the elder Rocklins stood.

"Where'd you learn to shoot like that, Preacher?" Noah demanded.

"Well, when you've got a single shot rifle, a family of ten children, and a widowed mother to feed with what you shoot, you learn pretty fast."

Charlotte reached her hands out, and he took them without thinking. "Pastor, we are in your debt!"

Noah huffed and said, "Good to see a preacher can be of some practical use around the place!" But he nodded, his old eyes grown warm. "Glad to have you at Gracefield. I hope you'll be here often."

Irons watched as the two moved away, and he looked around to see Amos Steele, who'd come to stand beside him.

"That was good thinking, Jeremiah," Steele said with a warm smile. "It was fast becoming a pretty bad situation. Good thing you can shoot like that!"

"God was in it, Amos."

"You sound like a staunch Calvinist. You think God's in everything?"

"By him all things consist," Irons said quietly.

"Well, I'm glad you've come to serve as pastor here. I love these people." Steele shook his head doubtfully, adding, "They don't care for me, because I'm an abolitionist. But they'll see the light one day. In any case, do what you can for them."

Irons said slowly, "Going to take more than a good sermon or two, Amos. The whole country is sitting on a powder keg. And the Rocklins are right in the middle of it."

Steele stared at the smaller man, a sober light in his hazel eyes. "It's a grand and awesome time, as the song says. I'm no prophet, Jeremiah, but as I've been told, Noah said yesterday, there's a cloud the size of a man's hand on the horizon. A dark cloud that I can't quite understand— but I do believe it's going to get bigger, and all of us are going to be under it."

CHAPTER FOUR

THE CHOICE

July was hot and sultry that year. The heavens withheld the rains, and fine dust rose in tawny clouds as wagons and horses traveled the roads around Richmond. Noah Rocklin did not bear the heat well, and it was on a blistering Thursday afternoon that he said to Thomas, "I'd like to be up North. So hot around here it sears a man's lungs! And look at that dust over there! I feel like I got hot mud in my chest."

The two men were sitting under a huge oak in the backyard drinking tepid lemonade. Thomas glanced at the rising dust, then back to his father. He was worried, for Noah was exhausted, and the constant cough that had plagued him all summer seemed to grow worse day by day.

"Maybe I ought to take you to Maine," Thomas suggested. "You always liked it there. Ought to be cool, Father. I'd like to get some good sea air myself."

Noah shook his head, started to speak, then went into a spasm of coughing that racked his frail body. Thomas sat there, helpless, until the old man gained control. "No, I don't want to die anywhere but on my own ground." He took a swallow of the lemonade, and as Thomas began to protest, Noah said with a trace of irritation, "Of course, I'm going to die. I'm like an animal, Tom. Can feel it coming on." A flash of humor took him, his black eyes gleaming faintly. "Heard about a place in Africa once, where the elephants go to die when they feel it coming on. Seems to me there ought to be some place for a man to go to and take care of it, too."

Thomas said nothing. He and the rest of the family recognized that Noah was growing weaker day by day,

51

and there was nothing the doctor could do. Finally he said, "Maybe it'll rain. Cotton could stand it, and so could I."

Noah nodded, and the two men sat there quietly. It was strange that the two of them had grown closer since Noah's illness. They had never been particularly close, for Thomas was not given to making Gracefield the greatest plantation in Virginia—which had been Noah's lifelong goal. Although Noah had never said so, he was deeply disappointed in the fact that none of his sons cared for farming. For a time Noah had hoped that Marianne would marry a man who could take over the empire he had built, but, like the others, Claude Bristol was more interested in fast horses and hunting than in raising cotton.

Noah thought of Amy's husband, Brad Franklin, who was as dedicated to the world of cotton as he himself had been. But Brad had his own plantation and could not leave it to come to Gracefield. Another spasm of coughing rose in his chest, but he quickly raised the glass and gulped the rest of the lemonade. He leaned his head back on the chair and mused quietly, "You know, Thomas, all this heat and dust we've had this summer, it reminds me of the election."

"You mean for president?" Thomas was quick of mind and caught his father's meaning at once. "Lots of heat and dust in the campaigns, you mean, Father? That's right. Who will win, do you think?"

"It won't be Van Buren," Noah said bitterly. "The country started going bankrupt the year he took office. The Whigs will win, and William Henry Harrison will be the president of the United States."

"He's a Virginian," Thomas noted with satisfaction. "He'll help us when he's elected. Lord knows we need it! I guess he's tough enough. An Indian fighter, isn't he?"

Noah suddenly smiled. "Don't pay any attention to the newspapers. They're saying that Harrison was born in a log cabin and loves cider. Trying to make him into a man the common people will love, like Andy Jackson.

But Harrison's no bumpkin, Thomas. He's from a prosperous Virginia family, went to college and studied law.
He'll win, and as you say, the South will have something
to say about the way this country is going."

They spoke for a short time of politics, then Noah
asked, "What's the latest report on the courtship?"

"Oh, I don't know, Father." Thomas shook his head
with disgust. "It's gone too far, and if Melanie doesn't
make up her mind soon, I think her father will lock her
up for a year."

Clay and Gideon's rivalry had grown as heated as the
climate and the political campaign. It had become, in
fact, a form of joke around Richmond. A cartoon had cir-
culated showing Melanie dressed in a hoopskirt juggling
the two young men in the air. Neither James Benton nor
Noah had thought it funny. The two men admired one
another and wanted to see their families tied together—
but both were heartily tired of the whole affair.

"I thought the Benton girl had more sense, Thomas,"
Noah said.

"Well, she's young, Father." Thomas shrugged. "Any
young girl would be excited to have two attractive men
after her. Can't blame her too much, I suppose."

"You'd like for Clay to win, wouldn't you?"

"Yes, I would. If she marries Gideon, Melanie will have
to leave home and follow him to his stations. It's a hard
life for a woman. Some of those forts out west are terrible
places, I'm told. But if she marries Clay, it'll be a tie between Gracefield and Briarcliff. The Bentons don't have a
son, so Clay would be master of the Benton empire
sooner or later. That would give us more land and slaves
than any other plantation in the South, I think."

"Not a very romantic approach to marriage," Noah
said.

"I suppose not." Thomas shrugged, then said, "Stephen
was always supposed to be the practical son, wasn't he?
And here I am, the 'romantic' son, trying to gain more
land by marrying my son into a wealthy family!"

Noah said carefully, "I've sometimes felt that you had hard feelings toward Stephen. Maybe I gave you some cause. I never wanted to show favoritism, but perhaps I did."

"We're not as much alike, you and I, as you and Stephen are," Thomas said slowly. "But I have no complaint, Father. Now that you mention it, though, I do think Clay feels a little antagonism toward Gideon. He's never said much about it, but I know him well. That's what worries me about this competition for Melanie. Clay's always tried to outdo Gideon in everything, and I've had the uneasy feeling that it's not altogether love for Melanie that's made him throw himself into this rivalry."

"You think he might want her just because Gideon's after her?"

"I hope I'm wrong, but Susanna and I have talked of it. Whichever one of them Melanie chooses, it's going to be hard. All in the family, isn't it? And the loser will have to look at his cousin as a 'winner' as long as they both live."

"Too bad!" Noah said, sadness touching his voice. "I wish she'd drop them both. That would answer. But I don't suppose she will."

"No. Gideon's coming next week. Maybe he's tired of the game, too. I got that much from Stephen's last letter. He and Ruth feel much the same as we do about it. So with a little pressure from us, from Stephen, and from the Bentons, maybe it'll be settled." He got to his feet, stretched, and shook his head. "Clay hasn't been worth a dime this summer. Done nothing but chase around with his crowd. He's got to settle down."

Noah said quietly, "I've been proud of the way you've taken hold of the place lately, Thomas. You've done a fine job."

The unexpected praise brought a flush of pleasure to Thomas's face, and Noah wished suddenly that he'd been quicker in the past to praise this unstable son of his. Sadness washed over him as he realized it was too late. *I guess all old men come to this,* he thought. *Wanting to go back and change the past. But it's always too late.*

"I think I'll go to bed for a while, Son," he said. "I'm a little tired."

Washington had suffered from the blistering July heat no less than Richmond had, and as Stephen brought the buggy to a stop at the hitching rack outside of the Orange and Alexandria Railroad station, sweat poured down his face. "Gid, if it's hotter in Richmond than it is here in Washington," he grunted, "you'll melt like butter in the sun."

Gideon stepped down, handed his mother to the ground, then answered soberly, "I'm not worried about the weather."

Ruth took his arm, holding on to him as if she planned to keep him from getting on the train. Ever since he had come in from West Point, stopping for an overnight visit on his way to Richmond, she had tried to get him to change his mind. Even now with the sound of the steam engine chuffing down the track, she pleaded, "Son, I wish you'd wait. There's no hurry about all this. Wait until fall, until you have more time to think about it."

Gideon looked down at her, smiling faintly. "You think if I stay away, Mellie will pick Clay, don't you, Mother?" Then he frowned, his square face growing sober. "That's what I'm afraid of. Clay's there all the time, and he's quite a romantic fellow. I'm just a plain soldier, and I'll be asking Mellie to leave her whole way of life."

"That's what your father and I are afraid of, Son," Ruth broke in, nodding. "Southern women don't transplant easily. And the woman you marry will have to follow you all over the country."

Stephen listened as Ruth continued to plead, but said nothing. He had talked with his son alone and knew there was no hope of changing the boy's mind. He was, moreover, less resistant to the match than was his wife. He liked Melanie very much, feeling that under her facade of light foolishness lay a strong woman who would make an excellent wife for Gideon.

An earsplitting shriek rose from the engine, and Gid quickly kissed his mother. "Good-bye, Mother," he said, then took the hard hand his father offered. "Thanks for the extra cash, Father." He grinned at Stephen. "I promise not to spend it on anything useful."

"Come back as soon as you can, Gid," Stephen said. "Now hurry, or you'll be left behind."

Gid turned and, plucking his carpetbag from the back of the buggy, dashed toward the train, which was already in motion. He caught the steel handhold with his free hand, hauled himself aboard, then turned and waved as the train picked up speed. When his parents were out of sight, he moved into the car and found a seat. All the car windows were open, and though it was hot, the wind on his face was welcome. The cinders that floated in and stung his cheeks were not, but they were a necessary evil of travel on the Orange and Alexandria Railroad. The car swayed from side to side on sleepers that gave slightly, for much of the line was new.

Gid leaned back, relieved to have his visit with his parents behind him. He had felt constrained to go and, in a brief conversation with his father, had laid bare his intention. "I'm going to get this thing settled, one way or another," he had said after his mother had gone to bed. "Mellie's got to make up her mind. I can't go on in limbo, and I don't guess Clay can either. So after this visit, either you'll have a prospective daughter-in-law, or Uncle Thomas will!"

As the train moved on, Gideon watched the Potomac roll beside the tracks. He went over his decision again. He had been, he knew, almost useless at the Point—his mind was on Melanie, not his work. And he was honest enough to admit that he had little hope of success with her. As the train made a quick stop at Alexandria, then turned west, he reviewed his chances, finding them not very good.

She'd be better off with Clay, he thought painfully. *I'll*

only be able to offer her a bare room in some outpost in Ne-
braska or some other wild place. If she marries Clay, she'll
have Briarcliff.

The train chugged along, crossing Bull Run Creek,
then Manassas Station. As it roared over the bridge that
spanned the Rappahannock River, Gid put his head on
his chest and fell asleep. He awoke occasionally, but by
the time the train pulled into Richmond, he had a painful neck and was bleary-eyed.

He made his way to a livery stable, rented a horse, and
soon was on his way out of Richmond. Glad to be off the
train, he kept the spirited bay at a fast trot, pulling him
up now and then for a drink at one of the creeks that
crossed the road. He passed the road that led to Briarcliff,
then pulled the bay to a halt. It was growing late, and he
was tempted to gallop right to the Benton place and put
his cause to Melanie at once. But there was a solid
patience in Gideon Rocklin, which some mistook for
dullness. That was one of the characteristics that made
him a good soldier. One of his instructors, Layton Fields,
had argued this with another on the staff who thought
Gideon was a plodder.

"Yes, he does plod," Fields had agreed. "But only until
he is certain of his ground. When he knows the enemy
and has assessed his own potential, he'll show enough
dash. It's those fools who rush blindly toward the sound
of the guns who scare me. Usually they manage to get
themselves and their men promptly slaughtered!"

So it was typical of Gid that he would pause and con-
sider every facet of the matter before he made a decision.
Clay, he thought with a wry grin, *would not have hesitated*
for a single instant. He would have spurred the bay, arrived at
Briarcliff with a spent horse, and flung himself toward
Melanie without hesitation.

"Maybe I am a plodder," Gid spoke aloud as he patted
the neck of his mount. Then he shook his heavy shoulders, spoke to the horse, and galloped down the dusty
road. The whippoorwills were calling faintly from the

woods as he reached the entrance to Gracefield, and when he dismounted, Highboy, the oldest son of Box and Carrie, came out of the stable.

"Marse Gideon," he said, his white teeth flashing. "I thought you was off soljerin' somewheres." Catching the reins that Gideon tossed to him, he asked slyly, "You come courtin' Miss Melanie?"

Gideon laughed suddenly, "Yes, Highboy, I have indeed." He well knew that the activities of the Rocklin family were the chief topics of conversation for the slaves and thought wryly that there were no secrets in the world of Gracefield. "How's Mr. Noah?"

"Real porely, Marse Gideon," Highboy said sadly. "De doctuh wuz here dis mawnin. I heard my maw tell Miss Charlotte dat she better git some medicines from Granny Sarrie."

"Grain this horse, Highboy," Gideon said absently, then walked toward the Big House. Granny Sarrie was a black woman of indeterminate age who trafficked with herbs and voodoo in equal proportions. Charlotte sometimes used the herbs, but scorned the rest of Sarrie's potions.

He was met at the door by his aunt Susanna and asked at once, "How is he, Aunt Sue?"

Susanna shook her head, saying, "Not well at all, Gideon. Come in." He followed her into the kitchen, where he was greeted by Carrie and given a glass of tea. "Most everyone's gone to Richmond, Gideon," Susanna said as he sipped it. "The Governor's Ball is tonight, you know."

"Forgot about it," Gid said. He looked at her carefully, then asked, "Can I see him?"

Susanna answered, "He was asleep a little while ago, but he wakes up often. Come along and we'll see."

He followed her to the bedroom on the first floor, and when they entered, they found Charlotte sitting beside the sick man. But Noah was awake and said at once, "Come in, Gid. And you two women can fix us a drink. A mint julep for me."

"I'll fix it," Charlotte said, and the two women left the room. Gid looked after them in surprise, for he knew that the doctor had forbidden liquor for his grandfather. *Not a good sign,* he thought, taking the chair beside the bed. *Almost as if they've given up.*

But he said only, "How do you feel?"

"Pretty bad, pretty bad," Noah said, then smiled faintly. "How come you're not at the ball?"

"Forgot about it."

"Well, you won't win any points that way," Noah said. He shifted in the bed, his thin hands pulling at his nightshirt. "How's Stephen and your mother?" He listened as Gid gave the news, then nodded. He examined Gid carefully. "You've got a look in your eye, Gid. What's on your mind?"

"Well, I've got to settle this business with Melanie," Gid said bluntly. He told his grandfather how he'd been practically useless, and then added, "It's got to be one way or the other." A streak of curiosity touched him, and he asked, "Which way are you betting, Grandfather?"

Noah grinned faintly. "Not sayin', boy," he stated. "But I will say that if that girl takes you, she'll get a winner." He laughed silently, adding, "I must be going fast. Got to saying nice things to everybody. Never was broke out with that, was I?"

"I remember when I broke the leg of that promising colt," Gid said. "You told me I'd wind up picking cotton for a living." He saw the memory bring a smile to Noah's lips, then added, "But when I went to the Point, what you said when I came to say good-bye has been a real help to me. You said, 'Boy, you're a fool, but all young men are fools. When you get that out of you, the man that's left is going to do the Rocklins proud.'" Gideon suddenly reached out and took the frail hand in his thick one. It felt as fragile as the bones of a bird, but he said, "That meant a lot to me, Grandfather. More than you know. Sometimes when I was ready to quit, I'd think of that—and it kept me going."

Noah's eyes glistened as he patted the strong hand of his grandson. "Glad you told me about that, Gid," he said simply. "I'm proud of you, as I was proud of your father." He lay there quietly, and then he said, "Whatever comes to this country, Gid, don't let go of the part of you that's here at Gracefield. I'll have your word on that, as an officer and a gentleman."

Gideon saw the fire in the old eyes and at once said, "You have it."

Noah relaxed, and the two men talked quietly until Charlotte came back with two mint juleps. She handed one to Gid, then helped Noah sit up. After handing him the tall, frosty glass, she stepped back, saying, "That's just about all the ice."

Noah sipped the concoction, then smacked his lips. "Gid, git out of here. Go give Clay a run for his money."

Gideon finished the drink, then rose to leave. "I'll see you tomorrow, Grandfather."

He left the room, and Noah said, "That's a good boy."

"They both are," Charlotte agreed. "I guess he's come to force Melanie to make a choice."

Noah was accustomed to her insight and merely nodded. "It'll be settled one way or another by the time he leaves. Which one will she have?"

Charlotte walked over and sat down on the bed. She smoothed his silver hair back from his forehead, then smiled at him. "You used to be smarter, Noah, than to try to guess what's in a woman's heart. I don't think Melanie knows herself—but she will have to choose now."

The color of Melanie's gown reflected the royal blue of her eyes, and as she swirled about the dance floor with Clay, she threw her head back and laughed at something he had said. He was the best-looking man at the ball, dressed in fawn trousers and a rust-colored coat. His black hair and olive skin set off his chiseled features, and as he spoke Melanie could sense the excitement that flowed through him. Aside from his good looks, there was a special quality that drew people to Clay. He seemed charged with some sort of energy, a life that seemed sadly lacking in most men. Though it was true that he often was quick to change direction, just now Melanie could feel her own spirit rising to meet his.

"I can't dance every dance with you, Clay," she protested. "You were absolutely rude to Lyle McIntire!"

"Let Lyle find his own woman," Clay said with a grin. "I've put the word out that I'll shoot any man who tries to dance with you tonight."

"You are awful!" Melanie exclaimed, but her eyes sparkled with excitement. "Very well, I'll sit out the next one, and you must ask Ellen to dance."

"She's got enough fellows chasing her." Clay cast a glance over his shoulder and, noting that Ellen had four of his friends surrounding her, laughed. "Look at them! Chasing after her like a pack of hound dogs with their tongues hanging out."

"Clay! Don't be crude!"

He was amused at her protest. "Mellie, any girl who wears a dress like Ellen has on wants to attract men."

Though she denied his words, secretly Melanie agreed. Ellen had appeared in a formfitting rose-colored dress, the front of which was cut extremely low. When Melanie had attempted to hint that the gown was immodest, Ellen had laughed at her. "It's what they're wearing in Europe, Mellie. I'm just introducing the newest styles. You'll be wearing one just like this at your next ball!"

Despite his protests, Melanie insisted that Clay dance with her cousin, so as soon as the dance ended, he handed her over to Taylor Dewitt, who saw Melanie to a chair, and went to Ellen. When he asked her to dance, at once she said, "Of course, Clay," and they waltzed off, leaving Bushrod Aimes staring after them in chagrin.

"Well, Tug, that is some stuck-up girl," Bushrod said half angrily. "Nothing but a Rocklin is good enough for her, I guess."

Tug Ramsey was wearing a tight collar, which made his

round face red as a rising sun—though, to be honest, some of the color was due to the contents of a bottle that he and the other young men sampled from time to time. "If she wasn't as juicy as a ripe plum," Tug said with a grin, "I guess we'd leave her alone. Wonder if—," he broke off, saying in a startled voice, "Look, Bushrod! There's Gid!"

The two of them watched as Gideon, resplendent in a dress uniform, came in through the double doors, looked around, and made his way to where Melanie was seated. They saw the astonishment steal over her face as she looked up at Gid. Then she arose and followed him through a pair of French doors that led to the outer court of the Governor's mansion.

"Ol' Gid looks dead serious, don't he now?" Tug remarked. "I expect he means business."

"I'd better tell Clay," Bushrod said. He waited until the dance was over, then, as Clay brought Ellen from the dance floor, moved close to him. "Clay, did you see Gid come in?" he murmured.

Clay gave him a sharp look. "No. Where is he?"

Bushrod grinned brashly. "Out in the garden, boy, with Melanie—and you know what that means! Better get yourself into action."

Clay gave Aimes a look of irritation, but said only, "I can't go busting out there now. Let's go have a drink. I'll head him off pretty soon."

But the drink turned out to be two drinks, then three. The pair of them were joined by Taylor Dewitt and Tug Ramsey, and the four of them got into a drinking contest. Dewitt, who could apparently hold any amount of whiskey with no discernible result, tried to caution Clay. "Better lay off this stuff, Clay," he said. "It's pretty potent. You don't want to get drunk."

Clay laughed rashly, tilted the bottle, and drank deeply. "I can hold my liquor, Taylor," he boasted. "You tend to your own business." He drank again, and laughed as he handed the bottle to Bushrod. "Put it down like a man, Aimes!"

On the other side of the mansion, Melanie was in a state of shock. She had been glad to see Gid, but when she started to tell him what she'd been doing, he had said, "I didn't come to Richmond to hear about the balls you've been to, Mellie." His words sounded a little harsh, but his eyes were gentle. "I came to ask you to marry me."

Melanie smiled. "You've done that pretty regularly for the past few months, Gid. In person and by mail."

Gid shook his head. The light that filtered through the French doors caught him, framing his solid shape and heightening the glow in his brown eyes. There was, Melanie saw suddenly, a determination in him that was somehow different than ever before.

"I'm worn out, Mellie," Gid said simply. "Life is difficult enough at West Point, and since I've had you on my mind, I've not done a blessed thing right. If something doesn't happen, I'll wash out." Then he took her hands, and held them in his. "But that's not the point, Mellie."

Melanie was sobered by his manner. His hands were so large that her own were lost in his grasp, and she exclaimed, "Why, Gid, you're trembling!"

He looked down at his hands and laughed shortly. "I didn't think there was anything in the world that could do that to me, Mellie. Shows you how things are with me." He took one hand from hers and used it to draw her closer. "You're so beautiful, Mellie!" he whispered. "But that's not why I love you. I'd love you even if you lost your beauty."

It was a thought that had not occurred to Melanie, and the sudden strangeness of it shocked her. She relied on her good looks, even took them for granted. Sometimes she felt sorry for plain girls, and now the thought came to her, *What would happen if I got scarred?* And she knew at once the answer: Most men would turn from her.

"I really believe you would, Gid," she said softly. "You really would." In that moment, though she had known Gideon Rocklin all her life, Melanie saw the strength of the man. It made her feel strangely safe as she stood within the circle of his arms.

"You know me, Mellie," Gid said. "I don't change much. Guess I'm not very exciting. But I'll never stop loving you. Not even if you choose Clay. When we are both old and silver-haired, I'll love you."

His simple words did more to Melanie than any she'd ever heard before. If some other man had spoken them, she could have put them away—but not this man. He was not dashing, true enough, but Melanie realized with a start that what she wanted, more than dashing manners, was a man who would always love her.

"I—I love you, Gid," she whispered, and stepped closer to him, reaching up to pull his head down. His kiss was sweet, but not demanding. She sensed the longing behind the light pressure of his lips and knew that he was holding himself in tight rein, thinking of her. And she now knew that she would trust herself to this strong, solid man for the rest of her life.

"I'll marry you, Gid, if you want me," she whispered, drawing back from him so that she could see his face.

His eyes burned suddenly, and his lips grew firm as he took a deep breath. Then he laughed and caught her close. "Great guns!" he exclaimed. "I thought I'd lost you!"

They were both trembling, and for the next few minutes they simply walked around the garden, oblivious to everything except each other and the decision they had just made. Finally Melanie laughed nervously, saying, "I feel married already, Gid!"

"Well, you're not," he said practically, then kissed her.

"Let's go make the announcement!" Melanie said, taking his hand.

"No! That's not the way, Mellie!" Gid pulled her back, then said soberly, "We've got to think of Clay."

Melanie flushed and dropped her head. When she lifted it to look at him, she tried to smile. "You see what a selfish girl you're getting? Yes, we must think of Clay. But I must tell my parents now."

"Good! After that, you must take Clay someplace

where it's quiet." Gid shook his head, adding, "It's going to be hard for him, Mellie."

"Oh, Gid, why did I ever lead you two on in such a senseless way?"

"That's past praying for, Mellie," he said gently. "The thing now is to make it as easy for him as possible. What I'd like to do is say nothing to anyone—except your parents, I suppose. Tell Clay you won't marry him, and don't even mention me. After he gets used to the idea, I can come courting again."

"Oh, Gid, that'll take forever!"

"But it's the best way, Mellie. Will you do it?"

Melanie nodded, then reached up and kissed him. "You're good, Gideon. Much better than I am!"

"That's true." He nodded with a twinkle of humor in his eye. "But you're young, and I can bring you up to my standards quickly enough. Now, go and tell your parents."

Gideon's plan was good—but it never happened. Melanie found her father and he was pleased enough with her choice. "He's a good solid man, Mellie," James Benton affirmed. "He'll be a general one of these days. You'll see!"

Melanie kissed him, then went upstairs seeking her mother. In her excitement, she forgot to tell her father to keep the engagement a secret, and as soon as she was out of sight, Benton went to the governor, telling him the good news. The governor, anxious to please Benton, called for silence, then proposed a toast to the engagement of the couple.

Clay himself got the news when he came into the ballroom with his friends. His face was flushed and his speech was slightly slurred by the liquor. He was stopped by a friend who said, "Well, you gave it all you had, Clay. Too bad you got beat."

Clay stared at the man, a tall fellow named Christopher Potter. "What—you talking about, Chris?" he asked.

"Why, about Melanie's engagement to Gideon," Potter said, then he saw that Clay's face had turned white. "Oh, good Lord, Clay!" he apologized. "I thought you knew about it!"

Clay Rocklin stood there, feeling the anger as it rose in him. He looked across the room for Melanie, but did not see her. He did see Gid, however, and at that moment if he had had a gun, he would have shot his cousin through the heart.

Gideon saw Clay and started across the room. But as he drew near, Clay gave him one bitter glance of violent anger, then turned on his heel and stormed out.

"That was bad," Taylor Dewitt said to Bushrod. "We better go with him." The two of them left at once, and for the rest of the night they trailed along with Clay as he made his way through the lowest dives and brothels of Richmond. When he was completely unconscious, Dewitt and Aimes took him to a hotel room and put him to bed.

Looking down on him, Dewitt said, "I've seen Clay when he was mad, Bushrod. But this is different."

"He's crazy, Dewitt," Bushrod agreed. "Maybe he'll feel better about it when he wakes up."

Taylor Dewitt shook his head, a doubtful cast to his lean face. "I hope so—but Clay was mighty set on that girl. If only it could have been any other man! You know how he's always been jealous of Gid."

"I guess if it were any other man, Clay would call him out. But he can't fight a duel with a member of his own family!"

"I don't know, Bushrod . . . just no telling what Clay will do. He's got a mighty wild streak." He suddenly struck his hands together and swore. "I wish Gid would take that girl and elope! Be better for everyone!"

But the pair knew that would never happen, and for a long time they sat up trying to think of a way to help their friend. But when the dawn came and Clay awoke, they saw the raw look of anger in his eyes. They both knew that there was not a single thing on earth they could do for Clay Rocklin.

CHAPTER FIVE
MELORA

"I DON'T suppose you ever thought of deer hunting as a ministry, did you, Brother Irons?"

"I never try to figure out how God might want to work."

Reverend Jeremiah Irons looked over his cup of steaming coffee toward Susanna Rocklin. The two of them were sitting in Gracefield's kitchen, which was, for once, unoccupied. It was so early that it was still dark outside. A chill September wind had numbed the preacher's nose and stiffened his hands on the ride from the parsonage to Gracefield, and he had found Susanna waiting for him with hot coffee. Now as the two of them sat at the table waiting for Clay to come down, he thought about the past two months.

He had spent a great deal of his time at Gracefield, not only coming almost daily to visit Noah, who was usually confined to his bed, but to encourage Charlotte and Susanna. They were both pillars in his church, and both were in the valley of the shadow—Charlotte because she faced the loss of her beloved and Susanna because of Clay's behavior. There was little he could do in a practical way for Noah and Charlotte, though his very presence there cheered both of them. But he had acted on Susanna's request to make himself available to Clay. This was, to say the least, difficult, for Clay had gone sour since Melanie had accepted Gideon.

Every attempt that Irons made to help Clay in a spiritual way was rebuffed. Clay did his work on the plantation sullenly, staying away from the family and leaving for Richmond to drink and carouse as soon as his work was done. Reports of his wild behavior came to Thomas and Susanna, and it was this that prompted Susanna to call upon her pastor for help. "He'll never come to church, Brother Jerry," she had said in desperation, and it was then that Jeremiah had been struck with the idea of getting next to Clay in another way.

"Maybe not," he'd answered Susanna, "so let's try something else." His plan was to get Clay to hunt with him, for both of them were avid hunters. Susanna had agreed at once, and the plan had worked to some extent. Clay had curtly refused the first invitation, suspicious of the preacher, but the second time he had gone duck hunting with Irons. It had been a strange hunt, Irons reported later to Susanna. "He had a wall built around himself a mile high, expecting me to preach at him." The minister had smiled at her. "When I didn't say a word about how he's been behaving, and I didn't mention the Bible—I think it sort of disappointed him. He was loaded for bear, Susanna. Just ready to bawl me out and stalk off. When he saw I wasn't 'on duty,' so to speak, he relaxed and we had a good time."

Now Irons sipped his coffee and looked at Susanna. "Clay's running from God, but Jesus Christ is on his trail."

Susanna had circles under her eyes, and there was a droop to her shoulders. The double difficulty of taking over most of Charlotte's work while the older woman cared for Noah and bearing the burden of Clay's behavior had worn her thin. But when she smiled and said, "I'm glad you've found a way to get close to him, Pastor," there was a light of hope in her fine eyes. "I thank God for sending us a pastor like you, Brother Jerry!"

Irons flushed at the praise and started to protest, but at that moment Clay came in, his eyes bleary and a tremble in his hands. He stopped and stared at them, his eyes defiant. "I told you not to fix breakfast, Mother," he said crossly. "I don't want anything to eat."

Irons said quickly, "Well, I do, Clay. If you don't want anything, you can sit down and listen to me eat." He spoke lightly, and began at once to eat the scrambled eggs and fried ham that Susanna set before him. As Irons had guessed, once Clay had made himself obnoxious—and when he saw that nobody was going to argue with him—he sat down and ate.

Susanna stood beside her son, saying, "Clay, you look like you've got a fever."

"I'm all right," he said shortly. "Just a cold."

When the two men were finished, Irons said, "Unless you know of a better spot, I thought we'd go over to Branson's Ridge. Buford Yancy got a big buck over there yesterday morning. He said there were plenty more he could have taken."

Clay nodded, muttered, "I don't care," and the two of them left the warmth of the kitchen. Taking care that Clay did not see, Irons winked at Susanna, and she smiled slightly in return.

Clay saddled a long-legged bay, and the two of them rode out of the stable. The air was chill and the horses were both spirited, so for the first mile they rode along at a gallop. Then they pulled down to a slower pace when they turned off the main road. Clay said nothing at all, but Irons spoke cheerfully of neutral things—mostly about hunting and horses and dogs.

They rode for an hour, then stopped at a rough house set at the edge of a thick, dense woods. "Have to walk from here, Clay," Irons said. "Looks like none of the Yancys are up yet. I told Buford we'd leave our horses here. He said he'd take care of them if we were late getting back." Then he looked closely at Clay and remarked, "You look washed out, Clay. Why don't we call this off until you feel better?"

"Nothing wrong with me," Clay said stubbornly. In truth, he felt terrible—but he dismounted in silence and waited for Irons.

They put their horses in a ramshackle corral containing a cow and two mules, then plunged into the thick woods. At first the going was fairly easy, but soon the heavy trees seemed to close about them, slowing them down. They were both gasping for breath two hours later when Jeremiah pulled up, saying, "Here's the creek. I think we can pick up something here. Why don't you take this stand, and I'll go on down a quarter?"

"All right."

Clay watched as Irons faded away into the darkness, wondering how the man moved so quietly over dry leaves and dead branches. Then he moved to a large oak, put his back against it, and waited. The ebony sky was beginning to turn gray in the east, and half an hour later a rosy glow emanated through the branches of the tree he stood under.

As Clay stood there in the silence that was broken now and then by the scurrying of small animals or the soft cry of a bird awakening, random thoughts came to him. He had been drunk the night before, reeling up the stairs and falling into bed without removing his clothes. Flashing bits of memory touched his mind briefly, like reflections in a pool broken by ripples of water. Some of them were from other nights spent in the fleshpots of Richmond—the sound of a woman's voice enticing him, the clink of glasses in a bar, the crash of a chair thrown in a fight.

But there were other memories, too . . . memories that he hated even worse. Memories of Melanie. Her face seemed to flash before his eyes, the way she had appeared to him once when he had brought her a huge bouquet of daisies—eyes bright and lips parted with delight. He shut his eyes quickly, giving his shoulders an angry shake. But he could not blot the images out for long. That was why he had sought oblivion in a bottle for the past two months. That, and his resentment and bitterness against his cousin Gideon.

Time and again he had tried to pull himself up, ashamed that he had no more control. But the bitterness was a drug, no less potent or addictive than the rotgut he was drinking. Even as the dawn spread faint ruby gleams over the small creek that murmured a few feet away, he struggled again to cast the envy of Gideon away, but with no success. It ate at him like lye, and nothing seemed to make it more bearable.

Grandfather is dying, he thought, staring at the creek without seeing it. *My parents are worried sick about me. All I do is go around mean as a yard dog looking for somebody to bite!*

He glanced down the creek toward where he supposed Irons was stationed. *The preacher knows better than to say anything, but if he only knew the truth . . . that nobody hates those nights in Richmond worse than I do! But I can't quit!*

Suddenly a buck stepped out from behind a huge oak on the far side of the creek, his head held high and his ears working. As always at such a time, Clay's breathing seemed to stop as if a huge arm had been tightened around his chest. He did not even blink as the buck stood there, suspicious, needing only a single movement to send him back into the woods. Time stopped for Clay; the very creek seemed to pause as the deer waited, and the breeze in the tops of the branches of the tree Clay stood under seemed to stop as if the world held its breath.

Then the deer took a step, halted, listened again—and walked delicately to the edge of the brook. He dipped his head, and Clay, waiting for such a movement, lifted his gun and pulled the trigger. The explosion seemed to rock the world, and the deer leaped sideways in a tremendous jump that carried him to the edge of the trees.

But Clay's bullet was in its heart. All of the animal's actions were sheer reflex, and he dropped down lifelessly.

Clay gave a yell, dropped his gun, and plunged toward the creek, pulling his knife from his belt. He had no control at such times and, in fact, did not want to control the emotion that welled up inside him. He reached the creek, took two giant strides, his heart beating madly— and then his foot went into a crevice by the brook's edge and he fell headlong into the cold water.

A cry of pain was wrenched from him, for the hole was

71

not soft dirt, but solid rock, formed by large stones which had been brought together by the action of the water.

A shock of ragged pain flashed through Clay, for his full weight had been thrown against his ankle, which was held as in a vise by the stones. He pulled himself up, pulling his foot free as he rolled over. But when he looked down, he saw that the foot was bent at an unnatural angle—and the pain was like a knife.

Sitting there with the cold waters of the creek soaking him, he held his ankle, clenching his teeth against the waves of pure pain that seared him. It was so great, that pain, that for a few moments he could not even pull himself out of the cold water. Then he tried to crawl, and a cry of pain escaped his lips.

"Clay! You get one?"

Iron's voice seemed to come faintly from far away, and it was all Clay could do to cry out, "Irons! Help me!"

He lay there on the bank, trying not to move the leg. Soon he heard Irons call out, "Clay? Where are you?"

"Over here!"

Then Irons was there, bending over him. "You didn't shoot your foot?" he asked in alarm.

"No—but I think I broke my ankle."

Irons began at once testing the leg with strong hands. "May be broken. But maybe not. I've seen some ankles twisted as bad as that without a break." Then he shook his head. "Got to get you out of here, Clay."

"I can walk if you'll let me lean on you, Preacher."

Irons looked doubtful, and when he had gotten Clay to a standing position, the first step brought a sharp grunt of pain from Clay's lips. "This won't do!" Irons protested. He helped Clay away from the stony creek bed and let him down on the soft earth. Standing up he said, "I can't carry you, so you'll have to wait while I go for help."

"I'll be all right," Clay grunted. He cursed and slapped the ground with his palm. "What a stupid thing to do!"

"We all take falls, Clay," Irons said. He stripped off his coat and handed it to the injured man. "I'll build you up a fire." He quickly gathered a supply of dead wood from a fallen tree, kindled a fire, and got it burning.

"Let's dry your clothes out," Irons said. "It'll take me a few hours to get back here with help. Won't do that cold of yours any good to stay wet."

"No. I'll be all right."

Irons looked at him doubtfully, but Clay's stubborn face told him there was no use in arguing the point. He turned and left at a fast trot, disappearing into the brush like an Indian. Clay looked after him, then picked up a rock and threw it at the creek angrily. Carefully he settled back and began the wait.

And it was a long wait, made worse by the discomfort of his wet clothes and the pain of his injured leg. As the hours passed by, Clay was able to get the wood the preacher had pulled close without much effort, but soon he began to shake with a chill. Painfully he dragged the limbs to the fire, but no matter how close he tried to get to it, the chill seemed to grow worse.

Finally he used the last of the wood, and when that burned down to a blackened pile of ashes, he drew his coat around him and tried to sleep. He did doze off from time to time, but the chills became so violent they woke him up.

Finally the sound of voices came to him, and he opened his eyes to see Irons and another man coming down the side of the creek bank leading a mule. "Clay?" Irons called out. "Are you all right?"

Clay sat up and tried without success to keep his voice steady. "All right," he mumbled, and was shocked at how feeble the answer was that came out of his mouth. As Irons came to where he sat, he tried to grin. "Had a little nap while I was waiting."

The preacher looked at him with alarm in his eyes, then shook his head. "We had to follow the creek. Woods were too thick to get the mule through." Then he turned, saying, "Buford, bring the mule up." As the man came up, he added, "This is Buford Yancy, Clay."

Yancy was a tall, thin man with greenish eyes, tow-colored hair, and a freckled complexion. He nodded slightly, saying only, "Howdy." But his hands were strong as he and the minister helped Clay to mount the mule. When Clay was set, he took the hackamore and turned the animal, speaking to him in a flat voice.

As they moved along the broken stones of the creek, Irons said, "Should have made you dry those clothes out, Clay. Didn't do you any good lying around wet all morning."

"I'll be all right when I get out of the woods," Clay said.

But by the time they got to the Yancy cabin, he was weaker than he thought possible. He staggered when he slipped down from the high back of the mule, and he heard Yancy say, "He can't ride that horse, Preacher."

Clay tried to protest that he could, but his head was swimming. Then he felt the two men, one on each side, guiding him across the yard, and they practically carried him up the steps.

"Mattie!" Yancy called out. "Git the bed ready for Mr. Rocklin."

Clay's vision faded as he went into the cabin, and he was glad when the back of his legs hit something and he was lowered by the two men into a rough bed. The mattress was rough cloth stuffed with cornshucks that rustled, but it felt better to him than the thick, fluffy featherbed he slept in each night.

"Be . . . all right," he mumbled, his tongue feeling thick and clumsy. "Jus' need to rest . . ."

The rustling of the shucks under him grew faint, and a soft blackness seemed to wrap him, like a warm ebony blanket. He felt secure as the sound of voices came to him from far away, like the faint cry of birds deep in the woods at evening.

Sometimes he was aware of light, but it was a watery sort of light, as he had seen when looking upward while swimming beneath the surface of the lake. The sounds, too, were muffled, as though he were deep underground in a warm cave sheltered far off from the harsh sounds of the world. Sometimes he would awake, and someone would always be beside him. Once he saw his mother, her face surrounded by an amber corona of light. She spoke to him, and he tried to speak back, but he was too tired. Hands would touch him, and the coolness that came to his brow and body was like balm.

Then, all at once, he opened his eyes and for one moment the room seemed fuzzy and out of focus. Then it changed, becoming clear and sharp. A young girl's face filled his field of vision. She had hair so black that it glistened in the lamplight like a crow's wing, and eyes that were large, almond-shaped, and of a peculiar greenish color.

"Hello," the child said, and she studied him so carefully that he thought she must be older than she appeared.

Clay tried to get up, but found that his arms seemed too weak to hold him. Even so, the fever that had burned in him was gone. He licked his dry lips, and whispered, "Water . . ."

The girl rose at once, picked up a glass from a table, and poured it full of water. Clay took it and drank thirstily, spilling some on his bare chest.

"Better not drink too much," the girl said. She picked up a cloth from the chair she'd been sitting in and, in a gesture much older than her years, reached over and mopped the water from his chest.

Clay blinked at her, then asked, "What's your name?"

"Melora Yancy," she said. "I've been helping take care of you."

"How old are you, Melora?"

"I'm six."

Clay peered at her, then ran a hand across his cheek, feeling a heavy growth of beard. He felt clearheaded but weak. "How long have I been here, Melora?" he asked.

"'Bout three days. Your ma, she was here right after you come. She brung the doctor with her."

Clay sat up carefully, noting that he wore only the bottom of a pair of underwear. "Hand me my pants, will you, Melora?"

"You better wait, Mister Clay," she said quickly. "Doctor said for you not to rush nothin'." Then she said, "I'll bet you're hungry."

At her words he was struck with a stab of hunger. "I sure am!"

"I'll feed you." She disappeared, and he managed to sit up in bed. His ankle was heavily bandaged, and when he tried to move it, he was pleased to find that though it was painful, it was not broken as he had feared. Carefully he got to his feet, but the room swayed in an alarming fashion, and he sat down abruptly, grabbing the side of the bed for support.

Melora came in with a plate, followed by a woman who had a cup in her hand. "You feelin' better, I see." She was obviously the mother of the girl, for she had the same dark hair and features. "You let Melora feed you, and I'll send my man to tell your folks you're all right."

"Hate to bother you, Mrs. Yancy." Melora came close and handed him the bowl of stew, and he took a quick bite. It was rich and nourishing, and as he gobbled it down, the woman told him of the last few days.

"The preacher came back with the doctor, and he bound your ankle up," she said. "But you was so sick he was afraid to move you. He axed could we set with you until the fever broke, and we did. Your ma, she's been here, and the preacher, too."

"I'm in your debt, Mrs. Yancy."

"Well, Melora here, she stayed with you most of the time. Fed you when you wuz awake and kept the cool cloths on you when the fever wuz burning." She gave Melora a fond glance, adding with a smile, "Reckon she's jest a natural-born nurse. Patches up ever stray kitten and varmint that come on the place."

Clay suddenly grinned and stopped eating long enough to say, "Well, I fit in that category, I guess."

76

"Oh—I didn't mean you wuz a varmint, Mr. Rocklin!" Mrs. Yancy said in alarm.

"Been called worse than that," Clay said. After the woman left to get her husband, he said, "Melora, I'm going to give you all my business when I get sick."

Melora was very serious and said at once, "You kin have some of my guinea eggs for supper. I'll cook them for you myself."

He ate all the stew, then at once grew very sleepy. Melora pushed him down, then pulled the rough coverlet up, saying, "You sleep some more, Mister Clay."

When he woke up later, he felt stronger, and Melora fulfilled her promise by cooking him six guinea eggs, which he wolfed down. After he ate, she sat down and said, "I guess your ma will be comin' to git you, won't she?"

"I guess so."

Melora said wistfully, "I wisht you could stay awhile, Mister Clay. It's been nice takin' care of you."

Clay reached over and took her hand. "Tell you what, Melora, I'll come back and see you after I get well."

"Oh, you won't either!"

"Promise! And I'll bring you a present. How about a new dress?"

Melora stared at him wide-eyed, then shook her head. "I'd rather have a book."

Her request took him aback, and he asked tentatively, "Well, what kind of a book?"

"One with knights in it, and dragons."

Clay was amused. "I think I've got a few of those myself. My mother never throws anything away. Seems like there's a box with all sorts of books I had when I was about your age. I'll pick out the best one and bring it to you."

Her strangely colored eyes glowed, and she hugged herself tightly. For the next hour she sat there talking to him. Clay had never been particularly drawn to children, but this girl's mind fascinated him. He discovered that her primitive world of cabin and field were small compared to the glittering world inside her small head. She told him tales that she had made up, composed of fragments of stories she had heard from her mother and from one book that contained a few romances—but mostly they were of her own imaginings.

Clay sat there for most of the morning, watching her small face as it glowed with excitement. He read to her out of the one book she possessed, then told some tall tales of his own. When his mother came in accompanied by Jeremiah Irons late that afternoon, he put his hand on Melora's shoulder, saying, "I don't know as I want to leave. My nursing has been so good here, I don't think I can expect as good at home."

Susanna was relieved to see that Clay's eyes were clear, for the doctor had feared pneumonia. She took a deep breath, then said, "Melora, thank you so much for taking such good care of my son. I'm sure God will reward you for it."

Clay walked out of the cabin and, finding Buford Yancy and his wife there with their other children, walked over and offered his hand. "Sorry to have forced myself on you two," he said, taking the man's hard hand. "I'm grateful to you all."

Buford Yancy nodded, saying, "Glad to be of help, Mr. Rocklin." His wife smiled nervously, and Melora came up to say, "Don't forget what we talked about, Mister Clay."

Clay stooped down and gave her a swift kiss on the cheek. "I sure won't! Be back soon as I can!"

As they rode back to Gracefield, Clay said, "That's some child, that Melora. Took care of me like she was a woman grown."

"What was she talking about when we left?"

"I promised to give her a book. Is that box still in the attic someplace, the one with the books all of us read when we were kids?"

"Yes. I'll get it for you as soon as you're able to go back." She hesitated, then said, "The wedding is next week. I don't know if you'll be well enough to go by then."

Clay said nothing to that, but he knew she was offering him an excuse to miss the event. That was not to be the case. He grew well rapidly, and when the day of the wedding arrived, he was there.

It was a big wedding, held in the Bentons' church in Richmond on Saturday morning. Clay felt like a fool, and his face was pale as he walked in with his family, but he had steeled himself for the affair. He did it so well that later he could remember little of the ceremony. He remembered going by to congratulate the couple, but it was a mechanical sort of thing. He shook Gideon's hand and even kissed the cheek of the bride, but the stares of the onlookers kept him stiff and unthinking.

"Thank you for coming, Clay," was all that Gideon said, and Melanie was too tense even to say that much.

As quickly as he could, Clay made his escape, avoiding the reception. As he rode out, Bushrod Aimes said to Taylor Dewitt, "Well, there goes Clay to get drunk. Bet it'll be a stem-winder this time!"

Clay, however, rode straight home and changed his formal attire for more simple dress. He caught up a large bundle that was in his room and went at once to his horse. Balancing the bulky package on the saddle horn, he rode along the road, thinking of the wedding and wondering how he'd ever be able to deal with the thing. His accident had brought some sort of catharsis to the bitterness that had driven him, but as he rode toward the backwoods, he knew that nothing had really changed. He was like a man who had caught a wild beast in some sort of trap and was holding the door for his life. He feared that if he relaxed for one instant, the wildness that had raged in him would burst out.

The air was keen, and he forced everything from his mind as he drew near to the Yancy place. The one thing that had sustained him for the past week had been the pleasure he had found in going through the old books he had read as a child. His parents had been lavish with books, and Clay rediscovered some of the pleasures he had known in the stories of Washington Irving. He read *The Legend of Sleepy Hollow* and *Rip Van Winkle,* and he knew that they would be a delight to Melora. He also found a copy of *Gulliver's Travels,* with gorgeous illustrations of the little people in the land of Lilliput and the big people in Brobdingnag. He included this book, knowing that though Melora would not understand the text for some time, she would devour the pictures. The same was true of *Pilgrim's Progress,* which he reread from beginning to end in one day's sitting. It brought back the days when his mother would gather them all at the end of the day and read of Christian and Faithful and how they came to the Celestial City.

He had sorted out at least twenty books and packed them into a box, and now as he drew up in front of the Yancy cabin, Melora came sailing out the front door, shadowed by the other children. She didn't speak, but her eyes were bright as diamonds, and when he stooped down to kiss her, she threw both arms around his neck and held on with all her might.

"Told you I'd come back, didn't I?" Clay straightened up, and when he saw the Yancys come to stand on the porch, he grinned. "Came to settle my bill with my favorite nurse."

It was a fine hour, taking the books out one by one and showing them to the family. Buford stood with his back against the wall, his wife beside him, and though neither of them said much except to exclaim over one of the books now and then, there was a brightness in their expressions. They led a hard life, eking a living out of the earth; to see the pleasure on Melora's face was meat and drink to them.

When all the books were laid out on the table, Clay turned to the other children and asked, "Do you all have birthdays?"

Royal, age eight, stared at him as though he were dim-witted. "'*Course* we got birthdays!"

Clay laughed and said, "Come with me." He led them

outside and took some small packages out of his saddlebag. "Happy birthday, all of you," he said, and he winked at Buford as they all tore into the presents.

"Mighty nice of you, Mr. Rocklin," Buford said, nodding.

Clay cocked his head then reached into the saddlebag, coming out with something he handed to Yancy, and he said, "Happy birthday to you, too, Buford."

Yancy stared down at the revolver in the calfskin holster. Slowly he pulled it out and held it in one hand. It was one of the new Colt .36 pistols, with a five-shot cylinder. They were rare as yet, and frightfully expensive. Buford Yancy lifted his eyes, but could not say a word, for he well knew that he would never in years of work have earned enough spare cash for such a weapon. Finally he said, "I thank you, Mr. Rocklin."

Clay laughed it off, saying, "Small enough gift for saving my worthless hide, Buford. Now, this is for you, Mattie." Digging down into the other saddlebag he pulled a bulky package out and handed it to the startled Mrs. Yancy. Winking at Buford as Mattie carefully untied the string and opened the package, Clay said, "Probably won't be worth a dime to you. I picked it out myself."

Mattie stared down at the folds of rich silk, green and crimson, in the package. She touched some of the buttons that Clay had gotten the clerk to include, then said without looking up, "It's right nice, Mr. Clay."

Clay wanted to ease the moment and said quickly, "Well, Mattie, if you'll make me a glass of that sassafras tea you do so well, Buford and I will go try out this new pistol. Then, Melora, you can show me how well you can read some of those books."

It was a fine day, and as Clay rode home at dusk, he wished that his own life were as simple and uncomplicated as that of Buford Yancy. But when he lay down on his bed late that night, he felt the magic of the afternoon slipping away. And as he tossed on the bed, he was plagued with bad dreams. Finally he got up and went to the window to stare out. The night was cloudy, and the oaks, stripped of most of their greenery, lifted clawlike branches to the dark skies. A rising wind keened around the house, then came to stir the tree outside his window. The branches clawed at the house and seemed to be trying to get at the sleepers inside. The moon slipped from behind a cloud, touched the tops of the trees with ghostly silver, then was covered as ragged clouds moved to cloak its brightness.

Clay stared out at the darkness for a long while, thinking of what might come. Finally, he took a deep breath and went back to lie down on his bed—but he found no sleep that night. He lay there until dawn, and when the first rays of the morning touched his window, he rose and dressed with a heaviness of mind and spirit, finally going out to meet the day.

CHAPTER SIX

A VISIT TO WASHINGTON

THE SNOWFLAKES that fell on Washington on Election Eve of 1840 were heavy and larger than dimes. They fell on the Potomac so thickly that the river was like a moving white highway. By noon the streets were carpeted with a blanket six inches deep. The snow glittered like diamonds as Gid and Melanie sat in a carriage that carried them across town.

"It's beautiful, Gid!" Melanie exclaimed, taking in the glistening spires of churches that flashed in the sunlight. "Even the ugly old buildings look like palaces!"

"Too bad we can't have Washington covered with snow all the time," Gid answered. He put his arm around her and gave a hearty squeeze. When she looked up at him, he said, "I enjoyed my honeymoon."

A flush rose to color Melanie's cheeks, but she lifted her lips for a kiss, then pulled him close, whispering, "I—I did, too!"

"Why, you shameless creature!" Gid laughed. "Weren't you taught that women are supposed to be passive and free from passion?"

Melanie pushed him away, laughter edging her voice as she said, "I'll try to be more formal in the future, Mr. Rocklin."

"Don't you do it! Stay just the way you are, Mellie," he said, smiling at her. Then he looked down the street. The horse was forging his way steadily along, and the driver was carefully keeping his eyes turned to the front. "There's the house," he said, then frowned and shook his head. "I wish we could have our own place here, but it wouldn't make sense since we'll soon be at our first station."

"I don't mind, Gid," Melanie said quickly. Their honeymoon had been brief, and it would not have been feasible for them to get quarters. Gideon had to return to West Point in a few days, and there was plenty of room at the Rocklin home, a large brownstone in the downtown area.

They drew up in front of the house, and the driver got down to retrieve their luggage. As Gid helped Melanie down, the front door opened, and Pompey, the Rocklins' butler, came down the snow-covered steps. He was a lanky, limber man with skin the color of chocolate and a pair of merry brown eyes. "I been 'spectin' you, Mistuh Gideon," he said happily, nodding his head. "Welcome home, Miz Rocklin!"

It gave Melanie a queer pleasure to be called by her new name, and she smiled warmly, saying, "Thank you, Pompey. But I think there'll be one too many ladies named Rocklin, so you can call me Miss Melanie."

"Yes ma'am, I will certainly do so! Now—" taking the bags from the driver, he said, "I got a big fire in the parlor, so you two go on in. Delilah will be bringing you something hot to drink right away!"

A few minutes later, the pair were sitting on an upholstered sofa in front of a blazing fire, drinking hot chocolate brought to them by Pompey's wife, Delilah. The beverage was almost the same color as the plump servant who beamed on them as they both exclaimed that it was the best chocolate they'd ever had.

"We'll have the good silver and the Dresden china tonight, Delilah," Gideon's mother said. "And be sure there's plenty of food for our guests." When Delilah left, she smiled, adding, "I hope you don't mind, but I asked a few people for dinner tonight." The ivory-colored dress she wore was exquisitely tailored, so that her extra pounds were not evident. Her hair was carefully and tastefully done, framing her round face in an attractive fashion.

"I warned Mellie we'd have company," Gideon said,

grinning at his wife. What he'd actually said was, "Brace yourself, Mellie. My mother loves to give dinners. I think she'd give a dinner to celebrate the end of the world!" But now he went over to his mother and gave her a hug. "Who are we having tonight? Can't be a politician. They'll all be drunk."

"Oh, don't be silly, Gideon!"

"Fact. The losers because they lost, and the winners because they won."

"You know it'll take at least four or five days to get the votes counted," his mother chided. Then she turned to her new daughter-in-law, saying, "I know you're tired, Melanie, but I did want you to meet a few people. Amos is so excited, Gideon," she said quickly. "You've heard of Charles Finney?"

"The famous evangelist? Of course I have. Don't tell me he's going to be here?"

"Yes! He's not speaking as much as he used to, now that he's teaching at the college in Oberlin. But he came to Washington just to preach at our church, and Amos persuaded him to have dinner with us."

"He's a pretty stout character, from what I hear," Gideon said cautiously.

"Oh, yes indeed!" Mrs. Rocklin agreed, her brown eyes alive with excitement. "I don't think you'll be bored." Then she glanced at Melanie with a sly smile. "There'll be a surprise for you at dinner, my dear! I think you'll like it very much."

She refused to say more and left at once to attend to the details. "I wonder what she's got cooked up for you, Mellie?" Gid mused. He put his back toward the fire, soaking up the warmth, and shook his head. "I told you how it would be. Mother is kind, but she lives from one party to the next. I think she's the most sociable person I've ever known." He came over and sat down beside his wife. "If you get tired of all her parties, we'll get you a place of your own until I graduate."

"Oh, no, Gid!" Melanie took his hands and held them.

"I'll enjoy meeting your friends. And after all, it'll be good training for me, won't it? I mean, we'll always be moving from post to post, and an officer's wife has to know how to handle people with tact, doesn't she?"

"Well, Mother can get pretty bossy," Gid said, but kissed her and grinned. "Do you good to learn how to hold your own with a strong personality." A thought came to him, and he added, "I'm looking forward to dinner. From what I hear of Rev. Finney, he's a potent sort of clergyman. Wouldn't put it past him to have us all on our knees."

"Oh, Gid! Don't be silly!"

They went upstairs and rested. Later in the afternoon, they drove around the city, Gideon pointing out the sites of interest. They returned to the house just in time to dress for dinner. Melanie wore a powder-blue dress, and Gid wore a dark blue suit. As she straightened his tie, he said, "Wonder what Mother's surprise is? Hope it's not something to do with more parties. I don't intend to waste all the time I've got left at boring dinners."

But Mrs. Rocklin met them at the foot of the stairs with a triumphant light in her eyes. "Now, you step into the library, both of you."

Gid allowed Melanie to go first and heard her gasp, "Ellen!" in surprise. He stepped into the large high-ceilinged room in time to see Ellen Benton being embraced by Melanie.

"There!" Mrs. Rocklin cried. "I knew you'd be glad to see your cousin, Melanie!" Then she turned to her son, and there was a slight hesitation in her manner. "Gideon, look who came to escort Ellen from Richmond."

"Hello, Gid." Gideon turned to his left, shocked to see Clay standing with his back to the wall. There was a sardonic light in Clay's dark eyes, and he looked thinner.

"Clay!" Gideon said quickly, going at once to shake his hand. "By George, I'm glad to see you." That was the simple truth, for bad reports had come from Gracefield of Clay's behavior. *And they were not false,* Gid decided as he clapped his cousin on the back. The unmistakable signs of excess marred his handsome face, and he looked thin and drawn. But Gideon was smiling. "Can't tell you how glad I am that you've come!"

Melanie had disengaged herself from Ellen and came at once to greet Clay. Putting out her hand, she smiled nervously, saying, "Yes, it is good to see you, Clay. I hope you can stay for a while?"

"I'm just a delivery boy," Clay said with a shrug. "Your father didn't want Ellen to make the trip to Washington alone and asked me to escort her." There was no ease in his voice, and it was obvious to all of them that he was stiff in his greeting to Melanie.

"I engineered the whole thing, I'm afraid," Mrs. Rocklin spoke up. "I thought it might be good for Ellen to spend some time in Washington with you, Melanie. When Gideon goes back to West Point, it'll be lonely with just us old folks here."

Ellen said, "It was good of you to invite me, Mrs. Rocklin." She looked very stylish in a green woolen dress that showed her figure to good advantage. She stepped close to Clay and lightly put her hand on his arm, adding, "Of course, I couldn't have come if Clay hadn't offered to bring me."

There was, Gid saw, something possessive in Ellen's manner. He didn't know the young woman well, but the thought came to his mind that James Benton should have had better judgment than to trust Clay on such a mission. But he said only, "Well, now we can have some fun! I've got two days, and we can turn this town on its ear before I have to go back."

At that moment a knock at the door sounded, and Mrs. Rocklin said with some agitation, "That must be Laura and Amos with Rev. Finney. I'll go let them in myself."

Gideon winked at Clay, a wry light in his eyes. "Did you know who our dinner guests are, Clay?"

"No."

"The evangelist, Charles Finney. He's pretty outspoken on the slavery issue, and he's made an ardent disciple of my brother-in-law. That's my mother for you, I'm afraid," he added, shaking his head in mock despair. "She brings in Clay Rocklin, a dyed-in-the-wool Southern planter, to have dinner with two abolitionists!"

Clay suddenly grinned. "Well, I hope we don't destroy each other, Gid."

"Just nod quietly and grunt every once in a while, Clay," Gid urged. "That's all I ever do at Mother's dinners. Makes life easier."

They waited somewhat awkwardly, but soon Mrs. Rocklin came in, shepherding her guests. She introduced Ellen to the Steeles, then said, "This is Rev. Charles Finney."

Finney was the most famous preacher in America, with the possible exception of Rev. Beecher of Boston. He was a tall man, spare of form and with the most commanding eyes a man could possess—a pale blue that seemed to burn with energy. He listened to the names, then spoke in a firm but restrained voice, seeming rather less than his reputation. He was a lawyer by profession, who had undergone a dramatic conversion to belief in Jesus Christ. At once he had begun to preach, and his meetings had grown so large that few buildings could hold the crowds that came to hear him. He was not, however, universally admired—many traditional ministers deplored some of his practices.

The group went in to dinner, and during the meal Stephen asked Finney about the opposition he had encountered. "Rev. Finney, I hear your methods had considerable opposition from your fellow ministers, but I don't know exactly what they oppose in them. They call them 'New Measures,' I understand."

Finney said evenly, "Why, some people call them that, Mr. Rocklin, mostly those who oppose them." He began to speak of his ministry, and it was obvious that he was not a ranting preacher, for he spoke fluently and well.

Clay, who was not enamored of preachers as a breed, was impressed as the man said, "I pray for people by name in the service. After the sermon is over, I ask those who feel a hunger for God to come to the Anxious Seat."

"The Anxious Seat?" Gideon asked, puzzled. "What is that?"

"Why, just a chair or bench," Finney replied. "When God begins to work in a sinner's heart, there will be anxiety. It's God's way of drawing sinners to himself."

"What happens when people go to—to the Anxious Seat, Rev. Finney?"

Finney gave a sudden smile, which made him look much younger. "Usually nothing dramatic, Mr. Rocklin," he said. "A minister or a believer will pray for him and read him some of the Bible. And then one of two things will happen—either he will repent and be converted, or else he will run away from God."

"Your critics mention that there's often what they call 'unseemly behavior' in your meetings, don't they?" Mrs. Rocklin asked.

"That is not a new charge, Mrs. Rocklin," Finney said. "Even in the ministry of Jesus, it was made. When the Savior was passing by and blind Bartimaeus began crying out very loudly for help, the crowd told him to be quiet, that his behavior was 'unseemly,' as we might put it. Every time a move of God comes to men, it is always the same. When John Wesley came and preached in the fields, men and women often were struck down by the power of God. The same was true with George Whitefield and Jonathan Edwards in our own country. There are always those enemies of the cross to cry out that such things are not dignified." Finney's eyes burned, and his voice rose as he said, "Would it be better to remain dignified and let sinners go to hell? No! There have been excesses, certainly, but when God moves upon men, there will be brokenness—and that brokenness will often be displeasing to those who must have their religion in orderly rituals!"

It was a strange dinner, the strangest the Rocklins had ever attended. Finney had one burning interest, the gospel, and there was such power in the man that the other guests sat spellbound, listening to his words.

Dinner was over when Amos Steele asked, "Have you heard about Rev. Finney's innovation at Oberlin?"

"What is that, sir?" Gideon asked.

"He has opened the doors to females," Steele said proudly. "The first college in America to do so!"

There was much interest in this, and Finney explained that in Christ there is "neither male nor female," so he was assured that both men and women were entitled to college training.

Clay suddenly asked, "Doesn't the Bible say there is 'neither bond nor free,' Reverend?"

Finney gave Clay a searching look. "You speak of the Negro race?"

"Yes, sir. Would you welcome them to your college?"

A sudden shock of silence filled the room, but Finney didn't hesitate. "The day will come in this country when we will see dark-skinned men and women in colleges."

"Not in the South!"

Amos said hotly, "The Negroes are human beings, Clay!"

Instantly Stephen said, "This would not be a good time to debate the slavery issue, I think."

Rev. Finney agreed. "No, but the time is coming when the question will have to be dealt with on a national level." Then he leaned forward and a gentle light came into his stern eyes. He addressed Clay in a voice that was kind indeed. "Mr. Rocklin, no man has the wisdom to know how this matter should be handled, so I will not try to impose my political view on you, and certainly not my feeling about slavery. All I can say is that the first duty of all of us is to make our peace with God. And that can only be done through the blood of Jesus Christ."

Clay was prepared for an attack from the minister, so the simple words disarmed him. He flushed, nodded, and said merely, "You are certainly right about that, Reverend."

Later, when Gideon and Melanie were alone, preparing for bed, they spoke of Clay.

"He's been drinking a lot," Gideon said. "You can see it in his face."

Melanie gave him a quick glance, then said, "Do you think he hates us, Gid? I couldn't tell much about him. He was always so lively. There's a sadness in him now."

"Well, he lost you, Mellie. That's enough to make a man sad." Gid paused, then said slowly, "I'm surprised that your father let him bring Ellen here."

"Ellen has a way with Father. She can wheedle him into doing what she wants."

"Well, what she wants now is Clay." Gid's face was heavy and he shook his head. "I see real trouble there for her. I don't think Clay will be interested in women for a long time."

Melanie nodded reluctantly, but there was a troubled frown on her face. "I suppose you're right, Gid—but she does have a way with men!"

CHAPTER SEVEN

THE WRONG BRIDE

CLAY Rocklin had never planned to stay in Washington for any longer than it took to deliver Ellen, but for some obscure reason not clear even to himself, he lingered in the city. He asked himself many times why he had come in the first place, for he was honest enough to admit he had not come simply to escort Ellen. She was well able to make the short journey alone, or her uncle could have found someone else to accompany her if he had refused the task.

He had no one to talk to, at least not about what was going on inside him. Except for Ellen, that is. The two of them had been thrown together much by necessity, and she had kept him busy seeing the city and attending the nightly parties that went on in his aunt Ruth's circle. It was due to Ellen that he stayed in the city, for she kept him busy, and Washington was more interesting than Gracefield in the winter. The two of them attended the theatre more than once, and it was on the way home from an evening at the Ford Theatre that she finally succeeded in getting him to speak some of the thoughts that had been bottled up inside.

The snow was still on the streets, and the air was biting cold as they drove through the silent streets late that night. A clock from the large Presbyterian church on Pennsylvania Avenue boomed out the hour as they passed. The sound was sudden, breaking the sibilant noise of the runners of the sleigh—and Ellen suddenly gave a start, grabbing at his arm.

"It's midnight, Clay!" she said, counting the strokes, then gave his arm a squeeze. "We'll be locked out."

Clay was feeling more relaxed than he had since coming to Washington, and the idea of having to wake his uncle and aunt amused him. "They might turn us away," he answered. "We'd have to spend the whole night in this sleigh." They had gone to a restaurant after the performance, eaten a late supper, then afterward sat there talking about the play. Clay drank liberally, and Ellen not a great deal less, so that when they finally left the restaurant, they were both giggling with their attempts to climb into the sleigh.

The sharp air numbed their faces but did little to sober them up. Suddenly Ellen moved closer to him, laughing up into his face. "I don't care if they lock us out," she declared. "We could sleep in the sleigh."

"Be mighty cold," Clay answered. They were passing under a streetlight, and the golden gleam of the lamp made Ellen look bewitching. Her eyes were half-lidded, which made them look sultry, and the rich swell of her full lower lip gave a sensuous cast to her face. He was acutely conscious of the pressure of her body as she leaned against him, and thought again of what an attractive woman she was.

Without thinking about it, he suddenly leaned forward and kissed her. The alcohol had loosened them both, and she put her hand behind his head, drawing him closer. Her lips, softer than feathers, had a pressure of their own, and he drew her closer, savoring the kiss.

Finally they parted, and he said, "You're what a man needs, Ellen."

She did not withdraw fully, but kept close beside him. "I know what it means to be disappointed, Clay," she said, her eyes dropping to study her hands. The kiss was not her first, for she had been pursued by many men, but it had shaken her. She had been drawn to Clay from the time she'd first seen him, and although she knew that he was a man who knew women well, she thought no less of him for that.

She didn't elaborate on her statement, knowing well

that men didn't want to hear about the troubles of a woman. "You've had a bad time," she said instead. "But it won't last forever. Things change."

Clay studied her curiously. There was some sort of knowledge in her that most women lacked, and it appealed to him. He knew little about her past, save that there was some sort of tragedy concerning her parents. Whatever it was, it seemed to have given her a toughness, which he admired. Now he said, "I thought love was supposed to be eternal. That's what all the poets say."

Ellen stirred against him, turning her face to look at him. A smile curved the edges of her lips upward. "All the poets who write about love are men," she said. "And they really know better. Love is for now, Clay. Poets may write about a love they lost years before, but I'd guess most of them want more than a poem in their bed."

"Now that's speaking right out," Clay said, smiling at her frankness. "So you think love doesn't last?"

"I didn't say that," Ellen said. She thought about it as they moved along the dimly lit streets. The corona of the street lamps glowed, but the feeble rays were swallowed up in the darkness, and there was something surrealistic in the sight of the street so busy by day, now deserted. "Love can last," she said, "but it can die, too. Look at your uncle and aunt. They were in love once, I suppose. Now they just live in the same house. I can't imagine them being in love, can you?"

Clay shook his head. "No," he replied slowly. "But we all get old." He said no more for a few blocks, then suddenly began to speak of himself. He was not entirely sober and the kiss had opened him to her. "I can't figure out what I'm doing here, Ellen," he said. "I didn't have to come. Mr. Benton could have gotten someone else to bring you to Washington."

"I asked him to get you to bring me," Ellen said suddenly. "I wanted you to come and see Gid and Melanie together." She had thought about telling him this for some time, and now seemed the best time. "I saw what you were doing to yourself, Clay, with all the drinking and carousing. It was destroying you."

"And seeing Gid and Melanie is supposed to cure me?"

Ellen ignored his sardonic tone, saying, "It's better to look at things straight on, Clay. I thought it would be better for you to see them married than to eat your heart out thinking about it. Maybe I was wrong—but I meant well."

Clay thought about what she had said, then nodded. "Maybe you're right, Ellen. It hurts like fury to see them together—but somehow it's not as bad as thinking about it. So thanks for trying. Don't know why you fool with a sorehead like me!"

"Don't you, Clay?" Ellen said, giving him a slight smile. "Well, it's been good for me to have you here. I may be some company for Melanie after Gid leaves, but she doesn't need me now."

"He's going back to the Point day after tomorrow. Guess I'll go back to Richmond then." He sighed heavily, adding, "Not much going on at the farm this time of the year."

Ellen had blinked when he announced his intention to leave, but said only, "We'll have to make the most of our time, then."

Gid and Melanie were too occupied with each other to give much attention to Clay, but on the morning of Gid's departure, they discussed him. Gideon was packing his suitcase, doing it methodically as he did most things, when Melanie came up behind him. Putting her arms around him, she held to him, pressing her face against his wide back.

"Oh, Gid!" she moaned. "I wish you didn't have to go! Or that I could go with you!"

He unclasped her hands, turned, and took her in his arms. His eyes were sober, but he allowed a smile to touch his broad lips. "That would make for an interesting life. Every one of the boys would fall in love with you." He stood there, holding her, hating the idea of leaving, but trying not to let it show. "You'll have Ellen for company, and it won't be forever."

"Yes it will!" she pouted. "And Ellen is no substitute for a husband. Besides, she's always with Clay."

"She sure is." He drew back, his eyes thoughtful. "I guess he'll go back to Gracefield, won't he?" Moving away from her, he picked up his shaving equipment from the washstand and placed it in the suitcase, then shut it. "I'm surprised he's stayed this long. I don't think I'd want to do it."

"Do what?"

"Hang around and watch you being married to another man. If you'd chosen Clay, I'd have gotten as far away from you as I could. He's a peculiar fellow, Clay is. I don't really understand him." Then he looked at his watch, saying abruptly, "I've got to go. Don't want to miss my train."

His departure was an event, with the entire family going out to the carriage. His parents bid him a fond good-bye, and all the servants came to wish him well. Finally he shook hands with Clay. "I'm glad you came," he said simply. He wanted to say more, but others were listening, and he could not have said it in any case. "Take care of yourself, Clay," was all that came to him, and he hated the inadequacy of the bare statement. He had tried more than once to put his feelings into words, but had not been able to break through the barrier that had risen between him and his cousin. He could not blame Clay, for he doubted if he could have handled such a loss as well.

"Good-bye Ellen," he said, taking her hand. "Take care of Melanie," he said, then got into the sleigh. "Let's go, Pompey!" He hated good-byes and had forbidden anyone to go with him to the station. He was actually relieved when the final words were spoken and the last waves were given. A gloom settled on him as the sleigh turned the corner, and he settled down in the seat, his face somber and thoughtful. He forced himself to think of his remaining days at the Point, wishing they were over and he was with Melanie at some distant station. But Gideon Rocklin was a practical man, not given to much wishing, and he left Washington determined to do his best at his job.

For a week after Gid's departure, Clay remained in Washington. Each day he got up determined to leave, for somehow Melanie alone made his loss more bitter than when she had been with Gid. He grew morose and silent, and if it had not been for Ellen he would have gone home the day after Gid left. But each morning she would meet him with a new plan, something that was taking place in the city that would entertain him. But it actually was something inside of Clay himself that kept him from fleeing Melanie's presence.

Stephen Rocklin pinpointed the young man's problem one evening after Clay had taken Ellen to a party. Melanie had gone to bed early and he and Ruth were sitting in front of the fireplace. "I wish Clay would go home," he said abruptly, breaking into his wife's account of some problem with one of the servants.

Ruth looked at him in surprise. "Why do you say that?"

"He's mooning around like a lovesick puppy," Stephen answered. "The trouble with Clay is that he's gotten everything he wanted up to now. And that's not good for a man." He got up and went to peer out the window into the darkness. Framed by the window, he looked sturdy and powerful. Finally he turned, saying, "I may have to talk to him about leaving."

"Oh, Stephen, don't do that!" Ruth shook her head quickly, adding, "Clay needs a little time, that's all."

"He needs to get away from here, Ruth. I wish he hadn't come at all."

"Why, I thought you liked Clay."

"I do like him, Ruth. That's why I want him to go. He's not helping himself any hanging around here. He's

97

drinking too much, and he's going to make a fool out of himself if it keeps up."

His words were not intended to be prophetic, but Clay had seen the disapproval in his uncle's face. "I've got to leave, Ellen," he said that night when they returned from the party. "I'm like a ghost at the party."

Ellen said quickly, "Well, not tomorrow. You promised to take me to see the Ethiopian Eccentricity—whatever that is."

She had seen a poster advertising a performance by Alex Carter's Black Face Minstrels and had forced him to agree to take her.

"Well, all right," he agreed, "but I'm catching a train out of here on Tuesday."

Melanie noticed that Ellen was in a strange mood all day Monday. She had none of her usual cheerfulness, but seemed to be thinking of something else. "Don't you feel well, Ellen?" she asked as the other woman was getting dressed to go to the minstrel show.

"I'm fine," Ellen answered, but when she left with Clay, Melanie was worried about her. She knew that Clay would be leaving and was astute enough to know that Ellen would miss him. She felt sorry for her cousin, but was relieved that Clay was going back to Virginia. The strain had been greater than she had anticipated, especially since Gideon had left. *Clay will be better off at Gracefield*, she said to herself firmly. *And maybe Ellen can see more of him when she goes back after her visit here.*

Ellen was bright and filled with excitement that evening. She carried Clay along with her, making him laugh at her outrageous comments on the minstrel show, which proved to be no better or worse than average. A pair of white artists with cork-blackened features clogged "Old Zip Coon" and "Possum Up a Gum Tree" with such noisy enthusiasm that the audience broke out into gales of applause. "Misto' Interlocutuh" wagged his preposterous woolly head and flung a series of conundrums to various members of his entourage. Mr. Alex Carter came on to sing, first "Blue Juanita," a long sentimental ballad, and next a catchy tune called "Buffalo Gals." A pair of real Negroes then executed a very brisk buck-and-wing as a finale, to the evident enjoyment of the audience.

After the show was over, Clay and Ellen went out to eat, and as usual Clay drank quite a bit. After the supper, he was feeling the effects of the liquor. "I'm drunk, Ellen," he remarked owlishly.

"No, you're just feeling good," she said at once. Then she leaned forward, smiling, to say, "Did you know there's a boxing match tonight?"

"A boxing match? No, I didn't know it."

"Well, there is. It's in a big warehouse down by the river. And we're going to see the match."

Clay laughed at her. "Women don't go to see such things, Ellen!"

"This one does!"

Shaking his head, he argued, "They wouldn't even let you in. No women allowed, I tell you."

"But I'm not going as a woman. Didn't you see the bag I put in the carriage? It's got men's clothing in it. I'm going to change this dress for a suit, put my hair up under a derby, and we'll be two young fellows at the fight!"

Clay stared at her. "You're not serious!"

"You just wait here, Clay Rocklin." Ellen grinned. "Give me half an hour, then meet me at the carriage."

She left at once, and Clay sat at the table, not believing what he had heard. He took several drinks from the bottle, then when the half hour had passed, he got to his feet—somewhat unsteadily—and went to pay the bill. When he got to the carriage, he took one look and laughed out loud.

Ellen had done exactly what she had said and now stood beside the carriage looking for all the world like a young man. "Hello, Clay," she greeted him in the deepest voice she could muster. "Let's go to the fight."

Clay grinned broadly, amused at her audacity. She had done a good job and looked like a young dandy. She had obtained a suit that was somewhat too large and a brown overcoat, so her figure was concealed. Her abundant hair she had managed to cover with a large bowler hat, and the effect was of a rather effeminate young man with large eyes and a smooth complexion.

She climbed into the buggy, saying, "Come on, we'll be late," and Clay got in and took the reins. "I even brought a flask," Ellen said, pulling a leather-covered bottle from her side pocket. "Have a blast, sport!"

Her attempts to emulate a young dandy brought a laugh from Clay. He took a drink, then said, "Here we go!"

The liquor was working on him, and he was delighted by Ellen's strange antics. He only wished that Taylor Dewitt and Tug Ramsey were along for the fun. It took some time to find the warehouse, and he stopped and re-filled the flask at a saloon.

"You better keep that hat on," he warned Ellen as they entered the old warehouse. "This is a pretty rough place."

Ellen gave him a dig with her elbow. "Give me a drink, chum," she said roughly. Her eyes were sparkling, and he saw that she was having a fine time. She took a swallow of the liquor, then said, "Let's get close to the ring."

Clay had seen many fights, and knew what to expect. He thought at first that the coarse language of the specta-tors would offend Ellen, but she seemed to pay no heed to them. He was also apprehensive that someone would see through her disguise, but fortunately no one did. Clay paid little heed to the fight. By the time it was over, he had finished the flask, and was almost too drunk to walk.

Ellen caught at him as he staggered getting into the car-riage, and said, "I thought you could hold your liquor better than that, Clay Rocklin!"

The remark offended him, and he said belligerently, "Can drink all I want! Let's go—find a place. Not too late."

The rest of the evening was a blur to Clay. He was

aware of going to a bar, then to another, but he soon lost all ability to make decisions. He laughed a great deal, hung onto Ellen for support, but the world began to lose focus.

He became dimly aware that night had gone. The morning sun was up, almost blinding him as they left one saloon, and he knew that he was supposed to do something. But he seemed like a man in a dream, and as he moved from one place to another, guided by Ellen's firm hand, he could not pull his thoughts together. There were some people around, and he spoke to them, but his words didn't make sense—even to him.

Finally he found himself being led into a room, and when the door closed, the sound was faint and far away. Then he heard Ellen's voice, saying, "All right, Clay. We're here."

He didn't know what that meant, nor did he know where he was, and when her hands touched him, he fell forward. But the fall was never complete, and instead of touching the floor or a bed, he fell endlessly, never stopping until the warm darkness enveloped him.

The darkness rolled back and Clay awoke slowly, sluggishly. A rough blanket was over his face, and he threw it off and lay there with his eyes closed, fighting a fierce headache, trying to think. Shreds of memories floated past his mind—a few snatches of conversations, a quick flash of one moment of the fight, Ellen's laughter as he tried to get into the carriage—but they all jumbled together in a meaningless fashion.

Then another memory came to him, and the abruptness of it caused him to open his eyes and look around the room wildly. It was a strange room, with one large window through which the sun was filtered by an opaque shade. The wallpaper was white with small red flowers, and there was no furniture in the room except the bed and a washstand.

A hotel room, he thought. Then the memory came back,

unmistakable, and turning his head, he saw that the pillow beside him was rumpled and dented.

Ellen!

He threw the covers back and got to his feet, ignoring the pounding at his temples. Moving to the washstand, he poured water into the basin with an unsteady hand, then splashed his face with the cold water. He found his clothing thrown on the floor. He grabbed his clothes and dressed as rapidly as he could, then moved to the mirror and stared into it.

His eyes were bleary, underscored by circles. He had no comb, so he tried to use his fingers to push his wild hair into place. Even as he was engaged in this, the door suddenly opened and he turned to see Ellen enter.

"Why, you're up at last!" she said at once. Her face was pale and she looked drained. She was wearing the dress she had worn to the minstrel show and was carrying a tray with a white napkin covering the contents.

"Sit down and have some breakfast," she said nervously.

"Don't know if I can keep anything down," he mumbled. He felt as bad as he had ever felt, and worse than the physical misery was the knowledge that he had made a fool of himself. He could not bring himself to look at Ellen. In an attempt to disguise his self-disgust, he sat down on the bed and picked up the cup of coffee from the tray. It was hot and strong, and he muttered, "Thanks, Ellen. This is what I needed."

"Try some of the eggs," she said. "I've already eaten."

Clay picked up a fork and pushed the eggs around listlessly. The situation was abominable, and he wished he had never come to Washington in the first place. The Bentons were old family friends of the Rocklins, and he felt he had betrayed them.

Finally he said, "I've been a fool, Ellen."

She suddenly reached out and caressed his cheek, saying, "I guess we both were pretty carried away. But I'm not sorry."

Clay shook his head. "I took advantage of you. Wish I hadn't done that."

The apology seemed to hang in the air, but she sat down beside him. Putting her arm around him, she squeezed him, saying, "I'm happy, Clay. And you must be happy, too." She drew his head around, and her eyes were intense. "This isn't the way I planned to get married, but we have each other, so it doesn't really matter."

Clay sat there, still as a stone, doubting his ears. "Married?" he asked hoarsely.

Ellen looked at him strangely. "Why, yes. Don't you remember?"

Clay shook his head, trying to free it from the cobwebs. His mind was reeling and he wanted to run out of the room. "Ellen, marriage is a serious thing. What we've done was wrong, but it's not—"

"Clay! We are married!" Ellen rose and moved to pick up her coat. She retrieved a paper from the pocket and handed it to him. "Don't you remember?" She watched as he stared at the paper. "It's our marriage license. I wanted to wait, to have a nice wedding at Gracefield, but you wouldn't listen."

Dimly Clay remembered a trip to some office and an argument with some official, but it was vague and fuzzy. "But—we can't be married!" he protested. "It takes more time than a single night to get the papers done."

Ellen shook her head. "You bribed him to set the dates back, Clay."

Suddenly Clay came to his feet, despair and confusion on his lean face. "Ellen! We've got to get it annulled!"

Ellen stood before him silently. Her eyes were enormous, and there was a vulnerability in her that seemed to make her smaller. "And do we annul what happened here?" She gestured at the tumbled bed, then quickly came to him. "Clay, I love you. Maybe you don't love me much, but I'll make you forget Melanie!" She began to weep, and suddenly she was in his arms.

Clay held her, feeling her grief, and for the next hour

they talked. He tried to tell her that it would never work—but she clung to him, begging him not to leave her. The guilt that gripped him weakened him, and—despite his past—there was a strong streak of honor in Clay that wouldn't let him just walk away.

Desolate, defeated, he said wearily, "Ellen, we can't do this. I'd be ruining your life if we go on like this. I'm not fit for you."

But in the end, she had her way.

The next day they were on their way back to Gracefield. They didn't deceive Stephen and Ruth about being together the night before. Indeed, they didn't try. They only agreed to say nothing of their marriage. After listening to what had happened, Stephen had said only, "Clay, don't be hasty."

Later, when they were alone together, Ellen urged, "Let's get married by the minister at Gracefield. We'll get a better start that way."

And that was what happened. A week after they returned, there was a wedding at Gracefield. Such a hasty marriage could not help but cause talk, but it was inevitable that people would say Ellen was getting Clay on the rebound.

Thomas and Susanna went through the ceremony with smiles, but when they were alone, they could not conceal their grief. Still, nothing could change what was happening, so they put the best face they could on it.

"It'll be all right, Thomas," Susanna said. "Marriage will settle Clay down. Ellen will help him."

But it was Taylor Dewitt who spoke the sentiments of most people. As Clay kissed the bride, Dewitt leaned over and whispered into the ear of Tug Ramsey: "I hate to say so, Tug—but I'm very much afraid that Clay got the wrong bride."

PART TWO
INCIDENT IN MEXICO—
1846

CHAPTER EIGHT

THE GUNS OF MONTEREY

A BLISTERING gust of wind heated by the white-hot sun overhead washed over the face of Second Lieutenant Gideon Rocklin as he stared across a wide plain broken by a crooked arroyo. He looked down the line of blue-clad infantrymen, then took a sip of water from his canteen. It was tepid and tasted strongly of rubber, which was not strange since that was what the canteen was made of. The putrefying smell of decomposing corpses seemed to have somehow gotten into the water, and even in the food. At least, so it seemed to Gid.

Two hundred yards out on the rocks lay strange bundles—dead men who had turned black and swollen to such proportions it seemed that they had been pumped up like huge balloons. Their legs burst the seams of their pants. Many of them lay face upward, their arms lifted in eloquent gestures toward the pale sky that looked down on them pitilessly.

"You reckon we might move up again, Lieutenant?" The question came from Sergeant Boone Monroe, a tall, rawboned man of thirty from the hills of Tennessee. He had been with Gideon since they had left Texas as part of General Zachary Taylor's small force back in March.

"Looks like it, Sergeant," Gid said, nodding. Looking down the line again, he noticed the ragged uniforms and torn boots of the men. He looked at the men's faces, burned with the Mexican sun and thinned by poor rations. He hesitated, then said, "The men are pretty tired, Boone."

Monroe spit an amber stream of tobacco juice that hit a small brown lizard directly on the head. He admired his shot, grinned, and said, "Shore am glad those greasers can't hit with them artillery pieces like thet!" Then his face sobered. He shook his head slightly, saying, "We come a long way, Lieutenant, since we left Palo Alto." He studied the thin line of troopers carefully through half-closed eyes, then added, "Some of those boys we lost on the way here . . . it sort of eats at a man, don't it, Lieutenant?"

"They were good men. None better."

As Gideon turned his gaze across the broken field, he thought of home, picturing the green grass and cool breezes of New York. But the war with Mexico had exploded—and had destroyed his world. He had known, they had all known, that the war was coming—but few of them were prepared when President Polk asked the Congress to declare a state of war in early May, 1846.

Only four months ago, Gideon thought, his eyes burning from lack of sleep. *Seems like ten years! But I guess being in a war always does strange things to a man's thinking.*

He thought of how he and almost every other regular army officer had been gathered up with scarcely time to get their belongings together. No time for furloughs now! He had been stationed at Fort Swift in Dakota Territory and had barely been granted permission to take Melanie and their three boys back to his parents' house in Washington before leaving for Texas, where he had joined General Taylor's force. Officers were scarce, and Gid, like most of the other green lieutenants, was given command of troops with no experience in combat at all.

The experience had come soon enough. Taylor had driven his army to Palo Alto. The general was expecting a fight, but his small army, reduced by illness and desertions, now numbered only twenty-three hundred men. The Mexican army tallied over four thousand. Gideon thought of that fight as he stood beside Sergeant Monroe. He remembered how he had struggled with the unknown factor every new soldier faces in his first battle: *Will I fight—or will I run away?* Fear had been thick in his throat as he had led his men toward the battle, moving slowly with their supply train of two hundred wagons and the two eighteen-pound cannons that were drawn by twenty oxen each.

The scene came to him sharply—the Mexican line stretched a mile in length; infantry anchored on a wooded hillock to the right and extending left, interspersed with eight-pound cannon on massive carriages. To the left was a line of lancers, the sun glinting on their bayonets and on the razor-sharp lances from which bright pennants streamed.

He remembered General Taylor, "Old Rough and Ready," as he was called by the troops—sitting placidly on Old Whitey, his horse. Sergeant Monroe had looked at the general, then winked at Gideon as they had marched into the line of battle. "Looks like he's on a possum hunt, don't he, Lieutenant?" he had said. The easy manner of Monroe had braced Gid up, and he had grinned back, the fear gone.

But not for long. When the two armies had lined up no more than a few hundred feet apart, it had returned. When the bullets began to whistle past his ears, and when men began dropping abruptly out of the line, fear was replaced by a blind terror that weakened his legs and emptied his mind. Once again, it had been Sergeant Monroe, who had stayed at his side whistling a tuneless melody as he loaded and reloaded his musket, that had kept him in place. Gid never knew if Monroe was aware of his lieutenant's fear. He suspected he was, but the tall Tennessean never referred to it.

There had been other battles, and the glamor of war, what little there had been for Gideon Rocklin, soon faded. There was nothing glamorous in what he saw . . . or what he did. Eventually he had learned to accept the terrible wounds, the sickness, and the constant presence of death.

The sound of a running horse came from behind, and Gideon took his eyes off the long hills that lay between the American army and Monterey. A smile creased his dry lips as a smallish man pulled his horse to an abrupt halt and came to the ground.

"Hello, Sam," Gid called out. "Glad to see you, but the rear is the other direction."

Second Lieutenant Ulysses Hiram Grant, a cigar clamped between his teeth, looked over, found Gideon, and came to stand before him. "Thought I'd better come and see the show." Grant and Gid had been classmates at West Point. Ulysses—as he was fondly called—had been a silent man who kept to himself, but he and Gid had become friends.

Grinning at Grant now, Gid remembered some of the times they'd shared in their relatively carefree days as cadets. Sam Grant was not a colorful soldier, but there was some quality in the man that other men respected. Now he looked at Gid, allowing a small smile to touch his lips. "Things are pretty bad when a quartermaster has to lead you dashing young infantry lieutenants into a fight, Gid."

"How'd you get out of your duty, Sam?" Gid asked curiously. Grant was under orders to serve as a quartermaster in charge of supplies. The stubby soldier had tried every way he knew to get out of the hateful duty, but had not succeeded.

"My curiosity got the best of me, Gid," he said. "I couldn't stand being out of it all."

"You'll get court-martialed!"

"Well, maybe I'll get killed in this charge that's coming," Grant said lightly. "That would answer. Anyway, I had to come. This letter came for you yesterday."

Gid stared at the envelope that Grant pushed at him, then grabbed it and ripped it open. Just the sight of Mellie's handwriting brought her before his mind, and his hands trembled as he read the letter quickly, slowing down at the last paragraph:

> My dearest husband, I miss you more than I ever thought possible! I am one of those women who lose themselves in their husbands, I suppose, and even after nearly six years of marriage, I still feel

like a bride! I suppose that's foolish, but it's true, my dearest.

The boys are fine. You mustn't worry about them. I know your parents (and mine, as well) thought we should have waited to have children, but we did well. When I take the three of them out for a walk, people turn and stare at them. "Such fine boys!" they say. Tyler, Robert, and Frank all send their love. Every night we pray, our boys and I, and though they're only three, four, and five years old, I know their prayers for your safety will be heard! They all look so much like you it gives me a start!

I must close, with all my love. I enclose a letter I received from Ellen. It is not good news, and I thought perhaps I ought not to send it, that it might be a burden to you. I know you are very fond of Clay, and according to Ellen, he is not doing well at all. But I decided you should see it, so I enclose it with a prayer that he will wake up to the terrible ruin he is making of his life. He has so much! Yet he seems determined to throw everything away.

Be careful! Oh, be careful, my dear!

> Your loving wife,
> Mellie

Hastily Gid unfolded the other letter and scanned it. It was the letter of an unhappy woman, which Gid and Melanie had long known Ellen to be. It was three scrawled, poorly spelled pages, all with the same lament—Clay was acting like a fool! Gid let his eyes run over it, doubting if the situation was as bad as Ellen painted it. And yet he knew that his father had received similar word from Clay's father. He read a sentence: ". . . and not only does Clay neglect me, but he pays so little attention to the children! I hate to tell you, Mellie, but he's been seeing other women!"

"Looks like we're about to butt heads with them greasers, don't it, sir?"

Monroe's twangy voice brought Gid back to the present, and he looked quickly across the line, just as a bugle sounded. Gid thrust the letters back into the envelope, shoved them into his inside pocket, and licked his lips. "All right, Sergeant, let's show the general what Company K is made of!"

"Mind if I go along, Gid?" Sam Grant stood before Gid, a dusty, insignificant figure, but with the light of battle gleaming in his dark eyes.

"Glad to have you, Sam," Gid said with a grin.

The charge sounded, and the two lieutenants moved forward, Gid shouting commands. Colonel John Garland led the charge, striking down the center between the Citadel on the right and La Teneria on the left. They had not gone far before they were caught on the front and at both sides by a shower of canister that whipped and tore the long lines. The men ran forward, hunched over, shoulders drawn in, clutching their muskets. The wounded fell with screams; the survivors jumped over bodies, stumbling, falling, seeing iron cut the dirt in front of them.

Gid yelled out, "Colonel Garland, we're taking a lot of hits!"

The colonel was a short, fat man with a red Irish face. Battle fury was on him, and he yelled, "Never will I yield an inch! I have too much Irish blood in me to give up! Forward, men!"

But he had not gone ten steps before a bullet took him in the stomach, driving him backwards. Gid ran to him and held his head up, but Garland cursed him. "You're in command, Rocklin! Lead the men to the cannon's mouth!"

A gush of brilliant crimson blood spurted from his mouth, and his eyes rolled back in his head. Gid laid him down, called for two men to take him to the rear, then stood up and ran to where Grant was waiting. "Let's go, men!" Gid shouted and without a pause moved steadily into the musket fire. The Mexican front flickered up and down the line, and it soon became evident to Gid that they could go no further without support. A thin line of rock lifted in front of where they stopped, a lip of basalt no more than a foot or so high, but it was something. "Take cover!" Gid shouted, and the men dropped in behind it.

"Looks like they're moving toward us, Gid," Grant said. He had picked up a musket and laid it on the oncoming line of Mexicans, then fired. He looked back over his shoulder. "Looks like we have help coming."

Two pieces of artillery were on the way, and soon the fire of the light cannons drove the Mexican forces back. Then it was time to charge again. Four times Grant and Rocklin led the men forward over the field, until they finally were forced to retreat before the artillery of the Mexican forces.

The air was thick with smoke, and the K Company was pinned down. "Be suicide to charge into that kind of fire, Gid," Grant shouted to make himself heard over the roar of musket fire. Then he stared at something to his right. "By the Almighty!" he said in awe. "Look! It's General Taylor."

Gid turned to look, but his attention was on something else. "Sam! Look out there!"

Grant turned to see what Rocklin was pointing to, squinted his eyes. "Why, that looks like Major Fields!"

"I thought he was dead," Gid said. He stared at the tall figure in blue who had risen to his feet. "He doesn't know where he is!"

"Must be hit pretty bad, Gid," Grant said. He peered through the smoke and said in alarm, "Look, they're coming!"

Gid saw the line of enemy troops at the same moment. And he knew, as every man in the company knew, that Major Fields was a dead man! The rest of the company had good cover, but Fields, standing tall in the sunlight, would be either shot or bayoneted within the next few minutes.

Gid could never remember what happened next. He remembered no conscious decision to get up and run through the hail of bullets that filled the air—but he found himself doing just that, leaning forward against the enemy's fire as a man leans against a hard wind.

Grant and Sergeant Monroe were both shocked into silence for a moment, for there was no way a man could run into that kind of fire and live. Then Sergeant Monroe cried out, "Fire, boys! Give the lieutenant some help!"

It might have helped, for as Gid reached the major, who had slumped to his knees holding his side, he sensed that the line of Mexican infantry had faltered. He snatched the major up, throwing him up on his shoulders as if he were a rag doll. Just as he did so, he looked toward the enemy and found himself staring into the cold, black eyes of an enemy soldier. The Mexican had his rifle lifted, and Gid could see the creases on the man's brow. He was that close! He tensed his body, waiting for the bullet that could not miss—and then a small black spot appeared over the soldier's left eye and he went loosely backwards, the shot he fired going into the air over Gid's head.

Quickly, Gid whirled and ran back to the line of K Company, thankful for the great strength he had been blessed with. He ran in long, jolting strides, expecting each second to be struck in the back by a bullet, but it did not happen—not until he was five yards from Lieutenant Sam Grant and Sergeant Boone Monroe.

He saw the looks of amazement on the faces of both, and knew that he had been a dead man in their eyes!

And that was the last thought he had, for suddenly he felt something like the blow of a giant's hand striking him in the back. He grunted, irritated at the blow, then fell forward, thinking, *I almost made it! I almost . . . !*

Within a fraction of a second, Monroe and Grant were at Gid's side, Grant shouting, "You men, take the major back to the ambulance!" He and Boone picked up the limp form of Gid Rocklin and moved toward the rear.

Suddenly a man on horseback was in front of them. "How is he, Grant?"

Lieutenant Grant looked up to see General Zachary Taylor staring down with concern in his eyes. The general seemed to be oblivious to the heavy fire that rent the air. He asked quickly, "Is he alive?"

Grant had felt the strong beat of Rocklin's heart. "Yes, General, he's alive." Then he gave Taylor a direct glance, a hard look that second lieutenants do not customarily give to generals. "If he doesn't get a decoration for this, General, I'll come back to haunt you."

General Taylor's lips turned up in a slight smile. He was not a man of much humor, but he found something amusing about Grant's attitude. "You're off your post, aren't you, Lieutenant? Aren't you supposed to be with the supply train?"

Ulysses S. Grant did not flinch. "Yes, sir," he said loudly, his head lifted in a defiant attitude.

The general held his gaze, then looked down at the still form of Rocklin. "Write it up, Grant. Send it to me and I'll put it through with my recommendation." Then he rode on, calling out, "Let's go see about taking Monterey!"

The long, ragged line of blue-clad infantry moved forward, following the general toward the low-lying hills that concealed the city of Monterey.

Sergeant Monroe and Lieutenant Grant delivered Rocklin to the ambulance, then walked back toward the line of battle.

"He'll do to tote the key to the smokehouse, won't he, Lieutenant?" Boone Monroe said, giving Rocklin as fine a compliment as any Southerner could give, for only the most trustworthy people were given a key to the smokehouse.

Grant stared at Monroe, nodded, and then the two of them moved across the smoke-filled battlefield.

CHAPTER NINE

A DRAGON FOR MELORA

JANUARY 1847 was mild and benevolent. The year before, January had fallen on Richmond with all the ferocity of a half-starved timber wolf, freezing the rivers and drifting banks of heavy snow over the eyes of the houses. But Box, the blacksmith, assured everyone, "Gonna be nice and easy dis year. Shells on de acorns is thin as paper, and de woolly caterpillars ain't hardly got no fuzz at all!"

Box himself was a high, handsome man, a mulatto with smooth skin and hair that was straighter than most and tinged with auburn. His wife, Carrie, was black as night, an attractive woman of forty-seven. They were seated in the kitchen, visiting with Zander and Dorrie, helping with the preparation of the food for the birthday party of the twins, Denton and David, two of Clay and Ellen's children. The smell of fresh gingerbread wafting through the kitchen was pleasant, and all four of them were drinking hot chocolate.

These four were the heart of Gracefield in many ways. Zander—the butler—and Dorrie—the lieutenant of Miss Susanna—controlled the house, far more so than the white people suspected. Zander at the age of forty-eight was tall and thin, with a rich chocolate complexion. He was a man of tremendous dignity, rarely angry or upset, but stern enough to make the other house slaves flinch when he raised his voice. Dorrie, his wife, was somewhat heavy, in contrast to her husband's leanness. She had a pair of direct brown eyes and felt herself no less a Rocklin than any of the white people in the house.

If Zander and Dorrie controlled the house, it was Box and Carrie who stood first in the hierarchy of the field slaves. James Bronlin, the overseer, made a great deal of noise, but it was mostly sound and fury. The Rocklins had learned long ago that one word from either Box or Carrie would get more accomplished than a torrent of words from Bronlin.

"Dem chillun' gonna catch dey death of cold," Carrie remarked, looking out the window to where the children were playing a game out in the grape arbor. The party had been scheduled for three in the afternoon, but it was after four and the shadows were beginning to lengthen.

"No, dey all right, Carrie," Box disagreed. "Lak I tole you all, we ain't gonna have no bad weather dis year." He picked up the cup in his massive blacksmith's hand, sipped at the rich chocolate, then asked, "Marse Clay, he ain't come back yet?"

It was an innocent question, but in some way it violated the unwritten code that existed in the world of the slaves of Gracefield. The white people were the main interest of all the slaves, but the house slaves felt a greater degree of sensitivity when the Rocklins were caught in some error. It was almost as though Zander and Dorrie were the protective parents of the Rocklins, quick to take offense at what they felt was any criticism of their "charges."

"Don't you be worried none 'bout dat!" Dorrie snapped at Box, who blinked in surprise at her vehemence. "Marse Clay, he be comin' back in time for de party." She rose and went to the stove, opened the door to look at the cake that was baking, then slammed the door with unnecessary violence. She walked to the window, stared out, and said, "I reckon he got held up in Richmond."

"I guess so, Dorrie," Box said, understanding that he had violated one of the taboos of the little world he inhabited. To make his peace and show his good intent, he took a bite of gingerbread and commented, "Marse Clay is doin' bettah."

But this displeased Dorrie, too, and she gave Box an

irritated glance. "You worry 'bout Damis, Box," she said, referring to Box and Carrie's oldest daughter, "and let Marse Clay take care of his ownself!" She glared at the muscular Box and, seeing the embarrassment in his eyes, sat down abruptly, saying, "My mouth is too big. Don't pay no attention to me, Box." She saw the reference to Damis had hurt them both, and suddenly reached over and patted Carrie's hard, work-worn hand. "You know I didn't mean nothin', Carrie."

"Dat's all right, Dorrie," Carrie said heavily. But it was not all right, for Damis was a burden to her and her husband—and to Zander and Dorrie as well, for their friendship went deep. Damis had been a problem since she was fourteen years old and had turned into a truly beautiful child. Too beautiful, really, for by the time she was sixteen she had every male slave on the place watching her. And Damis had learned early in life that it was not just the slaves who noticed her, but the white boys and men who came to Gracefield as well. It had been inevitable that she would be introduced to the lower lusts of men, and it came as no surprise that she became pregnant when she was barely seventeen.

The shock was that the baby, a boy, was obviously fathered by a white man. Such things were not uncommon on plantations, but the Rocklins, aided by Dorrie and Zander, Box and Carrie, had exercised such strict control that it was almost unknown at Gracefield.

And the silence of the girl was unnerving, for Damis would never name the father of her child. Privately, all parties thought that was best. How would it help to know? Such knowledge could only shame the father—and the rest of his family. Damis had been hastily married off to a middle-aged slave named Leon, but the marriage had not stopped her from chasing after other men. Her son, a sturdy six-year-old whom Damis called Fox, was far more white in appearance than black. His most striking feature was his eyes, which were not black or brown, but a shade of gun-metal gray that sometimes looked almost blue. He was a fine little fellow, but set apart by his appearance so that his peers in the world of slavery had little to do with him.

The air in the kitchen had been made uncomfortable by Dorrie's unthinking remark. Box got up, and Carrie rose with him. Saying thanks for the treats, they left the kitchen.

"You shouldn't have said that, Dorrie," Zander said disapprovingly. "Dey can't help what Damis does—no more'n Miz Susanna kin help what Marse Clay does."

"I knows dat!" Dorrie said sharply, her face unhappy. "I'm jest worried about Clay." She hesitated, then the words flooded from her lips. "When he gonna git ovah Miss Mellie, Zander? It's been six years since she turned him down for Marse Gideon, and he still mad as a bear with a sore tail!"

"Well, he don't talk 'bout Miss Mellie, does he?"

"And so dat make everything all right?" Dorrie shook her head, a sadness in her dark eyes. "You men! You think if nobody says anything, why dey ain't nothing wrong. Jest cover it all up—and it'll go away!" She got up, went to the window, and looked out. "Look at dat, Zander." She waited until he rose and came to stand beside her, both of them looking at the group out in the yard. "Ain't dey a good sight? All dem chillun!" She named them off fondly, "There's Miz Marianne and Marse Claude with Marie. Ain't dat child a beauty! Jes' nine, but she gonna be a beauty! And Miss Amy and Marse Brad with them three fine chillun. Look like stairsteps, don't dey, Zander? Little Les is two, Rachel is 'bout fo', and Grant is six. Dey may be named Franklins, but dey is all three Rocklins!"

"Fine chillun, Dorrie," Zander agreed. "But I reckon Marse Clay and Miss Ellen's crop is jest as purty." He named them with pride, having been active in their raising. "Look at dem twins, Dorrie! I nevuh kin tell which is Dent and which is David! Dis heah is their fifth birthday, and dey bof' big enough to be ten!"

"Well, dey may look alike," Dorrie snorted, "but dey sho' don't act alike! Dat David is de sweetest thing! But if somebody don't take a cane to Marse Dent Rocklin, he gonna be hung someday!"

"He is a mess!" Zander agreed sadly. "Take aftuh his daddy, I reckon. Look at Lowell, ain't but one year younger dan them twins, and ain't half as big! But look how he taking care of the baby. He do love that little Rena!"

They stood there watching the children, and finally Dorrie said, "You sees what it is? Dere's Miss Amy wif her husband, and dere's Miss Marianne and her husband. And where's the daddy of them four younguns? I tell you whar he is—he's drunk and wif some bad woman, dat's whar he be!"

Zander could not meet his wife's fiery glance, and his thin shoulders stooped. "Marse Clay, he's gonna put his mammy and pappy in an early grave, Dorrie."

"If Miz Ellen don't shoot him first!" Dorrie snapped. "I'm jest glad Marse Noah didn't live to see the way his grandson actin'!" Then she shook her head, saying, "Well, we ain't gonna make things no bettuh by talking about it. Go tell 'em de cake and punch is ready."

"All right."

Ten minutes later, the dining room was filled with the treble sound of children's voices underlaid by lower, adult voices singing "Happy Birthday." The twins, Denton and David, sat at the head of the table, and when Dorrie brought in the three-layer chocolate cake with ten candles burning, they let out squeals of joy.

As the boys blew the candles out and the cake was cut, Amy said quietly, "Ellen, I'm sure Clay will be here." She was sitting beside Ellen, whose face was pale, and she tried to bring some assurance into her voice. "Perhaps the weather got worse."

Ellen Rocklin was no less striking than she had been when she married Clay six years earlier. The pink silk dress she wore for the party set off her figure, for even the birth of four children in that short period had not destroyed the lush curves. But there was a discontent in her brown eyes as she murmured, "Don't make excuses for him, Amy. I've done that long enough myself!"

"I know it's hard—"

"How can you know about it, Amy?" Ellen said, keeping her voice under control. "You've got a family. Brad is home with you and your children, which is what a husband is supposed to do, isn't it? And even Marianne, as sorry as Claude is with his liquor and women, doesn't have to put up with what I have to."

Across the room, Thomas and Susanna were very much aware of Ellen's unhappiness. Indeed, they both felt Clay's inconsistencies keenly. Thomas moved his lips close to Susanna's ear, saying, "I never should have let him go to Richmond yesterday."

"It's not your fault, Tom," she answered. "He gave me his word he'd be back early this morning."

"His word!" Thomas said bitterly. "No such thing! Can't be trusted to do a single decent thing!"

Burke Rocklin, at sixteen, was the youngest son of Thomas and Susanna. He resembled his mother greatly in appearance, and he could see no wrong in anything his brother Clay did. "He'll be here," he said boldly to his mother. "Wait and see!"

"I hope so, Burke. The children are beginning to feel it," she answered sadly. "Dent asked me a minute ago why his father didn't like him." Her hand touched Thomas's under the table. "It made me cry, Tom! I didn't know what to say to the poor child."

The eyes of Thomas Rocklin were burning with anger. "Clay's not too old for a thrashing!"

"Yes, he is." Susanna spoke bitterly. "We should have seen to that when he was much younger."

Thomas felt the power of her remark, and though he realized she was speaking of the two of them, he said, "You're right, but it was my responsibility. I failed him, Susanna." Bitterness rose in his throat, and he had to force himself to keep the anger from showing on his face.

The others, he realized, all knew what Clay was. Marianne, who loved Thomas more than the others, had tried to comfort him, but he had said, "Don't try to find an excuse for me, Marianne. I should have used the strap on him when he was younger. He's got a rebellious streak. All of us Rocklins have it, I think, but with Clay, it's almost like a demon!"

Thomas looked across at Marianne, saw her watching him. She always sensed his moods better than the others, and now he tried to cover his anger with a smile. She answered it, but both knew that the day was spoiled for most of them.

After the cake and punch, gifts were brought in, and the boys flew through them, sending the colorful wrapping paper flying. Both of them got exactly the same things, a few toys and some books. Marianne noticed that David snatched up a book and had his nose in it at once, while Dent was fascinated by a toy rifle. "That's sort of symbolic, isn't it, Claude?" she said to her husband.

Claude Bristol was of no more than average height, but he looked very much like the French aristocrat from whom he had descended. "David the scholar and Dent the fighter?" he remarked with a smile on his thin lips. "Yes, they are like that. Dent is like Clay, but I don't know whom David takes his quiet ways from."

"From his grandmother, I think. He's very like her." She looked toward the window, thinking of Clay, but saying nothing.

"I should have gone with him," Claude said. Then he saw something in his wife's clear eyes that made him drop his own. "But that would be like sending a fox to guard the chickens." A slight bitterness touched his fine gray eyes, and he added, "Is that what you're thinking? That I'm very much like Clay?"

Marianne did not deny his words directly. But she touched his hand, looked into his face, and smiled. "You and Clay suffer from the same temptations. But you are man enough to struggle against them. Someday, Claude, you'll defeat them all. And you're a fine father!"

He shook his head slightly. "I try, my dear. And I will always try, for I love you very much."

At that moment, before Marianne could respond, Brad Franklin said, "Here comes Clay!" He had walked to the window and was staring out into the front drive. Now he turned and said evenly, "He's in time for the cake." Amy's husband was a smallish man, under medium height. He was lean, with fair skin and reddish-blond hair and a hungry-looking, intense face. He owned Lindwood Plantation twenty miles from Gracefield—closer to Richmond, which suited him, for he was up to his ears in politics. Now he moved to stand behind his wife, touching her shoulders, then stepped back to lean against the wall. He didn't like Clay, or more accurately, he didn't respect him. More than once in his rather intense fashion, he had told the younger man to his face that he was a sorry excuse for a husband and a father. Clay had taken it badly, and the two were always on guard when together.

"Daddy! Daddy!" The four children began to squeal excitedly and would have gone to meet their father, but Ellen said sharply, "Get back in your chairs, all of you!"

Three of them obeyed, but Denton ignored her and ran out of the room. Ellen rose to go after him, anger in her eyes, but Susanna said quietly, "Let him go, Ellen. You can speak to him later."

Clay came in, his eyes bright but his speech slurred. He had Dent in his arms, and cried out, "Happy birthday!" as he entered. As usual he ignored Ellen, going at once to where David sat watching him with a pair of steady brown eyes. "How's my birthday twins?" Clay asked loudly, then picked them both up and squeezed them. Only then did he turn to face the others, and there was a defiant light in his dark eyes. "I got held up in Richmond," he said briefly, which they all knew would be his only apology.

"Dorrie, bring some cake for Clay," Susanna said

quickly. "Boys, show your father what you've gotten for your birthday."

Ellen said nothing, not to Clay, at least. While Clay exclaimed over the presents, she sat rigidly in her chair, her eyes fixed on him, unblinking and angry.

Claude said quietly to Brad, "Look at Ellen. She's mad enough to cut Clay's throat!"

"Guess she has reason," Franklin answered briefly. He got on well enough with Claude, but the Frenchman was too much like Clay and in Brad's opinion was partly responsible for Clay's life-style.

Claude said no more to Brad, and the two men stood back, letting the party wind down. Soon the children were hustled off to bed, and Thomas instructed Zander to have the evening meal set out. When they were all seated, Thomas asked the blessing. In his prayer, he said, ". . . and remember Gideon, Lord, and keep him safe from the enemy."

"What do you hear about Gid, Tom?" Brad Franklin asked, cutting the roast beef on his plate. "He over that wound he took at Monterey?"

"Stephen says so," Thomas replied. "Said he's going back to his unit in a couple of weeks."

"I don't believe in this war," Marianne said, her brow troubled. "Everyone knows President Polk brought it on, and it was Andrew Jackson who put him up to it." She took a bite of potatoes, then added, somewhat angrily, "Jimmy Polk never had an idea in his head that Andy Jackson didn't put there!"

"In that you are correct," Claude agreed, nodding. "Jackson was a man possessed when he was president. 'Manifest Destiny' was his creation, and he was convinced that God has given America a special place in history. He, and many others now, feel it's her right—her destiny—to take whatever lands she needs to become a great nation."

Brad nodded, his narrow face thoughtful. "He and Sam Houston were thick as thieves. Jackson needed Texas as a state, but he also saw it as a door to getting control of California."

"But Mexico owns California!" Amy protested.

"Of course, dear." Brad grinned. "And that's what this war is all about. Partly, anyway."

"The rest of it is slavery!" Clay said suddenly. He spoke thickly and was weaving just slightly in his seat.

"That's correct, Clay." Brad nodded. "The Missouri Compromise has got the North and the South in a bind." The now-famous act declared that slavery could not be introduced into any state north of the Louisiana Purchase territory. But the South had realized that there were more potential states in the northern area. Franklin said with a sudden passion in his voice, "Soon there will be more states in the Union that are opposed to slavery. They'll strangle us! So what Polk has done is open the door to more Southern states."

"You don't mean take Mexico!" Thomas said, a little shocked at his son-in-law.

Franklin hesitated. "That is not impossible. Some say Mexico is a natural extension of the South, good cotton country. But most thinking men of our part of the world are thinking of New Mexico and California. Mexico owns them, but they don't care about them. Already Polk has sent two forces to California to have our people in place when the Mexican War is settled."

Marianne was troubled. "Isn't that what we fought against England for, Brad? So we could have freedom?"

"Why, Marianne, there will be freedom! America must have that land, we must reach from shore to shore! And the good thing about it is that all this territory will become slave states!"

The discussion went on for some time, but finally Susanna said, "Well, I don't know about this war, if it's good or bad. But I do know that I'm very proud of Gideon."

Thomas added, "Stephen tells me the boy got a medal." A cry of approval went around the table, but Thomas noticed that Clay dropped his head to stare at the table.

"They don't give those away!" Claude said with admiration. "I read the report of the action in the papers. It was a bloody affair, taking Monterey. Do you have a report of what the boy did to get the medal?"

"Yes. I don't have the letter Stephen wrote, but it was a very courageous thing." He proceeded to relate the rescue of the major by Gid, and concluded by saying, "I'm glad a Rocklin is serving his country so well!"

Clay got up suddenly, looked around the room, then said, "So Gid's a hero! Well, soldiering is a pretty exciting life. Let him try to do something heroic around *this* place! He'd find it a little harder than playing soldier!"

He lurched away from the table and went to his bedroom, followed closely by Ellen. But when she started to berate him for missing the party, he said thickly, "Ellen, shut your mouth—or I'll shut it for you!"

"Go on, hit me!" she cried out bitterly, her fists clenched. She would have struck him, but knew better. "Do you think that would hurt me as badly as what you do all the time?"

He threw his head back, his eyes bitter. He had long kept his tongue over the way they had gotten married. At first, he had done his best to make a real marriage of what they had . . . but he was haunted by the memories of Melanie. And the memory of Ellen's behavior had become a sickness with him.

"You wanted this marriage," he said in a deadly tone. "Well, you'll have to take what you got!"

"You never loved me!" Ellen whispered. "Do you think I don't know?"

"Know what?" he demanded, tired of the scene. It was like so many others!

"That you're still in love with Mellie!"

Clay stared at her, saying nothing. Their words seemed to have released a storm of emotions, a Pandora's box of buried thoughts that he had kept so deep that he had almost forgotten they were there. He thought of Mellie as she had been when he had courted her, and when he saw the twisted rage on Ellen's face, he knew he was doomed. There was no such thing as divorce in his family. *I will be married to this woman,* he thought bitterly, *as long as I live.*

Suddenly he wanted to strike her. He wanted to scream, "You've ruined my life! I'm trapped—and there's no way out!" Standing with his fists clenched, he almost let the wave of fierce anger overpower him, but then he wheeled and staggered out of the room.

She heard his steps pound unevenly down the hall and then down the stairs. A weakness took her, and she sat down on the bed. But there were no tears. She had shed them all long ago. Now there was only a barren anger that fed upon itself, and she sat there until she heard the sound of his horse leaving the stable, picking up speed until he reached the road and the furious drumming of the hoofbeats faded out.

I hate him, she thought numbly, sitting with her hands clenched. *He'll go to Richmond, to those women! I smelled their perfume on him tonight! I hope someone shoots him at one of those places. I wish he were dead!*

Ellen almost got her wish exactly two weeks after the twins' birthday party.

It didn't happen, however, at a bordello. No, it was the jealous husband of a woman named Lorene Taliferro who shot a bullet exactly one quarter of an inch away from Clay's right ear. And then Clay put a ball from his dueling pistol into the left side of Duncan Taliferro.

A light snow had fallen, cloaking the harsh dead earth with a beautiful coating of white. The two parties had met at eight in the morning at a spot just outside of Richmond. Clay could have stopped it all with a simple apology, but he had lived in a state of drunkenness since he had last seen Ellen. He could not live with the knowledge that his wife knew of his love for Melanie—and since he could not have the woman he loved, any woman would do—even a silly one like Lorene Taliferro!

Clay had stood quietly, giving Taliferro the first shot, which had missed. He thought once of tossing the pistol down and walking away; all honor would have been satisfied. But then, in a gesture that he never understood—never!—he aimed at the man's side and pulled the trigger. Watching Taliferro fall backward, the pristine snow suddenly turned a violent crimson, he was suddenly shaken as he had never been. A feeling of self-loathing swept him, overwhelmed him, and he left the dueling field without stopping to see if the man was dead or alive.

For several days he tried to drown the knowledge of his own heart in a bottle, but never succeeded. He discovered that everyone considered what he had done an act of cowardice. Even Taylor Dewitt, his best friend, had left him in disgust, saying, "My God, Clay! What a cowardly thing to do!"

He had not gone back to Gracefield, nor had he been sent for. The loose women and his drunken friends in Richmond had laughed at the duel, but this only made him feel worse.

Finally the pressure got to him. One gray morning he left Richmond, riding slowly along the rutted tracks of the road, unaware of the beauty of the countryside. He could have reached Gracefield before dark, easily, but he dreaded the ordeal of facing his parents—and his children. He didn't care about Ellen, except that it was torture to be with her.

All morning he rode, his head down, his horse picking its way along the road. Blackbirds dotted the sky, making raucous cries, and a red fox came out of the brush, stared at him, then walked calmly away. Noon came, and by two o'clock he was sober. The sun was dropping and clouds were lowering in the west. He discovered that he had wandered onto a road that he didn't know, so he began looking for a house where he might ask for his bearings. It was nearly an hour later when he rounded a curve in the road and saw a child leading a calf. The yearling was not disposed to go, and the young person was having a hard time of it. Clay spurred his horse forward and brought him to a stop when he was ten feet away.

"A little balky, is he?"

The figure had a voice, and from it Clay deduced that gender was female. "Hello, Mister Clay."

Clay blinked, then peered at the shapeless figure. The girl was wearing men's trousers, a ragged bulky coat that was far too large, and a black slouch hat that came down to her eyes. He tried to see her features, but they were covered by a green scarf pulled over them, which was tied behind her neck. "You know me?" Clay asked.

The girl loosed the scarf, pulled it away. "Why, certainly I do! It's me, Melora, Mister Clay!"

"Why—so it is!" Clay exclaimed. He had seen the child several times since she had nursed him to health, but time had slipped by. He remembered the books, and asked, "Did you read all those books, Melora?"

Melora had a pair of remarkable green eyes, and they sparkled in her reddened face. "Lots of times," she said warmly.

Clay smiled, then said, "Calf stray away last night?"

"Yes, sir. Pa sent me to look this way."

"Well, it looks to me like he's more than you can handle. Give me that rope, Melora." He took the rope, then leaned over, saying, "Now, you." She hesitated, and he said, "Not afraid of my horse, are you?"

"N-no, sir," she said. She lifted her arms and he put his right arm around her. She was larger than she looked, heavier and more filled out. He laughed, saying, "You're a grown-up woman almost, Melora! Another year or so and I won't be able to do that. How old are you now?"

"Twelve."

"Twelve," Clay twisted to smile at her. "Time sort of slipped by me! I thought you were about eight or nine."

"No, sir. I was twelve last month."

Clay touched the horse with his heels, gave the calf a jerk that nearly upended him, then began to question the girl. By the time they had reached the Yancy place, he had gotten a full report on her parents and the other children.

"Well—if it ain't Mr. Clay!" Buford Yancy had come from the barn at the sight of the man on horseback, and there was a welcoming light on his face as he reached up for the rope. "Git down and be friendly!"

The warmth of Yancy touched Clay, coming after the cold treatment he was used to. "Might do with a cup of coffee if it's handy, Buford." He reached back to help Melora, but she slid to the ground on her own.

"Melora, go tell your ma to fry up some of that venison!" He ignored Clay's protest, saying, "No bother. Now, you come and let's put this feller where he belongs—then we'll get us some grub outta my woman."

After the yearling was put into a corral, Buford showed Clay around the place. He had added several buildings since Clay had been tended by Melora, including a stout barn and several smaller additions. Yancy was proud of his place, Clay saw, as proud as any Rocklin was of Gracefield with its thousands of acres. Finally they went inside, and soon Clay was seated at the slab table eating fresh deer meat. He had eaten little for several days and suddenly was hungry as a wolf. It delighted the Yancys to see him eat, and he found himself feeling at home with them.

After the meal, he had to see how all the children were doing, and was impressed. Royal was fourteen, a carbon copy of his father, thin as a lathe and with alert greenish eyes. Zack, age ten, was more like his mother, short and sturdy. And Cora, at nine, was like Melora. The younger children resembled their father.

Melora, though, was a shock to him. Though only twelve, she was already possessed of the beginnings of beauty. She sat back from the fire, saying little that evening, but taking in every word that Clay said.

Finally, Buford said, "Well, I guess it's bedtime. Mattie's got you a bed made, Mr. Rocklin. Real feather bed! You take this room."

Clay was tired and said good-night as Yancy and his

wife retired to the single bedroom at the rear of the cabin. Melora herded the children up into the loft with practiced authority.

Clay drank the last of the coffee, then sat in a hand-made chair, staring into the fire. He was so lost in his thoughts that he came to himself with a shock when Melora's voice came from close to his side.

"Can I get you anything, Mister Clay?"

"Why, I don't think so, Melora. I'm stuffed like a suckling pig right now." She half turned, but he stopped her. "I'd like to hear you read a little, if you're not too sleepy."

"Oh, no!" Melora's face lit up, and at once she moved to a rough bookcase on one wall. She came back with a book, saying shyly, "This is my favorite."

He took the book, smiled, and said, *"Pilgrim's Progress.* I remember this one, sure enough!" He saw that the pages were worn and the back loose. It had been in good condition when he had brought it to her. "Read me your favorite part," he said, handing the book back to the girl.

Taking the book, she sat down at his feet, the pages illuminated by the flickering flames. "I like the part best where Christian fights with the fiend Apollyon." She started to read in a clear voice:

> "So he went on and Apollyon met him. Now the monster was hideous to behold: he was clothed with scales like a fish, and they are his pride; he had wings like a dragon, and feet like a bear, and out of his belly came fire and smoke; and his mouth was as the mouth of a lion. When he came up to Christian, he beheld him with a disdainful countenance, and thus began to question him:

> "APOLLYON: Whence come you, and whither are you bound?

> "CHRISTIAN: I am come from the City of Destruction, which is the place of all evil, and am going to the City of Zion.

"APOLLYON: By this, I perceive that thou art one of my subjects; for all that country is mine, and I am the prince and god of it.

"CHRISTIAN: I was indeed born in your dominions, but your service was hard, and your wages such as a man could not live on, for the wages of sin is death."

As Melora read on, Clay was fascinated. She knew the book by heart, and as she read, she threw herself into each part. When she read the lines of Apollyon, she deepened her voice and frowned angrily; when she read the part of Christian, she spoke sweetly and firmly.

Finally she came to the section where the actual battle took place between Bunyan's hero and the dragon:

"CHRISTIAN: Apollyon, beware what you do, for I am in the King's highway, the way of holiness.
"Then Apollyon straddled quite over the whole breadth of the way, and said, "Prepare to die; for I swear by my infernal den, that thou shalt go no farther: here will I spill thy soul." And with that, he threw a burning dart at his breast; but Christian held a shield in his hand, with that he caught it, and so prevented the danger of that."

Melora, Clay saw with wonder, was caught up in the old story, and he remembered suddenly that he had been the same when he was her age. When she was finished and looked up at him with her eyes alive, reflecting the fire, she whispered, "That's my favorite part!"

"I think it's mine, too, Melora," he said. "I must have read it a hundred times when I was a boy."

"Did you, sure enough?" she asked wistfully, her lips parted. "Ain't that nice, that we like the same part! Do you want to hear my second favorite part?"

"Sure, I do!"

"It's the part about when Hopeful and Christian come to the Celestial City, but they can't get to it without they go through the River of Death first."

"I remember that part," Clay said, nodding. "It always scared me a little."

Melora began to read again, this time much slower, and her eyes were enormous in the firelight.

"Now I further saw, that betwixt them and the gate was a river; but there was no bridge to go over, and the river was very deep. The pilgrims began to inquire if there were no other way to the City; to which they answered, 'Yes, but there hath not any save two, to wit, Enoch and Elijah, been permitted to tread that path since the foundation of the world.'

"Then they asked if the waters were all of a depth. They said, 'No, for you shall find it deeper or shallower as you believe in the King of the place.'

"Then they addressed themselves to the water; and entering, Christian began to sink, and crying out to his good friend Hopeful, he said, 'I sink in deep waters!'

"Then said the other, 'Be of good cheer my brother; I feel the bottom, and it is good!'"

Melora lowered the book, and Clay saw that there were tears in her eyes. "I love Hopeful, don't you, Mister Clay? When his friend was afraid, he stayed with him and made him believe it would be all right. Ain't that grand!"

"Yes, Melora, it's a wonderful thing to make people feel good." He smiled suddenly, saying, "It's a thing you do better than anyone I know."

"Me!" Melora gasped, her hand flying to her throat. "Why, I don't do nothing like that, Mister Clay!"

Clay leaned forward and reached out for her hand.

When it lay in his own he said, "I think you do. Like when I was brought here so sick I could hardly breathe. It was you who took care of me. And like tonight. When I came here I was feeling very bad, Melora. But you've made me feel very good."

Her hand was warm in his, strong and firm for a child's hand. He could feel the callouses that had already formed, young as she was. Then he released it, adding, "Thank you for reading to me, Melora. Do you like any of the other books?"

She was staring at him, overwhelmed by his compliment. She remembered clearly every detail of every encounter with him, and she knew she would never forget this night.

"Yes," she said. "Not so well as this one, though. But the ones about the knights and the dragons, I like them real well!" She ran to the bookshelf, and for the next hour, she read from the Arthurian romances that Clay had given her.

Finally she closed the book. "I like the part where the men go and kill the dragons that are killing the people, don't you?"

"Yes. I've always liked those stories."

She suddenly gave him an odd look, then giggled. "Know what, Mister Clay?"

"No. What?"

"When I saw you come down the road today, on your white horse and all, I thought you looked like a knight! I really did! And I pretended I was one of those ladies in the book, and that you'd come to save me."

Clay smiled. "I'm not much of a dragon killer, Melora." Then a thought came to him. It drew his smile down, and the joy left his eyes. The thought of his life and its emptiness, and the futility of the years that lay ahead, laid its hand on him. He said quietly, "I'm not a good man like those knights, Melora. I'm a very bad man, as a matter of fact."

Her response startled him. She dropped the book and

seized his arms with both hands, shaking him with all
her strength. "You're not!" she cried, and he saw with absolute astonishment that tears were filling her eyes.
"You're not a bad man!" she cried again, then turned,
put her arm on the stones of the fireplace, and cried
against it.

Clay Rocklin had never been so taken aback. He stared
at the girl's slender form, shaking with a rage of weeping,
and had no idea as to what it was all about. Standing
there, however, a strange thought came to him. It was the
most incredible thought he'd ever had, and at first he
shook it off. But it came back, even stronger. It filled his
mind, and he told himself he was crazy, but it would not
budge. Rather it grew into a full-fledged plan as he stood
there staring down at Melora.

I'll go away from Gracefield, he thought. *I'll throw myself
into something that will take all I have. The war! I'll join the
army, go be with Gid. And if I'm any kind of a man at all, I'll
find out about it. If I'm not—maybe a thing like that will
change me! I'll do it, by the Lord!*

When the thing was settled, wild and fantastical with a
thousand perils, he touched the girl's shoulder, turning
her around. "Don't cry, Melora."

Tears left silver tracks down her smooth cheeks, and
her eyes were half-angry. "I don't like it when you talk
like that, Mister Clay!"

"Well, I won't say any more." He hesitated, then said,
"Melora, I've got to go away for a while, but I want you to
do something for me."

"Me? What can I do?"

He took out his wallet and removed all the bills in it. "I
want you to go into Richmond. Get your father to take
you. And I want you to spend all of this money on books."

She stared at the bills, then looked up at him with be-
wilderment. "But what books?"

"The ones you like," he said. "Get a library for you and
for the other children. When I come back, I want you to
read them to me—like you have tonight."

CHAPTER TEN

THE NEW RECRUIT

THE SNOW—not heavy and damp, but dry as dust—fell lightly on Washington, so lightly that it seemed the flakes played wild games, fluttering like miniature birds before coming to rest. Standing at the bay window, Stephen Rocklin felt a sudden unaccustomed twinge of fear as he watched Gideon playing in the snow with the boys. Stephen was not a man of great imagination; he spent little time speculating about the future. But as he watched his son make a snowball and toss it at Frank, the youngest grandchild, he suddenly was possessed of something like a vision. At least, it was as close to a vision as a man such as Stephen ever received. He suddenly saw Gideon lying dead on a battlefield in Mexico, his empty eyes staring blindly up into a merciless sky.

"What is it, Stephen?" Ruth had noted the sudden change of expression on his face. She was standing beside him, enjoying the sight of the children and their parents. "Don't you feel well?"

"It's nothing," he said quickly. They were not an overly affectionate pair, though the years of marriage had molded them into a solid couple. He had often envied the closeness that existed between his brother Tom and Susanna, the almost mystic relationship that they seemed to have. But he was content with his marriage. So he put her off with, "Just dreading to see Gid go back to Mexico."

Ruth's lips tightened, for the same thought was never far from her mind. Gid's convalescent leave had been so wonderful! His wound, not as serious as it might have been, had healed rapidly, and the house had been a happy place with him there. Ruth, for all her rather stiff mannerisms, had grown very close to Melanie, closer than she did to most people. She didn't know that Gid had told his wife, "Mellie, I know Mother is sometimes difficult, with all her parties and social climbing—but see if you can get close to her. She needs a real friend. Someone to talk to about something a little deeper than the next party."

Melanie had succeeded in this with little difficulty. She was a warm, outgoing young woman, and her years on the barren plains at Fort Swift had given her a desire to get closer to her people—and to Gid's parents. She came through the door now, snow sparkling in her blonde hair. Her eyes were bright, and she was laughing as she entered the drawing room.

"Oh, my hands are freezing!" She had Frank in tow and thrust him close to the fire that burned merrily in the fireplace, filling the room with a faint scent of fragrant apple wood. "You're going to be a snowman yourself if you don't thaw out, Frank!" She began stripping the mittens off the sturdy boy, who protested, "Not cold, Mommy!"

The door slammed and Gid came in, anchored with the other two boys. "What about something hot for these fellows, Mother?" he demanded. His face was paler than usual, and he moved carefully as he began pulling the wool coat from Tyler, who at the age of five was insulted and insisted, "I can do it, Daddy!" He struggled with the buttons while the middle son, Robert, submitted docilely to his father's help. He was four, and already it was evident he would have his mother's slenderness. Tyler, however, was blocky, like his father and grandfather.

Ruth laughed and left for the kitchen, saying, "I don't think anyone could make enough chocolate to fill you all up!" She returned with a pot of frothy, steaming chocolate and a platter of sugar cookies, which the boys promptly fell on like small pigs. "Tyler, don't stuff three of those cookies in your mouth!" Ruth scolded. "There's plenty to go around." Then she looked at her son and laughed. "No wonder he eats like a pig, Gid, when you're stuffing yourself. Didn't they teach you any better manners than that at West Point?"

"Well, I may have had some polish at the Point," Gid said with a grin, licking his fingers and reaching for two more cookies, "but I lost them all in Mexico. No white tablecloths and polished silver there." He told them how he had joined with his sergeant, Boone Monroe, in a raid on a Mexican farm, nearly getting shot by an irate farmer as they tried for his chickens.

The boys all listened avidly, but Stephen laughed, "We sent you to West Point to learn how to steal chickens? I'd have expected a little more for a decorated hero!"

Gid flushed—as he always did when anyone referred to his medal—and covered quickly by saying, "Sergeant Monroe has more sense than most of the officers down there. I got a letter from him yesterday. He says the company's been sent to join General Scott's force."

The nature of the war had taken a sudden change during Gid's convalescence. President Polk, displeased with what he considered the snail's pace of the war, had named General Winfield Scott to command a force that would bring the conflict to an end. The plan called for General Taylor to simply hold on in the north, and send most of his men to join Scott, who would land an army at Vera Cruz and penetrate to the heart of Mexico.

A shadow crossed Melanie's face, but she quickly hid it. "Will you have to leave soon?"

Gid hesitated, then nodded. "Next week. My orders came yesterday."

"Oh, Son, you're not fit to go back to the war!" Ruth cried.

"I'm fine, Mother," Gid said, going to give her a hug. "And it means so much to me that you and Father are taking care of Mellie and the boys while I'm gone."

His announcement dampened the joy of the day. Even the boys realized what was happening, and Tyler asked, "Daddy, take me with you. I can kill those old Mexicans!"

Gideon took the sturdy form of the boy, holding him close. "I hope," he said quietly, "that you never have to kill anyone, Tyler."

The family spent the day together, going out for a sleigh ride in the afternoon, and when they returned, Pompey met them as they came into the house. "Marse Clay is here, Mr. Rocklin."

A look of surprise passed across Stephen's face, but he said, "Well, where did you put him, Pompey?"

"In the library, sir."

Gid caught his father's glance and said, "Well, let's go welcome him."

Melanie took Gid's arm, holding it tightly, and he felt the tension running through her. When they entered the lofty room where Stephen kept his books, they saw Clay standing at the window, staring out. When he turned, Melanie noticed that he was thinner than she remembered, and that he seemed very nervous. That was unusual for Clay, and somehow she was sorry that he had come. She forced a smile, however, and noted that he didn't look at her after his first glance.

"Clay! What a surprise!" Gid said, stepping forward to give his cousin a hearty handshake and slapping him on the shoulder. "You should have let us know you were coming."

"Well, to tell the truth, Gid, I didn't know it myself until two days ago." He thought of the storm of resistance and shock at his announcement that he was going to join the war, then forced the memory out of his mind. "Everyone sends their best to all of you."

Ruth's social skills came in handy, for she bullied them all into the dining room for dinner as soon as possible. It was her notion that food could solve any problem—if properly served in the right setting. Or at least, it could put off any problem for a time.

The dinner went well, though Clay's remarks about Gracefield held a significant omission: he spoke of everyone except Ellen. They all noticed that he was under some sort of strain, eating little and speaking too rapidly. After the meal, he said quietly, "Gid, I've got to talk to you."

"Come to the library," Gid said at once. "Pompey, bring us some coffee." He led the way and made no attempt to force Clay to speak. When the two men had their coffee and Pompey closed the door with a sibilant sound, Clay said at once with a grimace, "Sorry to bust in on you like this, Gid."

"What's wrong, Clay?" Gid asked at once. "Trouble at home?"

"Yes, but I guess the trouble is mostly in here," Clay said, giving his chest a slap. He got up, striding back and forth, his face pale and his mouth grim. "I want to ask you for something, Gid—but before I do, let me tell you what's been happening to me."

Gid sat there quietly, listening to Clay's rapid words. He had learned much about men from his tour at Fort Swift; he had been forced to deal with the problems of his men constantly. As a result, he had become a good listener, which gave men confidence in him. He knew now that if he said little and waited long enough, a man would finally wade through the minor problems and come to the big one.

As Clay spoke frankly—and with disgust—of his life and his failures as a parent, Gid listened. When Clay said, "I've made a mess of everything, Gid!" he knew Clay had left something out, but he did not force it.

"We all do things we're sorry for, Clay," Gid said. "But you're a young man. There's time to make it up to Ellen and the children."

Clay shook his head stubbornly. "Not at Gracefield, Gid. I've got to get away and make a new start. Too many failures stare me in the face there."

"Leave Gracefield?" Gid was startled. He knew the feeling that Rocklins had for the land, and he shook his head. "You belong there, Clay. Running away won't solve anything."

Clay stared at him, then flushed. "I've got to get away, Gid. For a while, at least. When I get some order and peace in my life, maybe I can go back. And that brings me to the favor."

"Anything, Clay. You know that."

Clay stared at him. "You really mean that, don't you, Gid? Well, here it is—I'm going to enlist in the army. Can you fix it so I'll be in your company?"

Gid Rocklin was a hard man to shock, but Clay had succeeded in doing just that. He had imagined his troubled cousin saying all sorts of things, but nothing like this! He tried to collect his thoughts, getting up to face his cousin. Instinctively he felt Clay was making a mistake, but he saw the stubborn pride on Clay's handsome, sensitive face and knew that he must not fail the man standing before him.

"I think it's a mistake, Clay—" He saw the hurt and anger begin to form in the eyes of the other man, then added with a smile, "But I'll do what I can." He threw his arm around Clay's shoulders, adding with a laugh, "It'll be good to have two Rocklins in the company!"

Clay trembled slightly, the warmth and weight of Gid's heavy arm feeling good to him. "I—I won't let you down, Gid! I swear it!"

"Of course you won't!" Gid saw emotion building up in Clay and wanted to break the tension of the moment. "Let's go tell the family that you're going to be going along to keep an eye on me, Clay. They'll be happy to hear it!"

"Gid—thanks!"

"No thanks to it." Gid smiled. "You'll wind up hating me, I expect. Most new recruits don't love their officers too much. But I've got a job in mind for you that you'll be good at."

"What job, Gid?"

"I'll put you on a horse." Gid smiled. "Make a courier out of you. You were always the best rider in Virginia, so we'll put that talent to work for the U.S. Army. Look out, Santa Anna!" he added.

The idea fired Clay, and at once he felt the tension running out of him. *It's going to be all right!* he thought. *I knew Gid wouldn't let me down.*

The next two weeks were exciting for Clay. He spent every day with the Sixth New York Cavalry, learning the rudiments of military drill. He was careless about most of the restrictions, which displeased the sergeant in charge. But he was such a fine rider that his lax disciplinary habits were overlooked. He was popular with the men, too, being likable and, as a Southerner, an interesting specimen.

Still, though he enjoyed his time with the Sixth, he felt strangely restless when at "home" at the Rocklin mansion. He knew, of course, that the cause of his unease was being around Melanie—but he would never have admitted it. He simply kept his distance from her, physically and in every other way. Melanie realized what was happening, but she seemed to be the only one. Gid and the rest of the family seemed oblivious. Once Melanie tried to bring the subject up to her husband.

"Do you think it might be best if Clay stayed with the unit?" she asked one night after they had gone to bed.

"With the men?" Gid had been thinking of the day of his departure—dreading it—and the question caught him off guard. "I don't know. Do you think he's unhappy here?"

Melanie hesitated, then said, "He's a restless man, Gid. He's going to be unhappy wherever he is." She tried to find a way to say what had been troubling her, but could not find the words.

"What is it, Mellie? Something's bothering you."

"Gid . . . Clay still feels something for me."

A brief silence, then, "He hasn't—"

"Oh, nothing like that! It's the way he doesn't say anything to me, Gid. He barely speaks to me. If he were over being in love with me, he'd be more natural."

"Poor fellow!" Gid lay there thinking, then sighed.

"Well, we'll both be gone next week. He'll just have to get over it. I was hoping he and Ellen would make a better job of it."

"They were never suited. Oh, Gid, I hate to see you go!"

"I'll be back soon. This war won't last long." He reached for her then, and they forgot about Clay and the war and everything else but each other.

A week later, the two cousins were on their way to join General Scott's army at Tampico, a staging point for the invasion of Vera Cruz. As the train pulled out of the Washington station, Gideon threw himself down in the seat beside Clay. He had just endured a painful farewell with his family, and his mood was definitely gloomy. "This is the worst part of being a soldier, Clay," he muttered, staring blindly out the window. "Leaving your family."

Clay felt the pinch of guilt, for he felt like a young boy off on a hunting trip. He missed his children, but not much. The idea of a new challenge was like wine to him, and he said only, "It's hard, Gid. But we'll come back with chests full of medals."

Gid gave him a sudden hard stare. "Get that idea out of your head, Clay. War isn't like that. It's not romantic and thrilling. It's an ugly, painful business that no man in his right mind could enjoy. I just pray we get back alive and not maimed!"

Clay agreed at once, but he was thinking of the sound of guns, the waving of banners. *When I get back with a medal or two*, he thought, *things will be different. I may even get a promotion to second lieutenant*. He had a sudden picture of himself wearing the blue uniform of an officer, being met at Richmond by a brass band, and everyone cheering his name. *I'll show the folks who the real soldier is! Maybe Gid has a medal or two, but I could always outdo him!* His thoughts went back to the night he'd spent at the Yancy cabin, and a smile came to him as he remembered Melora and her idea about knights. She had mistaken him for one—well, he'd be one for her sake. Surely there

144

was a dragon somewhere waiting for him in the dusty land of Mexico!

So the two men went to war—together physically, but far apart in every other way.

CHAPTER ELEVEN

DEATH AT CERRO GORDO

CLAY'S dreams of cavalry charges with flags flying did not last long. When he and Gid got off the ship near Brazos Santiago, they were separated at once. Gid was thrust into the job of whipping K Company into fighting trim, while Clay was given the responsibility of grooming horses. At first he went at the task cheerfully enough, but there was no challenge to it—nothing but dirty work. By the end of the first week he was sick of it.

A young lieutenant named George B. McClellan arrived at the Brazos Santiago, having made the move with his command from Taylor's force. He and Gid had been classmates at West Point, and the two of them had a good time over supper. McClellan, a small, erect man of a dapper appearance, spoke of his journey. "There was some hardship, Gid, but we made our own fun. You never saw such a bunch! We sat around and criticized the generals, laughed and swore at the mustangs and volunteers, and it was a nice outing."

"When you get to be a general, George," Gid laughed, "you'll know from experience just what the men are saying about you."

McClellan laughed in response—but years later, he would recall that remark with some chagrin. "You say your cousin is here with your company? Not an officer?"

"No, Mac. To tell the truth, he's running away from troubles at home. I got him in for a short enlistment. He would never make a career soldier. Too independent."

"Well, Gid, I don't know what sort of trouble he's running from, but he may have jumped from the frying pan into the fire. I hear Vera Cruz is bristling with cannon.

Beats me how General Scott thinks we can take it with ships. Those shore batteries have thirty-pound cannon, some of them capable of firing hot shot. If a ship takes just one of those red-hot balls, it'll go up like tinder!"

"Well, we've got to get there first," Gid said. "With this weather, I don't know if the ships can transport this army to Tampico, much less Vera Cruz."

His words proved prophetic, for of the forty-one ships that Scott had requisitioned to ferry his troops and munitions to Vera Cruz, seventeen were delayed for a month by terrible weather. Another ten ships that were to sail to Gulf ports and embark troops for the expedition were canceled by mistake. Other ships simply never appeared. Despite these factors, by the first of March—eight weeks later than he had hoped—Scott concluded that he would never be more ready.

There were seasoned men in his army, including two regular divisions—one headed by General Worth, who had led the attack on Monterey—and the robust old cavalry commander who would fight a circular saw. Sprinkled through this army were some familiar faces: Ulysses Grant, the reluctant quartermaster; a newcomer worth watching—a middle-aged junior officer named Robert E. Lee; and Lieutenant P. G. T. Beauregard, a swarthy soldier from Louisiana.

If Clay had known action was immediate, he might have avoided the problem he found himself in just before the invasion. While Gid spent much of his time with the officers, Clay was thrown into a rough company—a profane, hard-drinking bunch of volunteers who were looked down on by the regulars with barely veiled contempt. One of the volunteers, an Englishman named Rodney Hood, was a remittance man—which meant that his family in England paid him to stay away from them! Hood was a hulking man, twenty-eight years old, black-haired, and beetle-browed. He organized gambling among the enlisted men, scrounged liquor to sell to them, and pretty much did as he pleased among the enlisted men. Being an expert gunner, he was tolerated by the officers, particularly since they were not overly concerned about the volunteers.

Hood had run head-on into Clay in an argument over cards. The larger man started for the thin young Southerner to pound him into the ground with his massive fists. He had awakened some time later with a lump on his head. Clay had simply pulled out his heavy Colt and brought it down on Hood's head.

"Well, want to try it again, Rod?" Clay said, smiling as the big man struggled to his feet.

Hood touched his head and stared at Rocklin with admiration. "No, Bucko," he said, grinning. "I admire any man who can put me down. Let's shake on it." The two of them became friends, making a strange pair indeed! It was Hood's influence that kept Clay involved in constant drinking and gambling. And, in an indirect manner, it was Hood who eventually led Clay into more serious trouble.

The pair of them, at the insistence of Hood, had slipped off into a Mexican cantina for a night's carousing. When they returned, they were hailed as they stumbled to their tents. Hood, wise in the ways of the game, slipped off into the darkness, but Clay was caught.

"Hold it!" It was Sergeant Boone Monroe coming out of the darkness, a lantern in his hand, his eyes hard. He had been instructed by Lieutenant Rocklin that no exceptions were to be made for his cousin, and he said, "Left the camp without permission? Well, you'll be sorry for that, I reckon. Come on, soldier."

Clay was just drunk enough to resent Boone's hand on his arm, and he swung, catching the tall soldier on the neck with a wild blow. The next instant he was driven to the ground by a tremendous hit that caught him in the temple. Lights flashed before his eyes, and he grew sick from the bad liquor. When he had finished vomiting, Monroe pulled him to his feet with an iron grip. "Come along and take your medicine."

Gid and McClellan were together in the tent they

shared when Monroe called out, "Lieutenant!" They both stepped outside, and Gid kept the shock that ran through him from showing on his face. "One of the men, Lieutenant. I caught him sneaking back from the saloon. Private Rocklin, it is, sir."

McClellan took the situation in at once. Rocklin had told him enough about the cousin from Virginia to let him know how touchy the situation was. He stepped forward before Gid could speak, saying, "All right, Sergeant. Put him in the guardhouse for three days, bread and water. Give him lots of exercise, though. Let him clean up after the horses."

"Yes sir!" Monroe hauled Clay off at the end of his long arm, and Gid stood there silently staring after them. Finally he turned and gave McClellan a smile. "Thanks, Mac. I was in a pretty tough spot."

"May be what he needs, Gid," McClellan said with a shrug. "I hope so. He's a good rider, I guess, but a courier has to be dependable. Better have a little talk with him, off the record."

Whether or not McClellan's advice would have been effective Gideon never knew, for the next day he was ordered to take a patrol out to screen Scott's action from the enemy. The order came so suddenly that he had no time for even a brief visit with Clay. It troubled him, but he thought, *It will only be a few days. Clay will be more reasonable when I get back. We'll talk it out then.*

But the patrol lasted a week, and Clay had other counsel during that time. Rodney Hood smuggled liquor in to him for the three days of his confinement. When Clay was released, Hood welcomed him like a lost brother.

"You see how these officers are?" he said angrily. "Your own cousin, and he lets you rot in that filthy sty of a guardhouse!" Ordinarily Clay would have had nothing to do with a man like Hood, but the shame of his confinement with drunks and deserters cut into him deeply. Hood's constant tirades concerning officers and the army in general had sunk deeper than Clay realized into his spirit. And when Gid finally returned from patrol, his cousin was in a vile temper.

"How's my cousin doing, Sergeant?" Gid asked Monroe the morning after his return. He was worn thin, and his wound was giving him some trouble, enough so that he was weary of spirit and not as sharp as usual.

"No disrespect to you, sir," Boone answered bluntly, "but he's poor stuff! Been hanging around with Hood and the others who cause most of the trouble in the outfit, acting like a snapping turtle, ready to bite anything that moves."

Gid soon discovered for himself the accuracy of that description. He found Clay brushing a tall bay and tried to joke the thing away. "Well, how's the veteran doing? Ready for the invasion?"

Clay looked up, his eyes cold with resentment. "I'll hold up my end, I reckon." He took a swipe at the horse, then turned to face his cousin. "I didn't sign up to clean stalls, Gid. And I thought you'd do better by me than to have me put in the guardhouse."

Gid stared at him, trying to find a way to get inside the man. Clay had always been touchy, and the discipline of army life was no place for that. "Clay, if Lieutenant McClellan hadn't spoken up—and he did it to save me embarrassment—you'd have gotten more than three days in the guardhouse! Sergeant Monroe told me you hit him. For that alone I'd have nailed your hide to the wall!"

"Sure you would!" Clay shot back. "You'd do anything to keep me from showing you up!"

Gid struggled to keep his own temper in check. "That's not so, and you know it, Clay. I want to see you do great things, and I know it's in you. But I'm an officer, and you're an enlisted man. Do you think the whole company's not watching to see if I give you special treatment?" Gid hated the scene and wanted to cut it short. He tried to smile. "Let's put this behind us, Clay. There's

150

a big job ahead of us. You'll be needed, and I'll do all I can to help you."

Clay could not get the resentment out of his system. He ignored the frank words, saying in the same cold voice, "I'll take care of myself, Lieutenant."

It was useless. Silently Gid stared at his relative, wishing he knew how to do better with him—but there was no way. He was locked into his rank, and his responsibility to his men and to his superiors made any concession to Clay impossible. "Very well, Clay," he said evenly, then walked out of the stable.

For the next few days the invasion was poised, and finally after a risky voyage through rough weather, Scott's armada arrived offshore from Vera Cruz. Scott surveyed the coast; from what he could see of Vera Cruz, the defenses were impregnable from the sea. The city was enclosed by walls fifteen feet high, and on the land side they extended from the water's edge south of town to the water again on the north. A massive granite seawall protected the waterfront, and more than a hundred pieces of heavy artillery—most of which had been cast in an American foundry across the Hudson River from West Point—were aimed seaward.

Every man on the transports was dreading the moment when they would have to row ashore in small boats and face those terrible guns. But on March 9, when the invasion began, a minor miracle took place. The nine-mile ride to the beach began, the tall ships of war sailing along under their topsails. The ships' decks thronged in every part with dense masses of troops whose bright muskets and bayonets were flashing in the sunbeams, and bands played loudly.

Gid, standing in the stern of one of the flatboats that was to deliver the troops through shallow water, expected the huge cannons to fire at any moment. He turned to George McClellan, saying, "No reason why we can expect to get ashore alive, is there, Mac?"

"None that I can think of," McClellan answered jauntily. At that moment a shot whistled overhead, and he added, "Here it comes! Now we'll catch it!"

But the shot had come from the other direction. An American ship was having a go at scattering a few Mexican dragoons who were visible on the shore. And there were no more shots from the land batteries! History would never explain why the Mexicans did not blow the American ships out of the water. Whatever the reason, the landing was made without a shot being fired, which pleased the general very much—but puzzled him and his staff as well.

When the troops were all disembarked, Gid was in a small group of junior officers directing the placement of the mortars. He looked up to see General Winfield Scott approaching, accompanied by some of his staff. Scott spotted McClellan and said, "Lieutenant McClellan, how does it look, the lay of the mortars?"

"Fine, General Scott," McClellan answered. As he pointed out the spots on the wall that would be the best places to attack, the dark-haired officer who stood close to the general walked around to survey the walls of the city from a different angle. When McClellan finished, the officer came back and Scott said, "Captain Lee, you'll be glad to meet a fellow Virginian. This is Lieutenant Gideon Rocklin, from Richmond."

Lee was the most handsome man Gid had ever seen. He had perfect features, and his form was tall and erect. "From Richmond?" Lee said with a smile. "I expect we have mutual friends, Lieutenant. I have many acquaintances there. Do you know the Chesnuts?"

"Yes sir, very well." Gid nodded. "Fine people."

Lee stood there, speaking quietly, and before he left, he faced Gid directly. "Lieutenant Rocklin, I read the report from Monterey. As a matter of fact, I submitted General Taylor's recommendation for decoration to General Scott. It gave me a great deal of pleasure that a man from my state performed so well." Lee's quick eyes saw that his remarks embarrassed Rocklin, so he said only, "I'll be seeing you, I expect. My congratulations, sir."

"I never met anybody like him," Gid remarked as Lee walked back to the group of officers with the general.

"There is something about the man," McClellan agreed. "General Scott thinks he'll command the entire Union Army before he's finished."

The capture of Vera Cruz was relatively simple. For some reason, the Mexican command decided to pull their main forces out, and morale inside the city collapsed. Scott kept the mortars firing, and on the twenty-sixth, his army marched into the city. His victory had been swift and unblemished. His losses were minimal, by the standards of war—only thirteen killed and fifty-five wounded. At once he began preparing for the march into Mexico. Still, it was almost two weeks before the first of his troops set off. His immediate goal was Jalapa, seventy-four miles up the national road to Mexico City, four thousand feet above sea level.

Santa Anna had pulled his army together and chosen a spot twelve miles coastward from Jalapa where the national road passed between commanding hills as it climbed into the highlands. He established his headquarters near the sleepy town of Cerro Gordo, or "Big Hill." It was named for the mountain that dominated it, which the Mexicans called El Telegrafo.

Company K found itself under the command of General Twiggs, and they marched rapidly toward Cerro Gordo. Twiggs was eager for action and didn't seem to notice that many of his troops were collapsing in the heat. On April 11 they reached the bridge across the Rio del Plan, about three miles downstream from Cerro Gordo. The next morning, Gid and the other officers were called to a staff meeting. Twiggs informed them that about four thousand Mexicans were dug into the hill that lay in front of them.

"We'll wait for General Scott," Twiggs informed them.

"Get your equipment and men ready. I think it'll be a hard fight."

Scott pitched camp near the bridge on April 14, but instead of attacking, he began a careful three-day reconnaissance of the Mexican positions. He learned that Mexican cannon occupied the high ground on both sides of the road. A frontal assault would be suicidal.

On the American left, the Rio del Plan ran through a gorge five hundred feet deep, which made an advance in that direction impossible. Scott's best hope was to find a way to attack on the right—the weak side of the Mexican position. Scott gave the job of blazing a trail in this direction to his engineers, which included Robert E. Lee, P. G. T. Beauregard, and George McClellan.

It was early in the morning when Captain Lee came to the tent McClellan shared with Gideon. The two men looked up, and Lee said, "I need one of you for a mission General Scott has assigned me. The general tells me that you are busy, Lieutenant McClellan, so I would appreciate it if you could help me, Lieutenant Rocklin."

"Yes sir! Of course!" Gid grabbed his gear and followed Captain Lee toward the edge of the camp. He spotted Clay holding a horse in readiness and waved toward him, but got no response.

"We've got a difficult job, Lieutenant," Lee said. He explained the need for finding a hole in the Mexican line. With a smile, he added, "I thought a Virginian might be good at sneaking through the rough country. Did you ever do any stalking?"

"Yes, Captain Lee, but I should tell you, I'm not really a Virginian. What I mean is, my parents moved to Washington some time ago, but I have a cousin serving in the ranks whose family is in Virginia. Thomas Rocklin is his father."

"I know of him. But in any case, we've got to crawl through some rough country. Get your side arm loaded, and we'll start right away."

Gid never forgot that wild trip. He and Lee soon outdistanced the small escort and about midmorning came upon a small spring ringed with trampled ferns. "Somebody's been here, Captain," Gid said, then stopped, for the sound of voices came to them.

"Quick, behind this log!" Lee whispered, and the two of them dropped behind a huge log near the water. A troop of Mexican soldiers appeared, drank from the spring, then sat down on the log, laughing and chatting. Ants and spiders began to chew on Gid, and he saw that Lee was in the same condition. They lay motionless for hours, scarcely daring to breathe, and it was almost evening before the soldiers left. The two men stood up, stiff and burning with insect bites, then made their way back to camp.

"Thanks for your company, Lieutenant Rocklin," Lee said. "I think we'll be able to attack tomorrow." His eyes were bright, and afterward Gid remembered how the prospect of battle had excited the stately Virginian.

"Thanks for letting me go with you, sir."

Basing his plans on Lee's report, Scott called for a two-faceted attack for April 18. General Twiggs's division of regulars, reinforced by Shield's brigade, would cut the Jalapa road in order to trap the bulk of Santa Anna's army. At the same time, General Pillow's brigade would mount a diversionary attack designed to convince Santa Anna that the American main effort would come exactly where he expected it—against the strongly defended promontories between the road and the river.

"I believe he'll fall for it, Lee," General Scott said, staring at the map in front of him. "Be sure that we have good communication. If any of our people get pinned down, we'll need to know about it right away."

"Yes, General. I'll see to it."

And see to it he did, by hunting down the best couriers available—one of whom was Clay Rocklin. As it happened, Lee came by the headquarters of Company K and found Gid hard at work. "I need your best courier," Lee said at once. "He must be dependable."

If Clay had not been there, looking on with hope in his eyes, Gid would have chosen another man. But he gave way to an impulse. "I have a Virginian for you, Captain Lee. This is Clay Rocklin from Richmond."

Lee looked toward Clay, saying with a smile, "Private Rocklin, I'm glad you're with us. We'll expect you to do the Rocklins proud, as your cousin has."

"I'll do my best, sir!"

As Lee left, Gid said, "It's a big attack, Clay. Be careful."

"I can take care of myself!"

Clay stalked away, resentment in every line of his body, Lee's remark about Gid burning in his ears and his heart. When he got back to his tent that night, his excitement over the prospect of seeing action was dampened by Lee's obvious regard for Gid.

He slept poorly, and early in the morning he had a frightful nightmare. He dreamed that he was dressed in armor, like a knight of the Round Table, and he was facing some dark, terrible creature. He could not see what it was, but a woman was weeping, and a great desire to help her came to him. He pulled the visor of his helmet down, lowered his lance, and rode full tilt at the beast, still not able to see the creature well. As he drew near, his horse suddenly reared up, and he was thrown to the earth. Unable to rise because of the weight of his armor, he saw the grisly beast emerge from a darkling wood—yet he was not afraid. Struggling to his feet, he drew his sword and cried out, "Come to me, and I will kill you!"

But when the beast drew near, he saw to his horror that though it had the body of a grisly beast, the face was his own! "I have come for you," the beast whispered, and it threw terrible arms around him, crushing him and filling his nostrils with its foul breath! Closer and closer the monster drew him to its rank body, and he felt the life flowing out of him. Despair filled him as he heard the woman still crying, and he began to die.

Clay awoke with a wild cry and sat bolt upright in bed. The sun was already breaking the darkness, and Hood, awakened by his cry, muttered, "What's happening, Clay?" He got out of his bed, then peered at Rocklin. "Bad dreams, eh? Well, we all have 'em, I suppose." He leaned down and fumbled for something, then found it.

"Take this with you on your little jaunt, Clay."

"Where'd you get it, Rodney?" Clay asked, staring at the quart of whiskey Hood had given him. "I thought you were out of the stuff."

"Got it off a Mexican last night. He says it'll take your skull off, so be careful. But a man's got to have a drink, now, don't he?"

Clay put the bottle in with his other things, saying, "Thanks, Hood. Don't get in the way of any bullets, you hear?"

"Not bloody likely!"

Clay mounted his horse and fell behind the line of infantry that moved slowly toward the Mexican position. The air was still that morning, and the flags hung limply on their staffs as the men marched out. There was no cheering, and Clay was depressed by it all. He had expected more than this.

The going was hard, with ravines so steep that men could barely climb them. Artillery was let down each steep slope on ropes and pulled up on the opposite side. Men grew thirsty and drank from streams, and many were limping by the time the action started.

Gid heard it first, then Boone Monroe. "That's rifle fire," Gid said with a nod. "Sounds like some of our advance parties have made contact."

They had indeed, for a rifle company on a reconnoitering mission at the base of the mountain had clashed unexpectedly with a troop of Mexicans. At once Twiggs commanded three companies to rescue the rifle company. Gid called out, "K Company, forward! Private Rocklin, stay fifty yards behind us."

The men followed Gid, and soon they chased the attacking enemy down the mountains—and straight into three thousand Mexicans. Outnumbered twenty-five to one, Gid saw there was no hope without reinforcements. He waved for Clay, who came pounding forward. Gid was watching the enemy and didn't notice how unsteady Clay looked or how flushed his face was as he reined up.

"Ride back to General Twiggs, Clay!" Gid yelled. "Tell him we've got more Mexicans than we can handle! Tell him if he comes in from the south, he'll wipe them out! We'll do our best to hold—now ride!"

Clay tore out, and Gid turned back to the fight, which was not going well. All afternoon they fought, and when darkness fell, Gid was shocked at their losses. "If we don't get help by morning," he said in quiet desperation to Sergeant Monroe, "we'll be chewed up and swallowed." Then he added, "But Clay is the best rider I've ever seen, and he's studied the ground. He won't let us down."

The fragile hope Gid was trying to keep alive would have died completely had he been able to see his cousin at that moment. For Clay was lying on the trail, halfway back to General Scott's headquarters. The Mexican who had sold the whiskey to Hood had sold several other bottles of the vile stuff to the men of K Company—and it was pure poison. Two of the men went raving mad for a time, and another lost his vision for three days. Everyone who drank it was hard hit. The liquor Clay had drunk had attacked his nerves. He had begun to lose his vision and finally had fallen from his horse. His stomach cramped and he blundered along the trail, unable to see. Finally he passed out, facedown, on the trail.

General Scott's advance scouts found Clay Rocklin at noon the next day. They took him to headquarters, and Scott said sternly, "You're drunk, Private!"

Clay gasped out, "Send troops . . . to Lieutenant . . . Rocklin!" It was all he could do, for his stomach cramped and he fell to the floor in agony.

Scott stared at him, a merciless light in his pale blue eyes. "Place this man under arrest. Now! Lock him up!"

"He's pretty sick, sir," one of the scouts suggested.

"He's drunk on duty! Put him in irons." As soon as they removed Clay bodily, he called out, "Lee! I want you!"

Captain Lee came at once. "Yes, General?"

Scott related what had happened, adding, "It's probably too late, but send a relief column to help Rocklin."

Lee nodded, saying only, "I regret this, General. I picked Rocklin myself."

Scott stared at him, then forced himself to relax. "No blame on you, my boy. We have to trust men—and sometimes they fail us."

"Yes, sir, but Lieutenant Rocklin is too valuable a man to be wasted. I'll get the relief column at once, a cavalry troop. They'll be there in two hours."

When the troops arrived they found one hundred men dead, shot to pieces. The reinforcements drove off the Mexicans, and at once the commander began to call, "Lieutenant Rocklin!"

"I'm here, Captain." The captain whirled to see a dusty officer step out from behind a large rock. "Glad you made it. But it's too late for most of my men."

Captain Steele said at once, "The courier didn't get through, Lieutenant. We found him just a few hours ago—dead drunk." His voice was thick with disgust, and looking around at the pitiful bodies in the clearing, he swore and cried out, "I'd like to be on the firing squad that shoots him!"

There was no firing squad, though. Word of the bad whiskey got about, and that was taken into account. And although no one mentioned it, the members of the court-martial all felt tremendously sorry for Gideon Rocklin. It was that, plus admiration for the lieutenant, that motivated the officers who stood in judgment over Clay Rocklin to bring in a verdict of guilty, but with a mild sentence: immediate dishonorable discharge.

Clay stood at attention as the verdict was read. He felt the eyes of Robert E. Lee, who was on the court, upon him and could not meet them. When the sentence was read and he was dismissed, he moved blindly to his tent. He knew the men hated him, blamed him for the senseless deaths of so many of their number. But none of them blamed Clay as much as he blamed himself. They had no idea of the shame he felt, a shame that turned the world black for him.

He left without seeing Gid, though his cousin looked for him. He moved slowly, like an old man, and as he boarded the boat that would take him home, he felt like a man who was condemned for life to a prison cell far under the ground. The court could let him go free, but it could not take away the guilt that burned in his belly like fire.

And he knew it would never stop. He had killed those men as surely as if he had shot or bayoneted them himself. And he could never bring them back to life. He could only live—for the rest of his life—with the knowledge that he was a murderer.

As the boat moved across the dark waters, he stared down into the depths, longing to throw himself overboard. But he did not. Instead, he left the deck and stumbled to his cabin, where he drank himself into a stupor.

CHAPTER TWELVE

THE END OF A MAN

"WELL, the Scripture says seven is the perfect number—and it looks like that's what you ladies have here!"

Reverend Jeremiah Irons had come for his twice-weekly visit with Charlotte Rocklin and, taking a short-cut from the stable to the house, had encountered what seemed to be a miniature school. Actually it was Ellen Rocklin with her four children and Melanie, Gideon's wife, with her three. Irons stood beside the two women, admiring the yelling band of children, all of whom were so much alike in appearance that it was almost comical.

"They'll never be able to deny their Rocklin blood," the preacher remarked.

Melanie smiled suddenly. "They call us the Black Rocklins, Reverend Irons." She was looking very pretty in her blue dress, and her blue eyes sparkled in the August sunlight. "Can you point out which are mine and Gid's and which are Ellen and Clay's?"

"I never let myself get trapped into a discussion of people's children," Irons said with a grin. "In Arkansas, where I come from, some folk get almost as upset if you insult their children as they do if you bad-mouth their favorite coonhound." He studied the children, who were engaged in some sort of game involving a wagon filled with rocks. They were trying to hitch a sad-looking bluetick hound to the wagon, but all he would do was lie down and scratch.

Those children certainly do look alike, Irons thought as he watched. *All of them have the same dark hair and dark eyes. And they're all the same age, or almost so. Fine-looking children . . . how sad that Clay's are in far more trouble than they know!*

But he said only, "I used to lie when women showed me their babies. I'd say 'My, that *is* a beautiful child'— and the baby would be ugly as a pan of worms!"

Melanie laughed in delight. "Do you still lie, sir?"

"Oh no," Irons said, his brown eyes filled with humor. "Now whenever a mother brings out her baby and it looks like seven pounds of raw meat, I point at it and say in my most admiring voice, 'Now *that* is a baby!'" He laughed at himself, then said, "I didn't know you were here, Mrs. Rocklin."

Melanie said quickly, "Oh, I wanted the children to have some time with their Virginia grandparents while Gid is gone."

That was not strictly the truth. She had come at Gid's suggestion. *Go for a visit to Gracefield,* he had written. *They're probably worried sick about Clay, and you could encourage Ellen. Take the boys and make a holiday of it.* So she had gathered up the boys for the visit.

When Melanie arrived, she had found Thomas and Susanna sick with grief. Clay had not been heard from since his dishonorable discharge. As for Ellen, she was as angry as a woman could be. Melanie sensed that Ellen's feelings went deeper than Clay's disgraceful act; somehow the fragile marriage of the pair had been destroyed. Melanie had tried to counsel Ellen to be forgiving, but the rage in Ellen was white-hot, and the best she could do was spend time with her children.

Irons gave Melanie a careful look. He travelled over the county a great deal, holding evangelistic meetings and visiting other ministers. The story of Clay Rocklin's dishonorable behavior was spoken of everywhere he went, and since he was known to be a close friend of Clay's, he was often asked about the matter. He never said one harsh word about Clay, but defended him as well as he could. Now he said carefully, "Well, I'll expect you and your brood in church Sunday. And I'm giving you the job of bringing Miss Ellen and her children with you."

It was a mild rebuke, but Ellen flushed with irritation.

"If you had to be father *and* mother to four children, Rev. Irons, you might not have so much time on your hands!"

Irons said gently, "I realize you have heavy responsibilities, Ellen, but the Scripture urges us to let the Lord bear our burdens."

"The Scripture teaches that when a man breeds children, he's supposed to stay home and take care of them, too!" Without another word, Ellen whirled and walked angrily toward the house, slamming the door as she entered.

"I'm sorry, Brother Jerry," Melanie said. "She's not herself."

"No word at all on Clay?"

"No. For all we know he may be dead."

"Oh, I think it's not that bad," he said quickly. *More than likely off on a monumental drunk*, he thought to himself, then said, "But he can't stay gone forever. He'll have to come home sooner or later."

Jeremiah Irons was no prophet, nor even the son of a prophet, but just as he had predicted, Clay Rocklin finally came home.

It was not the homecoming he had dreamed of. No medals. No crowd at the station to meet him. Which was just as well, since he made a sorry figure when he got off the train—his suit was torn and dirty and he had not shaved in a week. His step was unsteady and his eyes were red-rimmed as he made his way toward the stable across from the railroad station. He kept his hat pulled down low over his eyes, fearful that he might be recognized, and when Harvey Simmons, the hostler, greeted him, "Hello—something for you?" he realized that Simmons didn't recognize him.

"I need to rent a horse, Harvey."

Simmons leaned forward, peering at Clay more closely, and could not hide the shock as he said, "Why, Mr. Rocklin! I didn't know—" He broke off quickly, saying, "I'll saddle up the bay for you."

Clay did not miss the furtive looks that Simmons gave him. He knew Harvey to be the biggest gossip in Richmond. *Well, I won't have to announce my homecoming in the paper. Harvey will see that the news gets out,* he thought dryly.

He mounted the horse when Simmons brought him up, saying, "I'll bring him back tomorrow, Harvey."

"Sure, Mr. Rocklin." Simmons struggled to contain his questions, but had had little practice doing such a thing. "What was it like, Mr. Rocklin? Down in Mexico in the war?"

Clay settled himself in the saddle, then turned to give the hostler a hostile glance. "It was dandy, Harvey. You ought to go see for yourself."

As Clay rode out at a gallop, Harvey scowled. "Somebody ought to make that man give a decent answer!" Then he whirled and hurried down to the Hard Tack saloon, announcing as he entered, "Hey, Clay Rocklin's come back!"

The sun was hot, and the liquor Clay had drunk on the train brought the sweat pouring down his face, and the jolting of his horse made him sick. Pulling the animal down to a slow walk, he thought sourly about the weeks he had spent in Dallas—that was as far as he had gotten after getting off the boat—and none of his memories were good. Being a fair gambler, he had managed to stretch his money and his stay out for two weeks. Finally a bad night at cards had left him with barely enough for train fare, and he had reluctantly bought his ticket, along with a bottle to numb his memories.

He rode slowly, wanting to sober up before he got home. He finally decided to time his arrival after the family went to bed. He could clean up and make his appearance in the morning. To that end, he walked the horse at a slow gait all afternoon, almost going to sleep more than once. It was after four when he came to the cutoff that led to the Yancy place. He thought suddenly that he could go there and clean up before going home, and on a sudden impulse, he turned the horse down the narrow road.

The air grew cooler as the sun went down, but he had a raging thirst and stopped once to drink from a shallow creek that crossed the road. He washed his face in the clear water, then tried to push his hair into place, using his fingers for a comb. Then he looked down into the shallow water, saw his reflection, and stopped dead still. He stared at the image—saw the hollow eyes, the sunken cheeks—and knew that if someone looking as bad as he did turned up at the back door of Gracefield, he'd send him down the road.

Despair filled him as he sat back on his heels. A bird was singing close by, a happy, joyous sound, and the rippling water over the stones was a merry note. But the happy world around him only amplified the unhappiness within him. For a long time he sat there, his face buried in his arms. Finally he got to his feet wearily, then mounted his horse, his face set. "They'll probably run me off the place," he muttered, but, driven by some impulse, he made his way to the cabin.

Smoke curled out of the chimney, and he saw Melora at once. She was feeding some hens, throwing the grain with a graceful motion. As he rode up, she glanced his way, not knowing him, he saw. Then when recognition came, she came running to stand beside his horse. Her eyes were enormous in the gathering twilight as she looked up at him.

"Mister Clay!" she whispered with a tremulous smile. "You came back!"

Clay's lips trembled, for he saw that she was glad to see him. "Well, I didn't kill any dragons, Melora."

"That doesn't matter," she said. "I was afraid for you."

Clay would have answered, but her parents had come out on the porch, and he looked at Yancy as he came closer. He saw the surprise in the man's careful green eyes, but there was no condemnation. "Why, Mr. Rocklin!" he said quickly. "Git off that critter! You're worse than a preacher for gettin' to a man's house just in time for supper!"

Yancy, Clay saw, was trying to put him at ease, but he was sure that they all knew about his sorry part at Cerro Gordo.

"Like to wash up, Buford," he said with an effort. "I'm dirty as a pig."

"I'll heat you some water, Mister Clay," Melora said quickly. "We got a tub you can use."

"Don't want to be a trouble," Clay mumbled.

"How could you be that?" Melora asked, then turned and walked into the cabin.

Clay still sat on his horse, the shame cutting him like a knife inside. "Buford, you may not want me in your house after I tell you what I've been doing."

In letters, Buford Yancy was an ignorant man—but he was wise in things that mattered. He had heard about Clay's discharge, but he came from a line of men who held friendship sacred. He said quietly, "Get down, Clay. You can use my razor."

The simplicity of the rough mountain man's acceptance brought a mist to Clay's eyes, and he got down, trying to hide his emotions. He didn't have to say anything, for with a natural tact, the family cared for him. He took a long bath in a tub placed on the back porch, shaved with Yancy's razor, and put on one of Yancy's shirts while Mattie washed his own. It dried by the stove as they ate a supper of roasted rabbit, collard greens, and freshly baked cornbread. The buttermilk, cool from its home in the springhouse, did more to cool Clay's burning throat than anything he had tasted.

After supper, he and Buford sat on the front porch. Yancy did almost all the talking. Mostly he talked about hunting and fishing, about his children. He sensed that Clay needed to say little and took the burden of the conversation.

"You gotta see them books that Melora bought with

the money you give her!" He added proudly, "She's done read every one of them!"

Finally Clay rose and went inside, where Melora showed him the books, and he commended her choices. But when he caught sight of the tattered copy of *Pilgrim's Progress*, he grew silent.

Finally he put on his clean shirt, which was not quite dry. He looked fairly presentable, but he felt a reluctance to leave. There was an ease, a happiness in the humble cabin that he knew would be lacking at Gracefield. And he also knew whose fault it was.

"Got to be going," he announced. The family followed him out, and as he rode away into the darkness, they all called after him. And he was able to pick out Melora's sweet voice as she cried out, "Come back soon, Mister Clay!"

In the years that followed, Clay Rocklin often wondered what would have happened if he had gotten home an hour later. It was a fine point, but his life was changed by the fact that he arrived at Gracefield at nine-thirty.

For if he had come just one hour later, he would not have encountered Melanie alone. He would have seen her in the morning at breakfast. If not there, then someplace else—but someplace where they would have been with other people.

Melanie wondered with grief much the same thing in the years that followed. She went over it a thousand times . . . how she had stayed up late, which was very unusual for her . . . how she had gone downstairs to the library to read, not being able to sleep. She had never done that before, but that night she was worried about Gid.

She had put the children to bed fairly early, and being tired from a hard day's play, they had gone to sleep almost at once. Then she had sat down and talked with Charlotte, who was much weaker these days. Melanie did not think the woman would ever recover, and she spent as much time as possible with her.

Charlotte Rocklin had gone downhill quickly after

Noah died. It was as if there were an invisible cord between the two, and when that was snapped by Noah's death, Charlotte lost her vitality and her will to live. She was feeble, and the thought of Clay was heavy on her heart. She had not been told of his behavior at Cerro Gordo, but still she was a wise woman and knew that things were ill with him.

"Noah worried so about him," the sick woman whispered. "But he always believed that God would bring him back. There's a verse in the Bible about it. Noah found it one day. I remember it so plain! He came running in where I was making a cake and said, 'Look here! It's in the Bible about our grandson Clay!' He was so excited that day!"

"Do you remember the verse, Mother Rocklin?"

"Of course. It's in Isaiah, chapter 54, verse 13. It says, 'All thy children shall be taught of the Lord.' And Noah never forgot it, Mellie! One of the last things he said before the Lord took him was, 'Clay! Clay's going to come to the Lord!'"

"That's wonderful!" Melanie said, and for a long time she sat there as the old woman spoke of her children and grandchildren. Finally she dropped off to sleep, and Melanie tiptoed out of the room.

"You ain't in bed yet, Miss Mellie?" Dorrie was in the kitchen, cutting up the last of a chicken as Melanie entered.

"I've been with Miss Charlotte."

"Pore thing! She ain't got long, has she? Jesus gonna come for her soon!"

"I think so, Dorrie. And she'll be glad to go."

"She been like a lost chile ever since Marse Noah was took."

The two women talked for a time, neither of them mentioning Clay, and finally Dorrie finished and left.

Still not sleepy, Melanie went to the library. She chose a book, then sat down in one of the horsehair chairs and began to read. It was not a good novel, and she was about to put it down when she heard a horse come down the drive and go to the stable. She looked out the window, wondering who could be moving about so late.

She turned the lamp down and left the library. Then, as she crossed the foyer, the door opened and a man stood there. Startled, she asked, "Who is it?"

The answer sent a shock running through her.

"It's me, Mellie—Clay!"

"Clay!" Melanie went to him at once, holding out her hands. "I'm so glad!"

Clay took her hands, his mind reeling. It was like witchcraft, for he had been thinking of her as he rode from the Yancy place, of the days of their courtship and how sweet, how beautiful she was.

And now she had come to him, appearing out of the night like a phantom—a beautiful phantom, for she wore a light rose-colored robe of silk and her eyes glowed warmly in the dark.

"Come to the library," she said quickly. "I want to talk to you."

He allowed her to pull him down the hall, and as soon as they were in the dim light of the library, she asked, "Clay, are you all right?"

"All right?" he asked in confusion. "Why, I guess so."

"We've been so worried, Clay! Not a word from you since you left Mexico!"

Clay stood in the darkness, listening to Mellie's voice, unable to think. For years he had kept his distance from Mellie, for he was still in love with her. Though bitter that she had chosen Gid, he could not forget her sweetness, and as they stood there whispering in the dim light, every nerve was painfully conscious of her beauty. She looked up at him, her lips rich and full, and he suddenly reached out and took hold of her.

"Clay!" she cried out in alarm. "Don't—!"

But he was like a man who was caught in one of those terrible, vivid dreams in which reality and fantasy are so fused that he can't separate the two. He clutched her in his arms, and his lips sought hers. She was soft and fragrant, and he forgot his family, forgot that she was another man's wife, forgot everything except that she was all he had ever wanted.

Melanie, shocked and outraged, fought against him, but he was far stronger. Her cries, though, did not go unheeded, for suddenly someone was standing in the door, and Melanie cried out, "Help me, please!"

Thomas had heard Clay's horse approach and, getting out of bed, had caught a glimpse of the rider as he crossed to the stable. "I'm going down, Susanna," he said to his wife.

"Is it Clay?" she asked quickly.

"Might be."

Thomas struggled into his clothing and went down the stairs, leaving Susanna as she searched for a robe. When he got to the foot of the stairs, he was startled by a cry from the library. Not sure of what he would find, he picked up the iron poker that rested against the fireplace.

What he saw as he came in the door sent such a wave of rage through him that he could not control himself. He saw his son Clay, forcing Melanie—his nephew's wife!—toward the couch.

Years of frustration and rage suddenly spilled out, and with a hoarse cry, Thomas lifted the poker and brought it down twice on Clay's unprotected head.

Melanie almost fell as Clay went to his knees, the sleeve of her gown ripping at the shoulder. She drew the gown together and, seeing Thomas raising the poker again, his eyes mad, ran to him and threw herself against him.

"No! Don't kill him!"

"The dog!" Thomas cried out, trying to disengage her clinging hands. At that moment Susanna rushed in. Taking in the scene, she joined Melanie in restraining Thomas.

"You must not!" she said, holding him tightly. The two women were hard pressed to hold him back, and

Clay got to his feet, blood streaming down his cheek. The first blow had taken him on top of his head, the second caught him as he turned and had opened a cut from his eyebrow to his cheekbone. Stunned by the attack, he stood there, his eyes blank.

Slowly Thomas regained control. He took a deep breath, then tossed the poker to the floor. "I'm—all right now," he said with a trembling voice. "It's a good thing you were here. I would have killed him!"

Clay blinked, felt the blood running down his cheek, and raised one hand to touch it. He stared at the blood, then at the three who stood in front of him. He could not think clearly, but the look in his father's eyes told him that nothing he could say would matter.

Then Thomas spoke to his son in a voice as cold and hard as his eyes. "Get out of my house! You are no longer my son!"

Clay licked his lips, trying to reply, but there was no mercy in those eyes. He shook his head, then turned and walked out of the library. As his feet sounded on the steps, Susanna clutched at Thomas saying, "Oh, my dear, are you sure—?"

"He's not our son, Susanna!" Thomas said in an iron voice. "He is dead—and I never want to hear his name again!"

Melanie, Susanna, and Thomas stood there, and soon the sound of a horse's hooves came to them. They waited until the echoes died away, and to all of them the sound of it was like a death knell.

PART THREE
PRODIGAL'S RETURN— 1859

✳ ✳ ✳

CHAPTER THIRTEEN

THE SLAVER

A FIERCE gale had torn the tops out of the *Carrie Jane* and—even worse—had snapped the mainmast ten feet above the deck. Ignoring the biting wind that numbed his fingers and stiffened his face, Clay Rocklin drove the deckhands aloft to set the new canvas. He would have gone up himself, but one of the first things he had discovered when he had come aboard the ship was that he had little head for heights. He had mastered every other aspect of seamanship, and it grated on his nerves that young Carlin, who was only sixteen, could scamper aloft into the swaying tops, while he himself was confined to the deck by some bad gene.

"Better get every inch on her you can, Mr. Rocklin." Clay turned to find that Captain March had come from the wheel to look at the tattered canvas. He was a thick-bodied man, his white hair set off by a ruddy complexion. Though well over sixty years old, the captain could work any of the deckhands into a stupor. It had been the fact that he could not outwork Clay Rocklin that had drawn his attention to the young man.

Clay had been stranded in Jamaica, totally destitute and with no prospects. The *Carrie Jane* had glided into the harbor under half sail, beautiful in the sparkling sunshine. That night Clay had met Captain Jonas March, and the older man had gotten the outline of his story. "Never too late for a man to change," he had said. "God can do what you can't."

Clay had resisted his preaching but had signed on as a deckhand for a run to Africa. "You know our cargo?" March had asked. "No? Well, it's black ivory, mister."

175

"Slaves?" Clay had asked in surprise. "That's against international law."

"It ain't against God's law! The pay's good, but it's the Lord's work, too. It's all there in the Bible, in black and white . . . the sons of Ham, bondservants, the sweat of their brow. We're spreading the Lord's seed, mister!"

Clay had soon discovered that Captain March held with the ideology of most of the planters he knew, that the black man was blessed by slavery. That his lot as a slave in the South was better than the life he would have had in a hut in Africa. Even more important, this new life would expose the black man to the gospel, which would save his soul.

The crew of the *Carrie Jane* was a poor lot, but March had some education. He invited Clay to his cabin often, and they had become friends by the time the ship touched on the African continent. March had said, "You're young and strong, Rocklin, and you're smart. Now let me tell you, if you apply yourself, you can make something of your life. I'm no spring chicken, you know! And I been keepin' my eye out for a good young man. Don't see why you can't be him. I'll teach you the sea and ships, and you work hard. Sooner than you think, you'll be a fine seaman, and you can buy an interest in the *Carrie Jane*."

As the wind whipped across his face, Clay studied the face of Jonas March. Things had happened exactly as the old sailor had predicted that night in his cabin. Clay had applied himself, discovering that he had a natural gift for the sea. The years had gone by swiftly, and now he owned one-half of the ship and had a large bank account besides.

The pay was good, as Jonas had said—but life had not been easy. Even now, Clay could hear the moaning of the blacks below deck. He always heard it these days, even in his sleep. The years had hardened him to the sight of men, women, and children being chained and packed below deck like animals. He had learned to block what he was doing out of his mind. He had even reached the point where he could ignore the awful smell of filth and disease that clung to the ship. After he had become master's mate, he simply concentrated on counting his money, dreaming of the time when he would leave the ship.

The land summoned him, for—despite his abilities—he was not a sailor. He longed for the fields, the trees, and the rivers of Virginia. More than once he had almost taken the plunge, but then he would think, *Where would I go? Back to Gracefield? I can't do that! They've written me off forever.*

Clay looked toward the stern, noting that the sails of the British frigate were slightly closer. "She's gaining on us, Jonas," he spoke loudly over the sound of the keening wind. "I don't think even with the topsails repaired we can outrun her. Not with the mainmast down."

"Try it." As he said this, Captain March stared at Clay, a thought in his head. But he decided the time was not right and simply said, "Get the canvas on her, Clay!"

An hour later, the topsails were all in place, but it was obvious that the frigate was not going to be shaken off.

"What'll happen if they catch us, sir?"

Clay looked around to see young Carlin staring at the warship, his eyes big with fear.

"They'll confiscate the ship and throw us all in a rotting prison for the rest of our lives," he said harshly. "That's what you were told when you signed on. It's the risk you take on a slaver." Then he said in a softer tone, "Maybe she'll lose some of her sails. Ordinarily we could run away and leave her, but not without a mainmast."

Clay had no hope, for he was seaman enough to know the truth—they could not outsail the frigate with the sails they had. He knew another truth, too: he would never go to prison, not as long as he had a pistol in his cabin. Life was bad enough, but he knew enough of the English prisons to know it would be better to die than go to one.

He was standing on the deck when Captain March

joined him. "She'll be up with us in two hours, Jonas," he remarked.

"Aye, she will." A strange look was on the face of the old captain, and he said in a tight voice. "Get all the blacks up on deck."

"On deck? What for?"

"Just obey the order, mister!"

A thought crossed Clay's mind, but he put it quickly away. Captain March had been a slaver for many years; perhaps shifting the slaves around would give the ship another knot or so an hour. He obeyed the order, and twenty minutes later the deck was packed with the captives. They were terrified, of course, as they always were from the time they stepped on board.

What must it be like, Clay wondered, not for the first time, *to be snatched from your village, from your home? To be chained and whipped and driven away from all you've ever known? And then to be put on a ship, taken thousands of miles to a strange land where nothing is familiar. No wonder so many of them just give up and die!*

The wind was rising as Clay stood there, staring at the pitiful captives. There were mothers with babies, and children so young they could barely walk. And there were the men, whose bodies were striped by the whips of the slavers who had brought them to the ship. He saw one young woman, a beautiful girl of no more than sixteen or seventeen. She had a child, and she clung to it fiercely, her arms around him to cut off the cold wind. She was dressed in rags, as they all were, and the cold January wind must have chilled her to the bone.

Then he heard Captain March say, "Over the side with them, Mr. Rocklin!"

Clay's mind seemed to turn to ice. He stood absolutely still, refusing to believe that he had heard the captain's order correctly. The young woman with the child was staring at him with huge eyes, and he could hear the keening of the child, a thin cry that seemed to tie his stomach into knots.

"Did you hear me, Mr. Rocklin?" Jonas March's face was fixed in a flinty expression. "Quick! You know what will happen if that frigate takes us with this cargo!" The hard hand of Captain March grasped Clay's arm, and his voice was harsh. "We have no choice!"

Still Clay stood there, transfixed, his mind reeling. It was like a terrible dream, the face of the young woman growing larger and larger, the sound of the child's crying thin and faint.

Then Jonas yelled at the second mate. "Over the side, Jenkins!"

As Clay watched, the burly Jenkins lifted the man on the end of the chain and flung him over the side. The man screamed, and the weight of his body jerked the slave next to him over the side. Immediately horrible screams rent the air, drowning out the wind whistling in Clay's ears.

The young woman had her eyes fixed on him when the chain around her waist caught her, dragging her to the rail, and she clutched her baby tightly. Her eyes were filled with panic, but she didn't scream. She stared at Clay as if she expected him to do something, but he stood there unable to move.

Just as she went over, her body striking the rail, she took one hand from her baby and lifted it in a strangely eloquent gesture for mercy, and her eyes were fixed on him as she disappeared from his sight. He took one horrified glance toward the stern and saw the line of writhing bodies sinking into the churning wake of the *Carrie Jane*.

Then he whirled and ran to the bow, where he vomited so violently that he thought his rib cage would be torn apart.

The rest of the voyage was strange. The British frigate finally overtook the slaver and boarded her. The British captain knew what they had done, and in his cabin he excoriated Captain March and Clay, cursing them with every invective he could manage. But he had no evidence, and in the end he had to let them go.

March said little for the next two days. It was clear that his partner was in bad shape. Finally he sought Clay out, saying, "It was unfortunate, my boy, and we both grieve over the loss."

"How much money did we lose, Jonas?" Clay's voice was harsh as a raven's caw, and he stared at the captain with haunted eyes. "How many dollars went down to the bottom?"

Jonas March stood there, his eyes hurt. He was not a dishonest man. He lived according to what he thought was right—but the sight of those black bodies had shaken his theory, and now he said, "I—I wasn't thinking of dollars, Clay."

Clay stared at him, his body tense, then he saw the pain in the eyes of the old man. "I'm sure you weren't, Jonas," he said wearily. "But this is the end for me."

And so it was at the end of the voyage that Jonas bought back Clay's half-interest in the ship. The two men parted at the bank where they had settled the legal side of the business.

"Jonas, I thank you for your goodness to me. You've been more than generous."

March waved his hand. "No, my boy, no more than just. You've done more than I expected." He paused and asked before turning to go, "What will you do, Clay?"

Clay shrugged his shoulders in a gesture of helplessness. "Try to forget," he said, and he walked out of the bank.

CHAPTER FOURTEEN
THE END OF THE TETHER

MR. WARREN Larrimore sat back in his tan leather chair, framed a steeple with his fingers, and stared at the man across the desk from him. Larrimore was a lean man with a large head and a full black beard that concealed most of his features. In fact, that was precisely why he wore the beard—as a banker he had to make hard decisions, decisions that sometimes went against his own desires. As a young man he had allowed his naturally generous nature to dictate his business decisions, but a lifetime of dealing with men and money had taught him something.

"Tom," he said quietly, his mild voice more like that of a choir director than a banker as he spoke, "We've been over this before. Although I hate to remind you of it, you've gone against every bit of advice I've ever given you. I'm accustomed to that, for most men think they know more about their business than a stodgy banker. But I like to think that our relationship has been a little more than just banker and depositor. I've considered you a friend for a long time."

Thomas Rocklin sat across from Larrimore, his face pulled tight and his heart beating too fast. He tried to smile, but made a bad job of it. "Certainly, Warren! I feel that way, too." His collar seemed too tight, and he pulled at it nervously, trying to find a way to say what he hoped would change Larrimore's mind about the loan. "And you're right about the rest. I should have listened to you. But I thought the price of cotton would go up—and I still think it will. Where else is England going to buy cotton for her mills?"

Larrimore shook his head with a sharp impatience. "Tom, you're like all the rest of the planters. You think the world runs on cotton!" The blindness that Southern planters had developed about cotton was an old story to the banker. He had explained the problem to Rocklin before, but he tried once again. "It's always an evil to be tied to one source of income, Tom. You're bound to it and helpless in the long run. What can you do if the price goes down? Hold your cotton? No, because almost every planter I know borrows to the hilt to get the crop raised. So, you'll take whatever is offered. And if there's a war, what will you do with it? You can't eat it, and you can't make cannon or shells out of it."

"England will buy it," Thomas said stubbornly. "She has to."

Larrimore gave up, and though nothing showed in his face, he was sickened over what he had to do. But there was no way out—a fact he had known from the beginning. Drawing his eyes down to a stare, he said, "Tom, I've got to call your loans. It's not my decision, you understand. I have a board of directors to answer to. When the loan committee met, I tried everything I could think of to get them to extend the loans, but they voted me down unanimously."

"But, Warren, there must be something you can do!" A cold sweat appeared on Rocklin's brow, and he clenched his hands to control the tremor that suddenly came to them. "I'll lose Gracefield!"

"I think I can maneuver the thing so that you'll come out with something, Tom," Larrimore said. "Not much, but enough so that you and Susanna won't have to worry." He tried to put a good face on the thing, saying in an encouraging tone, "After all, it's time you took things easy. You can travel some, maybe buy a little place in town, just big enough for you and Susanna and for the grandchildren to visit."

Thomas blinked his eyes nervously. The thing he had dreaded had finally come, and he felt as though he were in a terrible nightmare. More than anything in his life, he wanted Warren Larrimore to suddenly laugh and say, "Now, Tom, I was just trying to give you a scare! Cheer up! You can have the loan!"

He knew, though, with a sickening certainty, that no such thing was going to happen. He sat there trying not to let the fear that clutched him show, but Larrimore saw it. A Christian man, Larrimore had more compassion than was prudent for a banker. "Tom," he said, "I've told you before, there's one way out of this. Ask your brother to help you. Stephen is a wealthy man. He's your older brother. I think he'd be glad to help you."

"No!" The banker was shocked at the vehemence in Rocklin's answer. "I won't do it!" He got to his feet, picked up his coat, and started for the door. He stopped abruptly, turned back and added, nodding, "I'll find a way out of this, Warren. There are other banks!"

As the door closed, Larrimore sat at his desk, grieving over the tragedy of the Rocklin family. None of them was fitted for the world of business—except Stephen, of course. Burke Rocklin, Thomas's younger son, was no help. He had hated farm work from the time he was ten years old. Thomas had spent a fortune educating him, and at the age of twenty-nine Burke was still "trying to find himself." Then there was Clay Rocklin. . . .

The door opened and a tall, heavy man with a smooth face and a pair of direct gray eyes came in. George Snelling was chairman of the board. He asked at once, "You tell him, Warren?"

"Yes," the other replied heavily. "He didn't take it well."

"Too bad! But it's been inevitable. You did all you could to help him, Warren. But a man's got to stand on his own two feet." He went to the window and watched the traffic, then asked, "He understands that he's got to vacate at once?"

"I gave him a month, George."

Snelling frowned. That was not what the board had instructed Larrimore to do. But then he smiled. He was a hard character himself, but he had learned to trust the small man sitting at the desk. "Well, you know best, I suppose." He studied Larrimore, then said again, "Too bad," and left the room. Larrimore did not move for more than five minutes. He sat there staring at the wall, until, in a rare gesture of anger, he suddenly raised his fist and struck his walnut desk an angry blow that sent papers flying. Then he took a deep breath, shook his head, and began to gather them up in a logical fashion.

Susanna knew that something was wrong with Tom the minute he returned. She saw him from the kitchen window where she was helping Dorrie. "Finish the rest of these potatoes, Dorrie," she said, and went at once to meet him, but he came in through the side door and went upstairs. When she went into their room, she was shocked to find him sitting on the bed, his face twisted as though he was having some sort of attack.

"Tom! What is it?" She rushed over to his side, and he suddenly reached for her. She held his head against her breast, fear beginning to rise in her. In all their years of married life she had never seen him like this! "Is it your heart?"

"No!" He pulled himself back and stared at her, his dark eyes blinking. She saw that he was on the verge of losing control.

She said nothing, but put her arm around him. He clung to her until, finally, he grew calm. He took a deep breath. "I've been to see Warren Larrimore," he said.

Susanna understood. "He's not going to renew our loan?"

"He says he wants to, but the loan committee turned us down." He bit his lip, then broke out, "Susanna, we're going to lose everything!"

Susanna knew at that moment that she was stronger than her husband. But then, she had always known that. "We'll be all right, Tom," she said evenly.

"All right? How can we be 'all right'?" he demanded, his control slipping. He stopped, put out his hand, saying, "I'm sorry. I'm just not myself."

"We've seen it coming for a long time."

"I know—but I thought something would happen!" He groaned and pulled at his hair nervously. "How am I going to tell the children?"

"Just tell them," Susanna said practically. The thought of leaving Gracefield was a sharp pain in her bosom, but she would never let Thomas or anyone else see it. "A family is more than a house, I do hope," she said. "The Rocklins have good stuff. We'll be all right."

Tom shook his head. "I talked to Brad yesterday. I thought he could help, but he's had a bad year, too. Oh, he offered what he could, but it wasn't nearly enough."

"We can't take money from Brad and Amy," Susanna said at once. "They're in debt as deeply as we are. Brad expanded too fast." After a while, she got Tom to sit down and talk. It was, Susanna thought with some bitterness, the first time they'd talked so long in years. *It takes a tragedy to get us together for an hour*, she thought. But all she said was, "We'll tell the family tonight, after supper."

"All right. It'll have to be done."

That night Thomas ate almost nothing. Susanna looked around the table at each face, wondering how they would take the news. She sat at one end of the table, Thomas at the other. To her right sat Ellen with the twins, Dent and David. On her left Burke sat next to his father, and beside him, Lowell and Rena. *Four out of the eight are Clay's*, she thought suddenly, then resolutely closed her mind to the image of her oldest child.

The talk at the table centered on the strain between the North and the South. As usual, Dent and Burke were the loudest. Burke was well built and tall and looked remarkably like Susanna; he was the only one of the children who resembled her. He had a round face, smooth dark hair, and black eyes. Actually he cared little for politics, but he loved to tease Dent, who was easily stirred. They

were arguing about a series of debates that had taken place
a few months earlier between two politicians in Illinois—
Stephen A. Douglas, a man of national prominence, and
Abraham Lincoln, a lesser-known figure.

"Steve Douglas is our man, Burke!" Dent said, waving
a fork with a large chunk of roast beef impaled on it.
"He's got the right idea—popular sovereignty!"

"And what's that?" Burke prodded.

"Why, the right of a state to tend to its own business!
You just wait, Burke," Dent said, his dark eyes burning.
"Steve Douglas will be the next president of the United
States!" Dent, at the age of seventeen, looked so much
like Clay had at that age that it pained Susanna to watch
him. He was like Clay in more than looks, too. . . .

Burke sipped his buttermilk, then said, "No, Lincoln
finished him off in those debates. I hear the railsplitter is
about as homely as a man can get, but he does have a
way with words! People listen to him. Why, I can quote
you what he said about all the trouble we're having in
this country over slavery. 'A house divided against itself
cannot stand. . . . I believe this government cannot endure permanently half-slave and half-free. . . . I do not expect the Union to be dissolved—I do not expect the
house to fall—but I do expect it will cease to be divided.
It will become all one thing or the other.'" Burke had always had a fine memory, and he had recited the words
with evident relish.

"If Lincoln means that," Rena said suddenly, "we'll
have a war." She was tall for a girl of thirteen, and her
dark brown hair formed the perfect frame for her fine
complexion.

"You don't know anything about it, Rena!" Ellen
snapped. "There can't be a war!" Ellen was on one of her
diets, struggling to keep her figure. She was an attractive
woman, but her features had sharpened as her figure had
grown fuller over the years. That she was here at all was
unusual, for she spent more time in Richmond with
friends on extended visits than she spent at Gracefield.

The argument went on for several minutes, then Lowell got up, saying, "I'm going over to the stable. It's time for the new colt to come."

He was caught when he was halfway to the door by his grandfather's voice. "Lowell! Come back. I have something to tell you."

Lowell at once showed a stubborn streak, going back to his seat and flinging himself into it. He was fifteen and a throwback to his great-grandfather Noah. He had all the good traits, such as kindness and generosity, and some less admirable traits—mostly a tendency to be bullheaded!

Thomas looked around the table, cleared his throat, then said, "I have some news for you. I'm sure you'll not like it. I didn't! But we have to face up to it."

"What is it, Thomas?" Ellen demanded.

"Well, I'm afraid that we're going to be leaving Gracefield." He saw the blank looks with which they regarded him—all except Burke—and went on lamely. "Times have been very bad ever since Buchanan took office in '57. We've had a depression that's shaken the whole country. And we've had poor crops for the last two or three years. So, we're going to have to sell out."

"But—where will we go, Grandfather?" Rena was a quick child. She picked up on the uncertainty in Thomas at once, and her own voice had a thread of fear.

"We don't know yet, Rena," Susanna said quickly, "but God will take care of us."

"Is it the bank?" Burke asked quietly.

"I'm afraid so, Burke." Thomas tried to put a good face on it. "We'll look around and find a nice place. Not as large as this, of course. Maybe we'll move to the coast. You've all liked our vacations there."

Susanna saw that all of them were frightened. Little wonder, for the one fixed point in all their lives had been Gracefield. Ellen, she saw, was pale, and her lips were trembling. Since Clay had left, Susanna and Thomas had provided for her—and Ellen had been far from inexpensive. Now she was faced with being a woman with four children and no income.

Dent was staring at his grandfather, speechless for once, and David looked stunned. He was the quiet one, the thinker, and Susanna knew he would not sleep all night. He would lie awake and think about the future—but then, she would do the same, she realized suddenly.

"We'll talk about it later," Susanna said quickly. "We don't have to move tomorrow. And God will take care of us."

"Will God let us stay here in our home?" Dent said, his voice hard. "Doesn't seem that's too much for him to do."

"Don't speak like that, Dent!" Susanna said with a direct stare. Then she said, "We'll talk more about it later."

They left the table, quiet and subdued.

For the next week, Thomas walked around the plantation like a man in a dream. They all talked, of course, but no one knew what to do. Finally on Saturday night, after they had gone to bed, Susanna said, "Tom, are you certain you don't want to ask Stephen for help?"

Tom seemed to freeze, and she knew it had been the wrong thing to say. She had always known that Tom resented his older brother, but not until now did she know how deeply rooted that resentment was.

"I'll *never* ask him!" Thomas said between clenched teeth. "I'd rather die!"

She hugged him tightly. "We won't die, Tom. God won't fail us. You'll see!"

CHAPTER FIFTEEN

A VISITOR FROM THE PAST

THE TALL man in the fawn-colored suit looked to John Novak as though he might be business. Novak had been hired by Stephen Rocklin years ago, when the foundry had occupied an old carriage house on the outskirts of Washington. A scrawny boy of fifteen with eyes that looked huge in his hungry, lean face, Novak had been thrilled to find a job, though it was only as a lowly clerk. He came from a family of fifteen, his parents still speaking English with a thick European accent. Novak always smiled when he recalled how, three mornings in a row, Stephen Rocklin had run him away. But persistence was a family trait for the young immigrant, and on the fourth morning, Rocklin had studied the lad carefully. "You want to work, boy?" he had asked.

"Yah, I work, mister!" And Rocklin had believed him.

The boy had attacked work like a hungry dog attacks raw meat. Nothing was too hard, no work too dirty for him. Stephen admired the boy's eagerness, and his belief in him became strong. He had paid for Novak's schooling, and the boy soaked up learning like a sponge! As the Rocklin Foundry grew, John Novak grew with it, so that now Stephen often said, "No need to worry if I die. Novak would keep the place running without missing a day!"

Novak knew every job in the foundry, and his post as assistant to Mr. Rocklin required, in part, that he filter out visitors who wanted to see the owner. Gifted with a natural ability to discern a person's intent and motives, John Novak turned many people away. But there was something about the man who had appeared suddenly at eleven o'clock on a Tuesday morning and asked to see Mr. Rocklin.

Novak noted the fine suit, the expensive black leather shoes, and the diamond that glittered on the visitor's right hand. He noticed the hand, too; it was brown and calloused, but well cared for. The man's face was strong—more handsome than a man's face should be, perhaps—and it was saved from any look of weakness by the tough line of the lips and the firm jaw. Novak considered a person's eyes "the window of the soul," and the visitor had a pair of the darkest eyes he had ever seen, with a direct gaze that took in the office and Novak carefully.

"May I ask your business, sir? Mr. Rocklin is quite busy this morning."

"Tell him an old friend from the past would like to see him for a few minutes."

Novak hesitated, then nodded. "I'll tell him, sir."

Novak entered the door behind him and found his employer engaged in studying a rifle that had been disassembled and carefully laid out on a pine table. He looked up with a trace of impatience, but his voice was even. "Yes?"

"A gentleman to see you, Mr. Rocklin. He won't say why, but he's top drawer." Novak shrugged his thin shoulders. "Says he's an old friend from your past."

"Blast it, I don't want to see anyone, John!"

"Might mean money," Novak said mildly. "He's got some."

Suddenly Rocklin smiled. "I sometimes think you can smell cash, John! Well, show him in—but come back in five minutes and tell me I have to do something. Can't waste much time on my 'old friend.'"

Novak nodded, but had already decided to do just that. He stepped outside and, holding the door open, said, "Please step in, sir."

Stephen had bent over the rifle, having put on his glasses to study the fine work of the firing mechanism. He was aware that his visitor had entered, but did not want to drop the screw that he was trying to put into the tiny hole. Finally he got it started, laid the part down, then looked up, saying, "Now then, sir, what can I do for you?"

The sunlight from a window was in his eyes, and he saw only the outline of a tall man who stood quietly in the center of the room. He blinked, adding, "I'm Stephen Rocklin."

"How are you, Uncle?"

Rocklin gave a start, then moved to one side so that he could see the man clearly. "Clay!" he said, blinking with surprise. "My Lord! Is it you?"

Clay smiled, but did not offer his hand or move any closer. "I'm afraid it is. Bad penny turning up again."

But the shock that had gone through Stephen passed, and he came forward at once to throw his arms around his nephew. He felt the lean body grow stiff, but gave him a hearty hug, then stepped back, saying, "By Harry, it's good to see you, my boy!"

Clay's face was stiff with the effort of concealing the emotion that had washed through him as his uncle embraced him. Stephen was older, thicker in body, and his face was lined. Otherwise, he seemed to be unchanged in appearance. Clay slowly relaxed, saying quietly, "I've been here in Washington nearly a week." His wide mouth turned upward in a faint smile. "Most of that time I've been trying to get up enough courage to come and see you."

Stephen waved his thick hand. "Why, there was no need for that, my boy! You should have come at once!"

"That's—kind of you, Uncle. But you were always that way."

Stephen saw that Clay was uncomfortable and said briskly, "Well, by Harry, this *is* fine. Now, first we've got to go out and have lunch. I've got the inside track on the best chef in Washington, Clay! He thinks I'm more important than I am, and I allow him to think so. Novak—!" He began to pull on his overcoat, and when the secretary came to the door, he said, "This is my nephew, Clay Rocklin. My brother Tom's oldest boy. We're going out to eat."

"Glad to know you, Mr. Rocklin," Novak said, perfectly aware of Clay's history but allowing no emotion to touch his smooth, dark face. "But you have an appointment with the board at one, Mr. Rocklin."

"You meet with them, John," Stephen said with a grin. "You always think you know this business better than I do."

Novak protested, but Rocklin grabbed Clay's arm, saying, "Come on, Clay. Let's get out of here!"

An hour later they were finishing steaks at the Arlington House, the finest restaurant in Washington. Stephen had kept up a rapid-fire account of the family, including Gideon's promotion to major and a detailed description of his grandchildren. He said, "It was hard, losing Mother." Then he stared at Clay. "You didn't know? She died about a year after you left. Then, seeing Clay's sadness, he said quickly, "Gid's stationed here, Clay. He'll be glad to see you."

Clay had said almost nothing, but now he set down the glass of sherry he had been sipping and looked at his uncle candidly. "You're a clever man, Uncle Stephen. You've made me feel—well, like a man again. But I won't be seeing Gid . . . or Melanie."

His voice faltered as he pronounced Melanie's name, and Stephen studied him carefully. He was not the same immature, rash man who had disappeared twelve years ago. He was thirty-nine now, but older in more ways than in years. A little heavier, but not much, and his olive skin had been darkened to a richer tone. He was strong and fit, and Stephen had noted that he had a sailor's walk, as if contending with a deck that rose and fell. Clay's eyes bothered him, though—for in their dark depths he read a pain that ran deep. Now he said quietly:

"I'm a fool to chatter on like a magpie, Clay. But I wanted you to feel at ease." Leaning forward, he shook his head, adding, "Melanie would like to see you. She's spoken of you many times. We all have."

"Even after I attacked her?"

Stephen ignored the harsh, brittle tone. "Clay, that was one act. You don't judge a man by one act, but by his whole life."

"Like when I let Gid's company down at Cerro Gordo? You think I could face Gid after that?" Clay's face had grown hard, and the memories that came to him brought a torment into his face. "No, I just wanted to see you, Uncle."

"Have you been in touch with your family at all, Clay?"

"I didn't write for years. I pretty well hit bottom, but then after I got on my feet, I wrote to my father."

When Clay broke off abruptly, Stephen asked quietly, "Did he answer you?"

"He—sent my letter back unopened."

"That was a mistake. I've tried to talk to him about it several times."

"I sent money, Uncle Stephen, and he sent that back, too. I did get one letter. A year ago I wrote again, asking if I could come and see them, but he sent back one line— 'Don't come to my house ever!'"

Just then a waiter came to say in a low voice, "Will you gentlemen have anything else?"

Clay looked up and, after studying the face of the man, said in a sardonic tone, "No, thanks. I've had enough."

Suddenly a thought entered Stephen's mind, an instant impression that seemed to grow into a full-fledged plan in a matter of seconds. It was what some call an epiphany, referring to a sudden insight that comes by something other than logic or even conscious thought.

Stephen was not accustomed to such thoughts, and it rattled him somewhat. He made an affair of lighting a cigar, and not until he got it going and sent a cloud of aromatic blue smoke in the air did he decide the idea was sound, even if it had come almost like a mystic vision.

"Come back to my office, Clay." He saw a refusal

forming and added quickly, "I have something there you should see. It won't take long, and there'll be no chance of meeting any of the family, if that's what you're thinking."

Clay stared at him curiously, then shrugged. "I have no place to go, Uncle Stephen." On the way back through the raw weather, Clay wondered what awaited them at his uncle's office, but did not press for any information. Stephen told him about the factory—how it was booming, always behind in orders.

"I suppose," Clay offered, "if the war comes that everyone's talking about, you'll make a lot of money."

"I'd rather not make money off the lives of people," Stephen said, and he happened to be looking at Clay as he spoke. He saw with surprise that his remark struck his nephew hard, for Clay's face grew pale and his lip were contracted into a thin line. *I said something wrong,* Stephen thought, but he had no idea what it was.

Novak met them in the outer office, saying, "The board voted—"

"Later, John," Stephen said briefly, and led Clay into his office. "Have a seat," he said, going around to sit in his chair. He opened his desk drawer and took out an envelope. "I got this two days ago, Clay," he said. "It's bothered me more than anything has in a long time. I just don't know what to do about it. It's from Warren Larrimore. Do you know him?"

"The banker in Richmond?" Clay asked, opening the letter.

"Yes. He's a good man."

Clay read the letter indolently, then he drew a sudden breath. "Why, this is terrible!"

"It will kill your father, Clay," Stephen answered grimly. "It's the end of everything for him."

Clay finished the letter, then lifted his eyes to meet the steady gaze of his uncle. "I don't understand. What happened? How did things get in such a mess?"

"It's the curse of the South, Clay, as Larrimore points

out. A one-crop system is economic suicide. And cotton planting is tied to slavery. It takes an enormous number of low-skilled people to make the crop, and the price of slaves has gotten exorbitant. I know you're from the South and feel differently, but in my mind slavery is an albatross around the neck of the Southern people! A damnable thing that's not only financially ruinous, but morally wrong!" He cut his words off with a brief apology. "Sorry, Clay. I know you don't want to hear that sort of talk from a Yankee."

To Stephen's surprise, Clay said slowly, "No offense, Uncle. As a matter of fact, I agree with you."

Stephen blinked his eyes, surprised. "Well, that's good to hear. But of course, your father and almost all the planters feel differently. And that's why we're on a collision course in this country!"

Clay was only half listening. "This can't happen, Uncle Stephen! It must not!"

"I'd help in an instant. As a matter of fact, I've offered. But as Larrimore says, your father won't take help from me." He shook his head, sadness in his eyes. "It's been a grief to me, Clay, the way your father resents me."

Clay said slowly, "You're everything my father would like to be—and never can be."

"That's not so! Tom is one of the finest men I know!"

"He's not a man to get things done, as you are." Stephen didn't answer, for he knew deep down that this was true. He was, however, surprised to hear Clay voice such a thing. Then Clay asked suddenly, "Why have you shown me this?"

Stephen leaned back in his chair, thinking about the matter. "I think a lot of your family, Clay. I love your father, and I've always been fond of you. You've gotten off on the wrong track, but that can happen to any man, my boy. I don't ask what you've been doing for the past few years, but I am interested in the years that lie ahead of you."

"I don't have a life, Uncle Stephen," Clay said. "Not in

the past, nor in the future." He leaned back in his chair, his eyes half-closed. "Some things a man can repair, but I'm past all that. I'm like Humpty-Dumpty. All the king's horses and all the king's men couldn't put Clay Rocklin together again."

Stephen hesitated, then said, "God can put any man or woman together, Clay." He did not press his argument, for he saw that Clay was not ready for it. He only added, "Jesus Christ will come to you one day. When that happens, promise me you'll stop running and let him have his chance with you."

"If Jesus ever comes, I'll remember what you say. But I think Christianity doesn't work for some of us." Clay shook his shoulders, then asked again, "Why did you show me the letter?"

"Haven't you guessed? I think you have."

Clay stared at his uncle with a strange intensity. "I think you believe that I can rescue Gracefield and save the family."

Stephen nodded. "I believe God has sent you here at just the right time. You need your family, and God knows they need you!"

"Why, my father would die before he'd take my help!"

"No, I don't think so. I believe all this has come upon my brother to save him from the bitterness that's been eating him alive ever since you left. He would never have given up on that bitterness as long as he had a choice, but now he has none. Or rather, he has one, and that's you, Clay."

Clay was half-amused and half-angry. "You think God is interested in all of this? With a universe to run, you think he cares about keeping track of a scoundrel named Clay Rocklin?"

"We're all scoundrels, Clay. Some may put up a better front than others, but inside we're all lost." Stephen came around the desk and put his hand on Clay's shoulder. "It's your last chance, Clay, just as it's your father's last chance. Will you do it?"

A hammer was ringing on an anvil, a rhythmic, pleasant sound. The clock on the wall in Stephen's office was ticking quietly. Neither man spoke, and the silence between them ran on. Finally Clay got to his feet, and there was a look of grim determination on his face.

"Uncle Stephen, I hope you've got faith in this thing—because I think it's insane." Then Clay suddenly brushed his hands across his eyes, and when he looked at Stephen again, he was as sober as a man could be.

"I'll do everything I can. If it were just a matter of money, it wouldn't be so bad. But you know it's more than that."

"I know, I know, my boy," Stephen said, a great happiness filling him. "You'll have a hard way. You'll not be welcomed back. Your family won't accept you. Your friends will all remember your failures—and they'll be waiting for you to make more mistakes. You'll be all alone." Then he threw his thick arm around the young man's shoulders, saying with a hearty voice, "But you'll do it, Clay! I believe God's in it, and when God gets in a thing and we let him do what he wants, why that thing is settled!"

"Well, all they can do is kill me, Uncle Stephen," Clay said with a slight smile. "And since I'm dead already, that won't hurt too much. Come on, let's see what we can do with the Rocklin clan!"

CHAPTER SIXTEEN

THE HOMECOMING OF
CLAY ROCKLIN

IT AMUSED Clay that Harvey Simmons met him at the livery stable, just as he had twelve years earlier. But this time, Clay saw, Simmons had risen in the world, for the sign over the barn read, "Simmons Livery Stable," not "Jacob Essen's Livery Stable" as it had those long years ago. Clay had taken the Orange and Alexandria Railroad from Washington, arrived at the station just after seven in the morning, and spent the morning walking around the bustling city.

He had expected the city to stay as he had left it, but since 1847, many changes had come, mostly commercial. New construction was sprouting up everywhere, and the streets were alive with people going to work. *Couldn't expect the old town to stay just as it was,* he thought as he wandered along the side streets. *And I guess I've changed even more than it has.* Every street held memories, some of them good and some bad. He saw that the Blackjack Saloon had fallen into even worse disrepair. The paint was peeling and the windows were filled with cardboard, but the same sign with the ace of spades over the name still swung in the wind. He thought of the night that he, along with Taylor Dewitt and Bushrod Aimes, had tackled a gang of hoodlums over a woman, and all of them had come out of the scrap looking like raw meat. *I expect that pair is respectable now.*

He had taken lunch at the Harley House and recognized only one or two people. One of them was the manager, Nolan Finn. But Finn had not noticed him, and Clay did not speak to him. *I'll meet him soon enough,* Clay thought as he left the restaurant and moved toward the livery stable.

He had spent the last month with his uncle Stephen—not at his home, for Clay refused to go there. He had taken a room at a hotel, and the two of them had kept the mails hot with letters to Warren Larrimore. It had taken a great deal of doing, for Thomas's affairs were in such sad condition and so many creditors had to be satisfied that it took every effort on the part of the banker to achieve what Stephen and Clay had asked.

Stephen had written, explaining the situation, asking him to keep Clay's name out of any conversations with the family. He had requested that Clay be allowed to buy the paper and mortgages, but this proved to be impossible. Some of the men who held the notes would not sell them back, for Gracefield was a good property and they didn't want to lose their chance at gaining possession. Also, Clay didn't have enough money to pay all the notes and finance another crop. In the end, Larrimore wrote, *We will have to agree with some of the demands of the creditors and, I might add, with my board. The creditors want the place, and my board will not renew the note we hold if Thomas is in control. I persuaded them to renew, and they agreed only on the condition that Clay be responsible for the financial end of the plantation. I don't know how Thomas will take this, but it was the best I could do.*

As Clay approached the livery stable, he thought of the nights he had lain awake, dreading the moment when he would have to return to his home. More than once he had almost fled Washington, but Stephen Rocklin had sensed those times and had stayed closer than a barnacle until they passed.

Even now he wanted to go back to the station, get on the train, and put Gracefield far behind him. But he did not. Deep inside, he knew that this was the only chance in the world for him, and he hailed the owner of the stable with determination in his voice. "I need to rent a horse."

Simmons stared at Clay uncertainly. The bright noonday April sun blinded him as he came out of the darkness of the stable, and he hesitated. There was something familiar about the tall man who stood there, but he couldn't put his finger on it.

"Know you, don't I, sir?"

"You did once, Harvey."

Simmons blinked, and as his vision cleared, he gasped. "Why, it's Clay Rocklin!"

"What's left of him. You're looking prosperous, Harvey. Own the business now, do you?"

"Well, yes. Old man Essen died five years ago, and Mr. Larrimore at the bank helped me buy the place." He shook his head, staring at Clay in disbelief. "Most people think you died, Clay."

"Have to disappoint them. Let me have a good horse, Harvey."

"You going out to Gracefield?"

"Yes." *Where else would I be going?* Clay thought.

"Well, you don't need to rent a horse, unless you want to. One of the niggers from your place is in town. Boy named Fox."

"I remember him. His mother was Damis."

"That's the one. He come in early this morning for supplies. He's coming back by here to pick up Mr. Burke's saddle any minute. You could ride back with him if you wanted to."

Clay hesitated, but then shook his head. "I'm in a hurry, Harvey."

"All right. I'll give you the best we got."

Clay waited until Simmons brought out a tall buckskin, and soon he was riding through the streets of the city. The town had edged out, taking the countryside, and he was impressed at the growth. A huge building, the Tredgar Iron Works, had grown like a mushroom since he had left. Other businesses filled the busy streets. It was not Washington, of course, but it was impressive.

He passed into the countryside, enjoying the feel of a

good horse. He had come to enjoy the sea, but he loved the feel of a horse much better than the rise and fall of the schooner. Traffic was heavy for a time, the road crowded with wagons bringing produce to market, farmers bringing their families into town, and a surprising number of people on foot making their way into Richmond.

There was something about the journey to Gracefield that made him uneasy, and as he rode along, he decided that it was the fact that he was going over the same ground he had followed twelve years ago. That time he had come home drunk and half out of his mind over his failure at Cerro Gordo. Now he was on the same road, going to the same house. And if the guilt over the dead soldiers he had murdered in Mexico had been heavy, the scene of the slaves going overboard into the freezing sea to drown was much worse. Ever since he had left the *Carrie Jane*, he had experienced terrible nightmares, especially one that involved the young mother and her baby. Even now, with the sun shining overhead and the beauty of the Virginia countryside surrounding him, the sight of her face tried to form in his mind. He shook his head and galloped his horse for a quarter, driving the image away.

A strong urge took him as he passed the turnoff to the Yancy place. As always, the thought of the Yancys gave him pleasure, but he steadfastly refused to turn his horse in their direction.

At four he passed onto Rocklin land and felt strangely at home. Despite all that had happened, there was a mystic pull in this black soil that he felt at once. It had always been there, no matter how far he sailed to distant lands, and now it came back—along with memories of many things and many people.

He slowed the horse as he approached the drive leading to the house, uncertain even now of how to proceed. Most of all, he dreaded seeing Ellen and the children. The memory of the children had been strong in him all his years of wandering, but he knew from what little

Stephen had told him that Ellen had brought them up to despise him.

No matter—or, more accurately, no cure for it now. As he turned down the curving drive, he had a sudden thought and pulled his horse off sharply, crossing into a grove of water oak that rose to the east of the house. Anyone approaching the house by means of the drive would be seen at once, but there was another way. One hundred yards into the grove, there was—or had been—a tiny house, a cabin really. Only two rooms, but snug and comfortable. The summer house, as it had been called, had been used for visitors and by the children for playing games.

He was pleased to find it still there and in fair condition. Stepping out of the saddle, he tied the horse and stepped inside. There was no lock, and he found that the inside was in poor shape. Evidently the roof had some leaks, for the furniture was warped and there was a decaying smell to the place. He turned and walked down the path, which was overgrown, coming to the side of the house. He glanced at the scuppernong arbor where he'd courted Mellie in the old days. The vines were still there, but thin and wilted in the heat. There was, he noted, a general deterioration about the place. Fences sagged and were patched just enough to hold together, and the sheds had not been whitewashed in some time. Even the Big House was in need of paint and some repairs—but it was not as bad as he had expected.

Coming to the side door, he hesitated, uncertain as to his next move. He wanted to avoid all the family except his parents, but if he stepped inside the house, he could encounter anyone.

Suddenly the door opened and he found himself looking at Zander. The tall black man stood stock-still, his eyes sprung so wide the whites were enormous. "Marse Clay!" he whispered.

"Hello, Zander," Clay said, and moved closer. Zander, he noted, had grown white-headed and was overweight.

But he was still sharp, for the brown eyes of the slave were studying him carefully, now that the shock was over. Clay said quickly, "Zander, I need to see my parents—but nobody else. Are they here?"

"Yas suh, they here. They both upstairs."

"Anybody else in the house?"

"Everybody gone. Camp meeting over at Spring Grove, and a party at Miss Amy's house." Zander stared at Clay, questions in his eyes, but he said, "You want me to tell them you're here?"

Clay hesitated, then said, "I'll go to the library. Go ask them if they will come down and meet me there, Zander."

"Yes suh."

Zander went back into the house, and Clay walked around to the door that led into the hall. The library was stuffy, and he moved to open one of the windows. He could hear someone speaking down the hall, and supposed that it was Dorrie or some of the other house slaves.

He forced himself to stand quietly, looking out the window, but felt his hands trembling. Quickly he slapped them together, then tried to make his mind stop fluttering. Never could he remember being so tense, and he was glad when the door opened.

His father came in, followed by his mother, and for one brief moment they all three seemed to be frozen. *We could be a picture entitled "The Return of the Prodigal,"* Clay thought. He was shocked at his father's appearance. The black hair he remembered was sprinkled with gray, and his face was worn and etched with lines. He was still a handsome man, but worry and care had struck him hard. Clay's mother, on the other hand, seemed little different than when he had seen her last.

Thomas said in a voice tight with emotion, "I thought I made myself clear about your presence here."

"Very clear, sir," Clay answered. He saw that his mother wanted to come to him, but knew that she would not do so—not with her husband in the room. "I would have respected your wishes, but I felt I had to come." He hesitated, then got right to the matter. "I've been in touch with Warren Larrimore, Father. About the difficulties with the loans."

"I'm surprised you'd find that of any interest!"

"You have every right to think that," Clay said evenly. "I've given you occasion to think it."

"I'll ask you to leave, sir!"

Clay said quietly, "I will leave—if you will give me ten minutes."

Thomas had been stunned when Zander had come with the news that Clay was in the house. He had thought at first the butler must be mistaken, but Zander had been adamant. His mind had reeled, and the bitterness that he had nursed over the years welled up. He had started for the door, but Susanna caught at him.

"Don't go to him like this, Tom," she whispered.

He had stood there, struggling with the demon of fury that rose in him, but she had prevailed. "Very well, Susanna. I'm all right. Let's go down."

Now he stood there, keeping a tight hold on his anger. "Very well, you have your ten minutes. No more."

"Yes sir." Clay had thought out what he wanted to say, and Stephen had helped him with how to say it. "We'll arrange it with Warren," his uncle had said. "Keep my part out of it. You just found out about the problem and wanted to help. If you mention me, it'll just get his back up even more!"

Speaking slowly, Clay now said, "I've been out of the country for many years. But when I came back last month, I heard a rumor that you were having trouble with finances."

"Who told you this?" Thomas demanded.

"Oh, just a fellow who knew the county. He said that quite a few planters were having trouble meeting their loans because of the low price on cotton." He evaded the question easily and saw that his father was satisfied. That kept Stephen in the clear. If only the rest could be as easy.

"After I left here," he said, "I went to the bottom. You

wouldn't want to hear about it. But I met a man who liked me. He taught me his trade and gave me every opportunity to rise. The venture prospered, and I made considerable money from it."

"What venture?" Thomas demanded.

"Why, shipping. I owned half-interest in a schooner. But I never really liked it, so I sold out last month." Clay hesitated, troubled by what was sure to come. But there was no way to put the thing except to come right out with it: "When I heard that you were having problems, I wrote to Larrimore, telling him I'd like to help."

"He never said a word to me!"

"I asked him to keep it confidential. I wasn't sure how the thing would go. But when he wrote and put all the facts before me, I made a decision. You won't like it, I'm afraid."

"What decision? And why should I be involved?"

"Larrimore said that you were going to lose Gracefield. I didn't want that to happen. So I asked him if I could help with the notes."

"You had no right to do that!" Thomas raised his voice. "You gave up your rights when you deserted your family!"

Clay dropped his head. "I can't argue that, because it's true."

His admission stopped the tirade that Thomas was about to launch. Susanna spoke for the first time. "What sort of arrangement did you make, Clay?"

Clay explained that he didn't have enough money to get the place clear, but that he had worked something out with Larrimore. "He actually did all the work, of course," Clay said. "I wanted to be able to get the place clear, then just leave the country. But Warren could only make the arrangements if I agreed to be responsible for the financial side of the operation."

Thomas turned pale, and his voice was reedy. "So, you've come back to be lord and master over us—is that it?"

It was the most dangerous time, and Clay said carefully, "Nothing was farther from my mind. The only way I could help was to take the bank's offer. But I won't be your master, sir! Never!" Then he lowered his voice, pleading as he never thought he would. "Let me do this thing, Father, please! Just let me stay until the place is clear of debt. Then I'll sign it over to you, and you never have to see me again!"

Susanna looked quickly at Thomas, and saw the rejection which he was forming. "Clay, leave us now. It's too sudden, all of this. Come back tomorrow morning."

"Of course, Mother." Clay left the room at once, and when he got outside he discovered that his heart was thumping harder than it ever had in battle or in a storm at sea! He made his way at once to where his horse was tied, but decided to sleep in the summer house. *I might be making only one more trip to the house,* he thought grimly.

Thomas and Susanna stayed up late, talking. At first Thomas was adamant—Clay would never come back to Gracefield! Not while he was there! But Susanna knew this man better than he knew himself. By the time they fell into bed, exhausted, she had won the day.

Thomas had agreed, but with iron terms. "He'll be no son of mine, Susanna! He can stay, and he can help. It's only right, for it's been his family he's hurt the worst. But I'll never forgive him!" Later he said, "Ellen will never have him back. And she's spent years drumming into the children's heads that their father is the scum of the earth. They'll never accept him, Susanna!"

Susanna did not argue. There was time for that later— and long after Thomas went to sleep, she lay awake, her hot tears falling to her pillow. *My son is home!* her heart said over and over. *Thank God! My son is home!*

Susanna Rocklin was the pillar that had held Gracefield together. She was at work by candlelight and sometimes in the dead of the night smoothing out troubles, watching the baking, the sewing, the soap and candle making, the births and deaths in slaves' cabins. Her manner was gracious, and she seldom raised her voice to a servant. She knew her Bible and trusted in God. She was a woman of charm and grace, with inner strength of tempered steel.

Now she was faced with a monumental task—to prepare the way for Clay's return to Gracefield. Thomas should have been the one to do this, but he withdrew from the matter, saying, "You'll have to tell Ellen and the children." So she had, and Ellen had stared at her as if she had announced that the world was going to blow up. "Clay? Coming here? No, Susanna, I won't have it!"

However, when Ellen discovered that Clay had come up with the money to save Gracefield—and thus preserve the comforts of her life that went with it—she submitted. "He needn't think I'll take him back! But he owes it to you and Thomas and to the children to help."

"He'll come to supper tonight," Susanna said. "Do you want me to tell the children?"

"Oh, yes, Susanna! I'm too nervous—and you know how to handle them!"

"I'll send him to see you first, Ellen," Susanna said. "Try to work things out with him."

So it went, with Susanna's deft hand guiding them all. She spoke to the children, together at first, then separately. They were astonished, angry—and tremendously curious. "Give him a chance," Susanna told each of them. "He's probably more nervous than any of you."

When Clay came at five, Susanna met him at the door. There was no one else there, and she held up her arms. He crushed her in a strong embrace, and the tears came to his eyes. He didn't try to hide them when he drew back, and she whispered as she wiped them away, "Welcome home, my own dear son!"

"Mother—!" was all Clay could say, and then she said, "It will be hard tonight. They'll all want their little bit of revenge. But you can stand it, Clay. Now, go to Ellen."

His audience with Ellen was short, but far from sweet.

She was not the woman he remembered at all; the years had not been kind to her. She was overweight, the slim curves he remembered now being hidden beneath pampered flesh. She still would be considered attractive to men, but there was a predatory look about her that he did not admire. At once he said, "Ellen, there's no point in my making apologies, but let me say I'm deeply grieved at the sorrow I've brought you."

She stared at him, then snapped, "You needn't think I'll have you back, Clay, so you can stop begging. . . !"

The rest of the interview consisted of her telling him what a rotter he was, then listing the things he would have to do if he were permitted to stay on. He had listened without comment, wondering at the changes in her. Finally he said, "You won't be troubled by me, Ellen. I'll be busy with the work here."

Downstairs, the children were gathered in the dining room, all of them trying to talk at once. Dent said loudly, "Well, I must say he's got brass! Stay away from us for years, then come breezing in as if nothing had happened!" He was angry and intended to give no quarter to his father.

David shook his head, saying moderately, "Dent, let's hear what he has to say. He may have had more problems than we know."

Lowell scowled, then muttered, "It's rotten! Why did he have to come home?"

Rena was so tense that her voice was strained. All her life she had dreamed of a father, which meant she had learned to resent Clay for not being there. Now she was like a cocked pistol, just waiting for her chance to tell the man who had robbed her of what every girl should have exactly what she thought of him.

But when she looked up and saw her father enter with their mother, she could not say a word. She had been only a baby when he had left, and the pictures she had seen were suddenly worthless. Clay stepped to the table, and he looked first at her. *He's so handsome*, was Rena's first thought. He was tall and very strong, with hair black as a crow's wing and a pair of dark eyes that seemed to see right into her. She stared back at him, and he smiled. Then she dropped her head, unable to meet his gaze. But as he took his eyes from her, she watched him avidly.

Thomas and Susanna entered, but did not sit down. They were all standing, and Clay said at once, "I know you're all embarrassed. Not so much as I am, though." He met Denton's hard gaze, then said, "Long ago I forfeited the right to be called your father. So the one thing you don't have to fear is that I've come back to make all sorts of demands on you. Your grandparents and your mother have done all the hard work of raising you, and I didn't come to take over."

"Well, then, why *did* you come?" Dent demanded, his face pale.

"That's a good question, Dent."

Suddenly David asked, "How do you know he's Dent? Maybe I'm Dent."

"No, you're David." Clay smiled briefly, then added, "Dent was always the one to attack. And you were always the quiet one." Then he said, "I've come back to serve my father. You know, I suppose, that things haven't been going well with most plantations. My father has had to bear all the burden since I ran out on him. Now I want to do what I can to help him make it through this crisis." He stopped then and looked straight at his father. "Your grandfather is master here—of all of us, but especially of me."

Susanna touched Thomas's arm, and he said hurriedly, "Now, that's the way it is. So let's have something to eat." Truthfully the words of his son had struck him hard, as had the look in Clay's eyes. *Can he possibly mean all that?* Thomas asked himself as he sat down. A faint flicker of hope ran through him as he looked at Clay, and he saw that Susanna had tears in her eyes.

The mood, of course, was strained. Clay said nothing at first, but when David said, "You've been outdoors a great deal, sir," he opened up. He told them about the schooner—omitting the fact that she was a slave ship—and told a story about a storm off the coast of Chile. He was a good storyteller, always had been, and despite their suspicion, the children listened avidly.

When the meal was over, they were all glad of it. Clay made no attempt to go to any of them, but as they stood up he said, "It's late for me to say this, but if I can help any of you in any way, it would be my privilege." Then he turned and left the room.

"Where's he going to stay?" Rena asked.

"In the summer house," Susanna answered.

Rena said stubbornly, "He's not my father, Grandmother! Not my real father!"

Susanna bent down and took Rena's face between her hands. "He'll be what you let him be, my dear. If you'll let him, he'll be a father to you. If you won't—there's nothing he can do about it."

Tears rose in Rena's eyes, but she blinked them away. She was confused and angry. "I don't need him! I don't!"

When she ran through the door, Susanna went to stand in front of Thomas. She leaned against him, weak from the tension that had built up. "It's not going to be easy, Tom!"

"We'll see. I don't think he's changed, Susanna. He's weak, as he always was. Oh, he's a charmer, I'll give him that! But he's not solid!" Then Thomas straightened his back and sadness touched his eyes. "He gets that from me, my dear!" he said, then left the room at a fast walk.

CHAPTER SEVENTEEN

THE OLD MAID

"WELL, shoot! What's he want to come back for, anyway?"

It was early, and Rena was in the yard looking for bantam eggs. The miniature chickens were allowed to roam free and found strange and bizarre places to deposit their eggs. The tiny eggs were delicacies that Thomas loved, and he assigned Rena the chore of finding them. Usually she liked hunting them. "It's like an Easter egg hunt every day," she confided to Susanna.

But today a cross frown marred the smooth perfection of the girl's brow, and she shoved Buck away roughly. The big dog ignored her and pushed his huge head close to lick her in the face. He was a formidable animal, a deerhound of almost mythological fame, but he was devoted to Rena, who treated him as if he had two legs instead of four. Her grandparents had found it deliciously funny, coming upon them playing when Rena was only four years old. She had dressed him in one of her father's old shirts, and the two of them were sitting at her small table having tea!

Rena had no close girlfriends. Her cousin, Rachel Franklin, lived close by, but Rachel was seventeen, and between that age and Rena's thirteen years a great gulf is fixed! Rena played with the slave children, but they had their work. Besides, it was becoming clear to Rena that an even greater gulf existed between herself and Maisie, the slave girl of her own age who had been brought into the house to learn the mysteries of being a lady's maid. Rena was close to her brother Lowell, but he was a boy, and that was another gulf.

So that left Buck, and more and more she spent her time with him, roaming the fields, dabbling in the creek—even sneaking him into her room to spend the night whenever she could manage it. If the dog could have talked, he would have informed the adults of the house that Rena was in need of attention. He knew all there was to know about the child, for she had formed the habit of talking to Buck aloud—and she did so now as he nuzzled her neck.

"Get away, Buck!" she said crossly, pushing at him. But he weighed almost as much as she did, and it was like shoving a tree. She sighed and surrendered. Handing him the basket she had trained him to carry by the handle, she said, "Come on, let's go down to the barn. I'll bet we'll find some eggs there." She ran across the front yard, the big dog loping at her side easily, keeping the basket between his great jaws. When they got to the barn, she slowed down, probing here and there in her search for the tiny eggs, talking with the dog.

"He's been here two weeks, Buck," she said with a frown. "And nobody ever sees him. None of us, I mean." She paused, picked up two eggs that were behind an old grindstone, and put them in the basket. "He stays with the slaves most of the time. Lowell said he likes them better than he does his own family. But I don't care! Do you, Buck?"

Buck said, "Wuff!"—which Rena took to mean he didn't care either—and wagged his tail.

"I asked Dorrie why he didn't eat with us, and she said he worked all the time, that he came in lots of times after we were all in bed, all dirty and tired. She said she saves him a plate from supper time." She paused long enough to go over to the fence and scratch Delilah's ears. The huge sow groaned happily, and Rena sat there, continuing her recitation. "I told Dorrie I didn't like him and wished he'd never come home, and she said I was a fool! I told Grandmother on her, but do you think she whipped Dorrie? No, she took her part! Blamed old nigger!"

Buck caught the displeased tone in her voice and began to whine. "Oh, I'm not mad at you, Buck!" Rena laughed, throwing her arms around him. "It's just that . . . everything's changed!"

What Rena didn't realize was that it was not the plantation or her relatives that had changed, but she herself. She longed for the simplicity of the past, when she had played with her dolls or with Buck and roamed Gracefield at her grandfather's side. In those days she had given little thought to the world outside her own sphere. That had been a happy time for Rena. Her mother had been gone most of the time to Richmond, but Susanna had been always there—and Dorrie, who, in some ways, was closer than her own mother.

But changes in Rena's body and in her emotions had come, and now she was confused and moody. Susanna and Dorrie had recognized her unhappiness, but could do little to help her. Dorrie had spoken their mutual thoughts only once. She and Susanna had been shelling purple-hulled peas on the porch late one afternoon, and Rena had walked by, her head down, with Buck at her side.

"Chile misses havin' a momma and daddy," Dorrie had murmured. "Gonna be a hard time comin' for her."

Susanna had not commented, for she knew well enough that all of Clay's children lived under a cloud. Their friends all had parents; but Ellen was no mother, and with the shadow over their father, all four of the children had grown thick shields around their hearts without knowing it. Dent bluffed it out, swaggering as a front, letting it be known that he didn't have any concern about his parents. David tried to do the same but, being more sensitive, could not quite bring it off. Lowell was hard to read. He had the tough self-assurance of his great-grandfather, Noah Rocklin, but Susanna saw the needs in the boy. It was Rena, though, who was the most vulnerable. Susanna had discovered the girl's longing for a mother and father when she read stories to her, for

Rena always loved those stories best that featured a child who had a father and mother who loved and were there.

The sun was rising quickly, peering at Rena over the top of the grove of water oaks where the summer house was located. Rena hesitated, then said, "Come on, Buck. We might as well go over to the grove. Some of these durned banty chickens may have found that place."

None of the chickens ever had wandered as far away as the summer house, but Rena insisted to the dog that they might have, and Buck gave her no argument. The two of them walked across the lawn, and the shade was cool under the trees. A startled possum scurried away as the pair surprised him, which made Rena laugh with delight. "Did you see her babies, Buck? They were all hanging to her tail! They looked like little pink mice!"

The sight of the possum cheered her up, for she loved the wild things of the woods. She always had some pet or other in a cage made by Box. Once it was a baby raccoon, which grew up to be the worst pest on the place, getting into everything, its clever little hands able to open any door or lock! Once it was a fox, another time a yearling deer. She always cried when they returned to the wild, but forgot her grief promptly when another wild pet came along. And so the circle of certain loss would begin again.

When she got to the summer house, she was surprised to see that the yard had been cleared and that new paint had been applied to the small frame structure. Cautiously she approached the cabin almost on tiptoe, ready to wheel and flee if her father should suddenly appear. But when she got to the window and peered inside, she saw that no one was there. He could have been in the bedroom, of course, but she didn't think so. Her eyes were caught by a stack of books that were strewn on the table helter-skelter. She loved books and tried to see the covers, but could not. Temptation suddenly came, and she struggled with it dutifully—but the sight of the books was too much, and going to the door she pushed it open and walked inside.

It was a favorite place for Rena. She and her brothers had used it for a playhouse for years, but the boys had outgrown it and Rena herself had not been here much since the previous fall. Carefully she advanced to the table and was delighted to see several magazines with pictures. She picked one up, gave a fearful look at the door, then, satisfied that there was no danger, began to look through the periodical. She was a great reader and soon was lost in the pictures—so lost that she came to herself with a start when Buck made a huffing sound. It was his way, she well knew, of announcing that someone was coming. In a sudden panic she threw the book down and dashed to the door, Buck right beside her.

Opening the door she dashed outside—and ran smack into someone who said, "What the devil—!"

Rena in a blind panic bounced off the newcomer and gave a small cry of fear.

"Why—it's Rena!" Clay looked down at her with startled eyes, but that was all he had time to do—for Buck had heard his beloved Rena cry for help, and he launched himself at the tall man with a terrifying snarl.

Clay had time only to push Rena to one side and get his hands up before the huge dog hit him in the chest, driving him backwards. He stumbled, then sprawled to the ground, and felt the fangs of the dog rip his hand. He caught the dog by the fur on each side of his head, but the animal was so strong that it was all he could do to hang on. The two of them rolled over and over on the grass as Clay tried to get away, and he knew that sooner or later the dog would break his grip.

Rena had been shoved to one side, but when she caught her balance and saw Buck going for her father's throat, she was petrified. She had seen Buck fight other dogs and knew that he was terrible when aroused. At once she threw herself at the pair, getting her arms around the dog's neck and screaming, "Buck! Buck, don't!"

The dog lifted his mighty head, and his terrifying

snarls cut short. He twisted his head and saw Rena, whereupon he began to whine and try to get to her.

Cautiously Clay held on, but when he saw that the dog was no longer trying to tear his throat out, he released his grip. At once Buck turned to Rena, trying to lick her face, for she was crying in a hysterical manner. Clay looked down to see that his hand was deeply cut by the dog's jaws and took out a handkerchief. Wrapping it around his hand, he said, "It's all right, Rena."

The girl looked up, tears running down her face. She couldn't speak, so great was her fear, and Clay said, "It's all right. I'm not hurt."

Rena dashed the tears from her eyes, but then as she released Buck, who watched Clay with a steady gaze, she saw the crimson stain on his hand. "Oh, he bit you!"

"He got me a little, but it'll be all right. I'd better clean it out, though." He moved around the pair, keeping his eyes on the dog, and entered the cabin. Going to a pitcher of water, he filled the basin and carefully unwrapped his hand. It was a deep gash, and the water was soon stained crimson. He reached for a bottle of weak lye solution that he had found in a box nailed to the wall. As he sat down and opened the bottle, he glanced up to see that Rena was standing at the door, uncertainty on her youthful face.

"That's a good bodyguard you have there, Rena," he said gently and smiled. Then as he took the lid from the bottle, he said, "Come on in. You can help me do the bandaging."

Rena hesitated, but then came into the room, saying, "You stay here, Buck!" She came to stand stiffly in front of the table, and when she saw the deep gash, which was still bleeding freely, she gasped.

"It's not all that bad," Clay assured her. "I got lots worse than this on board the *Carrie Jane*." He poured the lye solution into the cut and gritted his teeth while it burned into the wound.

"I'm—I'm sorry!" Rena whispered. She edged closer, her face pale at the sight of the wound.

"Don't worry about it," Clay said quickly. "I'm glad you've got a good fellow like Buck to take care of you. He thought you were in trouble, and he helped the only way he knows how. He may not like me very much for a while, but I'm glad you have a friend."

"He's the best friend I have," Rena said. She watched as he rose, went to a chest, and took out a shirt. When he tried to tear it, she asked, "Are you going to make a bandage out of that?"

"It's just an old one."

"I can do that," Rena said. "I always help Grandmother make bandages out of old underwear."

Handing it to her, he smiled. "I can't do much with one hand. Maybe you can use my knife, since we don't have any scissors." He fished out his knife and managed to get it open. While she cut the shirt into narrow strips, he put more antiseptic on the cut, but actually was watching the girl. *She looks like Ellen did when she was younger*, he decided. But there was a delicacy in Rena that her mother had never had. Rena was slender, like the Rocklins, and already her girlish figure was beginning to become more womanly. She had a beautiful face with deep brown eyes and long eyelashes, and her lips were rosy and expressive. *I'm a stranger to her*, Clay thought. *She'll be a woman soon, and I've missed out on it all!*

"I can bandage your hand, if you like," Rena said diffidently. "Last year Buck got a bad cut on his paw and I bandaged it all the time."

"If you're a good enough nurse for Buck," Clay said, smiling, "you're good enough for me!" As she took his hand carefully and began to wrap the strips of cloth around it, he saw that her skin was so fine it was almost translucent. When she tied the knots firmly, he lifted his hand and admired it. "Why, Rena, that's a professional job! Maybe you ought to consider being a nurse. You'd do fine at it!"

"I'd rather be a doctor," she said firmly. Then she

blushed. "I know there aren't any women doctors, but I used to pretend to be a doctor when I was a little girl."

"Well, someday there will be women doctors, I expect," Clay predicted. "And I don't see any reason why you can't be the first one." Seeing her fertile imagination beginning to work, he added, "I've got a book somewhere about medical work in Africa. May be a little dull for you—?"

"Oh, no, I like dull books!" she exclaimed, and seeing his smile, she blushed again. "I mean, I like all kinds of books, not just stories."

"You do?" he asked with mock surprise. "Well, that's odd—because I do, too. Spend half my money on books!" That was true enough. He had not been much of a reader as a young man, but the long voyages of the ship had been made endurable only by books, and he had collected many fine editions. He waved at a box that had come by train from Washington. "Maybe you'd like to help me unpack all those. Might be some you'd like."

Rena said quickly, "Can I really? I never get enough books!"

Two hours later Clay looked over the pile of books scattered on the floor and the table, then glanced at Rena, who was sitting cross-legged, deep into one of his travel books. He said, "Rena, does your mother know where you are?"

A startled look came into the girl's eyes, and she scrambled to her feet. "Oh, I forgot! I'm supposed to be gathering the banty eggs! Grandmother will kill me!"

"Maybe I'd better go along and take the blame," Clay suggested. He got to his feet, and Buck rose at once, still alert, his eyes fixed on Clay. The three of them made their way to the house, where they found Susanna upset and exasperated. She started to chastise Rena, but Clay said quickly, "Take it out on me, Mother. I kept Rena so busy working on my books, that's why she's late with the eggs."

Susanna saw the thankful look Rena shot at Clay, then

her eyes fell on his hand. "What's wrong with your hand?"

"Just a little cut, Mother."

"Come in and let me see it."

"No need for that." Clay winked with a conspiratorial air at Rena. "The doctor's already taken care of it." He gave his mother a smile, adding, "Rena's going to help me arrange all my books as soon as I get a bookcase. That all right with you?"

Susanna felt a thrill of joy in her heart at the sight of the two. "Yes, Clay, that's fine with me!"

Taylor Dewitt, keeping his eyes on the door that separated the bar from the restaurant, was paying only slight attention to Bushrod Aimes. The two men met often at the Harley House; it was the focal point for the planters who came to Richmond. The bar was only half-filled, for it was still early afternoon.

Bushrod, who at thirty-eight was a prosperous planter, had been telling Taylor about a new horse he'd bought. It didn't take long for him to see that the other was paying no heed. "Might as well talk to a tree as you, Dewitt!" he grumbled. "What's eatin' on you?"

"Thinking about Clay Rocklin."

He was not alone, for the return of Rocklin had been a staple item of gossip for three weeks. There was plenty to gossip about, too. Ellen Rocklin had been a fixture in Richmond for years. She still had that aura of sexuality about her, but she was a discreet woman. She had managed to keep her standing as a respectable woman intact, so that she still had entrance into the lower echelon of Richmond high society.

"Wonder if Ellen will go back to him?" Bushrod asked aloud, echoing what had been on most people's minds. Then he shook his head, answering his own question. "I don't think so, not after the way he's acted. She's got too much pride for that!"

Taylor knew Ellen better than his friend, and a sardonic

look swept his face. "Not sure about that, Bushrod. Ellen likes her fun, but she's gettin' a little long in the tooth."

"Why, she's about the same age as you, Taylor—or me, for that matter."

"Well, we're not getting any younger. Clay's not either. He's what? Thirty-eight or thirty-nine, isn't he? Wonder what he's been doing all these years?"

"Nobody knows, but he came back with money. Bought back all the paper his father had on Gracefield, with plenty left over—"

"There he is now," Dewitt interrupted Aimes, then straightened up in his chair as Clay Rocklin came into the room and headed toward them at once. Both men got up, and Taylor put his hand out to greet his old friend. "Clay! Why, you look great!"

"Hello, Taylor, Bushrod." Clay smiled at the pair, shook his head and said, "You two sure you want to be seen in public with a reprobate like me?"

The question made both men feel a little uncomfortable, for although neither had voiced it, each had thought that it might be embarrassing to pick up their old friendship with Clay Rocklin. Taylor, however, grinned suddenly. "Maybe we'll be a good influence on you." Then some of the old memories of his good times with this man came back, and he suddenly threw his arm around Clay's shoulders and said, "You old bandit! By the Lord, but I'm glad to see you!"

The three sat down, and as soon as a white-coated waiter took their order, Clay said, "Go on and ask me."

"Ask you what, Clay?" Bushrod lifted his eyebrows at the question.

"Ask me where I've been, how much devilment I've been into, how much money I brought back with me, if I'm going back to Ellen, and if I'm going to behave myself!"

Both Aimes and Dewitt broke into laughter. "You are a caution, Clay Rocklin!" Bushrod said finally. "Haven't changed much, have you? You look good, Clay! How come you're still lean and tough while ol' Dewitt and me are getting fat?"

"Clean living and a pure heart. But you two look fine," Clay said, and he meant it. Both of them were older, of course, but Taylor had not changed—still lean with an unlined pale face and the lightest blue eyes Clay had ever seen. He was well dressed, as was Bushrod, and Clay knew from talking to Dorrie and Zander that these two were among the leaders of the young aristocracy in the county.

Both men were thinking that Clay had become a different sort of man. He looked older, but was still smooth-faced and hawk-eyed. It was his manner that was most different. Clay had always been reckless and forward, but now there was a solid quality about him, and assurance emanated from him. Taylor said, "Everybody wants to know about you, Clay. Tell us what you want us to know. But first, I apologize for the way I let you down." He shook his head at what was a painful memory. "When you plugged Duncan Taliferro in that duel, I came down on you too hard."

"Forget it, Taylor."

"No, I was so blasted self-righteous! Then right after that you went off to Mexico and got in another mess. I always felt like if I'd not been such a self-righteous prig, it might have made a difference."

Clay shook his head, stared fondly at Taylor, but said, "When a man's bound and determined to make a fool out of himself as I was in those days, he'll do it one way or another. So forget it. Now, let me tell you about what I've been up to, and what I'm trying to do. Then you won't have to go to Benson's Barber Shop to get the gossip. . . ."

He told them as much of his story as he thought wise. He told them that he'd come back with some money and was trying to help his father make it over a difficult time. And he said bluntly, "Ellen wouldn't have me back, so I'm staying in the old summer house at Gracefield. My children don't like me much, and my father thinks I haven't really changed. My mother forgave me before I even got here, but she'd forgive Judas and Attila the Hun. End of story."

Both men knew there was more to it than that, but they accepted it as what Clay wanted to have known. "Glad to have you back. Now maybe we can have some fun," Bushrod said.

"Well, not the kind we used to have," Taylor said with some regret. "All three of us are married and have children. Still, Clay, we get together with Tug Ramsey and some of your other old friends and have a friendly poker game every week."

"Friendly!" Bushrod cried out. "Call it that if you like, but it's the biggest bunch of cutthroats since Captain Kidd was in business!"

The three men sat there, and Clay relaxed. He had missed these men. It had been years since he had had anything even close to the comraderie this group had enjoyed. He drank the frosty mint julep placed in front of him, then another, and finally Bushrod said, "Going to need you, Clay. Things are going to get tough around here."

"I thought they already were."

"If Lincoln gets elected next year, it'll mean a war," Taylor said evenly. He sipped his drink, then added, "We may as well get ready to fight, for the North isn't going to give us any choice."

"Why, it won't come to that, Taylor!" Clay said at once. He had heard such talk, but didn't believe it could ever happen. "They've got a little sense up North! When they see it's going to mean a war, they'll lower that blasted tariff and give the South some freedom from the pressure."

"No, we'll have to fight," Bushrod insisted doggedly. Then he said something that Clay was to get sick of hearing: "Any Southerner can whip six of those Yankee boys!"

"Besides, England would like to see the Union divided," Taylor said. "And she needs our cotton to run her mills. The North wouldn't dare risk another war with England when she comes in on our side!"

Clay listened carefully, but finally said, "Well, I didn't come home to fight a war, but to save Gracefield if I can. And I didn't know until I came here how much I missed you fellows. Thanks for taking me back."

Both men protested that it was too early for him to leave, but he laughed, saying, "You rich planters can loll around swigging mint juleps all day, but us poor workers have to be in the fields. I'll be at that poker game on Thursday. I can use some extra cash, and I could always trim you two!"

He left the Harley House, feeling better than at any time since coming back to Virginia. Several people hailed him as he went into Dennison's General Store to pick up supplies, but several more whom he recognized ignored him. He loaded his supplies, then reluctantly drove to the small rooming house where Ellen stayed most of the time. It was a large home, a mansion, really, that had been built by J. P. Mulligan, a prosperous stockbroker. But Mulligan had lost his shirt in the depression and, after blowing his brains out, was discovered to have left his widow, Harriet, nothing but debts. She had more fortitude than J.P. and made a good living renting out rooms to the better sort of clientele.

Clay was met at the front door by the landlady, and she smiled at him. "Clay! It's good to see you! Come in." She was a tall woman of fifty, plain but with a warm manner. "I've thought about you often. It's good to have you home."

Clay nodded, warmed by her friendliness. "I was sorry to hear about J.P., Harriet. I always liked him."

"Thank you, Clay." She hesitated, then said, "Ellen isn't here now. She left an hour ago. I'm afraid she won't be back soon." She was not a devious woman, but there was a strange hesitancy in her manner that puzzled Clay.

Then he suddenly realized the woman knew something about Ellen that she didn't want to mention. Nor did he want to hear it.

Clay nodded. "Could you give her a message for me?" He wrote a quick note, saying only, *Ellen, here's the cash you asked for. Clay.* Putting both the note and the money in an envelope, he handed it to Mrs. Mulligan, bid her good-bye, and left the house. For the rest of the afternoon, he drove around Richmond, taking care of business matters. It was three o'clock when he turned the buggy toward the edge of the city.

It was a perfect June day, not too hot, but warm enough so that he removed his coat. The clouds scudded across the skies in huge, billowy masses like moving mountains, and the countryside was alive with wild flowers. He looked down at his hand, smiling as he thought of Rena. She had come to his place the next evening, and the two of them had sat up until Susanna sent Maisie to get her. It was the one gain he'd made, so far as the children were concerned. David and Lowell were so dominated by Dent that they had come to feel it a weakness to show any warmth to Clay. Dent himself used every opportunity to show his insolence.

Clay's father had shown no sign of bending. Clay took every decision to him and received only a gruff approval for most of them. His mother said little, but her smiles kept Clay going, and he had become a good friend to many of the slaves—especially to Fox, the mulatto son of Damis. At the age of eighteen, the young man was far and away the brightest of the help. Though he had been standoffish with Clay at first, when he saw that the new master was fair, he had become invaluable. He not only knew the practical things about actual farming—such as when to plant and when to hold off planting—he had been trained to do some of the bookwork for Thomas. This irritated the overseer tremendously, and he had become the implacable enemy of Fox.

Clay let the horse pick his own pace, and it was almost

dark when he came to the small store where the poor whites did most of their buying. It was called simply Hardee's Store by most. The Rocklins did a little business with Lyle Hardee, a transplanted Yankee from Illinois, but his prices were higher than those of the larger stores in town. However, Clay remembered that Susanna had asked him to bring some quinine home, and he remembered it only as he saw the store. Hitching the horse to the rail, he walked up the steps and met a woman and two children who were coming out. All of them were carrying large sacks, he saw. The woman had turned to lock the door, and Clay asked, "Can you let me have a little quinine before you close?"

The woman turned quickly to look at him, and hesitated. "Sorry to be a bother. Guess it can wait," Clay said, and he turned to leave.

"No, it's all right." Unlocking the door, she went in, saying, "You and Toby wait here, Martha. I won't be long."

The only light in the store was a tiny flame in a single lantern, so that Clay could see almost nothing. Then she turned the wick up and turned to him. "How much quinine do you need?" she asked. The lamplight threw its amber glow over her face, and he saw that she was a young woman. Young and very attractive. So attractive with her enormous eyes and beautifully shaped lips that he said tardily, "Why—I don't know." He laughed ruefully. "That sounds dumb, doesn't it? How much would you think a lady with a large house and a hundred slaves might use?"

"A quart." Her manner was assured, but she stood there, examining him, as though waiting for him to add to the order.

Her self-possession brought a slight sense of embarrassment to Clay, which was unusual. Her lips were full in the center, and as he watched, the edges of them curved up in a half-smile. Her eyes smiled, too, he saw. "I'm Clay Rocklin," he said suddenly. "I've just come back. Guess I'll be seeing you here from time to time."

Still she watched him, and he could see a strange expression in her eyes, which appeared to be green. "Will that be all?" she asked finally.

"I guess so." Clay watched her as she took a very large glass jug from a shelf, then an empty bottle from beneath the counter. The jug was heavy, and she had trouble holding it. "Here, let me help you, ma'am," he said quickly. He reached over the counter, took the jug and added, "Just hold the bottle for me, if you will."

She held the bottle, and when it was full, she put the cork in it. Then she took the jug, put it back on the shelf, and turned to say, "That'll be a quarter, please."

He fumbled in his pockets, coming up with no change. Then he discovered that he had no small bills. She stood there watching him as he searched, then said, "I'll trust you for the quarter, Mister Clay."

Mister Clay! He looked up, startled.

The moment she said his name, he knew her and cried out, "Melora!"

"I've been hoping to see you ever since I heard you'd come home," she said with a smile.

Clay could not believe it. He stood there staring at her, finally saying, "I guess I expected you to stay twelve years old, Melora. You're—!" He was going to say, "You're beautiful!" but changed his words. "You're all grown up." She *was* beautiful. Now that he knew who she was, he realized she had not changed all that much, for she had been a beautiful child. But the years had made a woman of her. "How old are you?" he asked suddenly.

Melora laughed, a delightful sound. "Wherever you've been, Mister Clay, they didn't teach you how to talk to a woman! Never ask a woman's age!"

Clay shook his head. "You're twenty-four or twenty-five." This was a greater shock than he had thought it would be. This young woman was not the thin girl who had fed him soup and read to him out of *Pilgrim's Progress*. He felt sad in some strange way, for he had missed her growing up. He voiced this, saying, "I'm sorry

I haven't been around to watch you grow up into such a fine young woman." He looked around the store, asking, "Do you work here, Melora?" Then the thought of the two children came to him. He glanced at them, asking, "Or did you marry one of Hardee's boys?"

"I'm just filling in once in a while."

"Oh. Well, I'm keeping you." He stepped back, and she came with him to the door, pausing to lock it. "I suppose these are yours?" Clay said, for they looked much like her, both the boy who was about eight and the girl she'd called Martha who must have been about ten.

"No, this is my brother and sister, Toby and Martha." She paused, then said, "Well, it's been good seeing you, Mister Clay."

"Do you live far?"

"The same place."

"You're still with your folks?" Clay asked in surprise, thinking that something must have gone wrong with Melora's life. She was too attractive not to be married and yet was still at home. Perhaps her husband had moved to the home place. Then he asked, "It's getting late. I suppose you have a wagon to come to work in."

"Just a mule," she said. "We make it fine, don't we, Martha?"

The girl nodded shyly, but Clay said, "Well, I've got a whole buggy seat and some room in the back. Tie your mule on, and I'll get your things loaded."

"It would be a help, Mister Clay—but it's out of your way," Melora said.

"Be glad to see your folks," Clay said. "I've meant to come before this."

Soon the children were in the backseat, sucking noisily on two cherry lollipops that Melora had provided. As the buggy moved smartly down the road, Clay gave the abbreviated version of how he'd come home—heavily edited, as he had learned to do.

She sat there listening, and in the twilight shadows he saw that her face had that same stillness it had had when she was twelve—or when she was six, for that matter. She did speak from time to time, telling him a little about the farm, but said nothing about her own life.

"I guess you're married," Clay said finally.

"No, I'm an old maid, Mister Clay!"

Astonishment ran through Clay, and he blinked at her. "Well, I can't understand that," he said finally. "The men around here, they've all gone blind?"

"Mother died when Toby was born," she said. "When I saw that Daddy would never marry again, there was nothing to do but take care of the little ones." She laughed at his expression. "I'm really a widow with nine children, Mister Clay, so my prospects aren't too good!"

"Nonsense! Royal must be—how old now? Twenty-six or seven? And Zack and Cora are full-grown."

"But the rest of them are sixteen down to eight," she reminded him. "They need me."

He said no more, but was very quiet as they rode along the dusty road. When they got to the cabin, Melora said quickly, "I do have one suitor. I think you might remember him—Rev. Jeremiah Irons?"

"Why, of course, I do! But didn't I hear that he was married, with two children?"

"His wife died three years ago, Mister Clay." She got out of the wagon, saying, "Martha, you and Toby wake up. We're home." Clay helped the children to the ground, then as they stumbled toward the house, picked up the bundles.

She took one of them from him, saying, "That's Rev. Irons's horse tied there. He comes to court me." A humorous smile came to her, and she said, "Most of his congregation are against his choice—especially young widows or families with marriageable daughters. As a matter of fact, most people around here think he's lost his mind. He could marry anybody, instead of just me."

Clay took a deep breath, thinking hard. Then he said, "Melora, remember when I rode out of here years ago to slay a dragon for you?"

"I—I remember."

"Well, I didn't do any dragon killing—but you turned into a lovely princess, just like those in the stories we used to read!"

The warm darkness hid her face, but her voice was husky when she finally said in a whisper, "Thank you for saying that, Mister Clay!"

Then she turned abruptly, lifting her voice to cry out, "Daddy! Look who's come to see us!"

CHAPTER EIGHTEEN

MELORA'S VISITOR

A WHITENESS of snow. Whiter than the breasts of pigeons—
and stretching out to infinity.

This was one of the scenes that came, but it was spinning and wheeling so that the dazzling whiteness blinded him. He tried to shut his eyes, but the lids were frozen, or so it seemed, and he could do nothing but stare at the endless stretch of pale snow.

But then, the unrelieved purity of the snow was broken by a single flaw, a speck of crimson. Clay stared at it, and as he stared, it began to swell, spreading over the snow in an obscene blot of scarlet horror. He knew that it was blood and tried to shut his eyes, to run—but he was paralyzed, unable to move so much as an eyelid.

And then he saw him. A man was lying there, and it was his blood pumping out of a terrible wound that was staining the snow. At first Clay thought the man was dead, but then he lifted his face, and Clay saw that it was Duncan Taliferro! His eyes were pleading, and he lifted a bloody hand from his wound in a hopeless gesture.

And even as he did so, Clay was suddenly aware that he and Taliferro were being observed. He lifted his head and saw that they were in a huge amphitheater, and that thousands of people were watching, and all of them had great, staring eyes. Some of them he recognized—his father shaking his fist; Taylor Dewitt shaking his head; his mother weeping. All of them were crying out, "Shame! Shame!"

That was one scene, and he wrenched himself away, until the snow seemed to melt and all the figures faded into a mist, and Taliferro became a specter, then vanished.

But another vision was already forming, and he knew what it would be. He began running, and he ran over a thousand plains, but the farther he ran, the more terrified he became—for he heard the sound of the sea moaning in his ears.

The sky darkened, and he cried out as he felt himself torn from the land. He shut his eyes, praying that it would not come again. But it did come. Opening his eyes, Clay saw the lifting waves, capped with frothy white, and he saw the sails of the ship overhead, swelling in the wind that howled like a demented soul.

He tried to dig his way into the deck, but an iron hand caught him up and he found himself looking into the face of Captain March.

"Overboard with them!" the captain cried in a voice like thunder.

"No! No!" Clay whispered, but his voice was snatched away by the wind. And then he knew it was going to happen.

He saw the young woman with the baby. Her eyes were fixed on him, and she turned the ragged cloth back, then held the infant up for him to see. Her lips were forming the words, "Help me!"

But March was shouting, "Overboard with them!"

As he had done so many times, he moved to the woman. She watched him, hope in her eyes, thinking that he was coming to free her from the iron chain around her waist.

Then he put his hands on her, lifted her high over his head, and flung her and the child into the sea!

She sank at once, and the long line of slaves who were attached to her by the chain began to be pulled overboard. One by one they went, screaming as they plunged over the side and into the black depths.

Then March was laughing like a maniac and screaming, "Overboard with you, Clay Rocklin!"

Clay looked down—and saw the chain around his waist.

And then he knew. . . .

He was one of them! He was part of the living chain that was sinking into the sea. Suddenly, he felt himself jerked wildly toward the rail, caught by the weight of the dying blacks who had already been dragged overboard.

He hit the freezing water, and the darkness came as he died. But it was not so dark that he could not see the line of living beings as they kicked and waved their arms wildly in the murky depths.

Then he saw the woman again, but now she was laughing—and all the others had suddenly turned their sable eyes on him, and their mouths were open like gargoyles as they laughed and screamed.

"You dead too, white man! You dead like we are! Come down, come down to hell—!"

Clay began screaming, but the dark water filled his throat and his nose, so his screams were silent as he sank deeper and deeper, toward the hideous black hole that was opening up beneath him.

"No! No!"

Clay awoke with a start to find himself drenched with sweat and crying out in utter terror.

He came off the bed as though it were white-hot iron and staggered toward the door. When he lunged outside, he stood there taking great gulps of the cool night air. He was trembling so hard that he had to move to the maple tree and lean against it. The bark was rough, and he pressed against it, needing the sense of reality after the nightmare.

Finally he began to breathe normally, and the tremors stopped racking his body. He wiped the sweat off his face and stood there in the silence of the night. His cry had alarmed the night creatures, silenced the frogs that boomed their bass voices from the pond, and cut off the high-pitched singing of the crickets and katydids. The only sound, other than the heavy beating of his own heart, was the whine of the mosquitoes.

With a moan of despair, he struck the maple, then turned and went back into the house. Finding a match, he lit the lantern and then stared at the bottle of whiskey. It was almost empty, and his throbbing head told him he was beginning to feel the aftereffects of a drunk.

He grimaced at the sight of it, then went to the stove and poured cold coffee into a cup and drank it down. It was tepid and bitter, but better than whiskey. Glancing at his watch on the table, he saw that it was only three o'clock. At least two more hours until the world came alive.

He washed his face, dressed, and went outside, walking slowly down the path that led to the pond. The moon was huge in the velvet-black sky, and he could see his way clearly. When he got to the pond, he stood there staring at it, the silver surface rippled in spots by fish moving or by water striders. The stillness flowed into him, and he felt the weariness that came from loss of sleep.

For more than a week, he had not slept more than a few hours. The bad dreams had started without warning, coming every night, so that he dreaded to go to bed. He had never been a man to dream much, and there was something about these dreams that he knew was abnormal. They were so brilliantly clear! Not fuzzy and vague as most of his dreams had been. The sheer terror of them was beyond anything he had ever known in the real world. *There is something almost evil about them*, he thought as he stared at the water.

His eyes were burning from lack of sleep, and he knew that the day would be terrible. He had not mentioned his lack of sleep to anyone, and he had continued putting in long hours in the fields and about the place. But he was getting weaker, and finally he had given in to a desperate hope that liquor might make him sleep. But it had only made things worse—as bad as anything he had ever known.

"Can't go on like this!" he said aloud.

A frog at his feet hollered *"Yikes!"* and hit the water with a lusty splash.

Clay stood there for half an hour, wondering what to do, then walked around the pond slowly. He went back to the house, shaved, and made his way to the Big House at six. The sky was just beginning to turn pink, and he found his mother in the kitchen alone.

"Why, good morning, Clay," she said in surprise. "You are up early this morning." She smiled, but then something in his face made her ask, "What's the matter? Don't you feel well?"

"I'm all right. A little tired, I guess."

She stared at him, but said nothing until she had poured him a cup of hot coffee. "You're working too hard."

"That's why I came."

She moved to sit beside him and, after a moment's awkwardness, put her hands on his, the one that was bandaged. "You've done so well, Clay!"

He could not help saying, "I wish Father thought so."

"He'll come around. As the children will. Look how close you've gotten to Rena!"

He looked at her and mustered up a tired grin. "Well, that makes two of you I've won over. Only about ten thousand more to go in the county."

"That's not so!" she said. "Amy and Brad are so pleased with you, and the slaves think you're wonderful!" A question came to her eyes, and she asked it carefully. "You never liked the slaves before, Clay. Now you're so kind to them. What made you change?"

His hand tightened around the cup, and he evaded her question. "Just got older, I guess."

Then Dorrie came in, her eyes taking him in. "You ain't gettin' enough rest, Marse Clay! I gonna tie you in bed! See if I don't!"

Clay and his mother laughed, and he said, "I guess I'm like the boy they put in college. They put him there, but they couldn't make him think."

"What's dat got to do with you?"

"You can tie me in bed, but you can't make me sleep, Dorrie," Clay said.

"I'll fix you a toddy tonight," Dorrie said emphatically. "My toddies make anybody sleep."

Clay thought of the bottle of whiskey he'd downed the night before, but said, "Thanks, Dorrie. That'll probably do it."

Dorrie fixed breakfast, but Clay could not eat, at least not enough to please the two women. When he left, Dorrie said, "He ain't happy, Miz Susanna."

"No. Did you see his eyes? He hasn't slept for several nights."

"Fox says he's giving up. Says he's got something goin' on in his head that's gonna kill him if it ain't took care of!"

Susanna said quietly, "It's not in his head, Dorrie."

The slave was very quick. "You right about dat! He's needin' a good case of ol' time gospel salvation!"

"That's what Rev. Irons says, Dorrie. He's been to talk to me about Clay. He says about the same thing you do, that if Clay doesn't get some peace, he won't make it."

Dorrie nodded firmly. "Dat preacher has got some sense! Whut he say he gonna do? Git him to come to one of his meetins?"

"No, he said Clay wouldn't come. And he's right. But he did ask me to pray that he'd have a chance to give him the gospel in some way."

"Well, we gonna believe Gawd for dat!" There was nothing timid about Dorrie's faith, and she took Susanna's hand and the sound of her fervent prayers could be heard as far away as the slave quarters!

Jeremiah Irons was aware that Melora was laughing at him, though the only hint of this was a sly twinkle in her green eyes. Even worse, he strongly suspected that at least six of the other seven people who were sitting in the big room of Buford Yancy's cabin were also amused at him. He was sitting in a rocking chair made by Buford, listening to his host give his opinion on the heresy of universalism.

Scattered around the room in various positions were the rest of the Yancy clan, except for Royal, Zack, and Cora, the married children. As Buford droned on, Irons shifted his eyes around the room at the children, all with their father's tow hair and greenish eyes: from Lonnie, who at sixteen was a younger edition of his father, down to Toby, the youngest. In between, in rather a stair-step fashion, Bobby, Rose, Josh, and Martha were examining the good reverend as though he were some sort of alien specimen.

Melora was washing the last of the supper dishes when she turned and gave him a certain look—that was when Jeremiah sensed that she was amused at him, and her humor had been picked up by all the rest except for Toby, who was asleep, and Buford, who was wading through the heavy seas of Calvinistic theology with a knitted brow.

" . . . a man can't find nothing like that in the Bible, kin he, Parson?"

Irons suddenly realized that he had tuned Buford out and tried to fake it. He knew the arguments well, but was not inclined to argue over fine theological points of doctrine. "Well, Buford," he said, clearing his throat, "as I've said so often, the universalists do what most do with the Scripture. They take a truth, close their eyes to what the rest of the Scripture has to say about the matter, then blow that single truth up until it's swollen like a huge balloon. In this case, men take a verse such as Colossians, first chapter, verses 19 and 20. 'For it pleased the Father that in him should all fullness dwell; and having made peace through the blood of his cross, by him to reconcile all things unto himself; by him I say, whether they be things in earth or things in heaven.' Well, the universalist jumps on the phrase 'reconcile all things unto himself.'"

Buford blinked, then he brightened up. "That's it!

They claim that means that every soul who's ever been created will be saved, that nobody will be lost."

"They go farther than that, I'm afraid," Irons said. "They claim that even the devil will be saved at last."

Such a thought had never occurred to Buford Yancy's simple mind. He sat there staring at the minister blankly, then said with indignation, "Well, I'll be dipped! Can't they read, Parson? The whole Bible talks about people who go to hell!"

Melora had finished the dishes and took pity on the preacher. She knew her brothers and sisters thought it was funny that Reverend Irons kept coming to call on her and was always trapped in the single room with half a dozen small Yancys and forced to listen to her father discuss the Bible.

"I've got to go check on the new calf," she announced.

"I'll jist go along with you, Sister," Lonnie said with a gleam in his eye.

"You'll do no such thing, Lonnie," Melora announced firmly. "You'll do the rest of those problems on page 34." She gave the others a straight, hard look which shut down the works before they even started. "The rest of you finish up your work, too."

Irons got up hastily, saying, "I'll go along, Melora. I always like to see a new calf."

"They are a sight to behold, ain't they now," Lonnie exclaimed with a grin. "I allus like to go down five or six times a day and see all the new calves!" Then he caught his father's warning glance and sat down suddenly and lowered his head over his arithmetic book. When Melora and Irons left, his father said, "Lonnie, if you make fun of Rev. Irons and his courtin' one more time, I'll peel yore potato, you hear me, boy?"

"Yessir," Lonnie mumbled, but gave a merry wink at Bobby and Rose, who giggled. "But, Pa, there's something downright comical about it, ain't they now? I mean, I never thought of an old man like Rev. Irons courtin' a lady—and 'specially not Melora."

Buford Yancy did not allow a flicker of an emotion to show in his steady gaze, which he fixed on Lonnie. But he had felt more or less the same way when he had first discovered what was happening. When the minister had started calling, Buford thought Irons was making a pastoral call. But the man kept coming over a period of several weeks. Finally Yancy had remarked to Melora one evening after Irons went home having stayed most of the evening, "'Pears like the reverend likes to talk theology with me, don't it, Melora?"

"He's calling on me, Daddy," Melora had said, and she had laughed outright at the comical expression on his face. "How'd you like to have a preacher for a son-in-law?" she had teased him, but then had shaken her head and patted his arm. "It won't come to anything. He's just lonesome—and he wants a woman to help him raise Asa and Ann."

Now as Melora walked along the path to the barn, she knew that Irons was frustrated. "You ought to give up, Jeremiah," she said frankly. "I don't think any other man in the world would put up with such a thing—courting a woman under the eyes of a such a mob."

Irons suddenly chuckled, for he had a keen sense of humor. "I do it because it gives such fun to your brothers and sisters," he said. "And it's one way I can irritate some of my congregation without fear of getting run off."

They came to the wooden fence then, and Melora leaned on it, watching the calf come wobbling to her call. She put her hand out and enjoyed the rough texture of the beautiful creature's tongue. "You're a beauty, you are," she murmured, running her hand over the silky coat of the young creature.

Jeremiah watched her, the red-gold rays of the setting sun washing over her glossy black hair, the blackest hair he'd ever seen. Her skin was creamy and smooth as silk, and her large almond-shaped eyes were filled with delight at the calf. Irons was not a poetic man, but now he said without meaning to, "You're the beauty, Melora."

Startled she brought her gaze up to meet his, and a slight flush tinged her cheeks. "You've been a long time coming to that, Jeremiah," she remarked.

"I'm a slow man," he said. "I was a slow child, a slow young fellow, and now in my old age I'm as slow as ever."

"You're not old," Melora said quickly, almost defensively.

"I'm thirty-eight, you're twenty-five."

"That makes no difference. You married Judd Harkins to Della Mae Conroy last January. He was sixty-two and she was only seventeen."

"I thought Judd made a fool out of himself, too." Then he took her hand, marveling at the strength and smoothness of it. "But you go on talking like that, Melora. I need somebody on my side." Then he dropped her hand, took her gently, and pulled her forward. Her lips were cool and tender, and he thought once that he felt her respond to his kiss. But there was a reserve in Melora Yancy, which he had long admired—most young women were too forward. He had watched Melora coolly receive several young men, some of them substantial and sound. The community had been offended when she had refused them all, giving as a reason that she could not leave her brothers and sisters.

Now as she pulled back slightly and looked up at him, he saw that the kiss had not moved her—as it had him. She was watching him soberly with a steady gaze. "I'd like for you to marry me, Melora," he said quietly.

"I know, Jeremiah," she said slowly. "But I don't love you—not in that way."

"That can come later."

"I'd be afraid to gamble on such a thing. What if it didn't come? Marriage is forever. I can't think of anything worse than sharing a house and a bed with a man I didn't love with all my heart."

Her forthrightness made him blink, and he was suddenly out of words. Finally he summoned up a smile of sorts. "I'm slow, Melora, but I'm stubborn. You think I'll be so embarrassed by your refusal that I'll let the matter drop. But you don't know me as well as you think."

She smiled and patted his cheek. "Perhaps not, Jeremiah. But I hate to see you wasting your time." The humor that lay just beneath the surface of her lively mind leaped out at him. "You'd pass up the widow Hathcock for a chance to marry me? And her with five hundred acres of prime land?"

"Oh, Melora!" Irons groaned. "She's a fine woman, but she must weigh three hundred pounds!" Then he saw that she was teasing him, and he laughed despite himself. "A man would never be bored in a marriage with you!"

The moment had passed, and they sat down on a stile, talking freely. He came finally to speak of Clay Rocklin. "He's in big trouble, Melora," he said, shaking his head. "He's given his best shot to reforming his life—and it's not working." He had gone hunting with Clay once since his return, and Clay had spoken tersely of his bad dreams and his doubts of anything ever coming of his return.

"He's trying very hard," Melora said quietly. "Pa says the same as you, that he's not going to make it."

"I think he's at the crossroads, Melora. He's got to find God now, or I don't think he ever will."

"You've talked to him, haven't you, Jeremiah? You're a good preacher, but you're better, I think, face-to-face."

"I tried, but Clay's got the idea he's sinned away his day of grace. Some idiot put the idea of an 'unpardonable' sin in his mind, and he thinks he's crossed the line." He sat there silently, thinking of Clay, and finally he said, "I think you ought to talk to him, Melora."

"Me? Why, I couldn't tell Clay Rocklin what to do!"

"Yes, you could." The certainty grew in him, and he turned to face her. "He doesn't need complexity of any sort, Melora. No complicated theology—such as your father loves to talk about. I've heard you talk about your love for Jesus and his love for you. The power of God is in you when you do that. That's one big mistake people make. They think that the power of God comes when a preacher is up on a platform, yelling with all his might! Well, sometimes it is, but far more often I think people sense God when somebody like you speaks of Jesus."

"I—I want so much to see him find his way, Jeremiah!"

"You two are great friends, aren't you?"

"I've always felt close to him somehow. When I was a little girl I thought he was wonderful. Even when he went bad, I knew there was something good in him—and I prayed for him all the time he was gone."

"Talk to him, Melora. Perhaps, like another young woman, you've come to the kingdom for such a time as this."

When Clay Rocklin rode his big buckskin into the front yard two days after Irons had urged her to speak with him, Melora had one of the strangest feelings she had ever experienced. For one thing, she was absolutely alone, which had not happened more than half a dozen times in her life. A circus had come to Richmond, and her father had bundled the whole family up and taken them to see it. It was not a thing he had planned, but for some reason he felt constrained to do it. "By gum, every child ort to go to the circus once, and you young'uns are going if it harelips Virginia!"

Melora hadn't been feeling well and felt that the quiet would do her more good than all the excitement of a circus. But when Clay rode in, she began to tremble, for she had promised God that she would talk with Clay if God would make all the arrangements. She was a woman of faith, and this was beginning to look as much like a miracle as anything she had seen. As she went to greet him, she was agitated in her spirit.

"Hello, Melora," Clay said, pulling a package from one of his saddlebags. "I brought the worm medicine Buford asked me to pick up for the stock. Is he inside?"

"N-no, they're all gone to Richmond."

Clay saw that she was upset, the first time he had ever seen her shaken. "What's the matter, Melora?" he demanded.

Melora stared at him, tempted to let the moment pass, but she remembered Irons's words—and she remembered her promise to God. Her voice was not steady, and her lips were tight as she said, "Mister Clay, can I talk to you?"

"Why, certainly!" Clay felt that she was struggling with a personal problem and thought, *She's got nobody to talk to. I hope I can help.*

Melora turned and walked into the cabin, and when he followed her, she said, "Let's sit down at the table." When he sat down with his black eyes fixed on her, she walked to the bookcase and returned with the big black family Bible. It was worn thin and dog-eared, the pages brown with age. She put her hand on it, said a quick prayer, then gave him a tremulous smile, saying, "Mister Clay, I've always loved you."

Clay blinked, his jaw dropping. He could not speak, so shattered had he become.

She continued, "You've done so much for me, ever since I was a little girl!"

"Why, Melora, I've done very little!"

"Maybe you think so, but I don't. So I'm thanking you for the books and everything." He tried to protest, but she shook her head. "But that's not what I wanted to talk about. Mister Clay, you're having a terrible time, aren't you?"

"Why—I'm no worse off than lots of others, Melora!"

Melora shook her head, and there was something fragile, yet very strong, in her firm jaw. "You're dying, and unless you get some help, you're not going to make it. Isn't that the truth?"

Clay stared at her—this young woman knew what was happening to him. How? He couldn't tell, but he said heavily, "I guess you're right, Melora. I never really thought it was going to work, my coming back here. I guess my father is going to make it—but I'm going away."

"You mustn't!" Melora cried out, and the smoothness of her face was marred by pain. "You can't run away! You've got to stay!"

"It just isn't working, Melora," Clay said, defeat in his eyes and despair in his voice.

"Mister Clay," she said quickly, "can I tell you about what happened to me when I was fifteen years old?" She waited for his nod, then began to speak slowly. "I was so afraid that I could never be happy. I was all legs and arms and thought I was so ugly. And we were so poor! I wanted to have nice dresses and go to school . . . but I knew none of it was ever going to happen."

For a long time Melora went on, speaking softly, her eyes fixed on his. He sat there, seeing for the first time the life of the child he had thought was so happy and content. It had simply never occurred to him that Melora had problems that went so deep.

Finally Melora said, "I was so miserable, I prayed that God would take my life." She smiled then, saying, "But God was there! It was in this room, Mister Clay, right at this table. Everyone was in bed asleep, but I'd stayed up crying over my life. And then a wonderful thing happened. I was sitting right here in this very chair, when I suddenly felt—oh, I don't know how to say it! Have you ever been alone, maybe out in a field, and had the feeling that you're not really alone, that someone is watching you even if you can't see anyone?"

"Many times, Melora!"

"It was a little like that, but different, too, somehow. My mother was living then, and she was always so busy with all of us, but once when I was no more than seven or eight, I woke up after a nightmare, crying and scared to death. She came to me, took me in her arms . . . and all the fear left me! It was a little like that, Mister Clay. I just felt that God was in the room, and I began to read the

Bible. Right off I read a verse that said, 'Sirs, what must I do to be saved?' And then the next verse said, 'Believe on the Lord Jesus Christ, and thou shalt be saved, and thy house.'" Melora's eyes suddenly flooded with tears, and she brushed them away with one hand. "I didn't know what to do. I'd been so scared and lonely, and all I knew to do was ask God to do what my mother had done. I just said, 'Lord, I want to be saved! Will you please save me?'"

Clay watched her and saw that she was choked with emotion. "What happened then, Melora?"

Diamonds were in her eyes as she looked across the table at him. "Nothing really. I mean, I didn't hear any voices or anything. But something happened to me right here in this chair. Ever since that moment, Mister Clay, I've loved God. Jesus Christ has been as real to me as you are. And I've never been afraid or lonely."

Clay saw that she was finished and said, "That's a wonderful story, Melora. You've got such peace, more than anyone I know."

"Would you like to have that sort of peace?" Melora asked at once.

"Why, of course, Melora. But it's not for me. You don't know what I've done, the wrongs that—"

"Jesus died for those sins!" Melora insisted. "It says so right here." She opened the worn Bible and read a verse: "'Who his own self bore our sins in his own body on the tree, that we being dead to sins, should live unto righteousness: by whose stripes ye were healed.'"

For some reason that Clay could not understand, he became extremely nervous. There was no reason for it, for Melora was speaking in a very moderate voice. But it was similar to the time before a battle, when a man's hands would begin to sweat and his stomach would tighten. If it had been Jeremiah Irons, he would have given a list of reasons why he could not trust Jesus Christ. But Melora was different. She was no preacher, had nothing to gain from him. He felt free with her in a way he never would have with a preacher or a member of his family. "Melora, I can't understand it. How can a man dying two thousand years ago do anything for me? I'll never understand such a thing!"

"No, you won't," Melora agreed. "It's not a thing a person can understand. I didn't understand when my mother came to me and my fears all left. We never understand love, do we, Mister Clay? You love your mother, but can you explain what that is? No, but it's real, more real than some of the things you can understand, isn't it?"

Clay stared at her, then slowly nodded. "Yes, Melora. It is. But—surely it's not as easy as that? Surely a man has to do something before God will have him!"

"Do what?" Melora demanded strongly. "If a person could do something to get rid of his sins, why would God send Jesus to die on the cross? Most of the Bible is about people who thought they could do something to make God love them. But God just loves us, Clay. We don't have to earn it. I think all love is like that. Suppose you went to Rena and said, 'I'll love you, but only if you do certain things!' You would never do that! You just love her, don't you?"

Melora had touched a nerve, and Clay suddenly wet his lips. He clenched his hands to keep them from trembling. Suddenly he realized from her simple words what a thousand sermons had failed to make clear: God did love him! He dropped his eyes, for he could not hold her gaze. "Melora, I've been so rotten!" and then without planning it, he told her of his experience on the *Carrie Jane*. It was the first time he had spoken of it to anyone, and the bitterness of it all flooded over him. He spoke of the young woman and the baby, and when he got to the part when they were dragged overboard, his throat grew thick and his eyes burned with unshed tears.

He looked up, expecting to see disgust and rejection in her—and saw that she was weeping. He cried out suddenly, "Melora! I'm a murderer! God help me! I can't forget those poor people I killed."

Clay Rocklin had never wept, not since he was a child,

but now his body was racked with great sobs. He stared at her helplessly, tears running down his cheeks.

Melora saw that he was paralyzed by his guilt, and at once she got up and went to him. She took his head, holding it against her breast for a moment. She felt the terror that was shaking him, and waited for a few moments. Then she drew back and knelt beside him.

"You can't undo the past, Clay. Those who died are in God's hands. But you can't carry such a load!"

"Melora . . . what *can* I do?"

"You've been a proud man, but now you've got to do the one thing that's hardest for a strong man. You *must* do it!"

"Do what, Melora?" he asked thickly.

"You have to receive, Clay. God wants to give you a precious gift. He wants to give you life. Life in Jesus Christ. You've already confessed you've been a sinner. Now, will you ask God to put your sins on Jesus? And will you let Jesus come into your life? That means more than going to church. It's like a marriage! You'll be part of the bride of Christ, and a bride loves and honors her husband above all things. Will you do that, Clay?"

Clay Rocklin felt that he was standing on a tremendously high precipice. He felt that he must turn and run or he would fall off. Yet somehow he knew that his only hope for peace was to throw himself off the cliff. As Melora continued to speak to him, not of doctrines or creeds, but of Jesus Christ, the man of Galilee, he felt a rising faith that was like nothing he'd ever felt in church. It was a quiet and powerful thing, as real as the earth or the sky.

Suddenly he knew he had no choice—not really. He lifted his head and, in a husky whisper, said, "I'll do it, Melora! I'll follow Jesus as long as I live!"

Melora said, "Let's pray, then, and you tell God that you want to receive the gift he's giving you. . . . "

Three hours later, when Clay walked into the kitchen at Gracefield, he found Dorrie and his mother there, planning the meals for the next week. When he entered, the greeting on his mother's lips died, and her face turned as pale as paper. Dropping the book she was holding, she ran to him, crying out, "Oh, my boy! My boy!"

As he held his mother, Clay saw Dorrie throw her hands into the air and heard her shout, "Glory to God! Glory to God! My chile's done come home! He's found de glory!"

And then she began to do an ecstatic dance of joy around the kitchen. It was not a graceful sort of dance, but it was the most beautiful dance Clay Rocklin had ever seen!

PART FOUR
THUNDER OVER
SUMTER—1860

✸ ✸ ✸

CHAPTER NINETEEN

THE WINDS OF WAR

LATE in the afternoon of October 16, 1859, John Brown reached the Maryland Bridge of Harpers Ferry. Brown, looking much like an Old Testament prophet—and believing himself to be the chosen vessel of God for freeing the slaves—had come with a grandiose plan for a death blow against slavery. For two years he had waited, raising money to set his dream in motion. Now the time had come. His lips compressed, his eyes shining like polished steel, Brown marched at the head of his "army"—which consisted of sixteen whites, four free blacks, and one escaped slave.

"Men, we will proceed to the Ferry," he proclaimed, a fanatical light in his great staring eyes. He led the group through a cold drizzle, crossing the Potomac River on a covered bridge that took them directly into Harpers Ferry. Brown posted two guards on the bridge and sealed off the other bridge leading into the town, then the party moved toward the U.S. arsenal on Potomac Street.

It all went with remarkable ease. The watchman at the arsenal was taken by surprise, then the raiders captured the nearby Hall's Rifle Works. Next, Brown sent a few of his men to seize some prominent hostages, particularly Colonel Lewis Washington, a prosperous slaveholder and a great-grandnephew of the first president. Following explicit instructions from Brown, the contingent brought back not only Colonel Washington, but also a sword belonging to him that had been presented to George Washington by Frederick the Great. Brown strapped the weapon around his waist and waited, expecting slaves by the thousands to rally to him. Once he had armed them from the arsenal, they would march on in his campaign of liberation.

But the slaves did not come. Instead, the town roused up and began to fight, and soon telegraph wires all over the East hummed with exaggerated reports like "Negro insurrection at Harpers Ferry! Fire and raping on the Virginia Border!"

Several militia companies formed, and when they got to the town they pinned Brown and his men down in Hall's Rifle Works. The raiders suffered the first casualty. Dangerfield Newby, a black, was killed. Townspeople dragged his body to a gutter and cut off his ears and let hogs chew on the corpse.

The battle went on all afternoon. At one o'clock, Brown sent two men out to negotiate under a truce flag. They were shot down. The battle went on, with several of the raiders shot or wounded. In the melée, the mayor of Harpers Ferry was shot dead, and in drunken rage the townsmen hauled out a raider whom they had captured that morning, killed him in cold blood, and used his body for target practice.

Word soon came that a company of marines from Washington was on its way. As the night wore on, Brown and his men spent a cold, hungry night in the engine house, listening to desultory gunfire and a drunken ruckus in the town. By then, Brown's son Oliver had been wounded, and he lay beside his brother Watson, both of them dying in terrible pain. "If you must die, die like a man," Brown replied in cold anger. Some time later he called to Oliver and got no reply. "I guess he is dead," said John Brown.

"What is it, Gid?" Melanie came out of the bedroom, pulling a green silk robe around her shoulders. She had wakened at once when the banging on the front door came, but waited until Gid threw on his own robe and went to answer it. There was some muffled talk that she did not understand, and when she heard the front door close, she went to meet him.

Gid's hair was mussed but his eyes were wide open, and she saw that he was aroused. "I've got orders to go to Harpers Ferry, Mellie," he said. "Help me get ready."

As he shaved, she pulled his kit together, listening as he told her what little he knew. "Some maniac named John Brown has captured the arsenal at Harpers Ferry," he told her. "That's about all I know. I'm ordered to go with the marines to capture the raiders."

Melanie always dreaded such moments. They had been stationed in Washington for over a year, and it had been a wonderful time for her, for both of them. But now he would be facing danger, and when he left her, she kissed him and held him with all her might, saying, "I'll be waiting."

"It won't be long, I think. You'll have to tell the boys." Then he was gone, and she watched as he moved out into the darkness, his body strong and upright in the blue uniform. When she could no longer see him, she went back to bed—but not to sleep.

When Gid got to company headquarters, he received another shock. Colonel Barrington, his commanding officer, met him, saying, "You made good time, Major. Now, come with me. I want you to meet your commanding officer." He led Gid across the yard where men were running about in what seemed to be wild confusion, but was only the normal manner of men called into sudden action. Barrington led Gid inside the quartermaster's building and moved to where two officers were leaning over a map on a desk.

"Colonel Lee, this is Major Rocklin. He'll accompany you as an aide."

Lieutenant Colonel Robert E. Lee turned and faced Gid and at once recognized him. A smile came to his lips, and he nodded. "Well, Major, it's been a long time since our venture in Mexico."

Gid returned the smile. "Yes sir. I'm glad to see you again."

"This is Lieutenant Stuart of the First U.S. Cavalry, Major. He'll be in our command." Lee waited until the two men shook hands, then said, "We'll move at once." He hesitated, his eyes on Gid, and said, "Well, it's always good to have a man who's been decorated along." When Gid moved his shoulders slightly, he said contritely, "I remember now. You never did like to hear anyone speak of your medal. But in any case, I'm glad to have you."

Later as they rode rapidly at the head of the column, Lee mostly kept his silence. Once, though, he did ask, "I don't want to bring up unpleasant things, Major, but what became of your cousin, the one we had to discharge?"

Gid explained briefly that Clay had led an unfortunate life, then added, "He's back in Virginia now, helping his father with the plantation. I have hopes he'll do well."

"Men can change, sir," Lee answered, and he said no more until they arrived at the arsenal. He took charge at once, spoke with the officer in charge of the militia, then sent Jeb Stuart under a white flag to demand surrender and promise protection for the raiders. Gid was standing slightly behind Lee and watched as Stuart talked to Brown at the door. After five minutes, Stuart jumped aside and waved his hat as a signal for the marines to charge.

It was soon over, but Gid always remembered the charge. He had led the way and heard the familiar sound of bullets singing in the air. He pulled his Colt and fired at the door and was with the first two or three men who crashed through to confront the raiders. The rifleshots rattled around the bricked-in engine room like firecrackers set off in a stone jug, and there was the harsh stink of sweat and powder.

Brown fired and missed, then fell to his knees, the sword in his hand bent double. A private snatched it from Brown and rained blows about his head.

From beginning to end, the charge took only fifteen minutes. Later as Lee, Stuart, and Rocklin stood watching the soldiers put irons on Brown, Stuart said, "Well, that was easy! But I'm glad it's over."

A shadow crossed Lee's face. He said quietly, "It's not over, Lieutenant. In fact, I'm afraid this is just the beginning."

Lee was correct. Brown was hanged forty-five days later and promptly became a martyr to the abolitionist cause—and a dark omen to the South. He inspired the North, and the day would come when men would march off to fight, singing "John Brown's body lies a'moldering in the grave. . . ."

For over a year John Brown's body did molder in the grave, but when the election of 1860 came, the cause for which he died was very much alive. The nation seemed to be poised on the brink of some climactic change, and when the announcement was made that Abraham Lincoln was the new president, both North and South reacted strongly. Springfield, Illinois, went wild, and there was dancing in the streets in Washington.

In the South, there was a strange reaction. The general populace felt a deep anger and a sense of being abused by the North. But there was also a sudden sense of release, a sense of some sort of bondage being lifted.

The Rocklins felt it as they drove to Richmond for a dress ball. The election was still in progress, though they were expecting to hear the results before the night was out. Clay drove Ellen and the children, and he was strangely oppressed as they drove through the crowded streets of the city. Ellen seemed oblivious to Clay's mood, as did the children. There were bands on the streets and buildings were decorated.

Ellen said with satisfaction, "It's so exciting! And Mr. Breckinridge will surely come to Richmond after he's elected."

"He won't be elected, Ellen," Clay said. He had explained to her twice that the Democratic party had committed political suicide by their refusal to agree on a

candidate. Instead the Party had divided into camps
favoring three men: J. C. Breckinridge, John Bell, and
Stephen A. Douglas. "Lincoln couldn't beat any one of
those, but when the party split three ways, he couldn't
lose," Clay had explained.

But Ellen said, "If you were a true Southerner you
wouldn't talk like that!" Then she began to talk to Dent,
who agreed with her. She was wearing a new dress that
was far too youthful for her and much too ornate. The
fact that Clay was coming to the ball with her at all was
some sort of a victory. Since his return, he had not shown
any inclination to join the social life of Richmond. But
she had insisted, and Susanna had said mildly, "I think it
would be nice if you'd make an appearance with the family, Clay. For the sake of the children."

So he had agreed, but as he helped Ellen down from
the carriage and led her into the ballroom, he was wishing he had not. Since his return to Gracefield he had
been isolated completely from her—especially after he
made his conversion known. Ellen had laughed at him,
saying, "It's just another of your fancies, Clay. It'll never
last!" But somehow, as the months passed and Clay
worked away doggedly at restoring Gracefield—and
slowly gained the respect of the community—she resented the change in him. It was as though she wanted
him to fail, and Clay soon began to realize that was her
true desire.

The ballroom was beautifully decked. Flanking its
long sides were chairs of all descriptions and degrees of
comfort, with scarcely an inch between them. Here and
there the line of chairs was broken by stands of Boston
ferns. The ferns had been washed to look fresher, and the
stands were sashed in broad bands of colored silk tied
with elaborate bows. Large branches of magnolias with
dark brown limbs and dark green leaves were set in tin
tubs that had been tinseled over and so gave back the
light of the huge chandeliers and the two hundred candles that brightened the hall.

There were already people everywhere, and soon the dancing began, but only waltzing; the formal sets had not yet been called. There was a general air of coming and going, and spectators staked jealous claims to the chairs that would afford the best views of the dancing and flirting. The ladies did much traipsing up and down the stairs with the excuse of leaving wraps or repairing hair and faces.

Ellen proved to be very popular, which did not surprise Clay. She was still an attractive woman, if one liked the lush type. She was claimed at once by a man he didn't know. As she floated off, he left the dance floor and made his way to the billiard room, where he found, as he expected, some of the men with whom he played poker. Bushrod Aimes was talking, as usual, waving one hand around wildly and holding a glass in the other. He spotted Clay and cried out, "Clay, come and wet your whistle!"

Clay moved forward and took a glass of wine from one of the white-jacketed waiters. He had learned long ago that it was easier to take one drink of the mild wine and nurse it along for hours than to fight off the constant demands of his friends that he join them in drinking.

Taylor Dewitt grinned at him. "You look pretty as a picture in that outfit, Clay. Now if you drop dead, we won't have to do a thing to you, except stick a lily in your hand."

"What's that I smell?" Clay frowned, ignoring Taylor's words.

"That's me!" Tug Ramsey said proudly. "Ain't it elegant?" He was as fat as a bear, but still had the baby face he'd had at eighteen. Shy to excess with women, he had remained a bachelor, the only one of the old group who had done so.

"He got that lotion from a Frenchman on Bourbon Street in New Orleans," Taylor explained, grinning.

"I did not either!" Ramsey protested indignantly. "I bought it at a fancy store right here in Richmond!"

The mood of the room was light, and Taylor Dewitt stood there, thinking, *Well, it took over a year, but old Clay has made it! Never thought it could happen!* He, along with the rest of the close-knit world of wealthy planters, had expected Clay to do well for a time. But it had come as a pleasant shock when he had kept to the task of restoring the fortunes of Gracefield. Dire prophecies had gone forth, stating that sooner or later he would break out, as he always did. But it had not happened. And Taylor was convinced that Clay was over the terrible part of his life. Oh, he had no life with Ellen, that was plain, for Taylor knew that she was unchanged. He himself kept his distance from her, but one of his friends, a boastful fellow named Jake Slocum, had informed him that the Rocklins did not live together as man and wife. Slocum, a stallion of a man with bulging arms and legs, had nudged Taylor in the ribs and given a sly grin, saying, "Woman's got to have a man, ain't that right, Dewitt? If Rocklin can't take care of his woman, reckon it's all I can do for him to take the chore myself!"

Slocum had taken a savage pleasure in throwing pointed jibes at Clay on the rare occasions when they were in the same company. Taylor had been alarmed on the first of these occasions. He had taken Slocum aside, saying, "Jake, I wouldn't take that line with Clay. He's been known to plug one or two fellows who took liberties with him."

"Rocklin? Aw, Dewitt, ain't you heard? He's on the glory trail! A good Christian like him can't take a shot at a fellow, can he now?" Slocum had taken every opportunity to push at Clay, and most of the crowd had been disappointed in Clay's reaction.

"You want him to shoot Jake, Bushrod?" Taylor had asked the fiery Aimes, who had expressed his wish to see Rocklin put a stop to Slocum's jibes. "That's just what Clay needs, isn't it? A duel! That's what got him off on the wrong foot in the first place, you blockhead!" Then he had said thoughtfully, "I might call Jake out myself."

Bushrod had stared at him. "What for, Taylor? He ain't insulted you."

"I may shoot him for being so stupid!"

The talk came around to the election, but Clay took no part in the heated discussion. He found a seat beside the wall, had the waiter bring him a cup of hot coffee, and relaxed. The sound of music drifted in from the ballroom, and for the next hour he sat and enjoyed the company. Though he refused to talk about politics, he did talk about farming. He shocked the small group that gathered around him by his remark that he was changing from cotton to corn, at least partially.

"Why, Clay, there's not the money in corn that there is in cotton!" Devoe Tate exclaimed. He was a short, muscular man of thirty who had become friendly with Clay over the past few months. "And this is cotton country. Too hot for corn."

"Tell you how it comes out next fall, Devoe," Clay said with a shrug. But when Devoe pressed him, he finally said, "Not going to tell you your business, Devoe, but corn would really be even better for you than for Gracefield." When Devoe pressed him, he went on to explain, a little self-conscious because several other men had gathered around to listen. "Well, you've got a smaller place, for one thing, and not nearly so many slaves. Cotton wears land out fast, which we all know, and it takes a lot of hands to make the crop."

"Well, I was thinking of buying more slaves and more land," Devoe said, scratching his chin.

"You could do that, but do you know the price of a prime field hand?"

"About three thousand dollars, I reckon."

"How much cotton will he have to raise before you make three thousand dollars clear?"

Devoe did some rapid calculation, then said, "I'd say about fifty bales, Clay, maybe more. But I'd have him for years."

"If he didn't die or get sick."

Clay sipped his coffee and Tug asked, "Are you against slavery, Clay?"

"I'm against losing money, Tug," Clay remarked, turning the question away. Then he went on, "Devoe, you wouldn't have to buy another acre or another slave to raise corn. Maybe you wouldn't make as much cash. I can't say about that."

Devoe looked a little embarrassed. "You know, my folks moved here from Missouri. Know what they did there? They raised corn and fed hogs, then sold the hogs. Did real good at it." He sighed, adding, "Pa told me the last time he was out of debt was back in Missouri. Said the first slave he bought put him in debt, and he's never been out since!"

Bushrod laughed and slapped Tate on the back. "You going to be a pig farmer, Devoe? You can't court that Debbie girl of yours smelling like pigs!"

A laugh went around the room, with Devoe Tate laughing at himself, but Clay noticed that he was sober the rest of the evening. As they all moved out of the billiards room later, Devoe said quietly, "Clay, be all right if I come over and talk to you this week?"

"Any time, Devoe."

The ball was in full swing, with the dancers moving across the floor to the sound of music. To Clay's surprise, Ellen came to him at once, demanding, "Dance with me!"

He had no chance to refuse, for she had practically thrown herself into his arms. She was a marvelous dancer, and as they moved around the floor, she was humming along with the waltz tune. There was a happy expression on her face, and in the candlelight she looked much younger. Suddenly she looked at him, asking, "Why are you staring at me, Clay?"

"Didn't mean to, Ellen," he apologized. "I'm not much of a dancer, you know. Have to keep my mind on it or I'll be walking all over your feet."

"You're a good dancer," she answered. She had forced him to dance with her simply to make their charade more believable. One of her women friends had taunted her, "That good-looking husband of yours doesn't pay enough attention to you, Ellen. You better keep a tighter rein on him, or he might run off with one of these Richmond belles!"

This was the closest she had been to her husband since he'd returned to Gracefield, and it gave her a queer feeling to be in his arms. *He is fine-looking,* she thought, looking up into his face. But then he always had been the best-looking man she'd ever known. He was one of the tallest men in the room, and his coal-black hair gleamed richly, complementing his rich tan. His face was still smooth and unlined, his features strong and clear.

His arms were strong and more than once he pressed against her in the dance, causing her to examine him carefully—but he had a preoccupied look on his face. When he had come home, she had assumed that he would eventually come back to her. She had informed him that she would never have anything to do with him, but as the weeks wore on, she had known she would relax as he tried to make up to her. Finally, she would permit him back into her life and into her bed. That had been her plan, but it had never happened.

He had remained in the summer house, fixing it up and giving every indication of staying there on a permanent basis. He was always polite and even considerate to her, but never showed the least interest in her as a woman. This had irked Ellen, and once or twice she had pressed against him on some pretext, but he had never seemed to notice. She feared that he had heard of her affairs in Richmond, but he never mentioned it if he had. Then she began to watch him closely, suspecting that he was seeing some woman, but it was obvious that he was not. He never went anywhere except to church, and then always with his parents, and with their own children when he could persuade her to send them.

He looked at her, smiled and said, "It's a nice dance. And you look very attractive." His compliment gave her an unexpected pleasure. She moved closer to him, but then the dance was over and he took her to the refreshment table.

He was getting her a glass of punch when there was a muffled shout, and when they turned to look, Sam Decosta, the editor of the *Richmond News*, came running into the room, his hair wild and his eyes wilder.

"Lincoln has won!" he shouted, waving a telegram over his head. "It's all over! Lincoln is the new president."

The room was alive with talk, but not with cheers. A man shouted, "Let the baboon be president! He won't be *our* president! We'll take care of that!"

A roar went up, and for the next hour there was bedlam. Clay marveled at what was happening. The entire South hated Lincoln, and many leaders had vowed that if he was elected they'd lead their states out of the Union. Yet here the people of Richmond were, shouting and yelling and drinking toasts as if they had won a great victory!

He spoke with his uncle, Claude Bristol, about it. He had always liked Claude, preferring him to Brad Franklin, his hotheaded brother-in-law. "I just don't understand it, Claude," he said, speaking loudly to be heard. "What's everyone so excited about? Don't they know this probably means war?"

Claude cast a weary eye over the crowd. He was fifty-five years old, and years of hard living had worn him thin. He had been a sorrow to Clay's aunt, Marianne, for there was little substance to him. He was, at the core, a degenerate—but there was a genteel quality in his manner that caused him to be so discreet in his affairs that they never became public. He had charm and, surprisingly, some insight. "It's a release, Clay," he said. "The tension is gone. Nobody knows what the future will bring, but at least the pressure is gone. From now on the South knows what it will do, and it's always easier when you've made up your mind."

Clay was depressed, and as soon as he could, he collected his family and took them back to Gracefield. He sat glumly as Dent spoke excitedly about the future. *Was I ever that young and so sure of everything?* he wondered, feeling about a thousand years old.

His parents were still at the ball, and Clay was glad that Highboy, the oldest son of Box, the blacksmith, was there to unhitch the team. "Good-night," he said, and moved away down the path that led to his house. It was not, he thought as he entered, *the summer house,* any longer, but *Clay's house.* The slaves called it that, and the family had taken it up.

He built up a small fire and made a pot of coffee. He removed his suit, then put on a pair of old cotton trousers and sat down at the table. He was tired, but not sleepy, so he worked on the books for the next hour.

The sound of a tapping on the door startled him, and he came to his feet quickly. It was unusual for anyone to come to his house this late, so he picked up the pistol he kept on top of the mantel and demanded, "Who is it?"

"It's me—Ellen. Let me in, Clay."

He opened the door and she came in at once. "What's wrong?" he asked, turning to replace the pistol.

She was wearing a thick wool coat, and her cheeks were flushed. She looked around the room, saying, "I haven't been here in a long time. We stayed here once, you remember? When we had the reunion and the house was full."

He nodded, but asked, "Is something wrong, Ellen? One of the children sick?"

She seemed embarrassed and shook her head. "No. Nobody's sick. I just wanted to talk to you."

He studied her thoughtfully, thinking it strange that she would come so late. "Well, sit down. I've got some coffee on."

He got her a cup of coffee, but when he brought it to her, she took only a sip, then set it down absently. She began to talk of the ball and how exciting it had been. Her cheeks were red, and Clay knew she had been drinking, but he said nothing.

Finally she said, "It's hot in here, Clay," and threw off her coat. She was wearing only a cotton robe over her nightgown, and when he stared at her, she said quickly, "I was in bed, but I couldn't sleep, so I just threw on my overcoat and came here."

Then she got up and began walking around the room, talking aimlessly about the books, the furniture, and how well he'd fixed the place up. She seemed nervous, which was unusual for her. She had taken extra care with her hair, and she smoothed her hand over it as she spoke. Finally she seemed to run out of words. She bit her lower lip, then came over to stand in front of him. He got to his feet, and she suddenly leaned forward.

"Clay—!" she whispered, pulling at him, "I'm your wife! Doesn't that mean anything to you?"

It was a trying moment for Clay Rocklin, for he had lived a long time without women. Her body lay against him, and her lips were parted as she whispered, "Love me, Clay! Like you used to!"

Clay knew that Ellen had no love for him. He guessed that she saw him as a challenge, that she wanted him only to prove that she was still desirable. And she *was* desirable, no denying that! Clay stood there, struggling with the hungers that he had kept under strict control for so long. There was nothing wrong in taking her, she was his wife, after all.

Yet he knew instinctively that he must not touch her. She represented a way of life he could not share. If he resumed his relationship with her, he would be in a bondage that he knew he could not endure and would never escape. She would devour him, as a female praying mantis devours her mate.

"Ellen, we're past all that," he said and stepped away from her. He tried to make his rejection less harsh by saying, "You don't need me. I'd make you miserable. It's better if we keep on just as we are."

If he had touched her with a hot iron, the effect would not have been greatly different. She turned pale, and after one moment of standing before him in shocked silence, not moving at all, she suddenly drew her hand back and slapped him across the face, screaming curses at him.

Clay stood there, not moving, and she slapped him twice more. Then she grabbed her coat and ran out of the house. He could hear her curses as she ran down the path. They grew faint, and still he stood there, until finally he turned and walked slowly to the chair. He sat down in it, his face rigid. He knew this was not the end of it. She would never let him have a moment's peace, not now.

Finally taking a deep breath, he picked up the Bible he kept on the table and began to read.

When Deborah Steele heard that her uncle Gideon was going to move his family to Virginia, she immediately mounted a crusade to get herself invited. Deborah, at the age of eighteen, had learned to get what she wanted as a rule. She got some of that from her father, Amos, who was a minister but also an abolitionist. He had taught his three sons, Patrick, Colin, and Clinton, and his daughter as well that it was displeasing to the Lord to go at anything halfheartedly. "Whatsoever thy hand findeth to do, do it with all thy might," was a Scripture that had molded his own life. He had managed to pass that message along to all his children except Colin, who took life less seriously than his father liked.

Deborah had been educated at Reverend Charles Finney's Oberlin College, where she had become an admirer of the great evangelist. The two strongest men she knew were both devoted to freeing the slaves, and it was not surprising that she became an abolitionist at an early age.

When she had gone to Oberlin at the age of sixteen, she had been one of the youngest students. If her father had not been one of Finney's strongest supporters for years, she would not have been accepted. Even then, the president had examined her long and hard, testing her morals, her intelligence, and her determination. In the end, he had admitted her.

Life at Oberlin had been exciting; Deborah had met the men and women who were at the head of the abolition movement, including William Lloyd Garrison, Frederick Douglass, and Theodore Parker. Deborah's youth and beauty made her stand out, and when she proved that she could hold her own intellectually with the best at Oberlin, she was busy and happy.

But college was over now, and Deborah found that there was no excitement in being a former student. She accompanied her father to meetings, but he was a busy man, and she felt that she had been marooned on a desert island.

Then her cousin, Tyler, Uncle Gideon's oldest son, had told her that his father was being transferred to South Carolina, and his mother was going to visit Uncle Thomas and Aunt Susanna before joining Gideon at Charleston. It was like a light coming on in a dark room!

I'll go with them and study the terrible lot of the slaves first-hand! Deborah's fertile imagination at once pounced on the germ of a thought, and within two hours, her plan was fully grown. She had to convince her own parents and her uncle and aunt, but she had no doubt of success. Being a very honest young woman, she freely acknowledged that she had learned early to get her own way. Being the only girl among six boys (counting Gideon and Melanie's three boys and her own three brothers), she had been a spoiled pet all her life. It had not ruined her, but she had learned that there were certain things she could do to get her own way. Though she had never formulated this knowledge into a written code, she practiced the principle of it on certain occasions.

In this case, success fell to her like a ripe apple. She had simply gone to her father and smiled at him, twisting the button on his coat, and said, "Father, do you think I could be of any help to the movement by doing some primary research on the terrible life of the slaves?" He had thought she meant in a library, but she had fluffed his side whiskers, saying innocently, "That's been done, hasn't it? But do you know what I thought of? I could go to Richmond with Aunt Mellie. She's always begged me to go with her for a visit. Perhaps I should do it. Then I could see slavery firsthand, and just think of the material I could get for your book!"

Amos Steele could handle a large congregation, an angry mob, or almost anything else—but he was easy pickings for his daughter. Before she was finished with him, he was totally convinced that the whole thing had been his idea! He plunged in with his abnormal energy, and before the sun went down, he had convinced his wife that Deborah should go; visited his sister-in-law, Melanie Rocklin, and admitted that he had been wrong to prevent Deborah from visiting her family in Richmond; gained Gid's permission for Deborah's visit; and bought a new set of luggage for her.

Deborah threw her arms around his neck and kissed him warmly. "Oh, Father, you're so wonderful!"

Steele hesitated, then said, "Deborah, you know the Scripture says a beautiful woman without discretion is like a jewel of gold in a swine's snout. So you must be discreet while doing your work there for the movement."

"But, Father, they know I'm an abolitionist!"

"Yes, but you don't have to wear a sign that says in bold print 'I am here to study the cruel treatment of slaves'!"

Deborah got a sudden vision of herself wearing that sign and giggled. "Of course not, Father. That would be silly."

"I'm serious, Deborah. You could do great harm to our relatives there if anyone found out about your study. You are a very impulsive young woman, and you'll see things there that will anger you. You'll want to step in and right the wrongs. But you must not! You must always remember that you can serve the best interests of those poor people by taking the long view. The book will stir the people of our country, both in the South and in the North. There need not be a war, for the South can be reached and won without bloodshed."

"I'll remember, Father." Deborah nodded.

She left the next week, on the twenty-first of November, never suspecting as she got on the train with the rest of the family that her uncle Gideon had been assigned to serve under Major Robert Anderson. And she did not know that Major Anderson was ordered to man a fort located at the entrance to the harbor of Charleston, South Carolina.

Nor did she know that this fort—Fort Sumter—would be the first place to feel the winds of war.

CHAPTER TWENTY

KISSING COUSINS

DEBORAH Steele came to the South with an adamant predisposition to dislike everything there, but she found that she could not do it. For one thing, the Rocklins of Gracefield were such open, warmhearted people that she could not help liking them. The twins, David and Denton, were gone on a hunting trip, but she found Lowell and Rena to be as well bred as any Yankee children their age. Her great-aunt, Susanna Rocklin, was especially charming, and by the end of three days at the big plantation Deborah felt that she had known the older woman forever. She liked Thomas Rocklin, too, but realized almost at once that he was a man to be pitied. She was too close to strong men, such as her father and her uncle, Gideon Rocklin, to miss the fact that the head of Gracefield was a weak man—but she could not deny his warmth and generosity.

It was Clay Rocklin, though, who fascinated the young woman. She had heard stories of his wild youth, his long exile, and his dramatic return. A lover of novels, Deborah was possessed of a powerful imagination, and the drama of Clay Rocklin's life would have made an excellent novel. He even looked like the hero of a romance, lean and darkly handsome.

Strangely enough, it was Deborah who discovered the rather unusual friendship between Clay Rocklin and Melora Yancy. It happened quite accidentally, actually. Deborah had always loved horses and had her own mare in Washington. When she lamented one morning that she missed her horse, Clay said at once, "That's no problem. Come along with me." He had led her to the stables and to her delight assigned a beautiful mare named Lady for her use while visiting at Gracefield.

"Oh, what a beauty!" Deborah cried out with delight. "May I ride her now?"

"Get dressed and I'll give you a tour of the place."

Deborah had dashed away at once, borrowing one of Susanna's riding habits. Soon she and Clay were riding across the fields. Clay watched her carefully, aware that the mare was spirited, but soon he was satisfied that the young woman would have no trouble.

"You're a fine horsewoman," he said. "Lady's been known to throw her rider a time or two, but I can see you can handle her." The fields were dead and brown, filled with the brittle cotton stalks from the last harvest. "I wish you could see this field when the cotton is ready to harvest, Deborah," Clay said. "It looks like fields of snow."

"Maybe I can come back for a visit then," Deborah said, smiling. She gave him a glance, admiring his rugged good looks, and added, "It's a lovely place, Mr. Rocklin. And everyone is so nice."

He suddenly turned his head and gave her a shrewd smile. "You didn't think we would be, did you? Nice, I mean." He laughed at her expression. "The daughter of Amos Steele and a graduate of Oberlin College wouldn't be expected to like Southerners. I expect you thought you'd find some pretty grim monsters. Beating slaves to death every morning before breakfast."

"Oh, no—!" Deborah protested, then laughed, though she was blushing. "You're pretty clever, Uncle Clay." She smiled. "I suppose that *was* what I expected." She sat on her horse, unaware of what a picture she made. She had hair that was almost blonde, the only light-colored hair in her family, and her eyes were large, well shaped, and a beautiful pure violet. She had a heart-shaped face with a widow's peak and a beautiful complexion. Even in her aunt's riding habit, her slim but well-curved figure was evident. For all her beauty, though, Deborah was not a vain young woman. Her mirror—and many young men!—had told her that her appearance was good, but she did not trade on it.

That was what made Clay admire her. It was unusual for such a beautiful young woman to ignore the tricks that most of her sort used on men. As they talked during that ride, he quickly discovered that the reports he had heard of her intelligence had not been exaggerations.

She looked at him now and asked directly, "Do you ever beat your slaves, Uncle Clay?"

"No." Clay thought about the thing, then shook his head. "I hate slavery, Deborah. If I had my way, I'd set every one of the slaves here at Gracefield free today."

His simple statement stunned Deborah. She stared at him, but saw that he was completely serious. "I wouldn't have believed it," she said finally. "But you're not a typical Southern planter, are you?"

"No, not really. But there are more like me than you think. Robert E. Lee, for example, feels the same way. Of course, most planters are blind to the evils of slavery, just as they're blind that our peculiar institution is leading us to economic disaster." He talked quietly as they rode over the plantation, and Deborah was forced to rethink her position on the question of the Southern slaveholder. She sensed a generous spirit in Clay Rocklin, which did not fit with her previously firm opinion that all slave owners were cruel men.

Clay led them down a narrow lane lined with first-growth fir trees that arched over them. "Somebody I want you to meet," he said as they turned toward a cabin that lay in a clearing. "You've met the so-called aristocracy of the South. You've met some of the slaves on the place. But I want you to meet another class of people. I think you'll like them."

Deborah asked no questions, but was soon being introduced to the Yancy family. Buford Yancy welcomed Clay and, when introduced, beamed a welcome to Deborah. "Come in, Miss Deborah. Always glad to meet Mr. Rocklin's kin."

Deborah tried to sort out the children, who only stared at her shyly at first, then came out of their shells as she smiled and began to talk to them. All of them looked like Buford. She said to the tall woman she assumed was the mother, "You have beautiful children, Mrs. Yancy." Then she was startled to hear the Yancy children all break out in giggles. Buford Yancy grinned slyly, saying, "Now I hope you take notice of that, all of you. Your pa looks so young he gets mistook for his own daughter's husband!"

"Oh, I didn't—" Deborah blushed, throwing a horrified glance at the dark-haired woman. She was no more than twenty-five, and she was a beauty. But there was a twinkle in her green-gray eyes.

"Melora *is* a mother to the children—a second mother," Clay said, with a fond look at the young woman. "Actually she's Buford's oldest daughter."

"Don't be embarrassed, Miss Steele," Melora said, smiling. "You're not the first to think as you have." Then she turned to Clay. "I don't think you've ever come here any time except just before mealtime, Mister Clay."

"My mama didn't raise no fools," Clay said, grinning.

Soon Deborah was seated at the crowded table. She tasted what Melora called "winter crab gumbo," which she dipped from a large aromatic pot onto a bed of freshly steamed rice. There also was cold ham and cheese with toasted biscuits. The fresh milk was rich and sweet, and when Melora set down a huge slice of pumpkin pie, she held up her hands protesting, "Please, Melora—no more! I've got to get into my clothes when I get home!"

After the meal, Buford said, "Clay, I've got a new litter of pigs from that big red boar of yours. Turned out real good. Come on, I'll show you." The men left, and Deborah offered to help clean the dishes. Melora protested that they could wait, but soon the two of them were elbow-deep in the soapy water. As they worked, Deborah probed at her hostess. She was very good at such things, but Melora was equally adept at keeping her own counsel.

"How do you like the Rocklins?" Melora asked, and that kept Deborah talking for a time. She gave more information about herself than she knew, and as they finished, Melora said, "You haven't met Mister Clay's oldest boy, Denton. He's the one who's most like his father, but—" She broke off, and Deborah picked up on the fact that something lay between Clay and his son. By the time the men returned, the children all began prompting their father to take them to see the beaver dam as he had promised. Buford groaned, saying, "Seems funny to me that you kids can forget everything I say about the work around here, but you jist let me mention some kind of holiday in a passin' kind of way—and you'll nag a man to death." He finally agreed, and when the children all had donned their heavy coats, he asked, "Don't reckon you'd wade across twenty acres of briars to see a beaver dam, would you, Miss Steele? No, I didn't think so. Well, come on, you kids!"

Melora set a cup of coffee out for Clay, then poured two more for herself and Deborah. Clay sipped his carefully, then asked, "Got anything for me, Melora?"

A quick flush touched the smooth cheeks of the young woman, which aroused Deborah's curiosity. "Oh, not now, please. Miss Deborah doesn't want to waste her time."

Deborah was intrigued, and asked at once, "What is it?"

"Can I tell her, Melora?" Clay asked. When he got a slight nod, he said, "Melora has a real gift for writing, Deborah. She lets me read it from time to time." He turned back to Melora. "Let's see it. What have you got?"

Melora gave a helpless look at the pair, saying, "Oh, it's nothing. Just things that come to me." At their urging she went to a bookcase stuffed with books of all sorts, then came back with an inexpensive notebook. She handed it to Clay, but he shook his head. "Read it to us."

Melora gave Deborah a shy look, but opened the notebook and began reading in a clear, easy voice. It was a very simple essay, more like an entry from a journal, and at first Deborah thought, *What does Clay see in this?* But as the young woman went on, she began to find a beauty in the prose. Deborah had read Emerson and Thoreau, and Melora's style reminded her a little of Thoreau. It described a visit Melora had made to take some cool spring water to her father as he plowed in the fields. As Melora read on, Deborah realized that this young woman had a rare gift! She had the ability to choose just the right word—so that one could smell the rich loam of the earth or see the ragged clouds race across the sky. When she described finding a young raccoon with his paw caught in a steel trap and confessed how she had released him, Deborah was deeply moved. Then Melora read on, speaking of the coon as some sort of symbol of all men— and Deborah knew for certain that Melora had that special genius that was given to only a few: the ability to communicate truth and honest emotion.

As the three sat there, Melora reading and the other two listening, Deborah suddenly became aware that Clay was different. She had seen him with his family and soon discovered that he and his wife were totally alien. There was no mistaking the harsh light in Ellen Rocklin's eyes when she looked at Clay—nor the lack of any affection at all in Clay toward her.

Now, Deborah saw, Clay was totally absorbed in Melora. His coffee cup rested in his hand, forgotten, and his dark eyes were fixed on her face. He had built a wall around himself Deborah knew, but now the wall was down. He had forgotten that Deborah was there, and suddenly the girl from the North knew that Clay Rocklin felt a great deal for Melora Yancy—perhaps even more than was proper. She knew instinctively that this was a scene that had been repeated many times, the two of them together. Melora had spoken briefly of how Clay had been kind to her even when she was a child, bringing her books and small gifts.

Suddenly Melora lifted her eyes to look at Clay. She had forgotten the third party in the room, Deborah saw, and her face was open, filled with something that she kept hidden when she was aware of it. But it was evident, at least to Deborah, that her feelings for Clay Rocklin went deep—a fact that perplexed Deborah. Clay was so much older, and the young woman was attractive enough to have found a husband long ago. Deborah resolved to probe deeper, her romantic spirit and natural curiosity alerted.

"Oh, that's enough of this!" Melora laughed shortly, gave a quick glimpse toward Deborah, and got to her feet. "I feel like a fool reading my scribblings to you," she said, and she moved to replace the notebook. "Jeremiah asked me to write a Christmas play for the church," she said, coming back to sit at the table. Her eyes gleamed with a sudden humor, and she said, "I'll write a part for you, Mister Clay. You can be the innkeeper. You can rant and roar and throw poor Joseph and Mary out into the cold."

"Just let me at it!" Clay grinned. "I'll tear a passion to tatters! The stage missed something when I decided to be a cotton farmer, but now's my big chance!" He ran on, laughing at his own foolishness, the first time Deborah had seen him in such a mood, and she marked it as another piece of evidence that he was one man when he was at Gracefield, and another when he was at the Yancy cabin.

Soon they left the cabin, and on the way back home, Deborah spoke of the Yancys. "They don't own any slaves," she remarked. "Is it because they think it's an evil—or are they just too poor?"

"Both, I guess." Clay shook his head with a puzzled air. "It's odd, Deborah. Buford has told me many times he'll never own a slave, but he's also told me that nobody is going to tell him that he *can't* own a slave. There are lots of men like that in the South. If it came right down to it, they'd fight for the right to do as they please. That's what states' rights is all about, isn't it?"

When they arrived at Gracefield, she thanked Clay and insisted on taking the saddle from Lady and giving her a rubdown. She was engaged in this when Rena came in, dressed in a pair of overalls that had obviously belonged to one of her brothers. "Hello," she said shyly. "Did you have a good ride?"

"Oh, yes! Lady is a wonderful mount, isn't she? And your father showed me all over Gracefield. I expect he takes you riding pretty often, doesn't he? You're lucky to live here, Rena, with horses to ride and lots of things to do."

Rena gave Deborah a strange look and came to stand closer. "I guess so." She sounded so uncertain that Deborah gave her a closer look, and at once she saw that the girl was unhappy. Quickly, she said, "I'm through with Lady. Why don't you show me your room, Rena? I'll bet it's nice."

Rena looked surprised, but brightened up at once. "It's not much," she said diffidently. But when Deborah insisted, she led the way to a bright, cheerful room on the corner of the second floor. The room had a large dormer window and was decorated with white molding, which set off the yellow wallpaper. It was a child's room, with several stuffed animals on top of the furniture and the wallpaper featuring small ducks and white geese. Deborah made much of it, saying, "It's the very nicest room I've seen in the whole house, Rena!"

Rena looked around with surprise as if it were a room she'd never seen before and then said, "Would you like to see some of my pictures?" The two of them sat down on the bed, and Rena pulled out canvasses and sketch pads filled with drawings. They were very good, revealing a talent for drawing that Deborah praised. "I can't draw a stick, myself," she laughed, "but you have real talent. Do any of the rest of your family paint or draw?"

This led Rena to speak of her family, and she revealed a great deal of herself in her description. She spoke warmly of her brothers, but hardly mentioned her mother. When she spoke cautiously of her father, her eyes revealed what Deborah recognized as a deep longing. Deborah soon had the whole story, how Ellen Rocklin had in effect abdicated her responsibility as a mother years ago. If Clay had abandoned his family physically, Ellen had done the same emotionally and spiritually. Although Rena didn't realize it, she revealed to the quick mind of her guest how she had missed having a mother and how she had hated her father for leaving them. The story of Buck's attack on Clay came out, and Rena's eyes grew warm as she spoke of how her father had let her help him fix his books, and how he sometimes read to her. Then she said uncertainly, "Maybe I shouldn't spend so much time with him. Dent says it's wrong. He says that he doesn't deserve to be trusted."

What an awful, pompous boor Mr. Denton Rocklin must be! Deborah thought with a stab of contempt, but said, "Oh, I don't think that's right, Rena. I like your father very much."

"You do?"

"Why, certainly. He made some bad mistakes, but we have to give people a second chance, don't we? You know what I think?"

"What?"

"I think your father is a very lonely man. And I think it's fine that you're spending a lot of time with him."

A look of relief washed across Rena's face, and she smiled at Deborah, saying, "He's really changed! I know he has! And I'm going to tell Dent to mind his own business!"

Good for you! Deborah thought, but said no more. Then Rena asked, "Would you do something for me? Something really big?"

Deborah hesitated, but when she saw the eager look in the girl's eyes she said, "If I can, Rena."

"Ask Mama if I can go to the Christmas party in Richmond with you." She began speaking quickly, as if to forestall any arguments. "Mama thinks I'm such a baby! She says I'm too young for a ball, but I don't think fourteen is too young, do you, Deborah?"

"Well, I don't think so, Rena—but I can't go against your mother on something like this."

"She doesn't really care! She just doesn't want to have to watch after me. But if you tell her that you want me to go, and that you'll watch me, she'll say yes. Oh, please, Deborah! I don't want to stay home by myself!"

Deborah's father often said, "Daughter, your spiritual gift is meddling!" And she realized that it was true. Something told her not to get involved with the internal affairs of the Rocklin family, but she was not far enough away from the age of fourteen to forget what a trying time it was. The pleading expression on Rena's face was more than she could bear, so she suddenly laughed and hugged the girl. "We'll do it, Rena! And you can get your father to give you a new dress."

"Oh, he'd never do that!"

"Fathers will do anything for their daughters, Rena," Deborah said confidentially, nodding. "But you have to butter them up a little."

"Butter them up how?"

"Oh, sit on their lap, run your fingers through their hair, tickle their ears. They like that a lot." She laughed at Rena's expression and hugged her again. "It's something you can work on. Now, let's go talk to your mother."

Major Robert Anderson was a lean, clean-shaven, graying veteran, noted both for an excellent combat record in the Black Hawk and Mexican wars and for a mildly bookish quality that was somewhat rare among army officers. He was also a Southerner, of Virginian ancestry, and some of the officers at Fort Sumter told each other that he had been chosen by Secretary of War Floyd because he was proslavery.

Gideon stood with his commanding officer on the battlements of Fort Moultrie in Charleston Harbor. It was cold, with a stiff wind pushing against them, and Major Anderson had to raise his voice as he explained the military situation to his newest officer.

"A poor way to spend Christmas, Major Rocklin," Anderson said, "but we've got no choice." He went on to

explain carefully what he was doing in Charleston, most
of which Gid knew already. "South Carolina seceded
from the Union, as you know, five days ago. The next
step they will make is to take over these Union forts."

"You really think they'll attack, sir?"

"No doubt about it. And look at what we have—our
main base here at Fort Moultrie is completely vulnerable
to land attack from the rear." Anderson turned to face his
subordinate, remarking, "My father, Captain Richard
Anderson, defended this fort during the Revolution.
Now I have to defend it from our own people—and it
cannot be done!"

"I take it you have a plan?"

"Yes. Clearly the most advantageous place to make a
stand is Fort Sumter. It's an island fort, only about three
miles from Charleston, but we have heavy guns there.
Since we can't hold Fort Moultrie, we'll shift all the men
to Fort Sumter."

"Yes sir. When are you thinking of moving?"

Anderson was a sober man, burdened with an awesome responsibility, but he smiled slightly as he answered Gid's question. "Tonight."

Gid was startled. "On Christmas night?" Then he nodded. "No one will expect us to do such a thing. And I remember what Tom Jackson said when we were in
Mexico—always try to do what your enemy will never
suspect!"

Anderson nodded absently, then said quietly, "Take
charge of loading the equipment, Major Rocklin." He
turned to go, but hesitated, then said, "Merry Christmas,
Major."

"'And God bless us every one,' as Tiny Tim put it," Gid
replied, and then the two men moved away from the biting sea wind.

"I don't see why I have to keep track of an old abolitionist!"

Denton and David had come back from their trip late

in the afternoon, and Dent was informed by Susanna that he would be expected to escort his cousin, Deborah Steele, to the Christmas ball. Dent had other plans—he had been engaged in a lively contest with Jackie Terrel for the favors of Mary Ann Small. "She's probably as ugly as homemade soap," he grumbled, then brightened up as he thought of a solution. "Let David take her, Grandmother."

"He's taking Lorella Ballentine," Susanna said briskly. An impish thought came to her, and she said, "It will be a good deed for you, Denton. The poor girl is rather homely. I'd venture a guess that she never had a real live young man to take her to a ball. It's Christmas. You can bring some cheer into a dreary life. Isn't that what Christmas is all about?"

Dent grumbled, but he knew that he was doomed. He could get around his mother, but he had never been able to circumvent any plan that his grandmother decided on. He went off to dress, and Susanna quickly told the other members of the family what she'd done. David fell to laughing at once, and the others thought it would serve Dent right. He was always playing some practical joke on others, and it was only fair for them to get him back!

Susanna went to Deborah's room and said, "My dear, I've done a dreadful thing. . . . " When she told her story, Deborah laughed out loud, delighted at the chance to see young Mr. Denton suffer. Susanna said, "I'll come in and help you fix your hair. I want you to look like an angel tonight!"

David was not given to practical jokes, but he entered into this one. A few minutes before time for the carriage to leave, he went to the bedroom he shared with Dent. Putting a somber look on his face, he said, "Well, Dent, one good thing about this, you won't have to do it but once. I mean, Christmas only comes but once a year. And she'll be going back to Washington pretty soon, I suppose."

Dent stared at him. "She's pretty ugly, David?"

"Well, look at it like this, Dent," David said with a pained expression, throwing himself into his role, "beauty is only skin-deep."

Dent swore, then gave the desk before him a sound kick. "Well, why don't you go skin her, then?" He was deeply depressed, and raved about what an awful woman his grandmother was to force him into such a thing. Finally he was ready—at least he was dressed—but he stood there, his lip sticking out mulishly. "I don't think I'm well, David. Just go tell Grandmother—"

"You know that won't work," David broke in, shaking his head. "Come on, Dent. Might as well get it over with. Tell you what, I'll dance with her twice myself! Now there's brotherly love for you—considering what she looks like!"

Dent followed David down the stairs, and found the rest of the family waiting at the foot of the great staircase. "Well, why don't you go on and laugh!" he exploded when Lowell tried to stifle a giggle behind his hand and Rena grinned at him broadly. "Fine family you are!" he burst out bitterly. "Spoiling my whole Christmas!"

"You've got to learn to take your medicine with less fuss, my boy," his grandfather said. Thomas could scarcely keep his face straight, and when Dent looked down with a scowl, he winked at Clay. "I understand that the young lady makes up in scholarship what she lacks in personal attraction, Clay."

"Why, that's correct, Father," Clay said blandly. "She's quite a marvel in theology, I believe. Dent, ask her about her views on hyper-Calvinism and a second work of grace. I think you'll benefit from her knowledge."

Dent gave both of them an angry look, and then Lowell said, "There she comes!"

Dent was aware that the entire family was having a great time at his expense, and he hated it. Determined not to give them any satisfaction, he didn't even look up, but stared out the window. "Dent, this is your cousin,

Deborah Steele. I know you'll take good care of her at the ball tonight," Susanna said.

Dent knew that he'd have to look at the girl. He couldn't avoid that, of course! He lifted his eyes and, at the same time, started to mutter some fitting remark—but he could not get it out of his mouth.

The girl who stood before him was the most beautiful thing he'd ever seen in his life!

He felt as if he had been struck a blow in the pit of the stomach, and his brain seemed to go dead. His eyes were working, however, and he stared at her while waiting for his voice and mind to come back to life.

Deborah was wearing an evening gown of magenta silk, which was cut slightly lower than the going fashion. She had picked it out because she knew her father would never permit her to wear it, and even Susanna had been a little apprehensive. But the gown suited her somehow, bringing out her flawless complexion, and the tiara she wore was a dramatic touch that drew the eye at once. Her strange violet-colored eyes looked enormous, and her lips were full and rosy as she smiled at Dent.

"How do you do, Mr. Rocklin?" she asked demurely.

"Uh—fine!" Dent stammered. He was not usually shy, but the beauty of this girl affected him strangely.

"Your family has told me how much you've looked forward to taking me to the ball—"

Deborah never finished, because Thomas Rocklin let out a great whoop of laughter at the comical expression on Dent's face, and then all of the family joined in. Only Ellen didn't laugh, for she had not been in on the joke.

Dent stared around wildly, thinking his family had gone mad—and then it came to him. A rich crimson color came to his face, and then it ebbed, leaving him pale. He had the impulse to turn and leave the room, but somehow he could not do it. He saw that his grandmother was smiling at him, and managed to say reproachfully, "I didn't think you could stoop so low, Grandmother!"

The look on his face sent them all off into fresh gales of

laughter. Finally Deborah said, "I won't hold you to such a bargain, Mr. Rocklin. Practical jokes are always a little unkind, aren't they?"

Dent looked very uncomfortable, and managed to say, "I think I understand that now for the first time. I'll be very cautious about pulling one in the future." Then he said, "But now that the joke is over, I'm delighted to meet you."

Thomas found his grandson's reformation amusing. "You young devil! Miss Deborah, I suggest that you cast this fellow aside. I'll find you a suitable escort when we get to the ball."

Deborah smiled, and Dent was intrigued at the two small dimples that appeared in her cheeks. "Thank you, Uncle Thomas. That's very gracious of you." She didn't look at Dent as she added, "I suppose all Southern men can't be gallant, can they?"

Dent straightened his back and determined to escort the girl if it snowed ink! "Miss Deborah, I must confess that I've behaved very badly. But you'll surely give me an opportunity to redeem myself? I ask it as a favor."

You are a devil! Deborah thought. *And good-looking as sin! Better-looking even than your father, and that's saying a lot. I think you haven't suffered enough yet—* "Why, that's very gallant, sir." She smiled and took the arm Dent offered. "While we're on the way to the ball, let me tell you about some of the latest doctrinal problems that have come up in these trying days. . . ."

Dent knew she was tormenting him, but he didn't care in the least. He had completely forgotten that he was supposed to be contesting with Jackie Terrel for the favors of some girl—whatever her name was!

Deborah Steele was the belle of the ball. She was a Yankee and, some said, an abolitionist—but as one young man noted, "She can be a retarded Buddhist for all I care! With a face and figure like that, I'd just 'bout be ready to join up with the Yankees if that's what she wanted!"

Deborah had a wonderful time, enjoying the antics of the young men who vied over her dances. She tormented Dent fully, but she gave much of her time to Rena. She had helped the girl with a dress, and the two of them sat and giggled as often as Deborah could fight off her admirers.

She forced Clay to ask her to dance, then said, "It would be nice if you would ask Rena to dance, Mr. Rocklin."

Clay smiled. "I don't even know if she can dance."

"Of course she can! All fourteen-year-old girls can dance. It's born in them. And you two would look so nice!"

"I'll do it!" Clay stared at her, then shook his head. "Miss Deborah Steele, you're a caution!"

Deborah hesitated, then said daringly, "I can tell what you're thinking. Did you know I can read minds?"

"What am I thinking?"

"You're wishing that I were Melora Yancy!" Clay stiffened, and she saw that she had overstepped her bounds. At once her hand tightened on his arm, and she whispered, "I'm so sorry! I'm a witless fool!"

Clay blinked, amazed to see tears glisten in her eyes. She really was sorry, he saw. "I want to see Melora have something better," he said finally. "One of the finest men I know wants to marry her. It would be good if she'd take him."

He said no more, but the joy was gone out of his face, and Deborah was sorry she'd mentioned Melora. When the dance was over, she found Dent at her side, demanding a dance. But before it got well under way, he maneuvered her out of the ballroom into a hallway that led to a small sun-room with huge glass windows. It was empty, and he said at once, "I brought you out here to ask you to go to a ball with me." He was wearing a gray suit, and his black hair and fine figure made him quite dashing. "Next week, at my aunt's house. Will you go?"

"I don't think so," Deborah said. "We laughed at you

for not wanting to take a homely girl to a ball. I suppose that's common, so I don't really blame you for that. But I still won't go to the ball with you."

Dent was stung. "Am I too Southern for you?"

"Probably. But that's not it either." She looked up at him coolly and said, "I like your father very much. I think he's a fine man."

Dent stared at her. "Well, what's that got to do with going to a ball with me?"

Deborah said clearly, "I don't like the way you treat him, Mr. Rocklin. He made a bad mistake, but you're making a worse one. He abandoned his family, which is a terrible thing to do. But you're standing in judgment on him, refusing to forgive. That, in my opinion, is a worse thing to do."

Dent turned pale and said bitterly, "Easy for you to make judgments, isn't it, Miss Steele? But aren't you judging me, just as you say I'm judging my father?"

"Don't you see the difference? I'm a stranger to you. A few more weeks and you won't see me again. But Clay Rocklin is your father. You'll never have another one. I think you're headed for a terrible fall, Dent," she said. "Anyone who won't forgive is going to have problems."

Dent was furious—and deep down, he was terribly ashamed. He had struggled with his bitterness, but it had been a silent struggle. Now this snip of a girl had laid it bare!

Her very beauty made it worse! He stood there, fists clenched, then suddenly reached out and pulled her close. Her eyes opened wide with shock, and then he was kissing her. It was an angry kiss on his part, something to hurt her. If she had been a man, he would have struck her with his fist. But since that was out of the question . . .

And yet, even as his lips bruised hers, he felt something sweet in her. Despite all her puffed-up knowledge and wrong ideas, he felt himself change, loosening his tight grip, but keeping his lips on hers. Finally he thought he felt her respond, and when he pulled back, he said in an unsteady voice, "Deborah, you're an awful person in lots of ways, but you've got something that gets to a man!"

Deborah Steele had been kissed before—but never had she felt such a powerful emotion. She stared at Denton, wanting to hurt him, and finally said, "Well, we're kissing cousins, it seems! And I can tell you've had a great deal of practice."

"Deborah—!"

"Never mind. Let's go back to the ballroom."

Both of them were shaken by the experience, and both were angry. Clay saw them return, and said to his mother, "I think our Dent got his feathers singed!"

The ball went on.

Far away in Charleston, Gideon Rocklin was in a boat with a full load of soldiers. The water was cold, and the men were doused by the high waves that threatened to swamp the boats.

By dawn the next morning Gideon said wearily, "All the men are disembarked, Major."

Anderson looked at him, his own face gray with fatigue.

"Very well, sir. Now, we'll wait for them to come!"

CHAPTER TWENTY-ONE

"I CAN BE ALONE!"

THE YEAR of 1861 did not come in gently for America. Ferment in the North and in the South stirred, and angry men on both sides pushed the two sections closer to the brink of war. President Buchanan, never a strong leader and now a lame duck, was so out of touch with things that it was Senator Jefferson Davis who had come to his office and broken the news to him that Major Anderson had spiked his guns at Fort Moultrie and moved his garrison to Fort Sumter. The senator had added, "And now, Mr. President, you are surrounded with blood and dishonor on all sides."

But Buchanan seemed to be completely paralyzed and did nothing but wait for Lincoln to assume the burden. On January 5, General Scott sent the *Star of the West*, a merchant vessel, with two hundred troops to reinforce Major Anderson at Sumter. But the ship was driven off by cannon fire aimed by a South Carolina battery and had to make her way back home with the troops. All that had been accomplished was to pour oil on the fire. Robert Barnwell Rhett, the fire-eating editor of the *Charleston Mercury*, wrote that "powder has been burnt over the degrees of our state, and the firing on the *Star of the West* is the opening ball of the Revolution. South Carolina is honored to be the first thus to resist the Yankee tyranny. She has not hesitated to strike the first blow, full in the face of her insulter."

Major Anderson had not even been informed that reinforcements were coming, and when he had joined his staff at the sound of cannon fire, none of them knew what was happening. When they learned that their reinforcements were not coming, Anderson said bleakly, "Major Rocklin, our enemies may not have to take our position by attack. If supplies don't arrive soon, we'll be starved out!"

"They'll come, Major," Gid said confidently.

But they did not come, and the weeks passed with an agonizing slowness for the little company on the island fortress. The Southern states began to coalesce, with Mississippi voting eighty-four to fifteen in favor of secession, and ten days later, on January 10, Florida joined Mississippi and South Carolina. A day later Alabama left the union. Finally, in February, the secessionist delegates met in Montgomery, Alabama, to set up their Southern nation. Jefferson Davis was elected as the first president, and when the word of his election came to him, his face paled. He said then and repeated later that he had not wanted the office. Rather he had hoped for command of the Confederacy's army.

So it went, ponderously at first, like a juggernaut. From time to time, Melanie would ride out to Sumter and spend time with Gideon. She gave him reports on the boys. She told him of Deborah's visit at Gracefield, which had been extended.

"It can't go on like this, Mellie," Gid told her one cold February morning as she waited for the boat to take her back to her rooming house in Charleston. "It's like a powderhouse, and sooner or later one spark is going to set the whole thing off!"

Back at Gracefield, Clay was running into problems, too. He had made many friends since coming back to his home, but now he was losing them fast. He tried to be moderate, but after one of his oldest friends left him angrily, Clay said to Jeremiah Irons, "It's like the last judgment, Jeremiah. There are only sheep and goats— nothing in between. A man's got to either be all-out for this war and slavery, or he's a Yankee abolitionist."

Irons studied Clay carefully. They were riding toward

the Yancy place, meeting Buford for a hunting trip. For both of them it was an escape from the pressures of life, for the minister was in little better shape than Clay. He had tried to speak of patience, of trying to work things out with the North, and had been branded a traitor by some of his most prominent board members.

"What will you do, Clay?" he asked suddenly. "If war comes, you'll have to decide. As you say, there's no such thing as neutrality in this thing."

"I have no idea, Jerry. What will you do?"

Irons shrugged, and the two men rode on silently, both deep in thought. "I've got fine friends in the North, Clay," Irons said finally. "Hate to think about fighting them."

"And there are Rocklins who'll be wearing Union uniforms. How can I shoot at my own family?"

It was a discussion that was going on all over the country, and no one ever reached an answer. In the end, the two men veered away from the subject. "That young woman, Deborah, has certainly plowed up a snake!"

"You mean with Dent? She sure has. I expect those two will have to be separated before they shoot each other! They get into those awful arguments about slavery that serve no purpose. I like the girl, but she ought to go home."

Irons thought about it, then remarked, "Melora says she's attracted to Dent."

Clay stared at him, then laughed. "Well, she takes a funny way of showing it! Dent's been pretty cool toward me since I came back, but I feel sorry for the boy. He's so besotted with that girl he can't see straight, but he's got as much chance of getting her as—as—"

"As I have of getting Melora," Irons finished gloomily.

Clay glanced at his friend, not sure what to make of that remark. "Don't give up, Jerry," he said quietly. "Melora's worth waiting for."

"Clay, I don't think she'll ever marry."

They got to the Yancy cabin and found Buford ready to

go. To their surprise they found Melora dressed in her old overalls, obviously ready to join the hunt. "I'm not getting left behind this time," she declared.

"Who's going to watch the kids?" Clay asked.

"Lonnie and Bobby, that's who!" Buford declared grimly. "They don't deserve to go with growed-up men!" He refused to say what the boys had done to disgrace themselves, but it must have been serious. Buford shook his head, saying, "Do them good to learn to act like grown people instead of babies!"

They all got in the wagon that carried the tents and the supplies, and they drove for hours. The deep woods began to close about them late that afternoon, but they pressed on until dusk. Pulling the team up, Buford said, "You two fellers get the tents up. I'll do the important things—like catching some bullhead catfish outta that crick."

Clay and Jeremiah began to set up the tents, but made such a mess out of it that they began to argue, each convinced that the other was incompetent. Melora came over from where she was building a fire to cook the hypothetical fish that her father was to bring and began to laugh at them. "Two grown men, and you can't put up a tent!"

"Well, if the preacher would just do what I tell him to do—!" Clay sputtered.

"I was putting up tents when you were in diapers!" Jeremiah snapped back, which seemed unlikely since the two men were the same age.

Finally the tents were up, Buford returned with a fine string of catfish, which he cleaned, and in good time they were sitting around the fire eating fresh fish and hush puppies, washing it all down with strong black coffee.

"I think a few of those big black bugs hit the grease the fish were in," Melora remarked. "It was too dark to see."

"Anybody who objects to a few black bugs in his fish don't deserve no consideration," her father pronounced. Then he proceeded to ask Jeremiah, "What's the meaning of the beast that came up out of the sea in the thirteenth chapter of Revelations, Reverend? The one with the seven heads and the ten horns?"

"Buford, don't you start on me with your endless questions about prophecy!" Jeremiah protested. "Let's just hunt and fish and rest."

Buford was offended. "Well, it's important, ain't it? Wouldn't be in the Bible if it wasn't!"

"Yes, yes, it's important, Buford," Jeremiah said wearily, "but I just don't know what the blamed beast means!"

Clay and Melora looked across the fire at each other, smiling at the pair. They had often laughed at the dogged manner in which Buford asked question after question on the more obscure sections of the Bible, while Jeremiah was interested in more practical things—such as how to get his members to stop gossiping!

The four of them sat around the fire for a long time, listening to the occasional cry of a night bird and, more than once, the plaintive wail of a coyote. Melora kept the coffeepot going, saying little, listening as the men talked. Mostly they didn't speak of the war or of politics. Instead, they discussed farming, horses, and dogs—simple things that men enjoy. Jeremiah told stories of his boyhood in Arkansas, of the hard life in the back reaches of the Ozark mountains where shoes were a luxury.

Finally they went to bed, Melora in the small tent and the three men in the large one. Wrapped in blankets up to her eyes, Melora lay there, listening to the night sounds for a long time. Then she dropped off to sleep. She awoke to the smell of bacon and fresh coffee. When she emerged from her tent, she found her father cooking eggs in the bacon grease. "The preacher and Clay took off 'fore dawn," he remarked. "Thought they might get a shot at a buck down where we seen them big tracks. Here, pitch into this bacon, Daughter."

Melora took the plate, ate bacon and eggs, then sat back to drink coffee. The air was cold, but she liked it that way. "Funny the way you decided to come along on this trip," Buford said. "But I'm glad you did." He was watching her as she drank the coffee, and thoughtfully he remarked, "You ort to get married. I feel bad that you've spent your whole life taking care of the kids." He tossed the stick he was whittling on to the ground, his face as sober as she had ever seen it. He was not a man of deep thought, Melora realized, but something was troubling him. He sought for what was inside him, then said simply, "I should have got married again when your mother died. I could have done it."

"Why didn't you, Pa? Most men would have."

He was embarrassed at what was in his heart, and he struggled with it. Finally he said, "I never seen a woman I liked as much as I did your ma. She was . . . special, you know?"

Melora realized that poets had been writing about love that never died for thousands of years. But it was a rare thing, she understood. Now, here in the deep woods, she found it—not in a prince, but in Buford Yancy, with his stubble of a beard, rough hands, and rougher speech. She said quietly, "That's real sweet, Pa."

Yancy was embarrassed and hurried to say, "Well, I don't know about that, but I do know I've robbed you of your youth, Daughter." A question came to his lips, but after glancing at her, he seemed awkward and ill at ease. Finally he voiced it. "The preacher wants to marry you right bad."

It was, she realized, his way of asking her to share her feelings with him. But it was not easy—for she herself was confused about the thing.

"I wish he would find somebody else," she finally said. Now it was her turn to search for words. Like her father, she had difficulty putting into words the deep feelings that ran through her. Finally she said, "I like him so much, it'd be easy to just give up and marry him. The kids are old enough now so they aren't much trouble. I could help him with his two, and I guess I could learn to be a preacher's wife—but not a good one."

"Why not? You're a good Christian girl."

"Not the same thing, Pa," she said slowly. "I've been free all my life. Oh, I've had to do my work and watch the children, but a preacher's wife doesn't have much freedom." She smiled at him, adding, "For example, I don't think I ever heard of a minister's wife going hunting with a bunch of men!"

He said, "You could do it if you set your mind. I'd feel better about you, Daughter."

She got up and went to him and, bending over, kissed his cheek. "Don't worry about me, Pa." She left him at the fire, and there was no more discussion with him on that subject. But she knew that he was worried—and hated to cause him grief.

The weather warmed up, and for two days the four of them had a fine time. Melora didn't want to shoot anything, but she enjoyed walking through the woods. She had brought her notebook and filled it with her "scribbling" during that time.

On the third day Jeremiah took it into his head that he had to have a wild turkey. They had bagged everything else: coon, possum, a fat deer, even three ducks from a pond. "I've got a special feeling for wild turkey," Irons announced on the morning of the last day.

"Wild turkey's about the slyest thing in the woods, Preacher," Buford said, shaking his head. "Offhand, I don't think I see but one feller in this camp who can git one."

Both Jeremiah and Clay at once began to deride him, and after breakfast they all set off for a place that was stiff with wild toms, according to Buford. They made a bet that the one who got the biggest turkey got to tell the other two what to do. "I got some fencing that needs to be put up," Buford said with a grin. "I can see now that you two boys are just the pair to do it."

They left right away, riding the two mules that had pulled the wagon, Clay and Buford sharing one of the animals. Melora began to pack some of the gear, but about ten o'clock she took a line and went fishing in the stream. The fish were uneducated, and she caught enough for supper in thirty minutes. She went back to the camp, and ten minutes after she arrived, she was surprised to see Clay come riding in on one of the mules.

"What did you forget?"

"I forgot to watch where I was walking," Clay said. He slid off the mule and hopped on one foot as he tied the mule up. Then he hopped painfully toward the fire, his face drawn with pain.

"What's wrong with your foot?" Melora asked.

"Stepped in a hole and twisted my ankle," he said in disgust. "We stopped down by the river and poked around looking for bear sign. I stepped into a hole and darn near broke my leg! Your dad and Jeremiah wanted to turn back, but I wouldn't let them. No reason why my clumsiness should keep them from having a good time."

"Let's get that boot off," Melora said. "I'll heat some water."

The ankle was not badly twisted, but it was painful. As Clay looked at it stretched out before him, he remarked, "I always forget if you put cold compresses or hot cloths on a sprained leg."

"Hot," Melora announced. She had heated the water and began to put the hot cloths on the injured leg. "Be still!" she said. "You behave worse than Toby!"

"Well, those things are too hot," he complained. He watched as she held the compress in place, then said, "You've had to treat just about every sort of sickness and accident, haven't you, Melora?"

"Oh yes. Most doctoring is just common sense." She knelt at his feet, holding the compress and speaking of some of the aches and pains the children had had. He admired the firm set of her jaw and saw that she had a faint line of freckles across her nose that he'd never noticed. She was a slim woman, but there was a pleasing roundness to her. Despite the rough clothing, there was a grace about her, and Clay said suddenly, "Been a long time since you fed me soup and nursed me. You're all grown up now, but I still remember that little girl. All eyes and as somber as a tree full of owls. I'd never been around children then, and I thought you were normal."

She laughed then, her green eyes glinting in the sun. "Why, I *was* normal!"

"No, you were never normal," he said. "You've always been different, Melora." She looked up at him quickly and saw that his eyes were half-closed. "All those years I was gone, I dreamed a lot about home, but mostly about you. I guess I can remember every moment of those times. I went over them again and again. It was like—like having an album filled with pictures, Melora, those times with you. And I'd go over and over them, until I guess they became clearer to me than anything else in the world."

Melora stood up and held the compress in her hands. Her eyes fell, and she whispered, "I did the same."

"You did?" Clay asked quickly. "I never knew that!"

"I was always a romantic thing, I guess. Remember how I always wanted books about knights and castles? Well, life was pretty drab, I suppose, so I remembered your visits and how we read *Pilgrim's Progress* and *Gulliver's Travels* together."

She came to stand beside him, saying, "You've got to keep off that foot. Come on. I'll help you to your tent."

Clay struggled to his feet, saying, "If you'll get me a stick—"

"I will, but first you need to lie down and keep the weight off that foot. Lean on me, now."

Clay put his right arm around her shoulders, and she bore most of his weight as they moved to the tent. When they went inside, he started to let himself down, but his leg gave way, and the suddenness of it made him grab at her for support. He pulled her down as he fell and hit the ground with a grunt, still holding on to her.

Melora was lying across his chest, and when she lifted her head, she started to laugh. "You're clumsy—," she said, then broke off. His face was only inches away from hers, and she suddenly read the longing in his eyes. She caught her breath, but seemed unable to move. The pressure of her soft body on his was both a torment and a delight to Clay.

It was as though time had stopped for both of them. Clay was thinking, *No, this is wrong!* but at the same time, he was realizing that he had wanted to reach out and touch this woman for years. It came as a shock to him, for there was a picture in his mind of a child who fed him soup, or a girl of twelve who loved books. Now he knew that he could never think of her in quite the same way again.

And Melora was thinking, *At last he knows I'm a woman! He's always ignored the fact that I grew up. But I can see in his eyes that he's thinking of me as a man thinks of a woman.*

Then without thinking she lowered her head and put her soft lips on his. It was as natural to her as breathing, for she meant only to show how she cared for him, was grateful to him. That was the beginning, but it was not the end, for slowly she became aware that this was not the caress of a child. Something powerful and strong began to form within her, and she could feel his recognition of the same force. His arms tightened, and the pressure of his lips grew more demanding.

How long that kiss lasted, she never knew—nor did he. Nor did they ever know which of them first realized the potent danger of what was happening. But however it was, Melora reluctantly moved her head, and then she stood to her feet. But she did not leave. Something kept her there, and then Clay said, "That was very wrong of me, Melora."

"Wrong of me, too, Clay," she said quietly.

He struggled to a sitting position. "Come down here. I can't talk with you up there." He waited until she was kneeling and studied her face. With one hand he reached out and brushed her hair from her forehead. "Don't be upset by this, Melora. It's not your fault."

Melora said slowly, "I think you'd better know. I'm in love with you, Clay. I have been for years."

"Melora!" he cried out as if she had struck him. "You mustn't say such a thing. It's not true!"

She looked at him, her eyes enormous in the gloom of the tent. "You may not love me. But I'll always love you."

He stared at her helplessly, then suddenly groaned and pulled her to his chest. "God help me! I love you, too, Melora!" He held her for only a moment, then released her. She watched him calmly, and he said, "It's a sad thing, Melora, for both of us. In the first place, I'm too old for you. And besides that, I'm already married."

Melora said, "Yes, I know that. Not that you're too old. But that you have a wife. She's no wife to you, I know that, too. I know how lonely you get. I get lonely, too." She bit her lip, adding, "Clay, don't let my love be a burden to you. It's the finest thing in my life—the most real thing. I can never have you, I know that. I've always known that. But it helps to know . . . that you care for me."

She got up and turned to go, but then his voice caught her. "Melora, marry Jeremiah! Be a wife to him! He loves you."

Melora shook her head. "No. I'll never marry Jeremiah—or anyone else."

"You can't be alone!"

"Yes, I can be alone. I'm strong enough for that, Clay. I have God, and now I know that you love me. That's all I need."

She left the tent then and went into the woods. For an hour she walked under the thick foliage. Then she came back and found him sitting in front of the fire, his leg stretched out. When she spoke, her voice was without strain. "Let's be friends. As we've always been. We can have that, can't we? If we can't have anything else, let's have that."

"Wouldn't we have to be on guard? Wouldn't it feel odd?"

"No. Let's talk about books, and you listen to me read out of my notebook. Come and see Pa, and sometimes

CHAPTER TWENTY-TWO

BEFORE THE STORM

As THE air sometimes grows utterly still before the power of a hurricane is unleashed, so a time of peace came to Gracefield. Susanna commented on it as she and Deborah were walking across to the slave quarters. The two had become quite close, and the younger woman had learned to trust the heart of the older, even though she did not agree with her ideas on slavery.

Susanna said as they passed Box, who at the age of sixty-nine was still able to do some work at the forge, "I feel so strange, Deborah. The whole country is falling apart, with all the politicians screaming for war. And yet everything seems so peaceful." As they came to the row of cabins that housed the slaves, she added, "I'm afraid, for the first time. There's something ominous about this time."

Deborah nodded, saying, "I am, too. I got a letter from my father yesterday. He wants me to come home."

"I'll miss you, Deborah." Susanna turned a smile on the girl, adding, "But if you don't go home, you're going to drive Dent crazy. I've never seen anyone so lovesick. It's like something out of a bad romance."

Deborah didn't return the smile. "Aunt Susanna, I . . . I haven't told anyone, but . . ."

She paused, but the older woman nodded at once, her face gentle and filled with a sudden concern. "I know. You feel something for him, don't you, Deborah?"

"It's insane, of course," Deborah said quickly, her face slightly tinged with a flush that made her look very young. "We don't agree on a single thing, I suppose. Every time we get together it winds up in a blazing row."

She fell silent and then after a moment said with a burst of honesty, "But you're right, Aunt Susanna, I do feel something for Dent! It's not that he's fine-looking. I don't care about that. He's bursting with all this Southern pride . . . 'Any Southerner can handle six Yankees!' But I have this feeling that beneath all that bluster, there's something very real about Dent."

"You see his father in him," Susanna suggested. "You're very fond of Clay. Anyone can see that. And Clay's got the same stuff." Her eyes grew nostalgic, and she said, "When Clay was nineteen, he was exactly as Dent is now. Unfortunately, Dent's got the same weaknesses that Clay had then—he's too impulsive, too self-centered."

"But Clay got over all that."

"Yes, but God only knows what hell he had to go through to do so. And he's still paying for some of it."

"He and Ellen, do you think they'll ever put their marriage together?"

"I doubt it. They were never suited from the beginning, and she's grown . . . more careless over the years."

Deborah hesitated, then said, "I think he's fond of Melora Yancy."

Susanna was startled by the young woman's perception. She had long known that Clay was half in love with the woman, but she had said nothing to anyone. "It can never come to anything, Deborah. I know you won't say anything to anyone."

"No, of course not. I just feel bad for them."

Susanna gave her a sudden hug. "You're a kind girl, Deborah. I wish Dent were more mature."

"Maybe I could marry him and raise him right! Housebreak him and all."

"Never try that!" Susanna said with a wry smile. "If a man doesn't change before a woman marries him, she'll not be able to do anything with him afterward. These Rocklin men are stubborn, anyway. They have to beat their head against a stone wall to get any sense knocked into them. Now, come along, and we'll get all the chores done, then go into Richmond for a wild shopping spree!"

Jake Slocum was a man of little sensitivity. He did, however, have pride in one thing: his ability to handle women. From his youth, he had known how to get women to surrender to his attentions. Certain women, that is—and it galled him that he was being denied by Ellen Rocklin.

He had pursued her for some time before she had agreed to meet him, and of all the women he had known, she was the one he prized most. For one thing, she was of a higher class than most of his women. Slocum was a small-time planter, with only eight slaves on his relatively small plantation. He blustered and shoved his way into the small group of prosperous planters who owned the really huge plantations and hundreds of slaves. But he knew they only tolerated him. He had pursued several of the wives and daughters of these men, finding more pleasure in the fact that he was irritating the men than from his flirtations with their women.

Though Slocum was not a handsome man, he was powerful and bold, and some women were drawn to this. He was a large man, six feet two, and weighed 220 pounds. Always dressed in the finest clothing, which he bought in New Orleans, he was an impressive man physically. He had a shock of heavy, slightly wavy blond hair and a pair of aggressive blue eyes. His face was broad and his mouth wide in a sensual way. His reputation as a womanizer was equalled by his reputation as a fighting man. He steered clear of pistol duels, preferring to be known as a bruising fistfighter. It was what he liked best, and he had destroyed many men with his massive fists.

But Slocum was unhappy now, for his conquest of Ellen Rocklin had backfired. He had won her after a long pursuit, longer than he normally gave to most of his conquests, but it had been worth it to him. Slocum had little taste for finer qualities in women, and Ellen proved to be more troublesome than he had expected. She had been adamant about their meetings, controlling them so that they never became publicly known. This had displeased Slocum, who wanted the world to know of his victory in charming the wife of a prominent planter, but she had refused to be seen with him in public.

And now, without warning, she had dropped him, which was a severe blow to Slocum's pride. He had persuaded her to meet him in Richmond, and she had finally agreed. He had taken a room at a third-rate hotel, where the clerk could not have cared less who made their way up the rickety staircase to the seedy rooms on the second floor. He had given scarcely a glance at Slocum and Ellen as they had gone upstairs, but had leaned back and dozed off.

When the door closed, Slocum got a rude shock, for when he came over to put his arms around Ellen as she stood there, she said, "Jake, I'm not coming to you like this anymore."

He blinked, then anger rose in him. He turned her around, kissed her hard, then said, "Sure you are! You're as crazy about me as I am about you."

But she had simply waited until he released her, then turned and said in a sharp tone, "It's too risky. And I'm sick of these awful rooms."

"We could go to my place," he said. "It's a fine house, and nobody would know."

"Yes, they would," she said calmly. "You've got slaves and a housekeeper. Word would be out in Richmond the next day."

"What difference does it make? Who cares what the hypocrites say?"

"I care, Jake." Ellen turned away from him, thinking quietly for a moment, then added, "You men can do what you please and still be accepted. It's a matter of pride, how many women you have. But it's different with a woman. Clay and I are nothing to each other, but as his wife I'm accepted in the best homes in the county."

"People know you haven't been a saint," Slocum growled.

"They may think it, Jake, but they don't know it. Because I've been—discreet. That's why we can't meet anymore. At least for a while. You talk too much, and much as I like you, I'm not about to give up everything for you. Now if you want to marry me—," she said, turning to look at him, but his expression gave him away, and she laughed harshly, adding, "No, you want your fun, but you want me to pay for it. Well, you'll just have to wait until it's safer."

"I don't have to wait for a woman!"

"For this one you do." Her face was set as she adjusted her coat, a beautiful silver fox. "It's not going to be easy for me. Clay's not much, but at least he's safe. He doesn't need me, but he doesn't want any other woman either."

Slocum gave her a rough grin. "Don't be too sure about that, Ellen."

She had started to turn, but stopped to stare at him. "What's that supposed to mean?"

"You don't know about your husband and Melora Yancy?" Slocum saw the sudden shock on Ellen's face and knew he had found a way to bring her to heel. "I thought you knew," he said casually. "He's been chasing around after her for a long time."

"That's ridiculous! She's poor white trash!"

"I guess maybe she is, but she's mighty gorgeous trash."

"Clay's got better sense," Ellen argued. "He's no fool to chase around after a girl like that. Why, he's old enough to be her father."

"And you think men never make a fool of themselves over a younger woman?" Slocum retorted. "Happens all the time," he said, then threw in carelessly, "especially when a man's been married a long time. His wife can't satisfy him, so he goes out and gets him a young woman. You've seen it happen enough, Ellen. Don't see why you should be surprised."

A smoldering rage began to rise in Ellen. She had been filled with hatred for Clay since the night she had gone to his cabin. His rejection had cut her to the bone, but it had never once occurred to her that she was rejected because he had another woman. Now, standing there motionless, she began to remember that Clay did make a great many visits to the Yancy place. She had thought it was to hunt with Buford Yancy, but now as she called up a vision of the daughter, she was instantly convinced that Slocum was telling the truth. It was impossible for her to believe that men and women could simply enjoy each other's company, for she herself never had such simple motives. As she thought of Melora's youth and beauty, she wanted to kill her.

"You're wrong," she said, trying to convince herself.

"Why, honey, he went out in the woods with her for three days! You think they was hunting all that time?" Buford had shot a record turkey and in casual conversation had mentioned to a group of which Slocum was a part that his daughter had been on the hunt. He had said also that Reverend Irons had been along, but Slocum altered the story to rouse Ellen's wrath, which it did, of course.

"He can't make a fool out of me!" Ellen grated. She stared at Jake, and he could almost see the workings of her mind. And she did exactly what he had known she would. "Jake, you've got to do something! He doesn't pay any attention to me, but I want him hurt!"

Slocum knew he had his way. He smiled and came toward her. "I'll take care of it, honey."

"Don't fight a duel with him," Ellen warned. "He'd shoot you dead, Jake."

"There's better ways," he murmured. Then slipping her coat off, he grinned, saying, "You're not in that big a hurry, honey. . . ."

The shopping trip to Richmond was a bittersweet experience for Deborah, with far more of the bitter than the sweet. She and Susanna were joined by Dent, who invited himself along.

"I've got a few things to buy," he said blandly, and it secretly pleased both women, for he was a witty and charming companion when he was at his best. He kept them entertained all the way to the city, telling tall tales of his escapades at Virginia Military Institute, some of them concerning one of his instructors, Thomas Jackson. "He knows Uncle Gideon well," Dent said. "They were in Mexico together."

They shopped in the morning, had lunch at a fine restaurant, then Susanna left the young people and went to visit a sick friend. "Don't get into one of your terrible arguments," she warned.

"No chance of that," Dent agreed cheerfully. "A man would be a fool to argue with anyone as beautiful as this woman!"

"You're out to charm me, aren't you?" Deborah asked. She was wearing an attractive dress of gray and pearl stripe, but pulled on a royal blue woolen coat as they got up to leave the restaurant.

"Certainly!" he agreed. "I've got fine manners you've never even seen. Come along now—we've got a lot to see and do."

All afternoon they wandered the streets of the city, and Deborah had a wonderful time. Dent knew the city like the back of his hand and introduced her to so many people that she lost track.

It would have been well if they had not made their last visit, and later both of them wished they had not.

They were walking down Walnut Street when a crowd moving into a large building of red brick caught Deborah's eye. "What's that, Dent?"

"Oh, nothing much," he said and spoke so diffidently that she knew it was something he didn't want her to see. She looked at the front of the building as they walked by and saw a poster proclaiming that a firm named Ellis & Livingstone was conducting a sale of Negroes.

There it was. The evil that she had heard about all her life; that her father had devoted his life to destroying; that her teacher, Charles G. Finney, had spoken against with great passion.

"I want to go inside," she said impulsively.

Dent tried to dissuade her. "It's mostly men, Deborah. You'd be very uncomfortable."

"Dent, I'm going inside." Deborah's lips were tight and her head was held high in a stubborn gesture. "You can come with me or not."

Dent followed her reluctantly into the large room where the sales took place. He had been there many times, but now he was apprehensive. He was also on the defensive, for he knew her feelings and was aware that the slave market would only harden her views.

The room into which Deborah stepped was about fifty feet square, and it was bare of all furniture except for a few scattered chairs and benches. The whitewashed walls, which were about twelve feet high, picked up the light from the mullioned windows. A pair of steep staircases made of rough oak led to the floor overhead, and a single door at the back led, apparently, to some sort of holding room where the slaves were kept until they were brought out.

Two classes of people were in the room, and Deborah at once recognized that they might have been beings from two separate worlds! There were many men in the room who were dressed in dark suits and wore broad-brimmed hats. They were walking around, smoking cigars, talking to one another and examining some of the second group—slaves who were either standing or sitting on benches.

As Deborah moved around the room, she saw many of the planters give her a startled look; more than one of them made remarks of some sort to the other men but, seeing Dent standing behind her, kept their remarks muffled. Dent himself was unhappy and kept his chin high, ready to resent any sort of insult.

At the front of the room was a small raised platform, occupied by the auctioneer, who was watching a woman mount the three high steps. She was wearing a red dress with a white apron over it. When she got to the top of the platform, the auctioneer began the bidding.

"Here now, look at this prime specimen, gentlemen! Only nineteen years old and never had a sick day! She's healthy and ready to breed, so what am I offered?"

The bidding started at fifteen hundred dollars, but rose rapidly. The young woman was a mulatto and very pretty. She dropped her head as the bidding went on, and once a man stepped up on the platform and took her jaw, forcing her to open her mouth while he examined her teeth. He ran his hand over her body, then stepped down and raised the bid.

The woman was sold for forty-two hundred dollars, and Deborah heard a man close to her say, "That's Bartlett from New Orleans. He buys the pretty ones up for the bawdy houses there."

Slightly sick at her stomach, Deborah stood there watching. She saw a child sold to one buyer. The mother, who was sold to another, fought to keep her little girl but was cuffed into submission, and the little girl was picked up bodily by a rough-looking man and carried out of the building screaming.

"Take me out of here, Denton!" Deborah whispered. She swayed, and he took her arm quickly, holding her firmly as they left the auction house. When they were outside, she said, "I want to go home."

Dent said quickly, "It wasn't something for you to see, Deborah. I shouldn't have let you go in there."

"Would it not go on if I didn't see it?" Deborah asked. They walked along the street, not speaking. She was almost beyond thought, so revolted was she by the terrible sight she had just witnessed. As for Dent, he was well aware that what had just occurred could be death to their relationship.

They found Susanna waiting for them, and she took

one look at Deborah's stricken face, then asked, "What is it, child?"

"I—we went to the slave auction."

Susanna glanced at Dent, who was stiff-lipped, and said, "We'll go home now, Dent."

"You two go on. I'll come later."

He accompanied them to the carriage, handed them in, and nodded as Susanna spoke to the horses and they left him at a fast clip. The day had turned sour for Dent, all the more so since—before the incident at the auction—he had seen a warmth and acceptance in Deborah that he had sought ever since meeting her.

Frustrated and angry, he turned on his heel and made his way to the Water Hole, a favorite haunt of the young bucks of Richmond. He found several of his cronies there and almost at once began to drink. He was not much of a drinker as a rule, but the whole group was excited, two of them being in the militia and expecting to be off to war soon. They sat around, blackguarding the North until a poker game claimed their attention. Dent was a good card player, and he sat there for several hours, not realizing how much he was drinking. Finally he noticed that he was losing hands and laughed, "You boys are pretty sharp. You know the only way to beat me is to get me drunk!" They protested, but he took his winnings, stuck them in his pocket, and left the saloon with a promise to come back and let them have a chance to win some of it back the next day.

He made his way down the street, walking carefully, for he was in that stage of drunkenness when the earth is somewhat unsteady and the curbs do not remain stable. Suddenly he remembered that he had no way to get back home, since Susanna had taken the buggy. *Have to stay in town tonight*, he thought, and made his way to the Harley House. The room clerk looked up, a smallish young fellow named Dixon Morgan.

"Need a room for the night, Dix," Dent said. "Got stranded with no way to get home."

"Your father's in the bar, Dent," Morgan said. "He came in for supper with Taylor Dewitt and some others. Expect he'll be heading out pretty soon."

Dent stood there irresolutely. He didn't want any company—especially his father's—but he didn't want to spend the night in a hotel room either. "Thanks, Dix," he finally said. "You just missed a customer."

He entered the bar, a large room with what was reported to be the longest and finest bar in the South along one wall and tables in the center. White-jacketed bartenders and waiters moved about serving the customers, and Dent spotted his father at a table with several of his friends. He walked over, and when his father looked up with surprise at seeing him, he asked, "Got room for me when you go home?"

"Sure, Dent," Clay said. "I brought the small wagon in. Be ready to go pretty soon."

"Take a seat, Dent," Taylor Dewitt said. He had noticed that Dent was speaking in that careful way that a man will use when he's been drinking and is aware that his speech is slurred. "Saw you squiring that Yankee girl around this afternoon." A grin scored his thin lips and he winked at the others. "First thing you know, she'll have you converted. I can just see you now going around the North giving lectures on the horrors of slavery!"

A laugh ran around the table, and several of the men offered ribald suggestions to the younger Rocklin. Dent managed a sour grin, but said only, "Seems like you fellows have all the answers. Maybe you ought to hunt Jefferson Davis up and tell him how to get the Yankees out of our hair. Or maybe Abe Lincoln."

There was a congenial air around the table, and Dent had taken no offense. But suddenly a voice said loudly, "You Rocklins don't have much luck with your women, do you?"

Dent turned to find Jake Slocum grinning at him, and it was not a pleasant grin. At first he thought he had heard the man wrong, for his hearing was fuzzy. His senses were drugged with alcohol, and sounds came to him hollowly, as if he were in a steel drum. But as he focused on Slocum's broad face, he saw that the man was deliberately provoking him.

"Keep your mouth shut, Jake," he said angrily. The frustrations that had been boiling in him all evening suddenly rose like a tide, and he glared at the huge man with anger in his face.

He did not know that Slocum had been pushing against Clay for some time. Never a direct insult, but so insolent with his words and expression that Taylor had said, "Jake, you're offensive. Either straighten up or go find some other crowd." He had gotten a rough glance from Slocum, who had said only, "You're not president of anything, Dewitt."

Taylor had gone to the bathroom with Bushrod Aimes and taken occasion to say, "What's Jake up to? He's got some kind of a wild hair."

"Dunno. But if he says much more to Clay, it'll mean a shooting."

Slocum had prodded Clay Rocklin steadily, determined to start trouble. But he was smart enough not to let it become a shooting affair. He was aware of Clay's skill with a pistol and had no intention of dying for any woman. He wanted to use his fists on the man but had had no success in stirring Rocklin. Clay Rocklin was a steady man and was hard to provoke. But Slocum was determined that the provocation would come, so that when he smashed Rocklin beyond recognition, no one could accuse him of being the instigator. Now, however, he saw in young Dent Rocklin a new opportunity.

"What's the matter, Dent?" Slocum asked. "You can't get that Yankee girl's attention? I did a little better than that with your ma! Maybe I better give you a few lessons—"

Dent came out of his chair and lunged at Slocum who was waiting for just such a move. He brushed off the wild blow aimed at his face and drove his huge fist into Dent.

The wicked blow caught the boy on the forehead and dropped him to the floor senseless.

At once Clay came to his feet, his face contorted with rage. He recognized what Slocum was doing and knew that he was falling into a trap, but for one instant the volatile temper he'd always had flared up. But as he moved toward Slocum, Bushrod caught him, saying, "Watch it, Clay! You know how Jake fights! He'll gouge your eyes out! You can't fight him with fists!"

"That's right, Clay," Taylor said instantly. "Let it be pistols!"

Fear came into Slocum, but out of the fear he managed to say the one right thing, the thing that would inflame Clay Rocklin.

"He can't even take care of his own wife! He's too busy chasing around after that Yancy girl!"

A coldness came to Clay then, and he shook off Bushrod and came to stand before Slocum. Something told him he could not shoot the man, and he knew that he could never beat him in a roughhouse fight. But he was ice-cold now, and with a sudden motion, he picked up a bottle of whiskey, almost full, and before Slocum could move, he brought it down over the man's head, lifting himself on his toes to put more force into the blow.

Slocum was driven to the floor as the bottle struck his head. It broke as it struck, cutting a jagged slash across his skull. A muffled cry went up from his thick throat, and then there was a sudden silence in the saloon as every eye turned to watch.

The blow would have knocked a lesser man out, but Slocum had a thick skull, and he came to his feet, his eyes glazed and a bright river of crimson blood flowing down his cheek. He was confused, but still a formidable figure. His huge muscles bulged against his suit, and his neck was so thick that his head seemed to be perched on his broad shoulders. Some of the men watching looked at the frightening bulk, and—remembering how he had nearly killed men in this sort of fight—shook their heads. "Clay ain't got no show!" one of them said quietly. "Slocum will get him down and kick his head off!"

Clay Rocklin was the same height as Slocum, but lean rather than heavily muscled. He looked almost fragile against the hulking man. But there was a quickness about his movement, and he picked up a chair, raised it in the air, and brought it down over Slocum's head. It was a frightful blow, smashing the chair and knocking Slocum to the floor. He moved slowly, thrashing his arms like a man underwater as he shoved at the broken fragments of the chair, but then he slowly came to his feet.

"That's all right, Clay!" he said thickly. "That's all right! I'm going to get you now!"

The endurance of the man was unbelievable! He should have been unconscious, but he was advancing with his great arms outstretched. Clay picked up another chair and drove it with all his force into Slocum's face. One leg caught him in the mouth, knocking out teeth and driving his head backward. He staggered, spat out teeth and blood, then with his eyes dulled, moved forward, saying, "That's all right, Clay!"

"I guess we're even now, Jake," Clay said. He caught Slocum with a driving right that stopped him dead in his tracks. But Slocum was not out, and he caught Clay full in the mouth with a right hand that sent sparks reeling before his eyes. It was a disaster that shook Clay to his heels, and as he fell backward, Slocum cried out, "I got you!"

Clay sprawled flat on his back and saw the madness in Slocum's eyes, and he knew . . . he knew if he fell prey to those massive arms, every rib he had would be broken. He was helpless, but as Slocum launched himself to fall on him, he did the only thing he could. He raised his leg and, with all his strength, sent his heel into the face of Slocum.

It caught the man full in the face, breaking his nose and driving his head back at an acute angle. He fell on Clay, who scrambled frantically to get free, but Slocum was out.

Clay stood there, his mouth bleeding from the blow he had taken, his breath coming in rasps. The saloon was absolutely still, and there was something like fear in the eyes of some of the men.

"Clay!" Taylor burst out. "I think you broke his neck!"

"I hope so," Clay managed to say, then moved over to where Dent was struggling to get to his feet. Putting his hands under his son's arms, he hauled him to his feet. "Are you ready to go, Dent?" he asked.

"Y-yes." Dent had regained consciousness in time to see the last of the fight, but was still confused. He let Clay hold him up, and the two left the saloon.

"I never saw anything like that!" Bushrod said. He bent over Slocum, staring at the ruin of the man's face. "He ain't dead," he announced. "But he won't be a lady-killer anymore. Not with that face!"

"Clay should have killed him," Taylor said. "He'll have to now, sooner or later!"

The two Rocklins got into the wagon, Clay helping his son. Then they left town, saying nothing.

Finally Clay said, "I wish that hadn't happened, Dent."

Dent took a deep breath of the cool air. It was all like a bad dream, and all he could hear was the taunt of Jake Slocum about his mother. He had long been aware that she was not a good woman, but to have her spoken about in such a way, in a saloon, made it unbearable. He was hurt and confused, and he struck out at Clay blindly.

"It's all your fault! Why did you have to come back? You've brought shame on my mother!"

The unfairness of it struck Clay like a blow, but he said nothing. Hot words came to his lips, but he bit them back. There was, he knew, nothing that he could do to make peace with Dent. So he kept his hurting to himself.

When they reached the house, Dent fell off the wagon and lurched off blindly into the night, leaving Clay to stare after him helplessly. Finally he unhitched the team and went to his house. He was met by Buck, who had befriended him long ago. The dog whined and licked his hand, but Clay only spoke to him absently, then went inside and lay down.

He stared at the ceiling, despair welling up in his mind. He'd wanted to kill Slocum! He felt again the fury that had risen in him when the brute had spoken of Melora. He'd thought he had overcome his temper, and since becoming a Christian he had had little problem. Now he despaired, knowing that word would get back to Melora, who would be scarred by it.

And Dent was in even worse shape. He was shattered by the experience. Finally, after walking for what seemed like a long time, he came back, but could not stand to go into the house. Making his way to the scuppernong arbor, he slumped on one of the benches inside. He did not even see Deborah, who had been standing at one end, shaded from his view by a winter hedge.

She turned to go, not wanting to speak to him—and then she stopped dead still, for she heard the sound of sobs. Turning quickly, she saw in the moonlight that Dent's head was bowed and his shoulders were shaking. The weeping came in great gasping sobs, and they went to her heart. She had struggled all evening with what had happened and had made Dent the villain of the piece, throwing all the anger and bitterness that had come to her on him.

Now as she stood there, amazed that the bold young man who seemed so hard and tough was weeping, something came to her. Deborah was a compassionate woman, tender of heart, despite the manner that she sometimes wore. And she had seen in the wild young Rocklin something of this side of his character. Now the great sobs tore at her, and she moved toward him.

"Dent—what is it? What's the matter?"

He looked up, startled, his eyes staring and the tears streaming down his face. "Deborah!" he whispered. But he could say no more. He was ashamed at being discovered with his defenses down and could not say a word. Yet her face, he saw, was not filled with contempt for his weakness, as he had feared. Rather, her expression was soft with compassion as she came to sit beside him.

She took his hands and asked softly, "Can I help, Dent?"

"No, there's no help!" he said, unable to take his eyes from hers. Then he suddenly told her what had happened. When he finished, his voice was unsteady. "I . . . love my mother, Deborah. I know she's not . . . good."

He paused, unable to go on, and she answered him out of a full heart, for his brokenness had somehow washed away her own pain and bitterness. "I'm glad, Dent. And you must love your father, too."

Dent sat there, then said, "I love *you*, Deborah."

"No, you mustn't!" she said quickly. "We can never be together. You must know that." She stood up, shaken by his simple statement. When he stood up with her, she touched his cheek, adding, "I—have to go home, Dent. This is good-bye."

Dent Rocklin had led an easy life, with only minor problems. Now he was suddenly aware that without this girl, he would never be complete. A flash of desperation ran through him, and he caught her in his arms. She was sweet beyond anything he had ever dreamed, and he whispered, "I can't let you go, darling! I can't live without you!"

Deborah lifted her face to reply, but his lips fell on hers and there was such a desperate intensity in them that she felt her will grow weak. She felt her hands go behind his head, pulling it down, and for one moment she forgot all the mountains that lay between them. Then they came rushing back, and she pulled away.

"You'll forget me, Dent . . . and I'll have to forget you. Good-bye!"

Dent stood there, the silver moon washing the arbor with warm waves of light, watching her float away into the darkness. He had never felt so lost and alone in his life.

Finally he took a deep breath, looked toward the house, and said quietly, "War or no war, slavery or no slavery—I'm going to have you for my wife, Deborah Steele!"

CHAPTER TWENTY-THREE

THE CANNON'S ROAR

ON MARCH 4, 1861, Abraham Lincoln took his oath of office as the sixteenth president of the United States. He had addressed the South in conciliatory tones. "We are not enemies, but friends." He concluded with urgency in his voice, "We must not be enemies."

But he was in office for only one day when the simmering Fort Sumter crisis boiled over. He received a letter from Major Anderson declaring that his position was nearly hopeless; that he needed twenty thousand more troops to hold position in Charleston Harbor; that even if Sumter were not attacked, his dwindling food supply would soon force him to choose between starvation and surrender.

Lincoln had made a public pledge to defend Federal property, but members of his cabinet sabotaged his efforts to reinforce Sumter. On April 4, the president informed Major Anderson that a relief expedition was coming, but that it would consist of supplies only, no troops.

The letter reached Fort Sumter on April 9. Early that morning, Major Gideon Rocklin was standing on the parapet of Sumter speaking with Private Daniel Hough when his commanding officer received the letter. Gideon listened as Hough spoke of his home and family, but his eyes were on Major Anderson, who was tearing open the sealed envelope handed him by a messenger who had come on a small boat.

"So as soon as I get discharged, Major," Private Hough was saying, "I'm going home and get married." Hough, a tow-headed young man of twenty-two, had a cheerful smile and was a favorite of officers and enlisted men alike. During the long months of siege, the young Michigan private had never complained of the shortage of food, even though he was so thin that his uniform hung on him. "Did I tell you I was getting married, Major Rocklin?"

Anderson was disturbed by the news, Gideon saw. He was staring at the message glumly, his mouth turned down. "No, you never mentioned it, Daniel," Gideon said. He gave the thin young man a quick glance, wondering what he thought of what was happening. It was hard to tell, sometimes, with enlisted men. "What if the war starts? Will you still get married?"

"Why, sure I will, Major!" Hough said, his smooth face showing surprise. "Me and Carrie got it all planned. We've got us a little place my pa gave me, got a nice cabin, and we'll be startin' a family pretty soon. My enlistment's up in two months, so it won't be long."

Anderson beckoned to him, but Gideon lingered to ask, "But if the war comes, you'll serve your country, won't you?"

Private Hough said, "Why, Major, didn't I tell you? Carrie, my girl, she's from South Carolina. Got a houseful of brothers, and all of them's been real friendly to me." His brow wrinkled in a frown and he shook his head. "No, Major, I'm going to my farm, me and Carrie."

Anderson was giving him an impatient look, so Gideon said, "Well, I hope you and Carrie have a fine marriage, Private." He hurried over to the commanding officer, saying, "What is it, Major?"

"President Lincoln says he's sending us supplies." Anderson's eyes were weary, for the three-month siege had worn him thin. He looked across the bay to Fort Moultrie on Sullivan's Island, adding, "Beauregard's guns will blow any ships out of the water that try to relieve us."

"They could do it, I'm afraid," Gideon agreed, nodding. "My report is that he's got some big guns in place. Five of them that fire twenty-four-pound shot, some long-range cannon, and some heavy mortars."

"And he's got plenty of firepower on James Island as

well. Not to mention about six thousand men to storm our base. To tell the truth, Rocklin, we're in a tight spot."

Anderson was right, for Sumter was in no condition to fight a battle. The fort was solid enough—brick walls five feet thick rising forty feet above the water, designed to carry three tiers of guns. Anderson had forty-eight guns in position, but some of them could not be brought to bear, and there were not nearly enough men to fire the guns. He had only 128 men, 43 of them civilians. Anderson and his officers had done what they could to get ready for an invasion. The wharf was mined and could be blown to bits at a moment's notice, and various infernal machines loaded with kegs of gunpowder were ready to be dropped on the invaders.

"We'll give a good account of ourselves, sir," Gideon said. "The men's morale is high."

"Yes, and I give you and your lieutenants credit for that, Gideon," Anderson said, with a sudden smile. "You've done a fine job with them. But we can't go on for long." The food was practically gone, and they both knew that if the relief expedition didn't arrive soon, they would have to surrender. "Well, we shall see," Anderson concluded, and left to go below.

The next day, April 10, at one o'clock, Gideon heard one of the guards call out, "Boat coming from shore, Major!" He turned to see the same boat that had brought Lincoln's message coming across the choppy waters. There were several passengers, but no women, which disappointed him. He had hoped that Mellie might come, but she had told him it was getting more difficult to get permission from the officers in charge. He walked along the stones, thinking of her, dismissing the boat from his thoughts. Every spare moment now, day and night, he was taxing his brain, trying to find a way to defend the fort. Over and over he thought of the difficulties, looking for solutions but finding few.

"Hello, Gid," a voice said, and he whirled to see his

cousin, Clay Rocklin, who had come to stand beside the wall.

Gideon threw his head back, blinking with the shock of the meeting. But he recovered at once, and moved forward. "Clay! By all that's holy! I can't believe it!" He gripped Clay's hand and stood there, taking in the face of the other man. "It's been a long time, Clay," he said finally.

"Maybe not long enough," Clay said. He was searching Gideon's face, looking for a sign of displeasure. Gid was older, weathered by sun and storm, but otherwise he was the same—thick-shouldered, solid, and with the same square face, which was as open and honest as ever. "Gid, let me have my say, then you can ask me anything. I've come to ask you to forgive me." Clay's expressive lips tightened and he shook his head, saying sadly, "For all of it. For what I tried to do to Melanie, for killing all your men in Mexico . . . " He paused, then added, "Ever since I became a Christian I've wanted to come to you. And lately, I've felt it more strongly. Then last week, it came to me that you could get killed in this place and . . . "

Clay paused, his voice thick with emotion, and Gideon suddenly put his arm around his cousin. "Clay— I'm glad you're here. For years I've wanted to see you. Prayed for you. Forgive you?" He gave Clay's shoulders a mighty squeeze. "Why, I did that long ago! Long ago!"

The two men stood there, and some of the men watched with curious eyes to see their officer hugging the tall man. Clay smiled, saying, "That's like you, Gid! But I'm only halfway home. With your permission, I'd like to go to Melanie. I want to ask her forgiveness, too."

"She's in the Foster Hotel, room 221," Gideon said at once. "She's been praying for you, too, Clay." He looked suddenly across the bay, saying, "I'm worried about her, Clay. She wouldn't listen to me when I tried to tell her it could be dangerous here. This thing is going to blow up any day now, and there's some pretty wild Southern fanatics in Charleston. Anything could happen."

Clay laughed out loud. "I don't think Melanie would welcome me as a protector, Gideon."

"Yes, she would. Soon as you leave here, go see her. Right away."

Clay stared at him. "It's not that close, is it? These South Carolinians are hotheads, but I'm still hoping it won't come to a shooting war."

Gideon lowered his voice. "I think it'll come very soon. Lincoln is sending a fleet to relieve the fort. And the secessionists know it. Those leaders who want a war know about it, and they'll never let it happen! I think they'll begin firing in two or three days."

"What will happen?" He listened as Gideon told him what he thought. The two men walked around behind the guns slowly, and by the time they had made a circuit, Clay was depressed. "It's insane, Gid!"

"Yes. War always is. There haven't been any sane, logical wars." Gid suddenly said, "Mellie and I have been keeping up with you. Your mother's told us how well you've done since you came home. My father's more pleased with you than I've ever seen him!"

Clay ducked his head, then smiled wryly. "I wish my father was as optimistic."

"He'll come around!"

"I doubt it, Gid. He was pleased, but when this war started shaping up, things changed in Virginia. Every man who's not ready to grab a musket and charge to Washington to shoot the Yankees is a traitor! And that's pretty well what Father thinks of me. And a lot of others think the same thing."

"What will you do, Clay?" Gideon asked quietly.

Clay said gloomily, "I honestly don't know, Gid. I hate slavery, but I love my state. Right now, I'm in limbo."

"Well, so are lots of others—including Robert E. Lee," Gideon pointed out. "I've made my choice, but then it was easier for me. I don't have the land in my blood— Virginia land—as you do."

"Everyone knows what your choice will be, Gid. And how can I pick up a musket and fight you?"

Gideon was silent, and both men knew there was nothing they could say to make the terrible choice any easier. They walked for an hour, and then the boat handler called, "Passengers for shore!" Clay said, "I'll see Melanie. And if she'll let me, I'll look out for her. Any message?"

"Nothing very original," Gid said, grinning. "Give her my love." The two men parted with a final gripping of hands. "I'll write your father, Clay," Gideon said as the boat left the wharf. "He'll come around!"

Clay waved but didn't answer, for he had little faith in winning his father's approval. When the boat docked, he went at once to the Foster Hotel, but going into the lobby, he suddenly was struck by a fear that Gideon might be wrong. It was Melanie he'd attacked, after all, and a sensitive woman would not shake off such a thing easily.

"It's got to be now," he muttered, straightening his shoulders. "I told Gid I'd watch out for her." He walked resolutely up the stairs, paused one moment before room 221, then knocked on the door.

"Just a minute!" He stood there, bracing his shoulders, and then the door opened. She was as beautiful as ever, he saw as she opened the door. She stood there, her mouth open in surprise, her eyes startled. Then she said quietly, "Come in, Clay." When he stepped inside, she closed the door, then asked, "Have you been to see Gid?"

"Yes, I have." Clay was nervous and began at once with his plea for forgiveness. She let him speak, listening carefully. He was far more nervous than he had been with Gideon, but this made her warm toward him all the more. When he had finished, she said, "Clay, when we do a wrong thing, there are two things we can do about it. We can cover it up. Keep it inside. When we do that, it grows. And that's what's happened. What you did was wrong, but you've nursed that bad memory in your mind for years. Of course, I'll forgive you! But if you'd asked years ago, you wouldn't have had this on your heart all this time."

Clay wiped the perspiration from his forehead. His limbs were strangely weak, and his head felt light—but he felt free. He nodded. "Thank you, Melanie. You're right, but I was too big a fool to do anything so simple as just asking for forgiveness in those days."

"Now, that's over," Melanie said with a smile. "Please tell me about Gid. They wouldn't let me go to the fort today."

Clay gave his report, passing along Gid's final word, and the two of them sat there talking about the dangers. He saw that she was tense, and after what Gid had told him, he did not try to soothe her with false comfort. "I'm going to stay around for a few days," he said. "Maybe I can get a room here. I understand the war fever gets out of hand."

"Gid asked you to take care of me, didn't he? Well, to tell the absolute truth, Clay, there have been a few unpleasantries. The wives of Union officers aren't particularly popular in Charleston right now."

"I'll go see about a room. Then maybe you can show me a good place to eat."

The room clerk, a tall, sallow-faced man with a fierce set of whiskers, insisted there was no room available, but when Clay let a twenty-dollar bill be seen in his palm, he suddenly remembered a vacancy. Clay checked into the room, washed his face, then walked around the city until supper time. At six o'clock he returned to the hotel, where he found Melanie waiting for him. "It may be hard to find a place to eat," he remarked as they stepped out on the street. "The streets are packed."

"There's something in the air tonight, Clay," Melanie said with apprehension in her voice.

She was exactly right. The excitement and patriotic passions that had been building up since secession in December had reached fever pitch. Neither of them was hungry, and as they walked around the city that night, long parades snaked through the streets, drums rolled, horses' hooves clattered, and the leaping flames of great bonfires made dancing shadows.

Charleston that night was no place for moderation, no setting for trepidation. Charleston was in the hands of the fire-eaters. Clay and Melanie stood under a balcony, surrounded by a screaming mob, listening to Roger Pryor, a Virginian, speaking to the seething crowd.

"You have at last annihilated this accursed Union, reeking with corruption and insolent with excess of tyranny. Not only is it gone, but it is gone forever. As sure as tomorrow's sun will rise upon us," Pryor shouted, "so it is sure that old Virginia will be a member of the Southern Confederacy! Strike a blow! The very moment blood is shed, old Virginia will make common cause with her sisters of the South!"

Clay said, "Let's get out of this crowd, Mellie." She nodded, and with some effort they made their way down the street toward the hotel. When they arrived, she said, "There's a balcony with some chairs. Let's sit and talk for a while, Clay."

The balcony was small, and as they took two of the chairs, Melanie said, "I sit here quite often at night. It's cool and you can smell the ocean." For a time they sat there speaking idly, then Melanie said, "Your mother has written me several times. She's very proud of you." Then, being a very direct woman, she turned to face him. "How are you, Clay? Susanna told us about the fight you had with the man who insulted Ellen. Was there any more trouble with him?"

Clay shook his head. "Not with him, Mellie. I carried a gun for a few weeks, but he never tried to take the thing further." He hesitated, then said painfully, "Ellen blamed the fight on me." He looked at his hands, and his silence told her much. Finally he began to talk, speaking of his life and the difficulties that had risen in the past few months. Finally he said, "I guess I've come to the end of the road, Mellie. My family doesn't have much use for me. Can't blame them much, for I've treated them shamefully."

"Not all of them, Clay. Susanna tells me you've become very close to Rena."

He smiled and nodded. "My one victory. But the others haven't forgotten that I ran out on them. Especially Dent."

"He's in love with Deborah, Susanna says. She's a favorite of mine, you know. We spent a great deal of time together when we were stationed in Washington."

"A beautiful girl," Clay said. "I like her very much. But she's an abolitionist, and Dent's just the opposite. They'd make each other miserable!"

"What about Melora?"

The question caught Clay off balance. His fists clenched, and he closed his mouth suddenly. When Melanie said nothing, he relaxed. "I guess Mother's been writing you more than I knew." He sat there, looking down on the street, then began to speak of Melora. His voice grew gentle as he went over how he'd known her from childhood, and how when he'd come back he'd expected to find her married.

"I wonder why she didn't marry?" Melanie's voice was casual, but she was watching Clay carefully. "It's unusual for a beautiful young woman to stay single."

Clay made no answer to that, but said at once, "Mellie, I've not said anything to a soul, not even to my mother. I love Melora, but it's hopeless. Ellen is my wife, and that's all there is to it. As a matter of fact, I've told Melora she ought to marry the minister who's proposed to her. He's a good man, and she needs a family."

Clay said no more, but Melanie sensed the heaviness of his spirit. She longed to encourage him, but could not get around the truth that he had spoken. Ellen *was* his wife, though she brought him no pleasure and likely never would. Finally she said, "God knows our ways, Clay. You are doing the right thing—painful as it is for you. He won't forget that!"

They sat there, listening to the cries of the people, and finally Melanie rose, saying, "I'm going to bed, Clay. Not that I'll sleep, but I need the rest. Good-night." She suddenly leaned over and kissed his cheek. "I'm glad you're here. I feel much safer!"

Clay sat there for hours, listening to the city, thinking of many things. Finally he went to bed, weary in body and mind, but also with a small feeling of triumph.

At noon of the same day Clay had met with Gideon, three men had stood before Major Anderson and his aide-de-camp, Major Rocklin. They were Colonel James A. Chisholm, Captain Stephen D. Lee, and Colonel James Chesnut. The two Union officers had been formal, as were the visitors, but they all knew that this was the ultimatum. Major Anderson withdrew, discussed the situation with his officer, then wrote out his response.

The next day, Chesnut and his party came again at one o'clock. Anderson and his officers debated once more. At three o'clock in the morning, Anderson handed the envoys his response, which was not acceptable. When Anderson escorted the Confederates back to their boat, he shook hands with each one, saying, "If we never meet in this world again, God grant that we may meet in the next."

The bells of St. Michael's in Charleston were pealing four o'clock in the morning as Chesnut's party rowed up to Fort Johnson. Chesnut ordered Captain George S. James to fire the signal shell that would open the bombardment at four-thirty.

Everyone was waiting. Roger Pryor was offered the honor of firing the signal gun, but said, "I will not fire the first gun of the war." It was Lieutenant Henry S. Farley who jerked the lanyard that sent the signal shell arching high into the sky over Fort Sumter.

All day and into the night the crowds had gathered at the beach, looking out over the sea, waiting for something to happen. Clay and Melanie were there, and as the signal shell exploded, a great cheer went up from the crowd. But Melanie whispered, "Oh, God! It's started! It's started, and no one can stop it!" She turned to Clay blindly, and he held her while the crowd lifted great cheers. Then she pulled back, and with her handkerchief wiped away her tears. "I mustn't cry! It's too late for weeping, isn't it, Clay? Everything is out of control, and no one can stop it. Not Anderson or Lincoln or Davis. But God is still in his heaven!"

Gideon Rocklin did not flinch when he saw that signal shell. Nor did he falter during the entire action. It was a strange, tentative, melodramatic fight that bore practically no resemblance to the cruel headlong battles that would come later. The first Confederate shot hit the wall of the magazine where Captain Abner Doubleday and one other officer had only a scanty supply of powder bags. For hours the shells fell on Fort Sumter, and no effort was made by the Union forces to answer the bombardment. At six, the men ate a meal of salt pork, and then Major Anderson directed the return fire. It was Doubleday, at about seven o'clock, who fired the first Union shot, which was a miss.

For hours the duel went on, and noontime found Sumter withstanding the bombardment well. Gideon moved from gun to gun, directing the fire. Once he passed by Private Daniel Hough, and the young man gave him a smile. "Well, Major, I guess I'll be telling folks what a hero I was when I get back to Michigan!" he said, then turned to his gun, whistling "Buffalo Gals."

The exhausted Federals slept as they could that night, and in the morning they breakfasted on a little salt pork and some rice. By now the Confederate gunners were firing hot shot, and fires were beginning to break out. By ten o'clock the fire was nearly out of control, and Gideon had the men move their small supply of powder. His eyes burned, and many of the men lay prostrate to avoid the smoke.

Finally a Confederate shot knocked down the flagpole, and Beauregard sent three aides out to give Anderson and his forces a chance to surrender.

"We can hold out, Major!" Gideon insisted, his fighting blood aroused.

"No, we must save our men, Major," Anderson said quietly.

At one-thirty Major Anderson ordered his men to raise a white cloth.

And that was it.

Fort Sumter had fallen.

The next day, April 14, 1861, the defenders of Fort Sumter were allowed by General Beauregard to fire a hundred-gun salute. Gideon had to scrape the bottom of the barrel to find enough powder, but he found it. The salute began about two o'clock that afternoon. Thousands watched from boats in the harbor, among them General Beauregard.

Gid was walking down the line of guns, watching as each one was fired. His heart was sick, and he wished that the whole terrible thing were done.

Suddenly an explosion rent the air—not of a cannon being fired, but something else. Gideon turned to get a glimpse of men being lifted and thrown into the air like dolls!

One of the gunners had rammed another cartridge into his gun before the sparks from the previous round were thoroughly swabbed out. The spark prematurely ignited the cartridge and the explosion had blown the crew to the ground.

One body fell not five feet from Gideon, rolled over twice and came to rest almost at his feet. His face was black and his right arm was missing. Scarlet blood pumped steadily from the raw wound. Gideon fell to his knees, pulled out his handkerchief and, knowing it was useless, pressed it against the gaping hole in the boy's side.

"Major—"

Gid started and looked carefully at the blackened face. It was Private Daniel Hough!

"Major?"

"Yes, Daniel, what is it, son?"

Hough's lips were blistered and his tongue was

burned. He tried to raise himself, his eyes pleading. "Am I—pretty bad, Major?"

Gideon bit his lip, then nodded. "I'm afraid so, Daniel."

The life was ebbing, and the voice faded so that Gideon had to lean forward to catch the words of the dying boy.

"Tell—Carrie—tell her—"

And then the body went lax as Daniel Hough died.

He was the only casualty of the battle of Fort Sumter, but never did Rocklin forget that moment, nor the agonizing cry of the boy for his sweetheart. There would be others to die, many of them. But up until the moment that Daniel Hough died in his arms, the war had been abstract for Gideon.

Now he knew.

There would be thousands of Daniel Houghs dying.

There would be many, many Carries weeping wildly for their men.

Before the end came, the land would be red with blood—and perhaps some of it would be his.

CHAPTER TWENTY-FOUR

AFTER DARKNESS, THE DAWN

LONG shadows of a darkness that was just beginning enveloped the land as spring turned into summer. The untaught armies were gathering, small fights were erupting on the fringes like ominous flashes of lightning, and here and there people died. One of them was Stephen A. Douglas, the Little Giant and legendary opponent of Abraham Lincoln.

Stephen and Ruth Rocklin were informed of his death by Amos Steele at supper. Ruth had brought the family together. Gideon and Melanie with their three boys were there, along with Laura and Amos and their four children. It was the irrepressible Pat, the oldest son of Laura and Amos, who looked around the table and grinned. "There are thirteen of us. That's unlucky. We better send somebody away."

"Or go get somebody else and make fourteen," Gid said.

And then it was Clinton, age seventeen, who put his foot in his mouth. He grinned at his sister, Deborah, saying impulsively, "Hey, Deborah, maybe you could send for that rebel cousin of ours!"

It was a false note, and Clinton—who was very fond of Deborah—saw from the look on his sister's face that his remark had given her pain. He fumbled with his napkin in the silence that followed his statement, trying to find some way to cover up his awkwardness.

Laura glanced at Amos, both of them still sensitive over Deborah's behavior. She had come home from her visit pale and not herself. Both Amos and Laura had tried to talk with her, but she would say nothing about what had happened. Amos had said, "I think seeing the evils of slavery up close has been a shock to her, Laura. She'll come out of it." But he was mistaken, and finally Laura learned the truth from Susanna. She had gone at once to Deborah and discovered that her daughter was shattered, not over slavery, but over an attachment to Dent Rocklin.

Now as Laura watched her daughter, she thought, *It's not getting any better, but it will have to. She can't marry a man who's likely to be shooting at her brothers!*

Amos Steele felt Deborah's reticence keenly. The two of them had been very close, and he sensed that Deborah was pulling away from him. Looking at her, he saw that she was pained over Clinton's thoughtless remark and said quickly, "I forgot to tell you. Stephen Douglas died last night."

Stephen said at once, "I'm sorry to hear it. He was a gifted man."

"Do you know," Gid said thoughtfully, "he could have been president instead of Lincoln? Just a few votes the other way, and he'd have been in office."

"I wish he had been," Melanie said. "He was more moderate on slavery and states' rights than Lincoln. Maybe he could have kept us out of this war."

"No, he couldn't have done that," Stephen said sadly. "It's been building up for years—decades even—and no one man could have stopped it."

"I think that's right," Gid agreed. He sat back in his chair, and Melanie noticed that he had gained back some of the weight he had lost at the siege of Sumter. "There's a line of a song that keeps going through my mind—'We are living, we are dwelling, in a grand and awesome time.' I think that's true. Grand and awesome enough, but inevitable. We've had two nations here, headed in different directions. And now we're going to have to fight a civil war to decide exactly what sort of country this is going to be."

His words fell across the room, sobering them all. "Well, Father," Tyler said, "it won't be a long war. The South can't last long." At the age of nineteen, Tyler was already broad and strong, as his father had been at that age. He was also pugnacious and stubborn, and he thrust his chin forward, stating emphatically, "Why, it's ridiculous! The South doesn't have any factories, and wars are fought with weapons. And we outnumber them, too."

"That's right enough, Tyler," Gid said. "But they have some advantages. In the first place, they don't have to win the war."

Deborah looked at him curiously. She looked very pretty in a red-and-black striped dress. Her clear eyes, however, were troubled. "What does that mean, Uncle Gideon?"

"Why, it means that they don't want to invade us." Gid shrugged. "They just want to be left alone. So they'll be fighting a defensive war on their own territory. We'll have to invade them, and that means enormous supply lines in enemy territory. And we in the North are fighting for an idea, but they'll be fighting for their homes."

"And they'll have better leadership in the army," Stephen added. Seeing the shocked looks on the faces of his grandchildren, he explained, "The best of the West Pointers have resigned from the United States Army to go fight for the Confederacy."

"I'm afraid you're right, Father," Gid said soberly. "General Scott practically begged Robert E. Lee to stay and take command of our army, but he refused. So have a lot of other good men." He shook his head. "I don't envy the general who has to attack Robert E. Lee on his own ground!"

As Gid continued to speak of the difficulties of conducting a war against the South, Stephen was swept with a sudden sense of gloom. Looking around the table, he surveyed Gideon's sons—Tyler, nineteen; Robert, eighteen; and Frank, seventeen; then he glanced at the three sons of Laura and Amos—Pat, twenty; Colin, nineteen; and Clinton, seventeen.

All so young! he thought sadly. *The old men will bring the war on, but it'll be the young men like these who'll shed their blood*. Then he thought of Clay's sons, and Amy's—all young men, the same as these around his table. "Have you heard from Clay since you got back from Sumter?" he asked when Gideon finished.

"Yes, twice," Gid answered, nodding. A frown crossed his brow, and he shook his head. "No good news, I'm afraid. Clay is against the war. He thinks it's a lost cause before it begins. You can imagine how that goes over in Virginia right now! He doesn't complain, but I know what such a thing can be like."

"But what will he do, Gideon?" Ruth asked. "Will he leave Gracefield? I wouldn't think he could stay there."

"He'll never leave his home." They all turned to look at Deborah, who had spoken. "It's so sad! He'd made such a wonderful recovery—and then this awful war came along!" She got up suddenly and left the table, her lips pale and tense.

"She was very disturbed by what she saw in Virginia," her father said quickly. "The slave auctions and that sort of thing."

They all knew there was more to it than that, but were careful not to mention Deborah's problem. A sense of impending gloom fell across the room, and they all hastily rose and left the table. The Steeles left as soon as they could, and when Stephen and Gideon spoke later neither of them was optimistic about the future.

"Are you pleased with your new assignment, Son?" Stephen asked as they sipped coffee in the library. Gideon had been ordered to report to General Scott at once. The wording of his orders was vague, and Gideon shrugged pessimistically. "The general just wants me around to get my ideas on how the South is feeling—will they fight and that sort of thing. Mostly because I'm from Virginia, I think. But I won't be with him long." He smiled slightly, adding, "I've been doing a little politicking. A number of new brigades are being formed. They're putting several older units together, and I'll be joining them as soon as the general has pumped me dry."

"I suppose promotion will come quicker that way." Stephen drummed his fingers on the table, then said, "I'm worried about Deborah. About Clay, too. About all of us."

Gideon looked at his father, noting with surprise that he seemed much older than usual. *He's only sixty-two, and he's still strong—but he feels the same as I do,* he thought. "It's going to be a hard thing," he said gently. "Wars are all terrible, but a war between brothers is the worst of all."

The dinner at her grandparents' disturbed Deborah, though she tried not to show it. For the next three days, she threw herself into her father's work, staying up late and accompanying him on two speaking engagements. Amos was pleased, but Laura was not. "She's going on nerve, Amos," she said to her husband. "She can't go on long this way."

The next day was Friday, and Steele had an engagement in Philadelphia. He wanted to take Deborah, but Laura discouraged this, insisting that the girl needed rest. "Very well, she can work on the book," Amos conceded, and he asked Deborah to do so. She agreed, and when he left the next morning, she kissed him good-bye, saying, "I'll have a lot for you to see when you get back."

All day she labored in the library, working from the notes she had made while in Richmond. More than once a note brought a memory before her that caused her hand to stop—but at once she would press on with vigor.

"Deborah, you've got to rest," her mother scolded that night. It was after eight, and Deborah had not eaten supper. "Now, I've fixed you a late supper. You come and eat right now!"

Deborah protested, but Laura was adamant, so she surrendered. She haggled the steak her mother had saved, eating a few bites, then sat with her mother briefly. Finally she said, "I think I'll take a walk before I go to bed, Mother."

She kissed her mother, then put on a light coat and walked out of the house. It was a mild night, and the stars were putting on a glittering show overhead. The streetlights threw their gleam across the walk, and for an hour she walked the streets of Washington. She was not a moody young woman, and for that reason the black depression she had suffered since her return home had taken her by surprise. All her life she had been able to identify a problem, then attack it with all her might—and in almost every case she had been able to overcome the problem.

But she could not seem to shake off the unhappiness that had come to her, and she knew that it was more than the war—terrible as that was. No, it was both lesser and greater than the war. In one sense there was nothing she could do about the war, except her duty, of course. For a long time she had fought with others against slavery, coming to believe that the evil would never be struck down except by force. But that was an idea, an abstraction. Now she was painfully aware of the flesh-and-blood element. Her great-aunt Susanna had grown to be very dear to her during her brief stay . . . her world would have to be destroyed. *How do you destroy a person's world without killing that very person?* she wondered, turning finally down the street to her home.

As she approached the house, she thought of the night all the Rocklins had met for Thomas's birthday party. It had been a lighthearted, happy affair, with all the children and grandchildren gathered around the big table to celebrate the event. In her mind's eye, she saw the older relatives and then the younger family members. And she felt despair close about her as she thought, *They'll never survive this war! Never!*

Then she turned into the walk that led to the front door, and as she did so, someone moved out of the shadows and called her name.

"Who are you?" Deborah cried out, startled and suddenly afraid. Washington was not the quiet place it had once been, and the man who suddenly appeared out of the shadows was not familiar.

"It's me, Dent Rocklin."

Deborah stood still, her heart beating as rapidly as a bird's. "Dent! What are you—"

"I had to come, Deborah!" he whispered. He was wearing a dark suit and a broad-brimmed hat that shaded his eyes. He took it off and stood before her silently for a moment. Then he said, "I didn't mean to frighten you."

"I was startled—but what are you doing here?" Deborah was taking in Dent's face, noting even in the feeble, pale light of the street lamp that he looked worn and tired. She wanted to reach out to him, but knew she must not. "Have you been in the house?"

"No. I was afraid your parents might not let you see me."

"Well, we can't talk here," Deborah said. "Come around to the side of the house." She led him quickly to the small garden framed by hedge, and then turned to face him. "Dent, you shouldn't have come."

"I know that," he said wearily. He was changed, she saw at once. He had lost that lighthearted air that had made him so attractive. The dim light cast his face into strong planes, his high cheekbones and deep-set eyes giving his face a sculptured look. "Deborah, I'm in the Confederate Army."

"Dent!" Deborah whispered. "You'll be shot if they catch you here in civilian clothes! They'd say you're a spy."

"I'm not carrying any papers they could shoot me for," he said with a shrug. "I don't even have a uniform. My company won't be mustered for a week, and I had to see you, Deborah!"

She was not thinking clearly. His sudden appearance had unnerved her, and she tried to regain her composure. The very sight of his face had brought back the memories of his kiss, and she said unsteadily, "You can't stay here. It's too dangerous."

335

Dent suddenly grinned, his teeth very white against his tan. "Here I am going into the army to face shot and shell, and it's 'dangerous' to come and see my girl."

"It's not funny—and I'm not your girl!"

"Yes you are." He suddenly grasped her arms and leaned down. "Now it's time for you to tell me that it'll never work. Tell me that I'll probably get my head blown off. Your family would never agree. My family would never agree. Then tell me I'll be fighting against your brothers. Give me a dozen reasons why we can't have each other. Go on!"

Deborah was trembling in his grasp. "It's all true! Everything you say is true!"

Dent's face grew gentle. He suddenly put his arms around her, ignoring her struggles. "I know it is, Deborah. But I know one more thing. Something you've overlooked."

"What—"

He pulled her close and kissed her, cutting off her words. Again she felt the stirrings that had shaken her when he had taken her in his arms in Virginia. There was a wild sweetness in his caress, and she lay in his arms passively at first, then added a pressure of her own to the kiss.

He lifted his head, but held her close, whispering, "That's what you've forgotten, Deborah!"

Suddenly tears came to her eyes, and she laid her face against his chest. Everything that was in her longed to say, "I love you, Dent! We'll make it somehow!"

But she could not. The obstacles were too overwhelming. She seemed to see a huge set of balances, the sort with two thin plates hanging from opposite ends of a hinged beam. In one of the plates she saw her family— parents, brothers, and others—and all that she believed in and had worked for, including the freedom of black people.

In the other plate was Dent.

And she knew that all the joy that she felt in his arms

was not enough. She could not deny her family and her faith, not even for the love she felt for him.

Drawing back, she forced herself to say quietly, "I can never turn my back on my family, Dent."

He stared at her, his face pale and tense. "You don't love me, then."

"There are all kinds of love. Sometimes one kind of love works against another."

If it had been another man, Dent could have fought, but he was stopped by the look on Deborah's face. He wanted to take her in his arms again, but knew that she would not respond.

Finally he said, "Deborah, I love you. And I know you love me." A hardness came into his tone, and his jaw clenched. "I've got to go, but this isn't the end. When the war is over, I'll come for you."

"I can't promise you anything, Dent," she said, hiding the misery that rose in her at the sight of his anger.

He seemed not to have heard. Looking up at the stars, he seemed to be lost in thought. Finally he put his hat on, then said almost harshly, "I'll be coming for you. But first I've got this war to fight. And until it's over, there's no mercy in me."

Deborah cried, "You see what's happening?"

"I see that I've got one thing to do, and I'm going to do it no matter what it costs me or anyone else." He whirled and walked away, but paused and gave her one look, and his eyes were filled with regret. "Don't forget me, Deborah. After it's over, I'll be coming for you!"

Then he was gone. Deborah stood peering into the darkness. Overhead the full moon looked down on her, pouring silver bars of light across the arbor. And then a ragged cloud racing across the sky covered its face, and she turned and walked slowly into the house.

"Oh, isn't it exciting! I declare, Leona, that Denton Rocklin is the handsomest thing in his uniform I've ever seen!"

A group of young ladies had pushed their way (in a most unladylike fashion!) to the forefront of the city square. All of Richmond seemed to be gathered there for the commissioning of the Richmond Grays, and the air was filled with the brave tunes played by the band and the smell of coffee furnished by the ladies of Richmond.

Dent, in his ash-gray uniform, black boots that shone like a well-rubbed table, and a fine tasseled scarlet sash, was at the head of the formation, his second-lieutenant bars gleaming in the sunlight. He caught the eye of Lily Duprey, who had just commented on his appearance and nodded, smiling slightly. "Lily! He's watching you!" Maybelle Saunders whispered. "I heard that Yankee girl he was so taken with went back home. What Denton needs now is a good Southern woman."

Dent, however, was not thinking of a woman, but of his company. He called it "my company" to himself, for he had a queer possessiveness about the Richmond Grays. The unit took the place of Deborah in his mind, and in pouring himself into the company, he forced the images of her back into the secret part of his being.

And he was content that fine June afternoon. Very content! Looking down the lines as the men waited for the president to come and address them, he was pleased with what he saw. The lines were straight, the uniforms sharp, and the men alert. But he realized that they should be impressive, for it was an elite body of men. As soon as James Benton had announced his intention of organizing and equipping a company of young men, there was virtually a stampede to enlist. Oh, there were other companies being formed all over the South, some of them with ferocious titles: Lexington Wild Cats, Yankee Terrors, Southern Avengers, and Chickasaw Desperadoes, for example.

But the Richmond Grays were different. The ranks were filled with the cavaliers, sons of the cream of Richmond society. Choosing the officers had been most difficult, for there were only a handful of positions, of course, with dozens of young aristocrats who longed for the officer's uniform. There were elections, and James Benton was the colonel. Brad Franklin was the major, which was no surprise, since he had borne half the expense of equipping the troop. The captain was a man named Brandon Coldfax, owner of a fifty-thousand-acre plantation north of Richmond. At the age of sixty he was the only one of the officers with any military experience at all, having served in the Indian wars and under Zachary Taylor in Mexico. The lieutenants were Taylor Dewitt, Bushrod Aimes, and Denton Rocklin. Not all of the volunteers were wealthy, of course, but the flavor of aristocracy was strong in the Richmond Grays.

"Look fine, don't they, Dent?" Bushrod, standing to Dent's right, had pride in his voice. "They're ready to fight anything the Yankees send our way!" Aimes and Dewitt had been somewhat taken aback at the way that Dent Rocklin had thrown himself into the work of whipping the Grays into fighting trim. They both knew he had made some sort of a trip, and though Dewitt had an idea it was to Washington to see the Yankee girl, there was no evidence of that.

"Whatever happened, it sure did put gunpowder in his blood!" Aimes had exclaimed. True, Dent had made himself cordially disliked for his hard drilling sessions, but he seemed not to notice. Day and night he had been hard at work, and all the officers had given him full credit, especially Captain Coldfax, who had said, "That young man puts us all to shame, Colonel Benton!"

Suddenly a hush went over the crowd, for a tall, erect figure on the platform had risen and begun to speak. Jefferson Davis, the president of the Southern Confederacy, looked like a hawk with his lean cheeks, sharp features, and piercing eyes. He spoke slowly at first, but at the last of what was a stirring speech, he cried out, "I am ready to march with you, shoulder to shoulder, to shed the last drop of my blood for our holy cause!"

The crowd went wild, and the Richmond Grays lifted

their rifles, cheering their leader. Dewitt noticed that Dent frowned at this breach of discipline, and he whispered to Aimes, "The boys will get it for that! Look how mad ol' Dent is!"

As Rev. Jeremiah Irons, the chaplain of the Grays, came to pronounce a prayer, Dent looked over the crowd. The men had all pulled their hats off, and suddenly he spotted his father standing with his mother. He frowned quickly, the joy of the event turning sour. When Irons pronounced the amen, the company was dismissed. "There's a lunch for all heroes at the Dixon House, Dent," Taylor said, grinning. "Let's go show how well we can eat!"

The dining room of the Dixon House was crowded, and the tables were laden with food. Thomas came at once to Dent, saying, "My boy, I'm very proud of you!"

Dent said, "We haven't done anything yet, sir. But give us time." He noticed that his own father was holding back, and he asked suddenly, "Did you think the company looked well, sir?"

"Yes, I did. You've all done a fine job."

They found a place to eat, across from Colonel Benton and Rev. Irons. Benton said, "This son of yours is a slave driver, Clay! The Yankees can't be any tougher than he is!" A laugh went around the table, and Benton added, "Thomas, you ought to join my staff."

"I'm a little too old for that, James! Besides, all I know how to do is raise cotton. You can't fight the Yankees with a cotton stalk!"

The colonel joined in the laugh, but said, "Why, you're no older than I am, or Captain Coldfax! As for that, the captain is the only officer we have with battle experience. I wish we had more like him."

Suddenly a man in civilian clothes, a tall, dark, lean individual, spoke up. "Well, what about your son, Mr. Rocklin? He's had military experience, I understand."

The remark brought an end to the ease of the dinner. The speaker, whose name was Rafe Longley, was a close friend of Jake Slocum. He seemed to enjoy the discomfort he had created, and he added, "Of course, your service wasn't of high quality, Mr. Rocklin—but perhaps you've matured a little since those days."

Clay sat there, pressing his feet against the floor. Longley was insulting him publicly, daring him to take up the insult. And there was a desire to do just that. But he suddenly caught the steady gaze of Jeremiah Irons, who shook his head very slightly. He had told Clay earlier, "You're a sitting duck, Clay. As long as you don't join in with the crowd, somebody's going to take his shots at you. And if you fight them, you've dug your own grave."

Carefully Clay said, "I'm not proud of that time, Mr. Longley. What I did in Mexico was dishonorable. It certainly wouldn't qualify me to serve with these brave young men in the Richmond Grays!"

It was the right answer, and Colonel Benton said instantly, "It takes a strong man to face up to his mistakes. We've all made them, and I for one have been happy to see Clay Rocklin come back and make amends as best he can!"

The moment passed, but Thomas noticed that Clay ate almost nothing. Afterwards, the three of them walked out of the hotel together. They found the women waiting beside the carriage, and when they got there, Susanna said, "Was it a nice dinner, Tom?"

But Thomas had no time to answer, for Denton took an aggressive stand facing his father. His face was pale but his voice was clear as he said, "How much longer are you going to keep this up, may I ask?"

Clay looked at his son and made no pretense of misunderstanding him. "I know I'm an embarrassment to you, Dent. But you'll have to give me a little time."

"Time for what?" Dent asked sharply, his lips thin against his teeth. "Don't you know all our friends and half of Richmond are watching you? Do you have any idea what they're saying?"

"Probably that I'm either a coward or a traitor," Clay

said evenly. "But I can't let public opinion force me to make my decisions. I would be a coward if I let that happen."

"Dent, don't make a scene!" Ellen snapped. "Haven't you learned yet that your father's a weak man? Don't count on him for help!"

Thomas said at once, "Stop this! I won't have it! It's unseemly and undignified. Dent, if you have anything to take up with your father, this is no place to do it. We have a home, and you well know where it is. Come along and we'll talk this out in private."

But his words did not touch Dent. Standing straight as a ramrod, he said, "Sir, I apologize to you—but to you, sir—," he said evenly to Clay, "I have nothing at all to say. Except that it was a sorry day for the Rocklin family when you came back!"

He turned and left, leaving the family staring after him. "He'll get over it, Clay—" Susanna said quickly, taking his arm.

"No, I don't think he will," Clay said, his eyes brooding. "Even if I join the Confederate Army and kill a thousand Yankees, Dent will never get over it."

"Let's go home," Susanna whispered, and they got into the carriage and drove through the streets of Richmond. The sound of band music playing floated on the air, and cheers rose as they left the city.

Clay knew at once that something was wrong. He was helping Box shoe his horse when David, Dent's twin, came walking into the blacksmith shop, his face pale. At once Clay said, "I'll finish this job, Box. Why don't you go get some of the cool buttermilk Dorrie keeps in the springhouse. Bring me some, too."

"Yas, Marse Clay." Box could read faces as well as his master, or better. He'd been reading Rocklin faces before Clay was born, and he knew trouble when he saw it. Going to the kitchen he said, "Trouble." When Dorrie stared at him, he shook his head. "Gimme some buttermilk!"

Clay asked, "What's wrong, David?" This boy was the bookish Rocklin, the thoughtful one. Identical to Dent in appearance, he was almost the opposite in his ways. He was easygoing but, because he accepted Dent's leadership, he had not allowed Clay to come close to him.

He stood there, unable to find a way to say what had brought him to the blacksmith shop. He fumbled with the button on his shirt, as he always did when he was nervous, and finally said, "Sir, I—I don't know how to tell you!"

"It's never easy to give someone bad news, David. The easiest way is just to speak it out."

Still the young man faltered. Finally he swallowed hard, then said, "It's about—Melora Yancy."

Shock ran along Clay's nerves, but he let nothing show on his face. "What's wrong with her? Is she sick?"

"N-no sir, not sick. But, I'm afraid that Mother . . . " He paused and had a wretched look on his face. Clay saw that he was tremendously embarrassed. Taking a deep breath, David said, "Mother got the idea that—that you were having some sort of affair with the young woman."

"David, I want you to know that's not so," Clay said evenly.

David gave him an astonished stare. "Is that the truth, sir?"

"With God as my witness, there's nothing between us."

David bit his lip. "That—makes what Mother did even worse!"

"What's happened? Tell me."

"Mother got to drinking, I'm afraid. And she went to the store where Miss Yancy works. She cursed her out in front of all the customers, called her awful names, and then she started slapping her. Mr. Hardee pulled her off her and brought her home." David closed his eyes, trying to shut out the memory of what he had witnessed. "The servants had to carry Mother into the house."

Clay stood there until the anger that had blazed up in him ebbed. He was aware that David was watching him carefully, waiting for him to speak, to act. "Thanks for coming to tell me, David. Better to hear it from your own." He saw a new light come to his son's eyes and added, "Your mother is a bitter woman, Son. We'll have to be patient with her."

David's only thought until that moment was that his father hated his mother. Now he saw grief in the dark eyes that regarded him, but no hatred. "Yes sir. Can—can I do anything?"

Clay said, "I'm going to ride over to see the Yancys, David. Buford Yancy's been a good friend to me. I want to look them all in the eye and tell them your mother was mistaken. I'll make her apologies. Later, your mother and I will talk."

"Yes sir, that would be best." David hesitated, then he said slowly, "I'm sorry this happened, sir—but one good thing has come of it."

"What's that, David?"

"Well, sir—I've been wrong." David dropped his eyes and twisted the button. "I've never given you a chance, not since you came back. I'm sorry for that!"

Clay's eyes lit up and he did what he would not have dared to do before. He put his arm around David's shoulder, saying, "That means more to me than anything in the world, David!" Then he saw that the boy was shy, and so he said, "I'll talk with you when I get back."

"Yes sir!"

Clay rode the black horse hard, and it was almost dusk when he got to Hardee's Store. He swung out of the saddle, tied the sweating horse to the rail, and went into the store. Lyle Hardee was behind the counter, along with his wife, Sarah. Lyle peered at Clay over his silver-rimmed glasses and said in the flat Yankee twang, "Mr. Rocklin, I wish you'd leave my store."

Clay stopped, studied the pair, then said, "I apologize for my wife. She'd been drinking, I understand. What she said was wrong, and what she did was wrong. There's no finer girl on this planet than Melora Yancy, and I'm on my way to speak to her family right now. I thought she might still be here."

Hardee stared at him. He had been as angry when Ellen Rocklin had abused Melora as he had ever been in his life—but he saw the naked pain in Clay's eyes and revised his opinion of the man. "Maybe I was a bit hasty, sir," he said. "I don't like to lose my temper, and your wife made me do just that. However, I can see you're as upset about this as I am . . . probably more so. Well, Melora left twenty minutes ago, walking."

"Thank you, Mr. Hardee," Clay said, then left the store. He mounted the black, but went at a slower pace. Before long, he saw her walking along the side of the road, and as he drew near, she turned and stopped to wait for him. As he dismounted he saw the scratches Ellen had left on her cheeks and fought down the rage that came to him.

"I thought you'd come," she said.

"I'm going to talk to your father," he said quietly. "Are you all right?"

"Yes." She was wearing a simple gray dress and a thin cotton jacket. Her hair was blown by the late breeze, and she tucked a curl in, adding, "It makes things hard for you, Clay."

"No it doesn't." He stood there in the failing light, looking at her face. He dropped the reins of the black, knowing that the animal was too tired to run away. "Let me walk with you," he said.

"All right." They began to walk, and for a time neither of them spoke. Overhead the purple martins performed their acrobatics, and from the woods came the sudden barking of a dog. The air was cool and from the distant range of mountains a line of light seemed to grow.

Finally he said, "Melora, I have to tell you something."

She stopped and looked up at him, her green eyes wide. "I know, Clay."

"You do?"

"Yes." A smile touched her lips, and she reached up

and touched his cheek gently. "You're going to tell me that we can't see each other."

Clay set his teeth, his jaw clenched. Nodding, he whispered, "I can't bring more shame on you, Melora. And I have a family."

Dropping her hand she turned to look toward the distant mountains. Everything was still, except for the cry of a bird who made it back to her nest just in time, before the darkness caught her.

Melora said, "It's getting dark, Clay. But after a while, the sun will come up again, and it'll be a new morning. That's God's way, I like to think. Darkness and cold—and then the first streaks of light in the dawn. And soon the darkness disappears and the world is bright again."

He knew she was telling him to be patient, and he suddenly wanted very much to believe her.

"Do you believe that, Melora? That despite all that's happened—and all the darkness that lies in front of us—that somehow we'll see the sun again?"

Melora nodded, whispering, "Yes, Clay. I believe it with all my heart! I don't know how, but God will bring us through all this."

"Then—I'll believe it, too, my dear!" He hesitated, then slowly and with great care leaned down and kissed her lips. They were warm and soft, like a child's lips.

"That was good-bye, wasn't it, Clay?" Melora said evenly.

"Until the sun comes up again," Clay answered simply.

Melora nodded, then she said, "Well, we're not going to have a funeral service! Come on, Mister Clay! I want to read you some of my scribblings! Come on, now."

Melora laughed, and Clay smiled. "All right. Let's see if you can stay on this horse behind me. I never could abide a woman who couldn't ride!"

He mounted and, using the stirrup, she swung up behind him. "Here we are, the knight and his lady!" she said. "Remember those stories, Mister Clay?"

Clay Rocklin felt strangely happy. Nothing had

changed outwardly, but the spirit of this woman had lifted him.

"Dragons, you all look out!" he called, then kicked the horse in the ribs. Melora clung to him, and a red-eyed possum scurried out of the way as the black horse trotted down the road in the moonlight.

THE END

Be sure to look for the second book in The Appomattox series, **Gate of His Enemies.** *Here is a sample from the first few pages of that book.*

✷ ✷ ✷

Washington was dark as Deborah Steele walked slowly down the street that led to her home. The clock in the belfry of the Congregational Church her father pastored sounded out nine times, but the voice of the bronze bell seemed muffled by the darkness and the fog that enveloped the city like a thick mantle.

Deborah was tired. The news of the fall of Fort Sumter in South Carolina had brought a heaviness to her—as it had to Washington and the North. Some of her fellow abolitionists were celebrating the event, rejoicing that at last a blow could be struck that would set the slaves free. Most felt it would be an easy matter: Send a few of our fine Northern troops down and teach the Rebels a lesson! Won't take thirty days—then we'll have a land free from the awful bondage of slavery!

Somehow Deborah had sensed that the war would not be like that, and a heaviness had quenched her lively spirit. Though the April night was not cold, the dampness of the air and the thick canopy of fog sent a shudder through her. Finally she reached the walk that led to her home and paused for a moment, gazing into the darkness, remembering.

It wasn't that long ago, only a few nights, that she had come home on a night very much like this one—and a man had moved toward her out of the shadows, calling her name.

Deborah remembered how the sudden appearance of the man had sent a startling fear through her. Washington, since the fall of Sumter, had been filled with crowds drinking and celebrating the beginning of the war. Deborah knew there had been several nasty incidents.

3

"Who are you? What do you want?" she had demanded. The reply had astounded her.

"It's me, Deborah—Dent Rocklin!"

As she relived that moment, Deborah closed her eyes, feeling once again the shock that had rolled over her. Dent had moved toward her, telling her that he'd had to come, had to talk with her. Even in the murky darkness broken by a pale yellow gleam from the street lamp, she had been able to see the tension in his lean face. He was the best-looking man she had ever known—tall, lean, with the blackest hair possible and strongly formed features.

That night, though, he had looked worn and tired. She had wanted so much to reach out to him . . . but had known she must not.

Deborah moved restlessly. She did not want to remember any more. Passing a trembling hand over her eyes, she wished things could have been different. But it had seemed, from their very first meeting, as though Deborah and Denton had been destined to fall in love.

She remembered vividly every detail of her visit with her uncle Gideon's family, of her time in Richmond and at Gracefield, the Rocklin family home just outside of that city. She clearly recalled how startled she had been by the powerful attraction that had sparked between Dent and herself. Even the fact that Dent was a fiery advocate of slavery and secession while she had been active as an abolitionist hadn't weakened that attraction. There had been some violent arguments between them, and finally, to avoid the strong feelings that Dent was creating in her own heart, Deborah had fled back to her home in Washington.

In a scene that could still tear her to pieces, she had said, "You'll forget me, Dent—and I'll have to forget you!"

She had left then and come home. Once back with her family, surrounded by all that was familiar and safe, she had been sure that was the end of her encounter with Dent Rocklin.

Then, a few nights ago, he had shown up, right here by the gate in front of her home.

She had scolded him, telling him he should not have come.

"I know that," he had said wearily. Looking at him, Deborah had noted that he was changed somehow. He had lost his lighthearted air. Then he had spoken the words that struck her heart a fierce blow. "Deborah, I'm in the Confederate Army."

Deborah breathed deeply, struggling with the tears that suddenly threatened to overcome her. The Confederate Army. Dent was in the Confederate Army. How could she love a man who would be fighting to destroy everything she believed in?

She had sent Dent away that night, but not before he had grasped her arms and leaned down, his eyes fierce. She could still hear his words ringing in her ears.

"Now, you can tell me it'll never work. Tell me I'll probably get my head blown off. Your family would never agree. My family would never agree. Then tell me I'll be fighting against your brothers. Give me a dozen reasons why we can't be together. Go on!"

Trembling in his grasp, Deborah had answered, "It's all true! Everything you say is true!"

"I know it is, Deborah. But I know one thing more. Something you've overlooked."

"What—"

And then he had pulled her close and kissed her, cutting off her words—and filling her with the same stirring that had shaken her back in Virginia. Despite herself, Deborah had responded to Dent's caress.

When he had finally lifted his head, he had held her close, whispering, "That's what you've forgotten, Deborah!"

Everything within her had longed to say, "I love you, Dent! We'll make it somehow!"

But she could not. The obstacles were too overwhelming. There was more than just their love at stake. There was her family—parents, brothers, and all the others—and all that she had worked for, including the freedom of the slaves.

She had told him that, told him she could never turn her back on her family, told him that there were all kinds of love . . . and sometimes one kind of love works against another.

She had known Dent had wanted to take her in his arms again, but he had not. Instead, he spoke to her simply with a great determination.

"Deborah, I love you. And I know you love me. I've got to go, but this isn't the end. When the war is over, I'll come for you."

He had whirled and walked away, pausing a few feet away, almost hidden in the fog, to say, "Don't forget me, Deborah. After it's over, I'll be coming for you!"

Then he had disappeared, swallowed up by the fog.

Deborah stood now, peering into the thick grayness where he had disappeared and struggling with the emotions sweeping over her. Then a break in the sky allowed the full moon to appear. It poured down a silver bar of light . . . until a ragged cloud racing across the sky closed it off, and the darkness moved across the land as Deborah turned slowly and walked into the house.